a

beautiful

mess

T.K. Leigh

A BEAUTIFUL MESS

This is a work of fiction. Names, characters, places, and incidents either are the product of the author's imagination or, if an actual place, used fictitiously and any resemblance to actual persons, living or dead, business establishments, events, or locales is entirely coincidental. The publisher does not have any control over and does not assume any responsibility for author or third-party websites or their content.

Published by Tracy Kellam, 25852 McBean Parkway # 612, Santa Clarita, CA 91355

Cover Design: Cat Head Biscuit, Inc., Santa Clarita, CA

Edited by: Arianna Katherine

Female Cover Image Copyright Jose AS Reyes 2013

Used under license from Shutterstock.com

Background Cover Image Copyright Kibru Senbetta 2013

Author Photo Copyright Stanton Kellam, 2013

ISBN: 0-9897406-1-7
ISBN-13: 978-0-9897406-1-6

To Stan… My Always and Forever…

CHAPTER ONE

SOMETHING ABOUT TODAY

One week. That's all Olivia Adler could think about as she stood staring out the window of her office on the twentieth floor overlooking the Financial District of Boston. In exactly one week, her parents would have been dead for twenty-one years. Yes, twenty-one years seems like a long time. And it is. Twenty-one years is a long time to have no family.

As she was contemplating her shit life on that Friday in mid-August, she heard her cell phone buzzing on her desk.

Kiera: *Where are you? It's quarter after.*

Olivia: *Shit. Let me just put on some makeup and I'll be right down. Sorry.*

She groaned, wondering why she had agreed to go out with Kiera and a few of her co-workers that evening. Going out was the last thing she wanted to do. Most nights, she preferred to stay at home, snuggle on the couch with her cat, and drown herself in a bottle of wine.

Walking into the en-suite bathroom in her office at the posh wellness center she ran, Olivia checked her reflection. Her dark, curly hair was cooperating for once. Placing a bit of gel in her locks, she framed her pear-shaped face with loose ringlets, the rest of her hair cascading down the middle of the open back of her red silk halter-top.

She applied a hint of makeup, needing only a little eyeliner around her big brown eyes and some lip gloss. She rubbed

1

lotion on her lengthy olive-toned legs and finished the look with a pair of black wedge sandals that made her even taller than her five-nine frame. She took one more glance at the mirror before grabbing her purse and running out of her office into a waiting elevator.

"Have a good night, Libby," she heard as she ran past the security office in the lobby twenty floors below. Olivia stopped quickly to say good night to one of the building's security guards.

"Good night, Jerry. I'll be back later on before heading home for the evening."

"Where ya heading now?" he asked with his eyebrows raised. Over the past several months that Olivia helped run the new wellness center, he had learned her routine. And that routine never consisted of going out after work.

"Out for a few drinks with the girls."

A smile spread across Jerry's face, happy to see that Olivia was going out for once. "Well, if it's after ten, the main doors will be locked, so use your key card to get into the night entrance."

"Thanks, Jerry. See you later on." Olivia left through the big glass doors and walked outside to meet Kiera.

"Hey gorgeous," she said as Olivia exited the tall, shimmering skyscraper.

"Hey gorgeous, yourself," Olivia responded, smiling at her beautiful friend. Her light green tank top brought out the deep green of her eyes, which contrasted nicely with her vibrant red hair. Although she was shorter than Olivia by about six inches, only hitting five-three on a good day, her confidence made her seem so much taller.

Olivia had met Kiera during her freshman year at Boston College. She moved into the apartment across the hall in the building where Kiera had been living. Kiera was a few years older than Olivia and had been her rock for the past decade. She was the only family Olivia had left.

The two friends linked arms and walked the few short blocks to the bar. It was a beautiful evening in mid-August and the humidity that had been present earlier that afternoon had faded. The sun illuminated the tall buildings of the city Olivia had grown to love over the past decade, casting the sky a beautiful pink color. A slight breeze blew through the air and all was right in the world. Olivia actually looked forward to spending her Friday night with friends.

"I can't get too fucked up tonight," Olivia said to Kiera as they handed the doorman their IDs. "I want to try to get in a long run early tomorrow before the heat hits."

"Yeah, sure. Whatever you say," Kiera retorted. She didn't try to downplay Olivia's training schedule, but she was worried that her friend pushed herself too hard, not leaving anytime to enjoy life.

"I mean it. I've been slacking on my running lately. I have a marathon in two months and I'm trying to qualify for Boston." The girls walked into the brightly lit bar, the sound of people laughing and having a good time filtering though. Olivia quickly scanned the huge room in order to locate her co-workers.

"You workout like all day long at work. You should take the weekend off."

"That's what Sundays are for. Anyway, I don't workout all day. I teach a few group classes during the week, but that's really it," she informed her darling friend as she spotted a few of the girls she worked with sitting by the windows overlooking the street. Olivia started in their direction.

MacFadden's was a trendy bar in the Financial District of Boston that attracted many twenty- and thirty-somethings who worked in the vicinity. At six o'clock on a Friday night, the bar was packed with people grabbing a few drinks with their co-workers before heading home for the weekend.

It used to be a hole-in-the-wall Irish pub. A few years ago, the owner, Mac, came into some money and did a huge renovation project on the bar. There was gorgeous hardwood flooring throughout both levels, creating a homey feel. On the first level, the atmosphere was bright and airy. Instead of regular bar tables, there were posh couches with coffee tables. The glass windows out front ran floor-to-ceiling and on a beautiful night like that, they were wide open, letting the

Boston air float through the bar. The second floor housed a rather large stage and a huge dance area. Every weekend, the bar was packed with people there to see whatever band Mac had booked, who had excellent taste in local talent.

"Hey! You made it," Olivia's co-worker, Bridget, shouted at her, obviously already a few drinks in. She was around Olivia's age of twenty-seven, petite, with fair skin and dark hair and eyes. Like Olivia, she was not a Boston native, being born and raised in Chicago. She had come out to Boston for college and just never left. That seemed to happen quite a bit in this town.

"Yeah," Olivia replied dryly.

"Thanks for dragging her out!" Bridget shouted at Kiera, giving her a hug.

"Hey, I saw Simon here. I think he was looking for you," Melanie, her other co-worker, said as Kiera and Olivia sat down on the small velvet couch opposite Melanie and Bridget.

"Why would he be looking for me?" Olivia asked, her irritation showing. She really had no desire to see Simon that evening.

"Ummm, I might have mentioned you were meeting us here. He came over to say hi and all so I let him know you were probably going to be here." Melanie looked at Olivia, who was rubbing her temples. "What? Did I do something wrong?" she asked innocently.

"No, Mel. It's okay," Olivia breathed. "I didn't want to have to deal with this tonight," she explained.

Olivia had met Simon while she was working at the wellness center. He worked construction for one of the companies that had been hired to design and construct a new studio room. He asked Olivia out for a drink the first day he was there. And every day for the next month. On the day that the studio room construction was finished, he asked one last time. Olivia reluctantly agreed.

"Why not?" Bridget asked, sounding surprised. "I thought you guys were dating."

"Miss Olivia doesn't date, remember? She has sex with guys while remaining hopelessly unattached," Kiera explained, laughing as she eyed Olivia.

4

"Kiera!" Olivia shouted, playfully smacking her friend. "You make it sound like I'm a whore!"

"Oh, you're not a whore. Far from it. You just refuse to be in a relationship. *With anyone.*"

Olivia glared at Kiera who knew her reasons for never getting involved with the opposite sex. "I don't refuse anything. I just find relationships to be full of disappointment. Life is disappointing enough without the stress of a relationship."

"So, what's the deal with Simon now?" Melanie asked, trying to lighten the mood at the table.

"The sex has gotten to be way too boring. The first few times it was good, probably because I was drunk. But now, well, let's just say, it does nothing for me. I haven't come once. And the other night, he wanted to stay over." Her face cringed at the thought of waking up next to Simon. Or anyone, for that matter.

"What's the problem with that?" Melanie asked. Olivia had a great deal of affection for her friend. Melanie was younger than the rest of the girls, having just turned twenty-one a few months previously. She was tall, tan, and blonde — a college guy's wet dream. Her personality was perfect for her job; she worked at the front desk of the wellness center. She was a total sweetheart and one of Olivia's favorite employees, but sometimes she was naive.

"Oh, you don't know Libby's rules," Kiera laughed.

"You have rules?" Bridget asked, trying to hide her shock. She had been working at the center with Olivia for the past month as a personal trainer and they had gotten to know each other fairly well, but the subject of Olivia's sexual habits never came up before.

"Well, I don't do the relationship thing," Olivia explained. "But before I just get in the sack with anyone, I lay down the law. No sleeping over. I get my own space. I hang out with my friends. I have no desire to meet their friends. If they happen to meet mine, so be it. We only sleep with each other and we're honest when we want to move on. I'm really just looking for someone to get me off a few times a week and that's it. I don't do relationships, like I said."

5

"God, I wish I could be like that," Melanie said with a dreamy look on her face.

"No you don't, Mel," Olivia replied quickly. She knew it wasn't the healthiest form of relationship. She just hated getting too close to anyone. Once you did, they disappointed you one way or another. Or they would leave you and you're stuck picking up the pieces of your shattered heart. So don't get close and you won't ever have to deal with the heartache, so Olivia thought.

"Fuck, I need a drink now. You're too depressing," Kiera laughed, looking for a server, scowling when there were none in sight.

"I'll go grab a few drinks. What do you want?" Olivia asked, getting up from the table.

"The usual."

"Okay. I'll be right back. Anyone else need another drink?"

Melanie and Bridget shook their heads and she headed to the bar to get some drinks. There were quite a few people surrounding the bar, so she got in line to wait her turn to order when suddenly she felt two hands on her waist.

"Hey beautiful," someone whispered into Olivia's ear from behind. She turned around and saw Simon standing in back of her.

"Oh hi," she replied coolly, exhibiting no enthusiasm for him. She turned back around, not wanting to miss her opportunity to place her much needed drink order.

"I like this top," he said as he dragged a finger down the middle of her open back. "It's hot." She visibly cringed at the contact, but Simon failed to notice. "So's the skirt," he said, taking in her short black mini skirt. "You've got killer legs."

"Thank you, Simon," she replied over her shoulder. He was a good enough looking guy, his blond hair kept messy in a sexy kind of way that Olivia liked when they first started "seeing" each other. Although he was only a few inches taller than her, she didn't seem to mind. In a city like Boston, it was difficult to find guys over six feet tall.

Olivia sighed when Simon didn't take the hint that she was not in the mood to talk. It was obvious he was drunk and

Olivia assumed he had gone to the Sox game earlier, as he was in full Red Sox fandom gear and his breath reeked of cheap beer and hot dogs. Simon was a life-long Boston resident, complete with a thick Boston accent. Olivia didn't think the accent would bother her when they first got together, but it had become difficult to find him attractive in the sack when he kept saying "harder, harder" in that Boston accent. Maybe that's why she never came.

Olivia remained silent for several minutes, her irritation growing, while Simon caressed her back. She hated public displays of affection, but she let him touch her. *It's the least I could do because he knows I won't let him stick his tongue down my throat in public*, Olivia thought. Relationships were all about give and take she had learned — even her fucked up version of relationships. He slipped his hands in through the side of her shirt and slowly made his way up to her breasts.

"Simon, no!" she shouted, turning her head around and elbowing him in the stomach.

"Oh, come on, baby," he breathed onto Olivia's neck as he pulled her toward him, her back to his front. She could feel the erection in his jeans. "I haven't seen you since Monday. It's killing me. Let's get out of here."

"I just got here." Olivia pushed Simon away, ridding herself of his grasp. "I want to have a few drinks with the girls. I'll find you in a little bit. I'm going to order my drinks now if you're done groping me in public, you sicko," she sneered.

"Okay, Livvy. Whatever."

Olivia hated when he called her Livvy. It was Olivia or Libby. Certainly never Livvy. Well, at least not to him.

Simon walked away laughing, thinking she was joking. She wasn't joking. Simon was disturbing. There was definitely something off about him, but she could not put her finger on it. Time to end it, Olivia decided. But first, some drinks. Simon could wait.

After finally placing her drink order, she made her way back to her table with four tequila shots in one hand and two beer bottles in the other; her years of working as a bartender helping her with the delicate balancing act.

"Oh hey. Our server came by while you were at the bar, so we ordered with her, too," Kiera said.

"Good! There's no such thing as too much liquor. I think tonight's looking like a good night for some tequila. Who's in and who's out?" Olivia asked, sitting down and pointing to the tequila shots she had placed on the table. "There's something about today that makes me want to be hungover tomorrow."

"Let's do it," Melanie replied, laughing.

"Yup, although I know I'm going to regret this in the morning," Bridget said, grabbing her tequila shot.

"Wait, where's the lime and salt?" Kiera asked.

"That shit's for pussies." Olivia held up her shot glass. The girls followed suit. "Here's to you. Here's to me. Friends for life we'll always be. If we should ever disagree, fuck you. Here's to me." The friends clinked glasses and gulped the shot back. The silver liquid burned as it went down Olivia's throat. She felt the warmth in her stomach and immediately started to relax.

"Well, at least you ordered good tequila or I'd be heaving already," Bridget said.

"Nothing but the best for me. Life is too short to waste it on shitty alcohol."

"You should make a tee shirt with that saying on it," Kiera choked out with tears in her eyes, clearly having trouble stomaching the tequila.

"It's going to be a good night, I can tell."

~~~~~~~~~

"I need to use the little girls room," Olivia said several hours later, standing from their table. She headed to the bathroom only to be met with a line snaking around the long corridor. Scowling, she decided to go to the second floor to see whether that line was any better. Olivia climbed the stairs, which proved to be slightly more challenging than usual, owing to her chunky heels and the drinks she had consumed. She made her way down the dark back hallway, thankful to see no line at the ladies' room. When she finished up and exited, someone grabbed her arm, pushing her against the wall.

"You've been ignoring me all night," Simon breathed, using his body to crush Olivia's to the wall, pinning both arms on either side of her head with his hands.

"I haven't been ignoring you. I've been spending some time with my friends. Get off me so I can go back to them," Olivia replied forcefully, trying to hide the fact that, in all actuality, she was rather frightened. Simon had never been that aggressive with her before.

As she stood there in his grasp, she silently hoped someone would come to use the restroom soon so that Simon would let her go. She was not sure if she should tell him that she was done with him, given her current predicament.

Simon kept her pinned to the wall for what seemed like an eternity as he looked down on her, licking his lips like an animal stalking his prey.

"Simon, please," Olivia begged, terror flashing in her big brown eyes.

"Oh, Livvy. You really are beautiful when you beg." He planted rough kisses against her jaw line, grinding his hips against hers as he crushed her against the wall.

"Simon, I'm not going to ask you again. Please, let me go." Olivia closed her eyes, not wanting to look into his eyes anymore. She tried to free herself from his grasp, to no avail. He was definitely much stronger than her.

"What's going on here?" a familiar, deep voice broke through. Olivia opened her eyes and searched for the source of the voice. A wave of relief washed over her.

"Simon, please," Olivia whispered, glaring at him, her vindication returning.

"Fine. Stupid whore." He released her and stumbled down the hallway onto the dance floor.

"We're done, Simon," she said, raising her voice. He didn't even turn around, but it was obvious he heard her when he raised his right hand and flipped Olivia off.

She let out a huge breath and turned to the source of the voice, staring into the dark eyes of one of her old college friends.

"Mo," Olivia said.

"You picked a real winner this time, Livvy."

Olivia usually hated when people call her Livvy, but Mo was the exception to the rule. The only other person who ever called her Livvy was her father and Mo reminded Olivia so much of him, right down to the name. Giacomo. Most of his friends called him Jack, but Olivia called him Mo.

"Yeah, I know." Olivia walked over to Mo and into his arms, happy to see one of her oldest friends again. She felt a calming feeling as she stayed in his embrace, the memory of the night they met making her smile. Olivia worked at an area bar that his band played at. One evening, before the bar opened, she had finished her prep work early when she noticed that the band had already set up their gear. The bar was empty, so she stepped up to the piano and sang one of her favorite songs.

It was a song that reminded Olivia of her parents. Something about that moment made it seem like the right thing to do. Maybe her parents were looking down from above because, unbeknownst to her, Mo had been watching the performance. He was very impressed with her voice and asked her to sing a few songs with his band. She agreed, and throughout her years at Boston College, she always jumped on stage for a few numbers with the guys.

She hadn't seen Mo since she graduated and fled Boston. Olivia pushed him away after graduation, just like she pushed away everyone she was close to. *If you keep everyone at a distance, you can't ever really lose them*, she thought.

"It's good to see you, Mo. Really good. It's been too long." She pulled out of Mo's embrace and looked into his eyes, overwhelmed with a thousand emotions from seeing her dear friend once again.

"It has been too long. Five years, if I remember correctly." He eyed Olivia, his eyebrows raised. She lowered her head, feeling guilty for never getting in touch with Mo once she came back to the city. And for cutting him out of her life in the first place. "I'm glad you're back in Boston, but please stop dating assholes like that. You know I think of you like a little sister and the next guy that treats you like less than a princess, I'm going

10

to have to kill him, and I really don't want to go to prison right now. At least, not until the band performs tonight." He winked at Olivia, their eyes nearly even from both of them being the same height.

"You know I don't do the relationship thing, Mo."

"I know you don't, but that still doesn't mean you shouldn't be treated well, no matter what your relationship is with someone."

"Still teaching?" Olivia wanted to change the subject from her inability to have healthy relationships with people, something Mo was all too aware of.

"Yup. Instilling musical ability into the minds of our children on a daily basis. It pays the bills while I slum around on the weekends with the band, playing bars," he joked. Mo had been teaching music at the elementary school level for as long as Olivia had known him.

"You guys are playing tonight?" she asked with her eyebrows raised and her arms crossed.

"We sure are." He smiled, running his hand through his dark hair. "When did you get back into town?" he asked, changing the subject back to Olivia. He knew her too well and was more than aware of all her tricks.

"I've been living here for a year now," she admitted.

"You've been back a year and never got in touch with me? I'm hurt." He placed his hands over his heart, faking a broken heart.

"I know. I know. I'm a horrible friend."

"Well, I've known you were back," he smiled. "Kiera can't keep her mouth shut."

She laughed. That sounded like her friend. "She planned this, didn't she?"

He remained speechless while Olivia glared at him.

"You have a terrible poker face. You know that, right?"

Mo shrugged. "Come on, baby girl. Get back on stage with us. It'll make you feel better." He flashed his brilliant teeth, made even brighter against his olive-toned skin.

Olivia sighed, thinking about the last time she played with the guys. Her mind immediately flash-backed to that awful time in her life. Graduation. Wanting to celebrate that milestone of her life and having everything ripped out from underneath her feet. Again.

"Come on, Livvy," he pled while gently touching her arm, comforting her. "It'll be good for you. You need to start playing again. And in front of bigger crowds than at Open Mic night." He raised his eyebrows at her.

Of course. Kiera must have told him about Open Mic. *She totally planned this*, she thought. "Fine," Olivia huffed.

Mo hadn't seen Olivia in years, but it was like nothing had changed. He knew she was starting to shut down.

But Olivia's past was too painful to think about, so shutting down was the only way she could continue to survive. At that point, Olivia just wanted to survive.

Chapter Two

A Good Night Turned Bad

"Thank you!" Mo shouted to a captive audience that had swelled in size over the last hour. "Now, for a little surprise. In the audience tonight is our good friend, Miss Olivia Adler!"

The crowd roared at the mention of her name. Butterflies started to form in Olivia's stomach, nervous energy coursing through her body. Kiera grabbed her hand, knowing that she still got nervous before she performed.

"Those of you who have been following us for the past several years know that she used to sing with us. What do you all think about getting her up here to sing again?" The decibel level in the club sky-rocketed.

Olivia walked through the crowd and climbed onstage, looking over the sea of people standing in the large, dark room illuminated only by the bright lights of the stage. She immediately wondered why she had agreed to get on stage with Mo and the guys again. The room was packed with hundreds of people, all standing shoulder to shoulder, enthusiastically cheering for Olivia as she made her way to the center of the stage.

Taking a deep breath, she closed her eyes and shut everything out, finding her calm. She slowly opened her eyes and smiled as she walked up to the microphone, ready for her performance. "How's everyone doing tonight?" she shouted to overwhelming cheers. "I think we're going to take it back a little bit. For those of you who came to watch us when we gigged at a great little bar called Scotch, this will bring back some memories. Hit it." With that, the familiar sound of The

13

Rolling Stones' *Honkey Tonk Woman* filled the bar. Olivia was back where she felt most comfortable and loved it. She could forget about her past and just live in the moment of the music.

She looked over the crowd and saw Kiera, Melanie, and Bridget enjoying the performance. The entire bar rocked out to their rendition of the classic tune. It felt great knowing that she could bring joy to complete strangers with a simple performance.

Growing up, her happiest memories revolved around music. She could barely remember her parents, but she did recall sitting with her mother at the piano in the great room, playing and singing together. Olivia's mother tried to teach her to play piano when she could barely walk. Even at a young age, there was something about certain melodies that spoke to her.

After her parents died and she was sent to a boarding school, Olivia continued to learn everything she could about music, becoming proficient at a wide variety of instruments and excelling, particularly, at piano. Throughout middle school and high school, she was involved in musical theater groups and sang with various bands. There was something about performing that always calmed her. It almost felt as if she could be someone else for a short period of time.

They finished their rendition of *Honky Tonk Woman* and Olivia took a quick bow, thanking the audience for their enthusiasm. The crowd immediately started chanting her name, "Libby! Libby! Libby!" She looked toward Kiera, who was jumping up and down, clapping and chanting along with the crowd. Olivia was in complete shock at the people shouting her name.

"I think they want an encore, Miss Olivia," Mo said into the microphone. Olivia walked back to her microphone and shouted into it, "Do you want to hear something else?" The crowd roared in approval. "Okay. Who am I to disappoint my adoring fans?" The liquor she had consumed throughout the evening had made her brave and maybe a little cocky.

She conferred briefly with Mo about what to perform next. When he told her what he wanted to do, she laughed, glancing over at the enthusiastic crowd, knowing immediately that they would thoroughly enjoy what he had planned.

"Here's another one that we usually save until later in the night," Mo said into the microphone. "But since we have Olivia up here, I figured it would be nice to actually have a female singing the high part instead of Marcus having to suffer through that." The crowd laughed as he looked to Marcus, the band's piano and guitar player. "Let's rock it." Dale, the drummer, counted off and the band went into Meatloaf's *Paradise by the Dashboard Light*. The crowd danced and sang along, the men singing with Mo and the women singing with Olivia.

She ended up finishing the set with the band. Afterwards, the bartender sent a round of tequila shots to the stage for the reunited band and they obligingly took their shots together. "Here's to *Groove Delay* finally being back together," Willy, the bass player, shouted, raising his empty shot glass.

"It's definitely good to be back singing with y'all." Olivia looked around at the guys that she practically lived with during her college years. Besides Kiera, they were the only family she had left, although she had shut them out of her life the past several years. Why she had waited that long to see them again, she had no idea.

"So will you sing with us once in a while?" Mo asked with a hopeful look on his face.

"You know I can't tell you no," Olivia replied coyly, wrapping her arms around him. "Thank you," she whispered into his ear so no one could hear.

"You know I love you, baby girl." Mo squeezed her tight and gave her a quick kiss on the cheek. She pulled away, happy to have reconnected with him.

"Well, I should probably get back to Kiera and the girls before they leave without saying good-bye. Mo, let me know about rehearsals. I'll see you all soon, I promise." She gave Mo her cell number before waving to the guys, thankful to be able to perform with the band again.

Olivia walked through the large dance floor area as she searched for her friends. People kept stopping her, saying how much they loved the performance. A few people gave her a beer or shot and, while she knew it wasn't the smartest idea to take drinks from people she didn't know, Olivia felt invincible and on top of the world.

"You were amazing!" Melanie screamed as she wrapped her arms around Olivia once she had finally found her friends milling about the downstairs bar. "I had no idea you could sing like that!"

"Me neither," Bridget said, handing Olivia yet another shot.

"Thanks girls." The four friends raised their shot glasses and downed more tequila. At that point, they all had more than enough liquor in their systems. Olivia was not drunk, but she was definitely buzzed, or so she thought.

No. She was drunk.

"So, are you going to gig with them on a regular basis again?" Kiera looked at Olivia, raising her eyebrows.

"I think so. It felt good."

"Good."

The girls left the bar, it being long after last call. They stood on the relatively empty street and said their good-byes. Olivia waved, telling her friends that she had to go back to her office to grab her laptop and a few other things before she headed home for the night. Kiera gave her a worried look.

"I'll text you the second I get home. I promise!" Olivia said, turning down the street as her friends piled into a cab.

Olivia walked the few blocks from the bar to her office in her own little world. She kept replaying the night in her mind. She finally started to feel happy for the first time in years. Maybe it was okay to start letting people back in again.

Olivia reached the building and recalled Jerry telling her that the front doors were locked at ten o'clock every night so she would need to use the night entrance on the side of the building. She walked past the front doors and turned the corner. As Olivia looked down into her purse to find the keycard that would grant her access to the night entrance, someone grabbed her around the waist and pinned her body, face first, against the brick building opposite her own office building, slamming her head against the hard wall.

"We meet again beautiful." Fear rushed through Olivia's

body as her head began to ache and her vision became blurry.

"Simon, please. Leave me alone," she pled, her heart racing.

"Come on, Livvy. You weren't very nice to me before sweetheart," he slurred his words. Even drunk, he was stronger than Olivia.

"You're drunk. You'll regret this tomorrow. Just let me go." Blood began to trickle down her face. Olivia realized that Simon must have slammed her head pretty hard.

"You're making it difficult for me to do my job," he growled, pressing her even harder against the wall.

"What job is that, Simon?" Olivia decided the best thing to do was to just keep Simon talking. Distract him.

"I can't tell you, bitch. Don't you see?" he demanded forcefully, his breath hot against her neck. "But they know, Olivia. They know who you are. And they want their stuff. The proof."

"What are you talking about Simon? I don't know anything about that." She was so confused at what Simon was saying to her. He didn't make any sense.

"Don't mock me, bitch!" Simon reached into his pocket, keeping Olivia pressed against the building with his body, and grabbed a knife, putting it up to her throat.

She looked down when she felt the cold metal against her skin. Tears streamed down her face. "Simon, please. I think you're mistaken. I don't know what you're talking about. I swear."

Simon thought about Olivia's words. The people he worked for warned him that she may not remember, as it was so long ago. Then an idea came to him. It was a brilliant plan he was proud to have come up with, considering he was drunk. He knew it deviated from the plan he was told to adhere to, but he didn't care.

"Well, maybe one last fuck will help you remember. And for once it will be on my terms and not yours," he growled.

Olivia was confused and scared. "S-Simon. Please." Tears started to flow more steadily from her eyes as he pushed Olivia's skirt up. "Someone might see you," she pled quietly, closing her eyes and hoping she would wake up and the entire evening turn out to be a bad dream.

Simon grabbed onto her panties and ripped them painfully from her body. She screamed from the shock of it.

"You know I like a screamer, but now's not the time for that." Simon pressed one hand over Olivia's mouth, holding the knife against her throat with the other. Her entire body trembled under Simon's weight.

Her mind started to race as she assessed her situation. Simon had her pinned against the wall with his body. He easily outweighed her by a hundred pounds. But he was drunk. All she needed was a few seconds to get away from him and run. She couldn't move her back or her arms, and her legs were useless. She opened her eyes, but all she could see was the brick of the wall he had her pressed against. Her heart raced, fearful of what Simon was about to do to her.

Her head throbbed from being smashed into the brick wall. She felt dizzy and nauseous, probably from the combination of the head injury and the liquor she drank. The rage inside of her rose. She was not going to let Simon get away with this. She knew she needed to fight. Her eyes grew wide when she realized a way to get out from Simon's grasp. Parting her lips, she sunk her teeth into his skin, biting down hard on his hand covering her mouth. When she tasted metal, she knew she had drawn blood.

"Ouch! Fucking bitch!" Simon screamed, releasing Olivia. She kneed him in the groin and he fell to the ground. She started to run away, but Simon was fast. He reached his hand out and grasped onto her ankle. Olivia screamed as he pulled her to the ground, her cries becoming desperate and loud.

With her free leg, Olivia kicked him repeatedly. Simon was forced to release her other leg when she landed a hard blow to his head. He moaned in pain, clutching his head as blood streamed down his face. Olivia quickly raised herself off the ground, desperate to get away from Simon, and fled onto State Street. She frantically ran down the cobblestone sidewalk, crying out for someone to help her. The silence around her was deafening as fear consumed her body, her hands shaking. The normally busy street was barren, the last of the bar patrons long gone for the evening.

The clouds in the sky created an ominous feel. All of the buildings were eerily dark. Street lights dimly illuminated each corner, casting shadows on the vacant street. As she tried to find someone to help her, Olivia heard a noise coming from the direction of the night entrance and she started running again, adrenaline coursing through her entire body. She wasn't sure where to go, but she knew she didn't want Simon to ever touch her again.

Chapter Three

Penance

In the early morning hours of a Saturday in mid-August, Alexander Burnham found himself walking from his penthouse apartment on the Waterfront to his office building in the Financial District. He had trouble sleeping, as happened from time to time, so he decided to head into the office to see how a few of his security operations were going. He had been awoken earlier from a dream. A dream he hadn't had in years. He saw those brown eyes that he hadn't seen in ages. Those brown eyes he never thought he would see again. Those brown eyes he had let down. Why, after all these years, was she haunting his dreams again?

He left the leggy red-head in his bed and walked to his office building to clear his head.

As he walked down State Street, he heard a woman scream in the general direction of his office building. He immediately started to run, not caring about ruining his crisp gray suit. Closing in on the building, a tall woman with long, wavy hair came running out of the street where the night entrance was located, frantically crying for help.

He slowed, hoping that he wouldn't scare her even more than it appeared she already was. Then he saw someone chasing her. He doubled his efforts, his SEAL training kicking in. He noticed the knife her attacker carried and shuddered at what that man had done to the woman who fled so desperately. Within seconds, Alexander caught up to the man a block away from his office building. He quickly incapacitated him, knocking him to the ground.

When Olivia heard a commotion behind her, she glanced over her shoulder and saw a man in a gray suit attacking Simon, punching him repeatedly. She stopped abruptly, her heart racing and her breathing labored. She sank to the ground, shaking and relieved to have gotten away from Simon. Adrenaline still coursed through her veins, but she was exhausted and couldn't take another step.

Olivia watched in curiosity as the man in the suit restrained Simon with a pair of zip ties. She wondered why someone would need to carry such an item with him.

Alexander walked over to the frightened woman as she sat on the ground trembling against a storefront. "Are you okay?" He stared into her big brown eyes. *This must be a trick*, he thought to himself. Surely, it couldn't be. He had just seen those eyes in his dreams and now here he was, staring into what appeared to be the same eyes. He could recall only one girl ever having wide brown eyes like those, and she was long gone. He had given up hope years ago. "I think you might be in shock. I'm just going to place my jacket around your shoulders. You're shaking."

Olivia watched as he removed his suit jacket and took a few steps toward her, gingerly placing it around her back. She felt his hands linger on her shoulders for a brief second and a tingling sensation permeated her body. She looked into his beautiful green eyes, completely dumbstruck, a calm feeling overtaking her.

He stepped back again and Olivia was unable to take her eyes off his six-foot-five frame. She knew her reaction was completely inappropriate, considering Simon had just attacked her, but she couldn't control it. She couldn't remember ever being so attracted to someone.

He smiled, noticing her openly gawk at him, bringing attention to the boy-like quality of his face. Olivia wondered how old he could be as she took in his suit, his crisp white button-down shirt doing a bad job at hiding the muscular torso underneath. She licked her lips, staring at his chest, soft little tendrils of dark hair escaping from the top of his shirt. Her eyes made their way lower, her breathing increasing as she ogled the dark gray pants that fell nicely from his hips, matching the suit jacket he had placed around her.

Olivia all but forgot about Simon's attack as her eyes returned to meet his, a smirk on his face, before falling into a different sort of look. Maybe compassion. And something else, like he was searching his brain for a piece of information that was missing at a crucial moment.

"I'm sorry. I'm usually so careful. I don't know what happened." Olivia finally found her voice.

"Hey, hey," he said rushing toward her, kneeling in front of her. "You have nothing to apologize for." His voice was soft but firm.

"I know, but I was stupid to not have my keycard out and ready to go." She touched her head and felt blood.

"Do you want to file a report? I can have a detective come and meet us up in my office."

Olivia gazed at him, a look of hesitation apparent on her face. She had just been attacked outside of her office building by someone she thought she knew and now a total stranger asked her to go with him, alone, to his office.

"I'm one of the good guys, I promise," he assured her, noticing her reluctance. She looked deep into his green eyes. "You can trust me," he said softly.

Her brain flashed back, remembering those words from a childhood memory. She didn't know why, but she believed him. "What do we do about him?" Olivia asked, nodding toward where Simon lay on the sidewalk, unconscious and restrained.

"I'll take care of him." He fished his cell phone out of his pocket and punched a button on it.

"Martin. Burnham here. I need you to send someone down around the corner of the night entrance on State and detain the individual you see restrained. Please call Detective Wilder and escort her to my office the moment she arrives. There's been an incident outside the building this evening." He immediately hung up and turned to face Olivia. "My office is in that building," he said, gesturing to the same building where Olivia's office was located. She smiled. "I can take a better look at that head, too."

Olivia nodded. "Okay."

"Let's get you inside…" Alexander looked at the woman in front of him with a questioning look. She quickly realized he was asking her name.

"Olivia Adler. Libby." She reached her hand toward him.

He looked at her, unable to believe he just heard that name. It couldn't be her, surely. Same first name, but the last name was different. Still, she was taken from him over twenty years ago. If she was alive, he would have found her already. And why would his father lie to him and say that she didn't make it after that tragic day?

He took her outreached hand and felt a certain electricity. "Alexander Burnham. Can I help you up, Miss Adler?"

"Yes, please, Mr. Burnham." Still holding onto Olivia's hand, he placed an arm around her and gently helped her stand.

"I've never seen you here before," Olivia said to him as they walked down the block toward the office building. "I've been working at Downtown Wellness for the past few months." The pair turned down the side street, heading toward the night entrance to the building. He held the door for her after swiping his keycard, granting them both access.

"Well, I tend to work all sorts of strange hours." He led her toward the bank of elevators and swiped his card again before punching the button for the twenty-ninth floor. The penthouse.

Olivia immediately turned to look at him. She had always heard stories about the man who occupied the twenty-ninth floor, mostly from Melanie who told Olivia time and time again how "absolutely breathtaking" the guy was. She had also said that he was some sort of "Billionaire Super Spy." Olivia quickly brushed it off. Melanie clearly read too many romance novels.

"Who are you?" she asked with a curious look on her face. He just smirked at her with a sparkle in his eyes as the elevator continued to ascend the twenty-nine floors to his office. "Wait a minute. You're Alexander Burnham. *The* Alexander

Burnham?" Olivia exclaimed. "You run Burnham & Associates, don't you?"

"No. I own it," he replied, smirking at her even more. "That, and this entire building if we're being honest. And I feel partly responsible for what happened to you this evening," he admitted, his playful expression being replaced with a look of compassion. "I'll be changing some things around here next week."

The elevator doors opened and Olivia was immersed in a posh office. Alexander led her into the foyer and toward a small reception area in front of a large mirror glass wall with *Burnham & Associates* in giant block letters. Several modern black chairs surrounded a coffee table in the waiting area with large black and white art prints adorning the gray walls. It was understated and elegant at the same time.

Alexander punched several numbers into a keypad on a large black door in the middle of the glass wall before placing his thumbprint on a scanner. The door beeped and he opened it for Olivia.

"What is it your company does?" she asked, curious about all the security protocols in place.

"This is a private security company, ironically, among other ventures," he responded, punching yet another security code into another door after leading Olivia down a long corridor. *So he is a Super Spy*, Olivia thought.

The door beeped and he held it open for Olivia. As she entered the room, lights sprang to life. The room was enormous and palatial. Floor-to-ceiling windows covered three of the walls. To the right was a sitting area with a black leather couch, love seat, and a few lounge chairs surrounding a black coffee table. Adjacent to the sitting area was a wet bar. On the opposite side of the room sat a simple black desk, which Olivia assumed was his workspace. Unlike Olivia's office, there were no papers or files scattered across the room. It was neat and orderly.

"Does your office take up the entire floor? It seems like it." Olivia couldn't believe how large the room was.

"Kind of. The main offices of the company are on the five

lower floors. And this office is not the entire floor. I have a few other private rooms on this floor. Usually operation specific. I can't really discuss it. I'm sorry."

As she took in her surroundings, Alexander turned to her. "Can I take a look at that injury of yours?" He grabbed her hand and led her into his en-suite bathroom before she even had a chance to respond.

The bathroom was larger than Olivia's entire bedroom. The gorgeous white tile throughout contrasted with the deep black of the dual vanity. Olivia salivated over the large tub with multiple shower heads, thinking she would give anything to use his shower at that moment to clean Simon off her.

"I tend to spend a lot of time at the office, so I like to have somewhere comfortable to clean up when I need to," he explained to her, answering the question that was clearly etched on her face.

He led her to a cushioned vanity chair and had her sit down as he grabbed the first aid kit and a few towels out of a nearby linen closet. Running one of the towels underneath the faucet, he gently removed the now caked-on blood from her face.

"We were kind of seeing each other, I guess," Olivia blurted out after a few awkward silent moments. "I mean, we were sleeping with each other the past few weeks, but tonight I told him I was done with him. He said he was on a job and needed me to give him the proof, whatever that means."

Alexander stilled. He gathered his thoughts, staring at her for several long moments. Was her attacker simply drunk or was Olivia in more danger than Alexander had originally believed? "You don't have to tell me what happened." He looked deep into her eyes, sending undercurrents of electricity through her spine. With just one look, Olivia was convinced he could peek into her soul.

Olivia gazed over him again, words escaping her. His eyes looked so familiar, but she would have remembered beautiful eyes like that. They were full of something she had never seen in another person before, but she just could not put her finger on what. "I know I don't have to," she said, finally finding her voice. "But maybe talking about it helps. That's what my therapist tells me, at least."

He laughed and the sparkle in his eyes returned. She smiled, wanting to run her hands through his dark brown hair that went in every direction possible. It was messy but incredibly sexy as well.

"Mine used to say the same thing." Alexander wondered what she was in therapy for. Too many puzzle pieces were falling into place. But it was impossible. Alexander could hear his sister's voice in his head. *"You need to stop seeing her face in everyone you see. She's gone."* And Alexander had stopped over a year ago. Until that night.

"It wasn't a serious relationship," Olivia continued rambling, her nerves causing her to tell Alexander about herself when normally she wouldn't. Something about him made her want to open up to him and tell him about herself. And she didn't want him to see her as a helpless victim or a weak person. She was much stronger than that. "I have issues with serious relationships, I guess. But a girl has needs and I've always done the no-strings-attached type of thing."

He cocked his head and looked at her.

"Safely though," she interjected immediately. "I'm a stickler for protection." She blushed. Olivia never blushed. *Why am I telling this total stranger about my sex life?* she thought to herself.

Olivia greatly intrigued him. There was something so familiar about her. Even so, she was a beautiful woman who admitted she was not interested in a serious relationship. She could most certainly suit his needs as well.

"I have no idea why I'm telling you all this. I'm sure the last thing you wanted to have to do on a Friday night was rescue some idiotic girl from her drunken ex outside of your building and then have to hear about her sex life," she blurted out, overwhelmed by the handsome man standing in front of her. She looked down, tying her hands in knots on her lap.

"It's okay," he assured her, turning back to the first aid kit, grabbing a bandage and some Neosporin. He tilted Olivia's chin up, forcing her to gaze into his green eyes again. Leaning down, his lips were only inches from hers. "This might sting a little," he said quietly, sending shivers through Olivia's body.

Not only was the proximity overwhelming, but his husky voice forced a reaction from her that she had never experienced before.

He watched as Olivia opened her mouth slightly, her breathing increasing. He could smell her sweet breath. Alexander rubbed a little cream over the cut on her forehead, trying to hide that he was seriously checking out her fit body. She clearly worked out, and often.

"This cut could have been a lot worse. You won't need stitches." His fingers gently brushed one of her curls behind her ear and placed a small bandage on the treated wound. His hand lingered on her face, gently caressing her cheek and chin. *God, her skin is so soft*, he thought to himself.

Olivia stared back into his eyes, biting her lower lip, and she felt that strange tingling feeling again. It was an odd sensation. There was something about that beautiful man in front of her that made her want to drop all her normal defenses and get close to him. Who was this guy and why did he have this kind of power over her? That worried her.

Alexander's cell phone buzzed, breaking the growing tension, and he quickly removed his hand from Olivia's face, leaving to answer his phone in private. Olivia snapped back to reality and remembered her reason for keeping everyone away, the fear of getting close to someone and losing them resurfacing in her subconscious.

She turned to glance in the mirror and examined her injury. Even with the bandage, it was clear that there was a slight bump where Simon slammed her head into the wall. Other than that, there didn't appear to be any permanent damage.

"You'll probably have a bruise there," Alexander said, startling Olivia as he walked back into the bathroom. She turned to face him. "Detective Wilder is here. I'll give you some privacy to speak with her here in my office." The last thing Alexander wanted to do was leave that woman's side, but he knew privacy sometimes helped people be more forthcoming when making a statement.

"Umm, I'd prefer if you stay with me, if that's okay with you." She stood up, looking into his eyes as a smile spread

27

across his face.

"I'd like that." He grabbed her hand and led her into his sitting area where a petite woman sat with her laptop open. When Olivia entered, she looked up and smiled, her face warm and her eyes the same blazing green color as Alexander's. She appeared to be in her mid-forties and in good shape. Olivia immediately felt comfortable with her.

"Miss Adler, I'm Detective Wilder," she said, standing and extending a hand to Olivia. "I just want to talk to you about what happened tonight. We'll have you sign your statement and then we'll take Simon away for processing."

Olivia told the detective as much as she could remember about what happened that evening. Alexander filled in the blanks as best he could. She told her about her relationship with Simon, as it were, how they met when he was working construction, how he pestered her for nearly a month to go out with him, and then his strange words that evening. Detective Wilder acted in a very professional manner throughout and did not make Olivia feel uncomfortable with anything.

When they were done, Olivia signed her statement and gave it back to Detective Wilder.

"S. Adler?" the detective asked, her eyebrows raised.

"Yeah. Technically my first name is Sarah, but I've always gone by my middle name, Olivia," she explained, shrugging her shoulders.

Before she left, Detective Wilder explained what the next steps were. Simon would be arraigned for assault and attempted murder the following Monday. Most likely, a no contact protective order would be issued since this could be considered a domestic case. She told Olivia she would let her know the result of the arraignment.

"It was nice to meet you, Miss Adler," Detective Wilder said, gathering her belongings and heading toward the doorway. "Mr. Burnham, can you walk me out please?" she said gravely to Alexander.

When they were in the hallway and Olivia was out of earshot, Detective Wilder turned to him. "Alex. It's not her. So stop trying to save every girl you find whose name is Olivia.

She died. Dad said she died in the hospital from a head injury. That was over twenty years ago. This girl's real name isn't even Olivia, for crying out loud."

Alexander looked at his older sister. "I know, Carol. I know that. Call it penance. We failed her that day. I have to do this. For me. And for the little girl we couldn't help that day. That's all." *And did you see those eyes?* he wanted to ask her. She didn't have to look into those eyes as they took their last breaths in her dreams like he did.

"I know." She hugged him. "We were all torn about that day. Dad never got over it. But you have to start forgiving him. And yourself. Think about it." She walked into the reception area, leaving Alexander alone with his thoughts for a moment.

Snapping back to reality, he quickly returned to his office, his heart skipping a beat when he saw Olivia sitting on his love seat, deep in thought. "Do you need a ride home?"

She looked up and hesitated. "No. I'll be fine. I need to get my stuff from my office and then I'll just call for a cab to take me to my place."

He sat next to her. "You were just attacked outside of my building. I run a security company and I couldn't even keep people who work in my building secure. The least I could do is make sure you get home safe."

Olivia turned to look at his face and could see how badly he felt. "Fine," she conceded. "But only because it's after three in the morning and I don't feel like waiting for a cab."

Alexander smiled, happy to spend even a little more time with Olivia. "Great. I'll accompany you down to your office and have Martin meet us out front with the car." The pair headed out of Alexander's office and through the security door to wait for an elevator.

A tall, built man in his mid-fifties wearing a black suit sat in the reception area, standing immediately when he noticed his boss emerge.

"Mr. Burnham, anything else I can do for you?"

"Martin, this is Miss Olivia Adler. Miss Adler this is Martin."

"Pleasure to meet you, Miss Adler," Martin said, extending

his hand to Olivia.

"Martin, I will accompany Miss Adler to her office on the twentieth floor. Please bring the car around and meet us out front."

"Yes, sir," Martin answered as the elevator car arrived. They all stepped into the car and Martin pressed the button for twenty and the basement garage. In a few seconds they stopped on Olivia's floor. As they turned to exit the elevator, Alexander placed his hand on Olivia's lower back, leading her in the direction of the front door to the wellness center.

The placement of his hand sent even more intense shivers up and down her spine. Olivia took a quick inhale of air as she wondered how a simple touch could affect her so. Turning her head in his direction, she noticed him exhale very slowly before their eyes met. She thought to herself that maybe she had the same effect on him. Then she remembered that she just met this guy. No one fell for someone after just an hour. That only happened in romance novels, not in real life.

"This is where I work," she said as Alexander followed Olivia through the center and down a corridor to her own office. *Why did I say that?* Olivia thought to herself. Obviously, she worked there. She had a tendency to just talk when she was nervous. "Well, this is where I deal with paperwork. When I'm instructing, I'm in one of the studio rooms."

She kept rambling as Alexander stared at her, loving the way her mouth caressed certain words. He couldn't believe how breathtaking the woman standing in front of him was. There was something stirring within his depths, other than the obvious arousal. It was something more. "I'll just grab my stuff and we can get out of here."

Alexander walked around her office, glancing at the various motivational prints containing words of encouragement. That wasn't what he was interested in. No. He wanted to get a sense of her personality. He stopped when he reached a medal rack containing close to fifty medals, clearly from a variety of marathons and half-marathons.

"Wow," he said. "Run much?"

Olivia laughed. "You could say that."

"I'm impressed," he replied.

"So, you must be important to have a police detective at your beck and call at three o'clock on a Saturday morning," Olivia joked as she gathered her laptop and other items she needed for the weekend.

"Well, actually, she's my older sister. She helps me out from time to time."

"Ah, I see." After Olivia turned off the lights and locked her office doors, they headed back down the hall to the bay of elevators and waited. Once an elevator arrived, it whisked them to the bottom floor where they exited through the night entrance.

Alexander grabbed Olivia's hand, noticing her reluctance to return to the scene of her attack. He whispered into her ear, "You're safe with me. I promise. You can trust me." He looked deep into her brown eyes, urging her to feel safe with him.

There was that phrase again. *You can trust me.* Olivia searched her brain. Why was it so familiar?

The pair walked onto the main road where a black Escalade waited. Alexander helped Olivia into the back seat of the car before running around to the other side and climbing in next to her.

After Olivia gave Martin her address, he turned the car onto the empty Boston streets and drove toward the Back Bay. Alexander reached his hand across the seat and grabbed Olivia's, squeezing it. He needed the flesh-to-flesh contact. Olivia turned to look at him and he gave her a small smile. She didn't pull her hand away as she normally would have. She needed his touch, just like he needed hers. They held hands in silence during the short ride to Olivia's brownstone on Commonwealth Avenue.

When Martin pulled up outside her house, Alexander quickly exited the car and ran around to open Olivia's door for her. He grabbed her bags and led her up the front stairs, placing his hand on her lower back again.

Reaching her door, she turned to thank him for all of his help. "If you hadn't shown up..." she trailed off, the memory of Simon holding a knife to her throat returning after being blissfully absent for the past hour.

"I don't want to think about what could have happened if I didn't show up when I did. I guess my insomnia paid off tonight." He reached for Olivia's face and caressed her head where her injury was.

He flashed back to a summer at the beach house and a young girl falling down on the rocks by the beach, cutting her head. She had to get stitches. His eyes wandered briefly to the other side of her forehead and noticed there was a very slight red scar underneath her hairline. *Coincidence, Alex. It's just a coincidence.*

"Well, thank you, Mr. Burnham," Olivia said, grabbing her bags from him. She hated awkward situations like this. She wondered what the proper protocol was for saying good-bye to someone who just, literally, saved your ass.

After a brief pause, he placed a gentle kiss on Olivia's forehead where the old scar was and said good night. "People only have to call me Mr. Burnham in the bedroom," he whispered in her ear.

She gasped, her eyes growing wide.

He smiled, rubbing his thumb over her bottom lip. "Call me Alexander… For now." He winked as he pulled his hand away from Olivia's face. She immediately felt sad at the loss of contact. "And if you need anything, please call me. If you're scared or worried or just need someone to talk to, don't hesitate to call. I don't sleep much as it is, so I would welcome the distraction." He reached into his pocket and handed Olivia his business card.

"I'll keep that in mind," Olivia said, turning to enter her house.

"Miss Adler…" Alexander said, causing her to turn and stare back into his eyes again. He didn't want to leave her. And he didn't want her to walk out of his life just yet.

"Yes?"

Alexander hesitated. He contemplated asking her out. But like Olivia, he didn't date. He fucked. And that was it. "It was a pleasure meeting you. I do hope our paths cross again, but under better circumstances."

Olivia had no idea what to say to that. She simply nodded her head and turned to enter her house.

Alexander watched her close the door, amazed at how different his evening had turned out from where it began. He went out for a drink and ran into Chelsea, an old friend that he had hooked up with from time to time over the past decade. The tall red-head helped him forget everything for a few hours. He had been in total control of everything. That was what he needed. It was what he desired. Control made him happy. After that day all those years ago, he had decided to always be in control from then on. But now, after meeting Olivia, he was slowly starting to lose control over his own emotions. He wanted to know that girl, even if she didn't turn out to be *his* Olivia.

When Alexander heard the click of the front door, he turned and got into the SUV, directing Martin to take him back to the office.

Inside her house, Olivia walked to the kitchen, the hardwood floors of the old house creaking. She grabbed a bottle of water, filled the cat's food bowl, and walked up the stairs to the master bedroom on the second floor. She remembered how badly she wanted to wash the evening off her body. After taking a quick shower and getting ready for bed, she popped a few aspirin and collapsed on her soft bed. Her cat, Nepenthe, soon joined her. After the evening she had, she planned on staying in her bed the following day. Screw the long run. Olivia sent Kiera a quick text, letting her know she was home, before setting her cell phone on the charger.

Olivia drifted off to sleep fairly easily for once and dreamed of beautiful green eyes.

On the other side of town, Alexander entered his office and unlocked the wall safe. For the first time since his father was killed over five years ago, he took out an envelope addressed to him, recognizing his father's handwriting instantly. He debated opening it. And he sat staring at the letter all night, scared of what his father's last words to him would reveal.

Chapter Four

An Unexpected Surprise

"Sweetheart, hurry up. We need to get a move on!" a young Olivia's mother shouted at her as she grabbed a few last things from her summer home. They usually didn't leave their beach house until after Labor Day, but they had to leave early. Olivia didn't know why they had to leave so quickly. Olivia's mother said it was an emergency and that she had to be a brave girl. But she was only six years old.

Olivia sat in the back seat of the car, playing with Mr. Bear, her favorite stuffed animal, as her father sped away. Her mama must have been tired from all the packing because she had fallen asleep in the front seat.

The car merged onto the interstate and her father became more relaxed, although he checked the rear-view mirror more than he usually did. Out of nowhere, a dark SUV pulled up behind their car. Someone had found them. He tried to accelerate, but his sedan was no match for the SUV steadily catching up. His face remained calm, a staple of his CIA training. He was no longer trying to save his family. He was protecting his assets.

"I love you," he said to his sleeping wife. He turned around, his face neutral, trying not to scare Olivia in the back seat. *"We love you very much, Livvy."*

Olivia didn't look up from her bear. *"I know."*

Then a crash. Olivia's head snapped hard against the seat in front of her. She slipped into unconsciousness.

"Hey, Olibia. We need to get out of here, okay?" a boy with green eyes suddenly woke Olivia up as he tried to unbuckle her seat belt. Olivia knew this boy somehow. He always called her Olibia.

"My mama and papa…" Olivia cried, remembering that there was a crash and her head hurt. She hoped her parents' heads didn't hurt.

"*I know. But this is an emergency and you have to be brave,*" *the boy pled with her.*

Olivia wanted to be brave for the boy. "*Okay. I'll be a brave little girl.*" *She reached out her hand and he pulled her through the shattered car window. Although he was not very strong, he picked Olivia up, running as he carried her to safety. As he did, Olivia noticed her uncle looking into the passenger side of the crashed car, a scared look across his face.*

"*I don't feel so well,*" *she said to the boy. The world spun around her. Her head hurt. She didn't know what was going on.*

"*I know. We're going to get you help. We're going to protect you always, Olibia. Nothing bad will ever happen again. You can trust me.*" *And then nothing. Black. Emptiness.*

~~~~~~~~~~

Olivia woke up with a start, shaking. She hadn't had a dream like that in a while. It was always the same. Her parents always died in the dream. She usually never saw who pulled her to safety, but that time she did. The boy with the green eyes. She knew him somehow, but couldn't remember how. And those words. *You can trust me.* What did it all mean?

She tried to get her bearings. She was in her bedroom. She was laying in her large king size bed, Nepenthe curled up at her feet. The shades were drawn and it was pitch black. She heard a buzzing sound and realized that her cell phone was vibrating on the nightstand. She looked at the phone and saw Kiera's name and photo flashing. She answered groggily.

"Libby, oh my God. You're alive. Are you okay?" Kiera screamed into the phone.

"I'm fine," Olivia answered.

"It's almost five and you haven't been answering your phone all day long! I've been worried sick!" she chastised her friend.

"Kiera, I'm sorry. I didn't get to bed until after four in the morning last night. I'm exhausted."

"Oh, yeah? Did you break down and invite Simon over for one last fling?"

"God, no!" she shouted into the phone. "But something happened last night that did involve Simon," Olivia said gravely.

"What happened, Libs? I know he was drunk when he left the bar last night, but he left at like ten. I saw him get into a cab."

"Well, apparently he circled the fucking block because when I went to get into my office building after I left the bar, he was waiting by the night entrance." Olivia thought about why he would leave the bar just to come back. Something didn't add up.

"Oh my God! What happened? Are you okay?"

"I'm fine, Kiera. Just a little shaken up and minus a pair of my favorite underwear. He attacked me. It was so weird. I'm such an idiot." Olivia proceeded to tell her what happened the previous night. "I'm just lucky I got away and that a guy who works in my building saw me being chased and caught him."

"So he kicked Simon's ass for you?"

Olivia laughed, thankful her friend had lightened the mood a little. "He definitely did. I didn't get too close of a look at Simon, but he was unconscious, so…"

"Who was this mystery man?" Kiera interrupted.

"Just someone who works in my building," she said quickly, not wanting to get into any details about the gorgeous man she met the previous evening, excitement coursing through her veins just thinking about him. "Listen, I'm starving. Want to come over for a girls night? I'll order some Chinese. We'll pig out."

"Fine, but I swear to God, if you order anything with tofu, I'm no longer your friend."

Olivia laughed at her friend's response. Kiera despised tofu. Olivia loved it.

"Okay. Grab some wine on your way over, please. I think I'm out. Give me about half an hour to take a bath." She hung up and walked downstairs into the kitchen, grabbing her binder full of various take-out menus and finding their favorite Chinese Bistro. Thankfully they delivered.

Twenty minutes later, after a nice relaxing bath, Olivia was lounging on her couch on the first floor of her house, dressed in a pair of black yoga pants and a green tank top, when her doorbell rang. It couldn't have been Kiera. She didn't knock or ring the doorbell. She had a key to Olivia's place and usually just let herself in. And take-out wouldn't be arriving for another half an hour or so.

Olivia got off the couch, walking across the large, airy living room and into the hallway toward the front door. She looked out the peephole, a confused look on her face when she saw a man holding a bouquet of flowers. She opened the door and thanked the man, searching for a clue as to who they could be from. No one had ever sent her flowers before. There had to be a card somewhere.

"Who sent you flowers, girly?" she heard Kiera shout from down the street as Olivia turned to head back inside.

"I don't know," she replied, walking through her front door. She placed the vase on the kitchen island and found the card that was with the beautiful floral arrangement of calla lilies and yellow tulips. She opened the envelope and pulled out the card.

*Just wanted to send you something to
brighten your day and help you forget
about last night.
-Yours,
A. T. B.*

A smile crept across Olivia's face as she read the card.

"Who is A. T. B.?" Kiera asked, peering over Olivia's shoulder at the card.

"He's the guy who kicked Simon's ass last night," she replied dismissively, grabbing the Willamette Valley pinot noir Kiera clutched in her hand.

"Okay. I can tell there's more to this story than what you've been telling me. I mean, look at the type of flowers he sent you!" she said, toying with the arrangement.

"I have no idea what you're talking about. Why does it matter what type of flowers he sent?" Olivia grabbed a corkscrew and quickly opened the bottle of wine, needing the alcohol at that moment.

"Libs, he sent you yellow tulips and calla lilies. Calla lilies mean beauty, and yellow tulips symbolize hopeless love," Kiera replied with a dreamy look in her eyes.

Olivia rolled her eyes as she handed her a glass of wine. "Please don't read too much into the flowers. He probably just had his secretary send them or something." They made their way into the living room separated from her kitchen by a simple archway. Olivia loved the open floor plan of her home. It was an old brownstone house, but she had updated it with her modern and simplistic style. They sat down on the couch and Olivia turned on the television, hoping to distract her friend. "He helped me last night and just wanted to bring a smile to my face today. That's all."

"So what was he like? There's definitely something you're not telling me based on that stupid grin on your face."

Olivia looked at her friend and couldn't help it. "He's the most beautiful man I have ever laid eyes on," she blurted out.

"Aw, Libby!" she exclaimed, hugging Olivia and nearly spilling her wine. "You're actually attracted to someone! I didn't think I would ever see the day this would happen!"

"Hey! I've been attracted to guys before! I don't just sleep with anyone. They've got to be good looking." Olivia took a hearty sip of her wine, needing some liquid courage to get through that conversation.

"Yeah, but it's easy to have sex without feeling any connection to someone. Hell, that's all you've ever done. And there's a difference between finding someone good looking and finding them attractive. You can be good looking and not be attractive. Being attracted to someone isn't just digging them on a physical level. It's something more. It's opening your soul to someone, letting them in. Telling them your hopes and dreams and fears. Letting them know the real you. I know you have trouble with that, Libby, but don't you want to have that connection with someone so you know you're not all alone in this fucked up world?"

Olivia's older and wiser friend definitely had a point. "He sent shivers throughout my body every time he touched me," she gushed. "I had no idea what was going on. Maybe it was because I was just attacked by Simon and he saved me. Maybe

I've got like Stockholm syndrome or something," she joked.

"Libs, Stockholm syndrome is when you get kidnapped and want to bone your kidnapper. You definitely don't have Stockholm syndrome. What you've got is a bona-fide crush on a man!" She oozed excitement over the thought. "So tell me," she crossed her legs, turning to face Olivia. "What happened after he kicked Simon's ass?"

Olivia proceeded to tell Kiera all about Alexander taking her to his office, patching up her head, calling a detective to take her statement, and then driving her home. She left out all the details about him owning the building and having a posh penthouse office, as well as a personal driver and/or badass bodyguard.

She made a mental note to do some research on Alexander later when she had some privacy. She was intrigued to know more about him and how he could have such a successful company when he appeared so young. He seemed relatively quiet the night before, simply listening to her ramble on about her sex life. And he was so gentle when he took care of her. But then she remembered his husky voice saying, *"People only have to call me Mr. Burnham in the bedroom."* It almost seemed like there were two very different sides of Alexander. Snapping out of her thoughts, she told Kiera that he left his cell phone number with the specific instructions to call if Olivia ever needed to talk.

"Dude, you should totally call him!" Kiera shouted excitedly. She bounced up and down on the couch with an infectious smile on her face. Olivia worried that she would spill wine on the red sofa. "Come on. Do it right now so I can hear his voice, too." She giggled.

"I think after my last failed 'relationship,'" Olivia said, quoting the word relationship with her fingers, "I'm off men for a bit. Maybe the whole no-strings-attached thing isn't such a smart idea, anyway. When I don't get to know the person, I am blind to whatever propensities they have, you know?"

She paused for a moment and looked at Kiera who remained silent. She didn't have to say anything. Olivia knew what she was thinking just by looking at her eyes. Kiera was happy that her friend had finally realized her approach to relationships had been anything but healthy.

"Anyway, I don't want to talk about this anymore," Olivia said, breaking the growing tension in the room. "Let's rent a cheesy movie and drink wine, okay?"

"Okay." Kiera relaxed into the couch. Their food arrived a few minutes later. They watched a few chick flicks, drank a bottle of wine, and ate almost half of the Chinese feast Olivia ordered.

At midnight, Kiera left to go home. Olivia, however, was wide-awake, having slept most of the day away. So, she did what she had wanted to do all night. She grabbed her MacBook out of her bag, powered it up, and typed "Alexander Burnham" into the search engine.

Olivia was surprised at the magnitude of hits that were returned, her heart beating rapidly as she started to get an overall picture of the beautiful man with green eyes.

Alexander Burnham dropped out of Harvard after a semester and joined the Navy. He eventually passed SEAL training and had been deployed on a variety of special ops around the world. After his father died five years ago, he left the Navy to take over his security company at the age of twenty-four. He was able to use his SEAL training in building his company into one of the foremost private security firms in the world.

His firm provided security and military services across the globe. Its contractors had trained local militaries in Iraq and Afghanistan, as well as Africa and South America. In addition to training local militaries, its contractors often provided protection services for key staff members traveling abroad and domestically, as well as protection of important natural resources, such as the oil fields in the Middle East.

Apparently, it also assisted various government and private entities in conducting certain classified operations, which Olivia deducted was a nice way of saying covert and clandestine services. Further, his company had recently expanded its services to include military aviation support, offering air support, medical evacuations, and armed air escort to any location on earth.

In addition to its vast overseas presence, his company also provided security for a wide variety of clients on domestic soil, from dignitaries to celebrities. What caught Olivia's eye was the amount of pro bono work his firm did, offering protection services for victims of a variety of crimes, including new identities. He had offices all over the country and abroad, although he made the Boston office his home. All that and he hadn't even hit his thirtieth birthday. Her research showed that he was successful and compassionate at the same time. It was a unique combination of qualities that most men she came across didn't even come close to possessing.

Sighing, she got up from the couch and looked at the flowers he sent, reading the card again. She was about to put it back into the envelope when writing on the back of the card caught her eye.

Please call me. Anytime.

So he did send them himself and didn't just have his secretary send them, she thought to herself. Olivia glanced at the clock in the kitchen, observing that it was after one in the morning. She debated calling him. But what would her reason have been for doing so? To thank him for sending flowers maybe? But it was late. She decided to call him the following day.

Olivia closed her laptop and went upstairs to settle into her bed. Her mind raced thinking about Alexander Burnham. She closed her eyes and thought about what it would be like to actually have a relationship with someone who genuinely cared about her.

She recalled all of Alexander's accomplishments and her subconscious instantly told her that he was so far out of her league. He was beautiful and successful. And, while Olivia was attractive enough, she was still trying to figure everything out. Her past haunted her. She had trouble just making it through the day sometimes. She didn't have anything to offer any relationship. She wouldn't even know how to act in a relationship. With that thought, sleep enveloped Olivia.

~~~~~~~~~~

In the South End of Boston, a man answered his cell phone, his deep voice reverberating through the room. "Donovan."

"Mark, um, I mean Donovan, it's me. Simon," he said nervously.

"I thought I made it rather clear that you were never to call this number. Not unless you had good news. Do you have good news?"

"Well, no. Not really. I tried to get the information you wanted, and the bitch fought back, and, well... I'm in jail. I need a lawyer, man, and you've got to get me out of here."

"Fuck."

CHAPTER FIVE

A BEAUTIFUL SOUND

The sun seeped into Alexander's bedroom, waking him up on Sunday morning. Finally, a full night of sleep. He looked at his nightstand and glared at the envelope. "Not yet," he said to himself. "Soon."

Alexander picked his cell phone off the charger and saw that it was eight in the morning. He reluctantly got out of bed and made a cup of coffee in order to prepare for his morning run. Coffee in hand, he made his way into the study to get a few e-mails out of the way before going out.

As he sat at his desk, his thoughts were consumed by one woman. *Olivia*. His feelings for her confused him. He was attracted to her. That much was evident. But there was something more there. And he wasn't sure whether it was because he desperately wanted her to be *her*, the girl he failed to save all those years ago, or because they connected on a deeper level. Normally, Alexander would ask her out, sleep with her, and then never see her again. But something about Olivia made him want more than just a quick fuck.

After throwing on some running clothes, Alexander left his three-story penthouse apartment and ran toward Boston Common Park. Olivia lived right around the corner from the famous Boston landmark and he secretly hoped that she was heading out for her morning run at the same location.

After braving the Boston streets teeming with tourists, Alexander finally reached Boston Common, inwardly detesting the hot and humid weather that early in the morning, but he had run in tougher conditions in the past. As he ran through the large park, he couldn't stop thinking about the woman he met just a few nights before. Her eyes flashed through his memory. He smirked a little as he recalled the expression on her face during his attempts to hit on her.

As he rounded the corner, the crystal clear lake came into view. The Swan Boats were out as tourists clambered for their turn to ride the famous boats. In the corner of his eye, he saw a woman sprinting in his direction. He stilled, flashing back to Friday night. It all seemed so familiar, but there was something different. No, this time, the woman was running for fun and not because her life depended on it. It looked like her, but surely, it couldn't be. What were the chances?

Alexander continued to run toward the woman. It *was* Olivia Adler. He couldn't believe his luck as he full out grinned at her, hoping she would stop for a quick chat. But she was so focused that she wasn't paying attention to anything around her, including anyone running nearby.

"Whoa! Slow down killer!" Alexander shouted, causing Olivia to stop abruptly.

She turned around, taking her ear buds out, and searched for the source of those words. She knew instantly when she saw his eyes. Those beautiful green eyes that she had been dreaming about the past few nights.

"Mr. Burnham, I mean Alexander," Olivia said breathlessly, blushing when she recalled his words from the other night. "*People only call me Mr. Burnham in the bedroom*." She bent down and put her hands on her knees, trying to slow down her breathing. "Sorry. I didn't see you. I was in the zone."

"What zone is that? The heart attack zone? You need to be careful in this humidity," he said in a stern voice. *Olivia needed to take better care of herself*, he thought. It was careless to run with such intensity in that heat and humidity. Something could have happened to her. Why did he care? He didn't know what to make of the strange feelings he had for her.

Olivia looked up and stared at the attractive man in front of her, taking in the beautifully sculpted biceps threatening to bust through the arms of his running shirt. Licking her lips, she imagined how he would look with his shirt off, wanting to rub her hands all over the finely defined abs she could faintly make out through his shirt.

Alexander's face softened with a hint of amusement, noticing her eyes traveling over his body. "You're not from Kenya, so stop trying to run like you are."

Olivia laughed and it felt good. Maybe it was the nerves of being so close to Alexander again, but she didn't care. She couldn't remember the last time someone made her laugh like that.

"That's a beautiful sound," Alexander said as Olivia straightened up, finally having caught her breath.

"What is? A girl out of breath from trying to break the four minute mile?" She smiled as she took a sip from her water bottle.

"No. The sound of your laughter," he said softly. "I think it's quickly climbing on my list of favorite sounds." Olivia blushed at his words, dropping her gaze from his. He took a step forward, leaning down to her ear. "But I'm sure I'd enjoy the sound of you out of breath as well, just as long as it were my doing."

Olivia gasped, blushing again, as she turned her eyes away from him. Something about Alexander and his words made her blush like a teenager. She was normally so confident and sure of herself, but around Alexander, her stomach seemed to be all knotted up, never knowing what words were about to fall out of his sensual mouth. She found herself thinking about all the ways she wanted Alexander to make her completely breathless. She felt the possibilities were endless as her eyes roamed his body to his perfect legs.

"See something you like, Miss Adler?" he asked with a mischievous grin on his face.

Shit, Olivia thought. *He totally caught me checking him out!*

Alexander smirked, proud of himself for catching Olivia off-guard. For someone who seemed so confident, he could tell it was all a front to keep people away.

Avoiding his eyes and his last statement, Olivia turned, gazing at the lake. "This is one of my favorite spots in the city," she said, taking in the Swan Boats as they floated through the park that morning. She had no idea why she felt the need to share that piece of information with him. She was desperately trying to ignore the desire that had begun to grow within her own body, particularly after his previous comments. "I couldn't decide whether to run the Charles today or come to the Commons."

"Well, I'm glad you went with the latter."

Olivia turned to look at him and was met with a full beaming smile. There it was again. That electricity between them. After a brief moment of silence, Olivia felt that she needed to say something. "Thank you for the flowers," she said, crossing her arms in front of her body. "I thought about calling you last night, but it was one in the morning and I didn't want to disturb you," she explained nervously as she stood not even a foot away from Alexander, staring into his piercing green eyes. His proximity was overwhelming.

"I told you to call me anytime and I meant it," he replied softly, taking a step closer to her, their bodies almost touching. Olivia could smell him. He smelled of sweat and body wash, and a unique scent that she assumed was just him. A slight breeze ruffled through the trees, causing a few wayward curls to fall in front of her face. Alexander gently tucked a curl behind her ear and she immediately became self-conscious, not wanting him to be turned off by her flushed complexion or her sweaty body.

Olivia had no idea why Alexander affected her as he did. She never found herself completely speechless in front of the opposite sex before in her life. But something about Alexander made all notions quickly disappear, prohibiting her from forming any rational thought. Most of her life, she had shied away from any sort of real relationship, fearful that she would be left heartbroken and alone, but there was something about the man in front of her that made her want to get to know him better. And there was part of her that felt as if she already did.

"Well, I should finish my run," Olivia said, breaking her gaze from his eyes and taking a step back, hopelessly wanting to keep her distance from Alexander. "I'm planning to head to Beer Works later for the game," she explained.

"Oh? You're going to the game today?" Alexander piqued up. This was turning into a golden opportunity for him.

"I hadn't planned to. I just love the atmosphere by Fenway on game day. And I love the watermelon ale at Beer Works, so it's a win-win, if you ask me." Olivia took another drink of water.

"Well, I have Red Sox season tickets. If you want to watch the game, I can take you with me. I was going to take my brother, but he can go next time."

"I don't know. I wouldn't want to interfere."

Alexander reached for Olivia's hand and that spark was back. That feeling of electricity between them that Olivia had only read about in romance novels. That feeling she was convinced did not exist in real life. "If I didn't want you to join me, I would not have asked you," he said in a husky voice that just oozed sex.

Part of her wanted to refuse Alexander's invitation. Yes, he was sexy as sin, but going out together, alone, scared Olivia. She secretly wanted to invite him over so she could fuck him and get him out of her system. Then she could go on with her perfectly ordered, albeit lonely, existence. But she realized something about Alexander would make it impossible to get him out of her system.

"I promise I don't bite," he whispered. "Unless you want me to."

Fuck. How could she say no to that?

"Okay. I'll go with you. But I need to go to Beer Works first for a watermelon ale."

"Absolutely," he replied with a twinkle in his eye. "The game starts at four-fifteen. Why don't I pick you up at two? That way we can relax and have a few beers before the game."

"Okay," Olivia agreed, glancing down at her GPS watch. She had more than enough time to get in some serious running before he would pick her up.

"Please take it easy on the rest of your run." Alexander looked down at the woman in front of him, the stern look back on his face. Olivia didn't know whether to find it frightening or endearing that he seemed to care about her so much as to chastise her behavior. And there was something about that look and voice that made her want to obey him.

"I will." Olivia turned to finish her run. She briefly glanced back and waved at him, thinking about what she had just agreed to. She had never dated before and immediately became anxious as she thought about what she had gotten herself into.

Growing up, Olivia went to an all girls boarding school for as long as she could remember. She would spend her summers with her uncle, who was her guardian, and he didn't really allow her to date. He was a little over-protective, which was understandable considering her parents were killed when she was young. Even in college, Olivia didn't date. She would casually see people, but she never really let anyone in. This was her life and it worked perfectly until Alexander walked into it two nights ago. Thinking about his hooded eyes and the way his mouth caressed certain words made her stomach tighten in excitement. No one had ever made her feel like that before. And that scared her to death.

What was Alexander doing to her? She had known him for less than forty-eight hours and already he had her rethinking her relationships. Before meeting him, she was too worried about losing someone close to her to allow anyone in. She always pushed away anyone who seemed interested, refusing to fall in love. But now, something changed. And she wasn't sure how she felt about that.

~~~~~~~~~

Olivia returned home around noon and got ready for her afternoon with Alexander. After showering and going through the tedious process of straightening her thick, curly hair, she headed downstairs to the kitchen and prepared a quick spinach and quinoa salad. As she ate, she sat at the breakfast bar, staring at the flowers Alexander sent the day before.

The yellow tulips and white calla lilies were beginning to slowly bloom and Olivia thought that the flowers could be a metaphor for her feelings for Alexander. They were slowly growing stronger and stronger. But just like everything else in her life, the flowers would inevitably die. And she would just be left alone. Again.

She played around with her salad, regretting that she actually agreed to go to the game with Alexander. It seemed like a good idea at the time as his delicious body stood in front of her, his voice husky when he told her he didn't bite unless she wanted him to. But now in the clarity of her home, she knew it would just end horribly for all involved. Nothing ever worked out for Olivia. She was all sorts of crazy and it was only a matter of time before her crazy scared off Alexander. As she finished her lunch, she wondered why she even cared. She needed to clear her head.

Trekking up to the third floor of her house, she entered her huge music room, which took up the entire floor. It was her pride and joy. After she bought her house, she hired contractors to demolish all the walls between rooms, making the third floor one large open space. It was just her, so she didn't have a need for two additional guest bedrooms. One guest bedroom and one master bedroom was all she really needed.

Entering the large room, she smiled as she walked to the upright piano placed against the wall facing the street, a feeling of calm overtaking her body from being enclosed in the four walls of her musical sanctuary.

In addition to her piano, she had several different types of guitars, a keyboard, amps, and anything else a musician could possibly desire. Several framed posters of her favorite bands and musicians adorned the walls. Against the far wall sat a large couch as well as several lounge chairs. That room was her refuge when things got bad. Some weeks, it seemed she practically lived in there.

Olivia shuffled through her bookcase, searching for the sheet music to the song she had on her mind, not really even needing it, but it never hurt to have a guide. After several minutes of searching, she found it, making a mental note to organize her music. The room was a little stuffy, given the late August heat, so she opened one of the large windows to let in some fresh air, looking down at the street below to make sure Alexander wasn't there yet.

She walked over to the piano and placed the music in front of her. Olivia had one passion in life. And that passion was music. It was how she dealt with life.

Olivia sat down and started the song, the sound of the piano and her voice filling the large room, the acoustics perfect.

At that moment, Alexander pulled up in front of Olivia's house. He rang the doorbell. No answer. He rang again. Still no answer. He immediately became concerned. He tried the door. It was unlocked. He gingerly opened it, calling Olivia's name. His ears were soon met with a beautiful melody that could only be Olivia singing.

He immediately flashed back to his younger years. Spending time with family friends. Playing piano and singing along during the holidays. Then having those friends taken from him. They weren't the only victims that day. Part of Alexander died that day, too.

He walked up the stairs, listening to Olivia play piano, her voice soaring through the house. He could hear the pain and loss.

As Olivia sang, she thought about everyone she had lost in her life. She grieved for her parents, desperately hoping that she had made them proud. She grieved for the life she had before the accident. The life she couldn't remember. She wasn't sure if it was the loss of her parents that caused her so much pain or whether it was the loss of her life before that day. She tried so hard to remember her friends and family. She must have had friends. But who were they? And where were they now? Would they remember her? And why couldn't she remember them? No. The only clue she had about her life before the accident came to her in the form of her dream. The green-eyed boy.

Olivia finished the song, keeping her eyes closed for a few seconds, trying to deal with her emotions after singing the song that reminded her so much of her parents and all the loss she had suffered throughout her life.

She took a deep, steadying breath, becoming startled when

she heard a clapping sound in the doorway behind her. She screamed, jumping out of her chair and turning around. Alexander stood there, leaning against the doorway, a bright smile across his chiseled face. *God, he looks good*, Olivia said to herself, salivating over the man standing in front of her. No matter what, he definitely had good style, she thought, eyeing his crisp white polo shirt, plaid shorts and a pair of flip flops. *I love a man who can wear flip flops*, she smiled to herself.

"That was beautiful," Alexander said, breaking Olivia's stream of thought.

"How did you get in here?" She looked at him, crossing her arms defensively.

"I rang the doorbell and you didn't answer. I was worried something had happened to you. Your door was unlocked, so I let myself in. Then I heard you playing the piano and singing. I just had to listen to you."

He took a step forward, brushing a wayward strand of hair behind Olivia's ear, his hand lingering, trying to keep his eyes trained on her face. Her legs looked amazing in the short navy and white striped sundress she wore that she accented with coral jewelry. He thought about how it would feel to have those long legs wrapped around him. Snapping out of his thoughts, he smiled. "You're very talented, you know."

She blushed at his words, staring down at her feet. "Thank you." Olivia didn't take compliments very well, unsure of the reason why. She knew she was talented. She had been singing and performing for as long as she could remember. It was the only thing that truly gave her joy.

"Look at me, Olivia," Alexander demanded. Olivia snapped her head up, unsure of why she felt the need to obey him. But she did. "You are very talented." He held her chin in place and stared at those big brown eyes of hers.

"Sorry I didn't hear the doorbell. It's hard to hear it up here," Olivia said, interrupting the building tension that she started to feel all over her body, including between her legs. She turned around and folded the cover over the piano keys, needing to separate herself from Alexander before she invited him straight to her bedroom.

"Are you ready to go?" He held his hand out to her.

"Yes," she replied, grabbing his hand.

Alexander marveled at how small her hand felt when enveloped in his. They walked out the front door and she turned to lock up. She felt Alexander come up behind her, mere inches away. He whispered in her ear, "Please always remember to lock your front door, even when you're home. You can't trust anyone."

"I thought you said I could trust you." Olivia turned to face him, remembering his words from a few nights ago. She smirked while she placed her keys in her purse.

"You probably shouldn't, but I'd like you to." He smiled a sort of mischievous smile, caressing Olivia's forehead where her bruise was. She closed her eyes at the contact, enjoying the feeling of Alexander's hands on her face. Why did a simple touch feel so good? Olivia didn't want to think about what it would feel like if he were to touch other parts of her body. She thought she would explode.

Alexander stared down at Olivia, both of their breathing becoming heavy. He couldn't understand the pull that woman had on him. He led a life of few distractions, avoiding all serious relationships, just like Olivia. It was hard to maintain total control when in a relationship. Instead, he would see a few women on occasion. Women who knew and understood his needs. But Olivia made him want to change his mind.

"Do you feel it, too?" he asked, bringing his hand to cup her chin, tilting her head up.

"Yes," Olivia breathed, her voice husky. She was normally cool, calm, and collected. Around Alexander, she acted like a thirteen-year-old girl who had her first crush.

"Good," he said, turning and walking down her front steps, opening the back door to the waiting Escalade. Olivia needed to take a minute to steady herself so that she didn't trip over her feet. Once she was finally confident that she could climb down the stairs without causing serious bodily harm, she joined Alexander on the sidewalk and climbed into the car.

Martin sat at the driver's seat and greeted Olivia as she entered the SUV. "Good afternoon, Miss Adler."

"Hello, Martin."

"Looking forward to the ball game this afternoon?"

"Yes, I am. Thank you." The door opposite her opened and Alexander sat down, preparing for the short drive. He reached out and grabbed Olivia's hand.

Her skin really was soft. Alexander could touch her all day. "You look beautiful today, Miss Adler," he said softly as he stared into her eyes.

"Thank you, Mr. Burnham," Olivia smirked, thinking about how much she wanted to scream his name.

Alexander brought Olivia's hand to his lips and kissed it very gently. Her heart raced at the contact from his lips on her body. She stared into his eyes and realized she was falling for that man, as much as she didn't want that to happen. That was bad. Very, very bad.

CHAPTER SIX

PUZZLE PIECES

Olivia and Alexander arrived at Beer Works after a longer than normal drive from Olivia's house. She didn't live far from Fenway Park, but with all the fans out on the streets for the game, it took a little longer than normal, which was to be expected on game day in Boston.

There was already a line outside, but the doorman saw Alexander and permitted the pair to enter, nodding a greeting to him. As they made their way through the industrial looking microbrewery, Alexander was greeted by more people, shaking hands with some, stopping to take pictures with others. He must have been more well-known than Olivia originally thought.

Olivia had distanced herself so much from the social scene that she didn't realize she was in the company of a local celebrity. Alexander had recently been named one of the country's most eligible bachelors by *Esquire* magazine, but that wasn't something he really bragged about.

They made their way to an empty high-top table toward the rear of the large bar and sat down. A server came to take their order of two watermelon ales. As she waited for her drink, Olivia's mind drifted back to the song she was singing before Alexander arrived. She loved the feeling of sharing a beautiful song with someone. And she felt that she shared that song with Alexander, although she wasn't aware he was even standing there. She wondered if he was able to figure out the meaning behind the song, about how she lost the few parental figures she had in her life. First when she was six, and then again on the day of her college graduation.

"Penny for your thoughts," Alexander said, watching Olivia stare out into space, deep in thought, as a server dropped off two watermelon ales complete with watermelon slice.

"Sorry," she said, returning her eyes to Alexander. "I was just thinking about my college graduation."

"Oh yeah? What about it?" He took a sip from his beer and Olivia did the same. It was so refreshing.

"Nothing really. Just how it seems so long ago. Thanks for inviting me." Olivia anxiously wanted to try to steer the conversation toward him and his life.

"You're welcome." He smiled at Olivia, staring at her perfect plump lips. He wondered how they tasted. He desperately wanted to find out. But, for once, he wasn't going to rush this. He could tell that Olivia was someone with a past. If he scared her off, he would regret it. For the first time he could remember, he wanted more than just a one-night stand with someone. And he wondered whether she felt the same way.

Olivia shifted nervously in her seat, taking a sip of beer with her trembling hand, fearful that he would ask too many questions. Questions she didn't want to answer.

"So, Alexander," she said, looking into his eyes, breaking the growing tension. "Are you a big Red Sox fan?" She figured that was a safe topic. *Boys love their sports, right?*

"I am," he said, his smile widening. "I spent my summers on the Cape growing up and remember going to games with my Dad when I was little." Olivia was relieved when he started to share some personal information about himself. She was eager to learn more about the man sitting in front of her, even though she was hesitant to share anything about herself.

"I've never actually been to a game inside Fenway," Olivia said quietly.

"What?" he exclaimed, dumbfounded. "How long have you been living here?"

That was a relatively safe question, so she decided to answer him truthfully. "I went to Boston College for undergrad. I started there about ten years ago. After graduation, I left but I ended up coming back about a year ago." She smiled, but he could tell there was more to the story. After an awkward silence, Olivia continued talking. "I missed it here and this was the only place that really felt like home." She tapped her fingernails nervously against the metal table.

"Where did you grow up? I know you're not from around here, not with that accent." Alexander had been trying to place her accent all weekend. It had a soft twang to it, particularly when she pronounced certain words.

"Charleston, South Carolina," Olivia laughed. She looked at Alexander, who seemed to have a perplexed look on his face. "I'm a southern beach bum at heart," she said, trying to bring the smile back to his face that was there seconds before.

Alexander couldn't believe she said she grew up in Charleston. He remained silent and stared at her as if he was trying to put a puzzle together.

But there was really no puzzle to put together. Olivia was just a girl from South Carolina who lost her family and wanted to start over.

Before she could ask him another question and keep the attention off her, he asked, "How about your parents? Are they still in Charleston?" He needed to know. He needed the back-story. Too many pieces were falling into place. There had been too many coincidences. The age. The name. Where she grew up. The music. Most of all, the music.

She froze after Alexander's question. That was the part about forming relationships Olivia hated. She despised the look she received when she told people that her parents were killed in a car crash when she was only six and too young to remember. Alexander looked at her with intense eyes. She started breathing quick and fast. It felt like the room was closing in on her.

She needed to get out of there. "I'll be right back," she said, stumbling out of her chair and trying to act as normal as possible. "Nature calls."

Alexander watched as Olivia practically ran away from the table, not knowing how to react to what just happened. She clearly had a panic attack. All he did was ask about her parents. That was another piece of the puzzle falling too easily into place. What happened to her parents? He needed to know.

Safe in the ladies room, Olivia took a minute to calm her breathing, splashing some water on her face and willing her heart to stop beating so quickly. She had never figured out why she panicked when people asked about her parents. Her therapist seemed to think that Olivia was repressing some memories about them; memories that were painful, causing her to react that way. The doctor was obviously full of it, according to Olivia, because she had very few memories of her parents.

As she stared at her face in the mirror, Olivia was unaware how much time had passed since she abruptly left Alexander at the table. Slowly opening the door to the bathroom, she saw piercing green eyes staring back at her. Alexander grabbed her arm, leading her down the hallway, his face awash with concern. "Are you okay?"

"Oh no," Olivia spat out, crossing her arms. "You don't get to go all Navy SEAL interrogation specialist on me." He gave Olivia a questioning look. "That's right. I Googled you."

Alexander softened the intense look he was giving Olivia. "I bet you did," he smirked, raising an eyebrow. She couldn't help but to laugh in response. And not just a small polite laugh, but a gut-splitting, all-consuming laugh. *This feels good*, Olivia thought to herself.

That sound was like music to Alexander's ears. He decided right then and there that he would do everything in his power to make sure he could hear that sweet melody as often as possible. He pulled Olivia into his arms, stroking her hair, whispering, "Top ten favorite sounds."

Holy crap! He feels good, Olivia said to herself as she nuzzled her face against Alexander's broad chest, listening to his heart race. Hers was racing, too. She turned her chin up and stared into his eyes, feeling so small enveloped in his arms. He licked his lips and Olivia was certain he was going to kiss her.

Alexander gazed down at the beautiful woman in his arms. He wanted to kiss her so badly. She was asking for it, pleading for it with her eyes. With her mouth. Should he kiss her, even given his suspicions? What if he was right and it's her?

After a few intense seconds, he exhaled loudly, shaking his head, and released Olivia from his embrace, grabbing her hand to go back to the table.

Olivia was confused. Maybe he wasn't as attracted to her as she was to him. He was so sweet and caring one second, and the next she couldn't read his behavior. He was almost cold and removed.

They sat back down at the table where another round of beer awaited them.

"I ordered another round. I hope you don't mind." He glanced at Olivia but didn't hold her gaze.

"I'm sorry about that. I mean before, when I, well…"

"When you had a near panic attack?" He raised his eyebrow, taking a sip from his beer.

"I can't hide anything from you, can I?"

Alexander remained silent, not prodding her, but Olivia knew he wanted an explanation. After a few brief seconds and several gulps of liquid courage, Olivia took a deep breath before telling Alexander about herself. "I don't really have as many panic attacks as I used to. Talking about my parents usually triggers them."

"I'm sorry," he responded. "I didn't know. I would never have asked you about them if I knew it would harm you in any way. The last thing I want to do is hurt you, Olivia." The soft look was back in his eyes. Mr. Warm, Caring, and Compassionate was back. Olivia wanted him to stay. And she wanted to be the reason he had that sparkle in his eyes.

She continued to share some personal information with him. Information that took her years to share with Kiera and Mo, but something about Alexander seemed so familiar, as if he knew her story. "They were killed when I was six. Car accident. I don't remember anything. I think what hurts the most is that I can barely remember anything about my life before the accident, and I've tried. God damn it, I've tried so hard," she trembled as she took a deep breath. "The one thing I do remember is they never called me Sarah. I have no memory of that ever being my name. But I do remember my dad calling me Livvy." Tears threatened to spill down her face. "I was in the car when it happened. But I survived somehow." She thought about telling him about the boy with green eyes she had been seeing in her dreams the past few nights, but she couldn't be sure that he actually existed. None of it made any sense.

Alexander looked at her, torn about what to say. She just admitted her parents were killed in a car accident. And that her father called her Livvy. He remembered that. He was the only one that called her Livvy. Too many pieces were fitting into place. He could brush off maybe one or two similarities between the woman sitting in front of him and the girl he knew all those years ago. But there were too many coincidences now.

He was smiling on the inside. *Is it really her?* he thought to himself. But at the same time, if it wasn't her, this was still a girl who lost her parents so young and that had shaped the woman she had become. And probably the reason she seemed to keep everyone away.

"That must be very hard for you, even after all these years."

"It is." Olivia breathed a sigh of relief. It felt good to actually share that with him. "I just wish I could remember them. I feel like I should, but they died when I was so young. I have a few good memories of my mom, but I wish I could remember my dad. I don't even have that many photos of them. They say that photos can help trigger memories." She finished her beer and Alexander signaled a server to bring another round.

"I remember spending summers with my uncle, begging him for photos of my parents. And he got so angry with me. I never understood why I couldn't have any photos of them. And as the years went on, I started to forget what they even looked like. I'll never forget my sixteenth birthday. My uncle sent me a card and in it was a photo of me and my parents when I was little. He said it was taken just a few months before…"

Reaching across the table, Alexander grasped Olivia's hand, clutching it. "I won't pressure you to talk about anything you don't want to. I understand that even though this happened years ago, the pain is still with you. And it will probably never leave you. And it shouldn't. That way your parents will always be alive in here," he said, dropping her hand and placing his now free hand over his chest where his heart was.

Olivia imitated him, knowing that he was right. She could almost sense that Alexander had been through a terrible loss, too. There was something in his eyes as he spoke to her about her own loss that made it all too clear that he was still dealing with his own issues. "I saw a shrink for years and you've made more sense in a few minutes than she made in nearly ten years." Olivia laughed and he joined.

God, that's a beautiful sound, Alexander thought.

Olivia finished her story after a server dropped off another round of beer. "I was sent to a boarding school after my parents died. My uncle kind of took care of me. He wasn't really my uncle. I mean, I called him Uncle Charles, but he was a close family friend. So the title just kind of stuck. He was originally from Boston, I think, but had some property in Charleston and would come down from time to time, mostly when I was on school break. For whatever reason, he thought it was more important for me to stay in Charleston than to travel up north to him. The older I got, the more time I spent at my school during the breaks for various extracurricular activities, although he did keep a rather watchful eye on what activities I was allowed to be involved in. That infuriated me as time went on." Olivia took a deep breath.

"When I was applying to colleges, he suggested giving Boston a try, that way he would be nearby. I got into Boston College and he helped me find my own place. We weren't that close. I think it was painful for him to be around me because I reminded him of my parents, especially my mom." She paused, remembering him always keeping watch on her, even in college while she was bartending. She recalled leaving the bar many nights to see him sitting in his car. It really put a damper on her ability to take someone home with her for a quick fling.

Alexander grabbed her hand again and looked at her, letting her know with his eyes that she could stop talking whenever she wanted to. But Alexander hoped she wouldn't. There were more pieces falling into place. Or maybe he just wanted them to fall into place.

"The day of my college graduation, I got a phone call telling me that my uncle had passed away. He was in the wrong place at the wrong time and was shot by a stray bullet, according to the person on the other end of the phone." Olivia closed her eyes, remembering how she felt when she received that phone call.

Alexander did the math in his head. When Olivia opened her eyes, his eyes were closed and he was rubbing his temples with his free hand. She continued. "The only family I had left was gone."

Alexander looked at her and squeezed her hand. He was suddenly hopeful. But if it was her, then where had she been all these years? He immediately feared for her safety. He hoped with everything that he was wrong and it was just a matter of coincidence. A whole lot of coincidence. If it was her, his father had obviously tried to protect her identity, telling Alexander that she died in that accident. Now that his father was dead, who was protecting her?

"I'm sorry. I shouldn't have told you that whole sob story. We barely know each other and I'm like a freaking Lifetime Movie over here." Olivia tried to lighten the atmosphere.

Her trick worked. He smiled slightly. "Lifetime Movie?"

"Yeah," she replied, laughing. "You know. Poor pathetic broken girl with a troubled past that she just can't get over, so she refuses to form relationships with anyone so that she won't get hurt anymore. It's such a tragic cliché, but I can't control what happens to be my life."

"You have nothing to be ashamed of, Olivia. Your past made you the woman you are today. If one thing was different about your life, you may be on an entirely different trajectory." He looked into her eyes, bringing her hand to his mouth. Kissing it ever so gently, he murmured, "And then we never would have met, and that is a mother fucking tragedy." The twinkle in his green eyes sent Olivia's heart soaring.

Alexander didn't care if she was the girl from all those years ago; the one who stole his heart when he was a little boy and he never really got it all back. Because the girl sitting in front of him now was filling the pieces of his torn heart. And she was worth getting to know.

~~~~~~~~~~

Across town, a middle-aged man sat in a stark room with all metal furniture.

"Simon MacKenzie. My name is Paul Flinnigan. I've been hired by Donovan to represent you." The tall, lanky man motioned to Donovan who was sitting next to him at the cold metal table in a private room at the local jail.

"All right, listen up, Fucker," Donovan said, leaning into Simon. "I'm doing this to help you out. But here are the rules. This does not go to trial. You do not mention my name at all. My real name is dead to you. You will take a plea deal. Flinnigan will do what he can, but I don't give a shit that you may be facing possible prison time."

The towering, muscular man sitting across from Simon was very intimidating. He had only spoken to Donovan on the phone. Simon made a mental note to never cross him again. He got drunk and stupid. He should have been more patient, but he was so eager to get his hands on the rest of the pay-out money he was promised.

"Mark, I mean Donovan," Flinnigan said, winking at Donovan. "Don't worry. I can most likely get a plea with little prison time. Simon has no priors so his chances are extremely good. He's never even received so much as a parking ticket. I've talked to the D.A. and it's looking like it will be just an assault and attempted murder charge he'll be arraigned on. I've gotten guys to walk on worse than that." Flinnigan continued pouring over the case file as Simon sat silently across the table.

"There may be a slight hiccup that you should probably be aware of." Simon looked up, noticing that Flinnigan was speaking to Donovan and not to him. "The arresting officer. It was Wilder."

"What the fuck, Simon??" Donovan shouted. He immediately stood up and paced the short length of the room.

"Unbelievable." He ran his hand through where his hair once was before he shaved it off.

"What's the big deal?" Simon had no idea why that was so important. He never told Donovan that he had been subdued by a crazy man after he failed to get the information he needed from Olivia. Simon was simply in the wrong place at the wrong time. Just his luck lately.

"Yes. And the swearing witness, Donovan. None other than Alexander Burnham. Apparently, he was walking down the street and saw your boy wonder chasing one Sarah *Olivia* Adler as he was waving a knife after last call on fucking State Street." Flinnigan emphasized Olivia's name, giving Donovan a questioning look. "He was able to subdue and restrain Mr. MacKenzie here before calling in his sister to make the proper arrest." Simon wondered why they made a big deal out of the bitch that arrested him and the dude that knocked him out.

"Okay. Okay. We'll deal with it." Donovan paced back and forth. Then he stopped abruptly, clearly remembering something. "Actually, this could work. Are we done here?"

"Yes," Flinnigan responded as he gathered his belongings. "Simon, I will see you tomorrow." Flinnigan and Donovan turned to walk out of the jail together, leaving Simon behind.

When they were out of earshot and walking down the hallway to the jailhouse exit, Flinnigan finally spoke. "Mark, are you still on that Olivia DeLuca thing? I thought that was dead and buried, no pun intended?"

"It was. Until I got a phone call a few years ago. The guy that hired my Dad to fix this whole mess over twenty years ago found out she was still alive and being protected by Burnham, Senior. We tried to get her location, but nothing worked. We ended up killing the old man, hoping it would bring her out, but apparently she fled the city."

"So, it's really her? Does she know where the infamous box is?"

"It's hard to say. But if anyone would, she would."

"What's the plan?"

"We bail Simon out. Tomorrow. Let him stew for another day. He owes us big, so we let him do our dirty work. Then we bide our time. We don't rush into this. If what Simon said is true and she has no memory of her past, we need someone to help her remember. And once she remembers something about her past, she will lead us right to it. I'm sure of it. From what I know of this girl, she is so desperate for memories of her parents. So once she has that memory, she will lead us where we want." He winked and left Flinnigan speechless. He thought back to his law school days, wishing he had chosen a different path and hadn't been mesmerized by money.

"Wait. Mark!" Flinnigan shouted as he ran to catch up with Donovan. "How do you know all this about the girl?"

"I never reveal my sources, but let's just say Dad's client, the one who hired him to deal with the DeLucas all those years ago, has been in constant touch over the years. He's the one who actually found her a few months ago. Lucky for us she was in Boston."

When Donovan was safe in his car, he picked up his cell phone.

"Cheryl. It's Mark... Yes, it has been a while. I'm hoping you can help me out here. Target is Sarah Olivia Adler. I'll also be looking into her, but see what you can do to get close to her."

CHAPTER SEVEN

SENSELESS

After another round of beer, Olivia and Alexander made their way to Fenway Park to watch the game. During their walk down Yawkey Way and underneath the grandstand, Olivia held onto Alexander's hand and the spark between them intensified. The smile on her face grew.

Alexander's seats were fantastic! They were three rows behind home plate and the view was amazing as they sat watching batting practice before the game began. Olivia had always wanted to see the Sox and couldn't believe she had such amazing seats for her first game. It was getting late in the baseball season and Sox fans were starting to get nervous, hoping to either place first in their division or win a wild card. It didn't look like either was going to happen that year, but you wouldn't know that looking at the excitement of all the fans inside Fenway.

The first three innings passed quickly and Olivia's nerves began to settle. The Sox were beating the Orioles by two runs. Olivia had a huge grin on her face and enjoyed every little thing about being there, from the vendors walking up and down the aisles to hearing the crowd cheer for Big Papi every time David Ortiz stepped up to bat. Alexander couldn't help but smile as he watched Olivia get into the game, cheering for the Sox and booing the opposing team.

Around the fourth inning, the temperature started to drop, making it slightly more comfortable to be sitting outside watching the game.

"Do you want a beer or anything?" Alexander asked

between innings.

"A beer would be great," Olivia smiled as he stood up from his seat.

"How about a hot dog? You need the full baseball experience and part of that is having your very first Fenway Frank."

Olivia glanced down at her hands. "Umm... Thanks, but I don't eat meat."

"What?" he gasped at her.

"I'm not vegan or anything, don't worry. I just don't eat meat. I'll eat seafood, but that's it."

"Well, that I can deal with. If you said you didn't want to go out for oysters with me, say, Tuesday night, I'd be heartbroken." Alexander turned quickly before Olivia could even answer him. She was reeling from the thought of seeing him again.

Alexander felt giddy as he strolled up the aisle heading underneath the grandstands to find some decent beer. It was such a strange feeling for him. What self-respecting almost thirty-year-old professional got butterflies in his stomach? He did. And Olivia Adler put them there.

After Alexander left to get a few beers, Olivia felt her cell phone buzzing in the purse on her lap. She grabbed it to see who was texting her.

Kiera: *Oh my god! I'm at a bar watching the Sox game and you're on TV! PS – who's the hottie you're with? Dish, baby, dish!*

Olivia hastily texted a response to get her friend off her back.

Olivia: *He's the guy from the other night. We'll talk later, I promise!*

Only a few seconds went by before she received another response.

Kiera: *K. I didn't get a good look at him. All the bartenders keep saying that there's a hottie there (him) and I look up and you're there.*

WTF?!

A few seconds later, Olivia received yet another text.

Kiera: *Holy crap!!! That's Alex Burnham! He's like Boston's most eligible bachelor. They totally did an instant replay of him smiling at you, asking who the mystery woman is. Dude, you're gonna be famous! I can't believe you didn't tell me Alexander freaking Burnham saved you, you damsel in distress, you! Ask him if he has any friends for me!!!! LOL. Text me later. Love you!*

Olivia: *Will do! PS – he asked me to go out with him again on Tuesday! EEK!*

Within seconds, Kiera responded once again.

Kiera: *I bet he has a big cock… You'll have to tell me all about it tomorrow!*

Olivia smiled as she dropped her phone into her bag. Alexander returned with their beers and they continued to watch the game. At the seventh inning stretch, the Sox were up by five runs. Olivia would be thrilled if they won. Her first time at Fenway and a home team win – What could be better than that?

The game ended with the Red Sox wining by five runs. The crowd went wild, knowing that the team was that much closer to the top spot in the division. Alexander and Olivia left their seats as *Tessie* blared, all the fans singing along with one of the Red Sox's anthems, and headed out of the ballpark.

"Do you want to grab some dinner or something?" Alexander asked. "It's not even eight and, well, I'm not ready for this day to end just yet." He looked into Olivia's eyes, willing her to agree to accompany him to dinner. He desperately needed that woman's company, even for just a little while longer. He was also avoiding returning home because the only thing waiting for him there was that unopened envelope.

67

"Okay. I'd like that," she replied. Nearly every thought she had since she met Alexander Friday night had been about the man standing in front of her.

He beamed at her, grabbing her hand, and led her down Yawkey Way. They walked around the corner and Martin pulled up almost immediately. Alexander opened the back passenger side door and Olivia got in before he ran around to the other side to get in beside her.

He clutched her hand and told Martin to drive to the North End, intending to take Olivia to one of his favorite Italian restaurants in the city. She looked like she was part Italian, another interesting coincidence, so he assumed she would enjoy his choice for the evening. Traffic was a little chaotic getting out of the Fenway area, but neither one was in any rush for the night to end.

"Thank you so much for taking me to the game today," Olivia said, glancing at him. "I really enjoyed it." She smiled.

"I enjoyed it as well, particularly the company." He grinned at Olivia, making her heart melt with his dazzling smile.

"You're a big baseball fan, aren't you?" Olivia inquired, needing to focus on something other than her growing desire for him.

"I am. I love it. I love Fenway," he answered excitedly. "When I was overseas working for the Navy, one of the few things I missed, besides my family, was watching games at Fenway." He looked out his window, taking one last glance at the Green Monster as they drove by.

Fenway was like a second home to him. He recalled going to games all the time with his father. They rarely missed watching a game together, whether on television or live. It wasn't until that fateful summer twenty-one years ago that his father stopped watching games with Alexander. That summer marked the end of his relationship with his father. He became distant, blaming himself for what happened. Alexander felt guilty. His father would avoid him, or so he thought, deciding to spend his summers away from his mother and the rest of the family.

"That must have been difficult, being so far away from your

family and your home." Olivia brought him back from his thoughts. "How long were you gone for?"

"What? You didn't find that on the internet?" He laughed.

"No. I just wanted an overview." She blushed.

"Well, I was gone for about six years. My first few years, I was able to come home on occasion to see my family. But once I went for SEAL training and started to work special ops, I really didn't get to come home all that much. Maybe once or twice."

"Wow. That's admirable what you did. I mean, sacrificing your home time to do something worthwhile. Well, I just couldn't imagine." Alexander listened to Olivia speak, her voice soft and sweet like a song. "Most people are too selfish and self-absorbed these days to even think about putting something ahead of themselves." She looked over at him. He was blushing. Alexander Burnham did not take compliments well either.

"It kind of runs in the family, I guess. Growing up, my dad wasn't around a lot. He was always away on different protection detail assignments. You'd think running the company would give him wide berth to pick and choose his assignments or to manage from behind a desk, but that wasn't my dad. And now I look at a lot of the guys I have working for me training over at our center. They're willing to go overseas for who knows how long to work various protection details or even train foreign armies. It's mind-boggling."

"We're here, Sir," Martin said as he pulled up outside a small Italian restaurant on Hanover Street.

"Wonderful," Alexander said, leaving the car and running around to Olivia's side to open the door for her. He grabbed her hand, helping her out of the car, and led her into the small Italian restaurant typical of those in the North End of Boston. Olivia surveyed the quaint restaurant, the creamy yellow walls with deep mahogany trim reminding her of her trip to Tuscany just a few years before. There were only about thirty tables in the entire restaurant along with a small bar showcasing quite a few wines.

Antonio, the Maître D', saw Alexander and recognized him

immediately. "Buonasera, Signori Alex!" he exclaimed in a thick Italian accent, running up to Alexander and shaking his hand. "And who is this beautiful young lady?" Antonio turned to Olivia, wide-eyed and looking rather excited that Alexander was accompanied by such a beautiful young woman. Actually, Antonio was thrilled to see Alexander with a date at all, that being the first time he was not entertaining clients.

"Antonio, this is Miss Olivia Adler," Alexander said, placing his hand on the small of her back.

"Olivia, what a pleasure to meet you!" Antonio exclaimed, kissing both of her cheeks. "Please, follow me. I have the perfect table for you both."

Antonio led them past the bar and into a small dining room. They followed him to a table in a rather private window alcove. It was intimate and quiet. Alexander held Olivia's chair out for her before taking his own seat.

"Would you like a bottle of wine, Signori? The usual?" Antonio asked as he placed menus in front of Olivia and Alexander.

"That would be wonderful, Antonio. Thank you."

Antonio left to get the bottle of wine Alexander ordered. "The wine list here is fantastic. I ordered a super tuscan. It's amazing. I hope you like red."

"I do. Particularly chiantis." She smiled at him as she opened the menu, noting that they had a rather eclectic menu. She glanced around the restaurant to see what the food looked like. Everything looked and smelled amazing.

Antonio returned with the wine. "Bella Olivia, you will love this wine! Oh, I'm so happy Signori Alex is accompanied by such a beautiful young woman!" He poured the wine and left, giving Alexander and Olivia some privacy.

Olivia eyed Alexander as she tasted the delicious wine. "So, Antonio seems excited that you're here with me. Any reason for that?"

Alexander placed his wine glass on the table and grabbed Olivia's hand. "To be honest, it seems we have a little something in common, Miss Adler. I don't really do the relationship thing either. I like to fuck and leave all those emotional attachments out of it. I've certainly never taken a woman out like this before, apart from the obligatory charity functions I am expected to be at."

Olivia looked down, not wanting to hear what he was going to say next. She actually enjoyed spending time with Alexander and, for once, wanted more than just an occasional hook-up, but it sounded as though that was all he was interested in. But why the Red Sox game? Why the wine and dine? And why didn't he make his move at Beer Works when Olivia made it rather clear that she wanted him to kiss her?

Alexander continued speaking, breaking her away from her growing unsettled emotions. "But, there's just something about you, Olivia. You make me want to break all my rules. I can't quite put my finger on it, but I'm beginning to not care."

Butterflies erupted in Olivia's stomach at his words. She felt the same way. Looking up, she smiled as she met Alexander's eyes. "That doesn't mean that I still don't want to fuck you senseless, Miss Adler," he winked as the waiter arrived to take their order, leaving Olivia completely shocked.

"So, I have to ask," Alexander said abruptly after the waiter left. "Your house. Do you own that?" That would be another piece of the puzzle.

"I do," she replied, still reeling from Alexander's admission. "My parents left me a lot of money when they died. Mom came from money. My uncle took care of all my expenses when I was growing up. Once I turned eighteen, I was handed more money than I could imagine. My uncle helped me get in touch with a money manager, who is helping me manage some of my investments. I really don't have to work the rest of my life if I don't want to. But I'd be bored out of my mind, so I work part-time at the wellness center."

"What do you do there?"

"I teach a couple of classes. Circuit training, yoga and pilates. Stuff like that. I actually helped start the center. My partner, Linda, had a really great idea. We not only have a regular fitness center, but we also offer nutritional counseling, one-on-one private gym sessions, and menu planning, among other things. I loved the idea so much that I provided a good chunk of the startup capital, so I'm a partner." Olivia took another sip of her wine before continuing.

"Linda always hated to see a personal trainer or workout at the gym when she was trying to lose weight. She felt so out of place. So we offer private personal training in small studio gyms. We teach our clients different workouts to do and help them feel more at ease with different gym equipment and exercises so that eventually they don't feel overwhelmed when they actually go to the gym. Our goal is to help people get on the right track to living a healthier lifestyle. She's the brains behind the operation and I'm the bank." Olivia smiled at Alexander.

"Do you work a lot? I just find it odd that I've never seen you in the building before..." his voice dropped.

She grabbed his hands across the table. "It's okay. I'm okay, Alexander. I promise." She gave him a reassuring smile before dropping her hands in her lap. "I don't work a whole lot. Just when I'm teaching a class or I feel like going into the office. I have enough outside commitments to keep me fairly busy during the week." She laughed.

There was a brief silence before Olivia started drilling Alexander with her own questions. "So, tell me about your family. What are they like? I have none, so I need to live vicariously through you." She knew she shouldn't joke about the fact that the only family she had ever known was gone, but it was her way of dealing with it.

"Well, not much to tell. Mom is great. She does a lot of volunteer work these days. Lots of help with victims of domestic violence. Dad died a little over five years ago." He looked down, trying to figure out what to say next.

"I'm sorry. It sucks to lose a parent, doesn't it?"

He laughed. "It was difficult. Particularly because I was overseas for so long and I didn't exactly leave on the best terms with him. He was running the security company at the time and he died in the line of duty protecting the identity of a client. I think he knew it was going to happen because a few days before he was killed, he got in touch with me overseas and almost seemed like he was trying to warn me about it. When I

72

heard what happened, I was able to secure an honorable discharge and I came home to run the company."

"That must be difficult, knowing your dad died for someone else. I'd be pissed if that was me. But you don't seem like the selfish type."

Alexander just stared. He never understood why his father abandoned the family in order to protect other people. Why weren't they good enough for him? But if his Dad died protecting *her*, if his suspicions were right, then maybe he could understand it. He would have done the same thing.

Before Alexander could respond, their food arrived. It looked absolutely delicious.

"How is it?" Alexander asked after Olivia had taken a few bites of her seafood risotto.

"It's amazing. Thank you." She took another bite, trying not to stuff too much food into her mouth.

"I hope you like Italian," Alexander said as he brought a piece of pasta Bolognese up to his lips. "I didn't mean to be presumptuous, but who doesn't like Italian?"

"You're right. I do like Italian. Dad was actually Italian." She looked out the window. "Is it strange that it feels weird to refer to him as 'Dad?' I mean, I would usually refer to him as my father. Never really Dad. I guess Dad would make him a person and I just don't really remember him as a person."

"Hey," Alexander said, grabbing Olivia's hand. "It's okay. You don't have to talk about this. What helped me get over my dad's death was to think about all the good memories I had. The moments we shared together. Even if all you can remember is one small sliver of time, hang on to that. It's better to have known your parents and to have loved them, than to have never known them at all, don't you think?"

Olivia looked at him. He had a point. Why was she so intent on dwelling on the past, holding onto her anger of losing them? Was it anger, though, or was it something else entirely?

~~~~~~~~~~

"I think I am the selfish type," Alexander said out of nowhere on the car ride home after they finished their dinner.

"What do you mean?" Olivia asked.

"Well, when we were talking about my dad before. I was so pissed at him growing up. He was never around. He always put his work before his family. Before me. It drove me crazy. I left Harvard to spite him. He wanted me to go there. That's where he went. So after one semester, I joined the Navy just to piss him off. Then I decided I wanted to go for SEAL training and I was one of the few that made it through. I was good at special ops like my Dad, I guess." He smiled at Olivia as she reached for his hand, squeezing it.

"Like I said before, the last several years of his life, he was working on a protection detail. No one in the office knew what he was working on. When he was killed, none of us got any closure. A few months after I returned home and took over the company, a letter arrived that he had sent to me overseas. It was probably written a few days before he died. I still haven't opened it. I am not ready for his apologies just yet." He looked out his window, deep in thought. Alexander hoped the only thing in the letter was an apology and not information. He wasn't ready to face that letter. He didn't know if he ever would be.

"I'm sorry. I don't know what's worse; growing up without parents or growing up knowing your dad is too busy to even spend time with you." Olivia seriously considered who had it worse. At least she had good memories of her mother. Wonderful memories. Learning to play the piano and sing with her. All the fun they used to have at the beach house. After all these years, it still upset her that her parents were taken from her so early in her life.

The car pulled up to Olivia's house and Alexander ran around to open the door for her before walking her up the steps to her house.

Another awkward moment, Olivia thought as she unlocked the front door. "Would you like to come in?" she asked, her eyes brimming with hope.

"I don't think that's such a good idea."

His response was like a knife to Olivia's heart. She had never been rejected before.

Alexander noticed the disappointed look on her face and grabbed her chin, forcing her to look him in the eyes. "If you invite me in, I'm not so sure I can be held entirely responsible for what happens afterward." His eyes became hooded and he looked as though he was ready to devour her. Olivia's nerves stood on end from the intense look in his eyes, causing a strange sensation deep down in her stomach.

"I had a lovely time today, Olivia." He reached down and grabbed her hand gently with his own and, ever so softly, placed a chaste kiss on her knuckles. "Oysters. Tuesday. I'll pick you up at seven." It wasn't a question. It was more of a demand. And before she had time to respond, he turned, leaving her totally unsatisfied and wanting him, standing on her front stoop.

She watched as his car pulled away and noticed him blow her a kiss. Feeling like a teenager on her first date, she caught the kiss. It would have to do for the time being.

CHAPTER EIGHT

FALLING IN LIKE

Olivia woke up the following morning after having the same dream again. The boy with the green eyes was now a permanent fixture. With these dreams returning, she decided it was probably time to talk to her overpriced therapist again and get her take. She made a mental note to call her office sometime that week.

Shortly after nine, she left her house, making her way to catch the subway out to the local animal shelter where she volunteered every Monday. As she waited for the T beneath the busy Boston streets, the screeching sound of metal wheels on the train tracks echoing throughout the dark tunnels, she checked her phone for the first time since the previous afternoon. Mo had called and left a voicemail telling her that the band would be rehearsing on Wednesday and he wanted her to be there. She became excited during her short ride to the animal shelter as she thought about singing with the band again.

"Olivia! Great to see you!" Bethany exclaimed when Olivia walked in the front door of the brick building.

Bethany Jones had been single handedly running that shelter for as long as anyone could remember. Olivia had started volunteering when she moved to Boston for college, wanting to spend some time with animals. And once she returned to the city, she resumed her volunteer work.

"Of course. I couldn't miss spending time with my critters! Do we have anyone new?" Olivia dropped her bags and followed Bethany toward the kennels, the sound of dogs barking and yipping filling the room. It brought a smile to her face.

"Yeah. We picked up two dogs over the weekend as well as five baby kittens, all in the same litter. We're running out of room. We need to get some adoptions this week or..."

"Don't worry, Bethany," Olivia interrupted. "I can take a few home with me to make some space if I need to. Nepenthe won't mind." Nepenthe was a mangy eight-year old cat that Olivia fell in love with several months ago.

"That would be a huge help. We need to get some more foster parents trained and ready to take some of these critters." She was right. The shelter would be getting into its busy season soon. Winter was always the worst time of year. They had so many animals and just didn't always have enough room to shelter them all.

"Well, I'm going to take some of these guys for a walk," Olivia said, motioning to the dogs in the kennel. She did all sorts of things at the shelter from feeding, to helping with adoptions, to playing with all the cats. But her favorite was taking the dogs for their walks.

The morning passed by relatively quickly as she made sure all the dogs in the shelter got some exercise. After a quick lunch break, she got ready to take out the last dog. She always saved Runner for last. Runner was a pointer-terrier mix and her favorite. He was a little older so he wasn't on the top of anyone's list for an adoptable dog. Everyone always wanted a puppy, which was unfortunate for all the wonderful dogs available for adoption.

Runner lived up to his name. He loved to run. She always tried to take him out last so they could run a few miles together and then head to the dog park where she would tire him out with a round of fetch.

Olivia quickly changed into a pair of running shorts and a tank top before grabbing a few tennis balls. She threw them into her pack and headed toward Boston Common, Runner taking the lead.

That day, Runner was giving Olivia a good workout. She just did a long run the day before so her legs were a little tired.

They ran the mile up over to the Commons where there was an off-leash dog park. Without fail, Runner would always head straight there. They reached the area and Olivia let him off his leash. The dog ran free, sprinting up and down the gated area. There weren't that many other dogs there, so the pair had fun playing fetch, just the two of them.

After about half an hour, Runner was beat and Olivia was even more so. She pulled out his portable doggie bowl and filled it up from a fountain. He lay down on the ground after slopping up some water. She joined Runner, lying down on her back next to her favorite dog. He snuggled against her and they just enjoyed their moment together, savoring the feel of the cool grass beneath them.

After a few minutes of a rest, Olivia decided to head back to the shelter. She would never forgive herself if Runner missed an opportunity to be adopted. She leashed Runner back up and started to walk back to the shelter. "Come on buddy. Time to go back home."

~~~~~~~~~~

Alexander couldn't believe his luck. He was going over case reports from the previous week, unable to focus, when he decided he needed to clear his brain. That envelope still hung heavy on his mind. He left his office building and wandered the streets of Boston. Before he knew it, he found his way to Boston Common and sat on a park bench looking out over the Swan Boats and replaying the previous day in his head when he saw her. Again.

He watched with admiration as Olivia leashed up a great looking dog that she had been playing with. She leaned down and gave the dog a quick scratch on the head before she headed in his direction, smiling. He wondered if she would even see him sitting just a few feet away. All her attention seemed to be devoted to the white and brown spotted dog walking proudly in front of her with its tongue hanging out.

As Olivia walked Runner through the Commons, she felt a familiar electricity coursing through her body. It almost felt as if someone was watching her.

No one is watching you, Libby. You just wish he was here. That's all.

She looked up from Runner and stilled when her eyes met with his, her heart racing from seeing those beautiful green eyes so unexpectedly. She headed in his direction, seeing Alexander's smile widen as she walked toward the bench he was sitting on, the dog eagerly wagging his tail.

"Miss Adler. Why do we keep running into each other here?" he asked, standing up to meet Olivia.

"Alexander. I'm starting to think that you're stalking me," she joked, taking in his nice navy blue suit that he made casual, foregoing the tie. He looked amazing as always. "You are a professional stalker, so my point is valid."

"I prefer the term security consultant," he replied smoothly.

"I've heard it both ways," she smirked playfully.

He grinned at her. "Touché, Miss Adler. You have quite a smart mouth on you." He leaned in, closing the distance between them. "I can't wait to have that mouth on me," he whispered, his warm breath sending shivers up Olivia's spine.

She gasped.

"Well, who do we have here?" he continued as if he didn't just tell Olivia that he wanted her mouth on his body. How did he expect her to react to that? She could barely form a sentence in response, all her thoughts going to places that were probably not appropriate to be talking about in a public park with people walking by.

Alexander bent down and let Runner smell his hand. Runner obviously approved of him so he let Alexander scratch his head. Olivia was floored. That man had on a rather expensive looking suit, but he seemed to have no problem petting Runner, getting dog fur all over him. Alexander Burnham was a conundrum.

"This is Runner," Olivia said, finally finding her voice. "I was just tiring him out before having to take him back to the shelter," she explained, gesturing to the dog that was leaning into Alexander's hand, obviously enjoying the attention he was getting.

"To the shelter?" Alexander asked, straightening up and

admiring Olivia's obvious affection for the dog.

"Yeah," she replied as Runner rolled over, hoping to get a belly rub. "He's been at the animal shelter for the last few months. No one has adopted him yet. Everyone always wants a puppy. No one wants a four-year-old hound. It's sad, really."

"So you work at the animal shelter, too?" He took a step closer, surprised at the many different layers of Olivia.

Her breath caught, the proximity of Alexander to her overwhelming her once again. For a minute she forgot all about the dog rolling around in front of her. "I volunteer there," she finally replied, returning to the present. "I take the dogs on walks, play with the cats. Stuff like that. I just love spending time with all the animals. Speaking of which, I really should be getting on. It was wonderful to see you again, Mr. Burnham," she smirked as she gave Runner a biscuit.

Alexander grabbed her soft hand and kissed it as he always did. "The pleasure was all mine. I look forward to tomorrow evening, Miss Adler." Olivia started to walk away. "And I do hope you can find a good home for Runner." He winked.

"So do I."

Alexander watched as Olivia walked away from him, her hips swaying in a way that excited him. When she disappeared from his view, he grabbed his cell phone, needing to make an important call.

~~~~~~~~~~

"Thank goodness you're back!" Bethany shouted at Olivia as she walked through the door with Runner. They took their time returning to the shelter, mainly because Olivia's head was in the clouds after her chance encounter with Alexander.

"Sorry it took so long. I ran into a friend at the dog park. What's up? Is something wrong?" Olivia was worried they had gotten an order to destroy some of the animals due to lack of space. That was always her biggest fear.

"No. Nothing's wrong. Someone called a little while ago. They saw Runner on the website and asked to see if he was still available for adoption. They'll be here within the half-hour to fill out the paperwork."

"That's fantastic," Olivia replied, her lack of enthusiasm showing. She was a little disappointed, knowing that she would miss her Runner. He had been in the shelter the longest out of all their dogs. Olivia and Runner had formed such a strong bond.

She grabbed his leash, pulling him along behind her down a long corridor toward the kennels. "I'll go get him cleaned up then. He should have a nice bath so he looks good for his new family."

"Libby," Bethany said, placing her hand on Olivia's shoulder. "This is a good thing for Runner."

"I know, I know. I'm just going to miss him," she replied, her sadness about never being able to see Runner again evident.

Olivia took Runner into the back and started to run him a bath. Most dogs hated baths, but for some reason, Runner loved them. He loved water. He would make a good dog for any family, Olivia thought. She just hoped that whoever adopted him would be active.

Ten minutes later, she put the finishing touches on Runner's bath, tying a cute doggie bandana around his neck, when Bethany peeked her head in.

"He's here, Libby. And wow is he handsome." Bethany fanned herself. Olivia couldn't help but laugh. Bethany was pushing seventy, but she had no problem flirting with any good-looking man who came in.

"I'll bring him out in a minute," she replied. After giving Runner one last hug, she took a deep breath and walked down the hallway toward the large doggie playroom. As Olivia approached, she could see Bethany speaking to Runner's potential new owner through the large glass windows. The man was tall and dressed in a pair of jeans and yellow polo shirt. His silhouette looked rather familiar to Olivia. Surely, it couldn't be...

"Here's Runner," Bethany said as Olivia entered the playroom, nearly tripping over a squeaky football. The man turned around, causing Olivia to stop dead in her tracks, a look of surprise across her face. Her stomach fluttered as she took in his beautiful body yet again. She didn't think she would ever tire of looking at him, even with his clothes on.

"Libby, this is Mr. Alexander Burnham. He's looking to adopt our Runner here." Olivia just stared at Alexander, unable to form any coherent thoughts. She snapped out of her daze when Runner darted for Alexander, pulling her with him.

"I see that you two will get along famously!" Bethany exclaimed, clapping her hands. "Well, I'll leave you to do the paperwork with our Olivia here," she said, walking out of the room.

When she heard the click of the door, Olivia turned to Alexander. "What are you doing?"

"I'm adopting Runner. I've been wanting to get a dog for a while and there's something about Runner that I love." He bent down to give Runner a quick scratch on the head. Olivia unclipped Runner's leash and he immediately rolled over, giving both of them an open invitation to rub his belly.

"Silly hound," Olivia said, stroking Runner. Alexander bent down to rub the dog, meeting Olivia's eyes. There was that spark again. Olivia didn't know what to make of it. He wasn't even touching her, but just being in the same room as him gave her an overwhelming feeling of contentment.

"Well, normally I like to make sure you'd be a good match before approving an adoption," Olivia said, remembering she had a job to do. "But I think we're all set here. And plus, I know where you work so I know where to find and hurt you if you ever mistreat Runner here." She looked up, smirking.

"Good point." Alexander grabbed a tennis ball and threw it across the room. Runner immediately ran to catch the ball, bringing it back to Alexander but refusing to drop it on the ground.

"Oh. Runner doesn't understand fetch with just one ball. You'll need more than one if you expect that hound to drop the one in his mouth," Olivia explained.

Alexander smiled. "I think that can be arranged."

After they were finished with the paperwork, Olivia walked Alexander and Runner outside. "Now," she said, turning to face Alexander. "Runner needs lots of exercise so take him on your runs with you. He loves the dog park and…"

"I know, Olivia. He'll be fine," he said, brushing an errant curl behind her ear. "I'm going to take great care of our boy here." He winked.

I can't believe he referred to Runner as our boy! Olivia thought. Those two words were full of so much hope.

"And you have an open invitation to come and visit him anytime you want."

"Good. I'm going to hold you to that," she said, bending down and giving Runner one last kiss good-bye.

"You better," he replied before walking down the street, leaving her standing outside the front door of the animal shelter.

"I'm falling in serious like with that man," Olivia said to herself.

CHAPTER NINE

TOO MANY COINCIDENCES

Later that evening, Olivia returned to her house. After her hectic weekend, she wanted to unwind and have some much needed time to herself. As she prepared her dinner of tofu stir-fry, she kept glancing at the flowers Alexander sent her over the weekend. Feeling bold, she picked up her cell phone and sent him a text.

Olivia: *How's Runner?*

Across town, Alexander was speaking with his sister, Carol, on the phone in his home office about Simon's arraignment.

"I don't know, Alex. There's something about this guy that seems off. I don't want you to read too much into what I'm saying. It's not her. She's gone."

"I know that, sis, but I've been spending time with her this weekend and there are just so many coincidences." His voice dropped as he stared at the dark walls in his office. "Too many, really."

"I understand that. The name. The age. Her background. Losing her parents. I understand everything you've told me. So tell me this. Why would Dad say she died at the hospital? And why would he change her name?"

Alexander knew all too well why his father would do such a thing. He was unaware of it at the time, as he had just turned nine, but now it made sense. In fact, he had helped people fake their own deaths too many times to count in order to protect them for their safety. And he also knew that if it was true and her identity was ever uncovered, he could lose her again. He vowed to make sure that did not happen.

Just then, a text from Olivia came through over his cell phone. A smile crept across his face when he saw it, eager to get off the phone with his sister so he could respond.

"Alex, are you listening to what I'm saying?" Carol brought him back from his thoughts about the beautiful woman that had been occupying his mind lately.

"Sorry Carol, what was that?"

"All I'm saying is that something's not right about this Simon guy. His financials came back and he has no money. Nothing. He qualified for a Public Defender for crying out loud. But he's got an attorney. An expensive one at that, too. And someone posted his bail, which was set at a quarter of a million dollars. I'm going to do some more snooping around, get in touch with the bail officer, and see who posted it. It's just unusual is all."

"Well, what do you want me to do?" Alexander was worried. What if Simon came back after Olivia? He was surprised to realize he had such strong feelings for her, even though he had only met her a few days ago. It was such a foreign idea to him. He never wanted to protect someone as fiercely as he wanted to protect her.

"I don't know. He doesn't have any criminal record. None at all. He has a clean work history, strong family ties in the area. No one had anything but exemplary things to say about him. So why did he attack the girl? And what did he mean about the job he had to do?"

"It is a bit worrisome," Alexander admitted as he sat at his desk looking over the family photos adorning the walls, wondering if the little girl smiling next to him in most of them was the girl he met just a few days ago.

"Well, just keep an eye on her, Alex. That's all you can do. I called her office earlier, but she wasn't in. I'll alert her when I speak with her about what she should do."

"Thanks, sis. I must go. Love you." Alexander hung up his office phone and turned to his cell, eager to reply to the beautiful Olivia.

As Olivia finished preparing her dinner, she heard her phone beep. Her heart immediately swelled when she saw the picture Alexander had sent of Runner. He looked so happy, curled up in a ball on a little doggie bed, surrounded by all his new toys.

She texted him back.

Olivia: *He looks so happy.*

Alexander: *He is. But he misses you... So do I.*

Olivia giggled at Alexander's response.

Olivia: *I miss you, too. And Runner. Give him a big hug and kiss from me.*

Alexander: *I will. Do you have a big hug and kiss for me? ;-)*

Alexander Burnham just used the winky sign! Olivia exclaimed in her head. She grinned from ear to ear, unable to hide her enthusiasm for her growing attraction to that man. She looked down at her cell, eager to continue flirting via text, and typed out a quick response.

Olivia: *Maybe. You'll find out tomorrow.*

Alexander: *I'll wait with bated breath. Have a wonderful evening, Miss Adler.*

Olivia: *You as well, Mr. Burnham.*

Alexander enjoyed their text flirting, so he sent one last text before heading to the gym for his evening workout.

Alexander: *I'll see you in my dreams.*

Alexander left his penthouse, wondering if Olivia could even know how true that line actually was. If Olivia really was the girl from Alexander's past, he *had* been seeing her in his dreams.

He returned from the gym late that evening and spent several hours in his very own music room. Olivia would drool over his set-up, he thought to himself. He made a mental note to invite her over in the near future, grinning at the thought of Olivia giving him his very own private performance. He stepped over to his Steinway baby grand and checked the tuning on one of his guitars. After tweaking the strings a bit, he sat down to play Damien Rice's *The Blower's Daughter*.

He played through the song, relishing the last verse, thinking of Olivia because he couldn't get her out of his mind. And he wasn't sure he wanted her out of his mind either.

He played and sang for several hours that evening, wondering if he and Olivia were inspired to play music by the same person. He hoped they weren't and that all the similarities were just coincidences. But those coincidences had become too overwhelming for Alexander to ignore anymore. Still, he continued to ignore that envelope containing the letter.

~~~~~~~~~~

Olivia woke with a jerk after having fallen asleep on the couch. She had that dream again. She saw the boy with those green eyes. Why was she seeing those eyes after years and years of having that dream? Why was it suddenly different now?

She sat up on her couch and Nepenthe stretched, giving her a look like he was ready to murder Olivia for disturbing his precious sleep. She shut off all the lights and climbed the stairs to her bedroom. Sleep found her again quickly.

The sun woke her the following morning as it filtered through the bedroom windows. She began to stir and Nepenthe started to swat her face, his majesty's indication that he needed more food. Olivia checked the time and saw that it was a little after seven. Rubbing her eyes, she descended the steps to feed her needy cat.

Throughout her day, she kept thinking about Alexander and their date that evening. Time dragged mercilessly for Olivia, who found herself extremely nervous. Five minutes felt like an eternity. She had nothing on her schedule, but she tried to keep herself occupied. She caught up on her e-mails, spoke to her financial advisor, and called her shrink to schedule an appointment for later in the week.

Finally, she decided it was useless to sit at home all day waiting for the clock to strike seven. Olivia grabbed her bag and headed to the wellness center to get in a workout and review some paperwork.

"Libby! How was your weekend?" Jerry exclaimed when he saw Olivia enter the building.

"Great, thanks. Relatively uneventful, but that's how I like my weekends," Olivia lied as she pushed the call button for the elevator.

"Olivia, this is Richard. He's training to be the new night security guard. And I've got a few more guys I'm training later this week who will be taking the weekend shifts. We'll now have security here twenty-four seven. Apparently there was an incident over the weekend and the big boss man figured full-time security would be better." Jerry sat at his security desk surrounded by closed-circuit TVs, apparently going over an employee manual with Richard.

"Hi, Richard. Nice to meet you." Olivia shook the new night security guard's hand, smiling to herself, knowing she was the reason for the added security.

"I saw you on TV Sunday," Jerry said, making small talk. "I was watching the Sox game. You had great seats." Olivia blushed. Did everyone see her on TV? She needed to rethink ever going to another game with Alexander if she was going to be seen across the nation. "It's nice to see Mr. Burnham out with someone as sweet as you."

Olivia was shocked. She didn't know how to reply to that. Alexander was obviously Jerry's boss. He owned the building, after all. Thankfully the elevator car arrived and she was spared having to talk to Jerry about her non-relationship with one Mr. Alexander Burnham. Or about his sexy bedroom voice telling her how he wanted her mouth all over his body. Or about the way he constantly caught her checking out his body, making her entire being alive with electricity.

The feelings she was beginning to have for Alexander scared her. She still hadn't quite worked out a few of her issues with her shrink. Granted, Olivia wasn't the most devoted patient. She had been in some form of therapy as long as she could remember. When she was younger, she thought it was normal to go talk to someone every week about her parents and how they were taken from her. Therapy never really worked, though. She never coped with her parents' deaths.

When she moved to Boston, her Uncle Charles insisted that she see his therapist, Dr. Greenstein. She helped her uncle cope with Olivia's parents' deaths, apparently. While in college, Olivia made some headway, finally being able to form bonds with certain people in her life without the fear of them being taken away. Music became a healthy coping mechanism for her. Music was always her coping mechanism.

When Olivia's uncle was killed, she panicked. The only family she had left was taken from her again, or so she thought. Instead of dealing with the pain of losing anyone else she was close to, Olivia fled Boston. She moved from city to city for the next several years, not staying in one place for more than a month at a time.

During that time, she no longer played music. Sex and alcohol became her coping mechanisms. And to some extent, they still were.

When Olivia returned to Boston, she had no intention of staying. One night when Olivia was out at a random bar looking for someone to hook up with, she ran into Kiera. When she saw the hurt look on her face, Olivia finally realized how selfish she had been, pushing people away for fear of losing them.

After reconnecting with Kiera, Olivia decided it was time to lay down roots somewhere and Boston was the only place she had anything close to family. Within a month of returning to Boston, she bought a house. Kiera had a friend of a friend who was looking for investors for a startup and, after running it by her financial advisor, Olivia became a partner in the wellness center. It had only been open for six months but was already quite successful and popular in Boston.

Olivia still had fears of getting too close to people. The fear of her world being swept out from under her was still present, although sometimes buried several layers beneath her skin. It was because of that fear that she had refused to get back in touch with Mo. Olivia didn't want to admit it, but she was glad Kiera pushed to make sure their paths crossed. Music could be her coping mechanism again and maybe Olivia could finally be normal, whatever that was.

Olivia snapped back from her thoughts when she walked through the front doors of the wellness center and was greeted by a smiling, chirpy Melanie.

"Libby! How are you?" she asked, running from behind the registration desk and giving Olivia a hug. The girl really did have a lot of enthusiasm.

"I'm good, Mel," she responded, weakly returning her hug. Olivia was not a big hugger, but she did it for Melanie. Melanie loved to hug.

"Here, let me give you your messages. You have a few." She returned to her desk, handing Olivia a stack of missed calls. "You know, you really should set up your voicemail so that I don't have to track you down all the time."

Olivia smiled. "I know. I'll work on it. Thanks, Mel," she said, turning down the hall to her office. She popped her head into Linda's office on the way.

"Hey, Linda. How's everything going?" Olivia asked her business partner while she sat in her office, smiling through her vibrant blue eyes. She motioned for Olivia to come in as she threw her blonde hair back into a ponytail, taking her reading glasses off her face. The wellness center was her baby; Olivia was just the money behind it. When she agreed to back it, Olivia made her agree to let her teach, having already been certified to lead a few different classes. And of course, she made sure that she had her own office there as well.

"Great!" Linda replied excitedly. "It looks like we're going to post some big numbers this quarter. Enrollment is up two hundred percent. We may have to hire some new staff to keep up with all the people that have signed up for coaching."

"That's fantastic. Just keep it up!"

"Will do." Olivia left Linda's office and went down the hall to her own office where she grabbed what she needed for her workout before getting to it in the state-of-the-art gym.

After an intense two-hour workout, Olivia returned to her office, dripping with sweat, and grabbed her messages to sort through. Most of them were relatively mundane and nothing she had to deal with right away. The last message caught her eye. It was Detective Wilder, probably calling to tell her the result of Simon's arraignment. Olivia had almost forgotten about what happened Friday night, having been living in a bit of an Alexander-induced daze.

Taking a deep breath, she grabbed her phone and dialed Detective Wilder's number. She picked up after the second ring.

"Hi. It's Libby Adler. Olivia. I'm just returning your call from yesterday evening, Detective Wilder."

"Miss Adler. How are you doing? Is everything okay?"

"Surprisingly, yes. I had actually forgotten about Friday night until now, if you can believe that." Olivia laughed nervously.

"Well, I'm sorry to have to be the one to reopen that wound, but Simon had his arraignment yesterday. The first thing I need to tell you is that he was issued a no-contact protective order. That means he cannot contact you in any way. If you are both at the same restaurant or bar or whatever, he is under a court order to leave immediately. You do not have to leave. You can if you want, but he is the one required to leave. He cannot approach you under any circumstances. He must stay at least fifty feet away from you at all times. If you initiate contact with him for any reason, he must walk away from you. But if I was you, I would stay far away from him. Do not call him. Do not engage him at all."

"Don't worry. I have no intention of ever speaking to him again," Olivia replied, trying to hide her nervousness.

"If, for any reason, he violates this protective order, he can be charged with an additional felony on top of the other charges of criminal assault and attempted murder. If he violates it by trying to contact you, you must call me immediately. Do you understand?"

"Yes. I do. Thank you. So what's the next step?"

"Well, as I mentioned, Simon was arraigned on assault and attempted murder charges. The judge set his bail at a quarter of a million dollars. He had an attorney with him and someone posted his bail, other than a bail bondsman. I'm still looking into this. According to his financials, he was eligible for a public defender, so I have no idea how he is able to afford an attorney or post bail."

That was a little disconcerting, Olivia thought. Simon did not make a lot of money and his friends didn't have any money that she knew of. Then again, she didn't really know Simon that well.

"In the meantime, this case will be assigned to a district attorney who will be in touch with you. If, for some reason, Simon does not accept a plea deal, this will have to go to trial and you will probably have to testify. Do you understand this?"

"Yes, I do. I'm fine with that." Olivia sounded braver than she felt. She was nervous just thinking about having to tell a courtroom full of people about Simon.

"Just one last word of caution. There's something about Simon that rubs me the wrong way. He seems like a nice guy at first, but I don't know. There's something off about him, Miss Adler. That protective order won't prevent him from harming you if he really wants to. It will only enhance any sentence he's given on the assault and attempted murder charges. What I'm trying to tell you is to be very careful, at least until this is all settled."

"I will be. Thank you for the update, Detective." Olivia's voice was clearly shaky now. The detective must have noticed.

"It's my pleasure. And if you need anything, please contact me."

With that, Olivia hung up, suddenly nervous. Detective Wilder's warning concerned her. Why did she feel the need to go out of her way to tell her that something about Simon seemed odd? Olivia had thought the same thing before brushing it off as nothing. But now, maybe she should be worried about Simon, roaming the streets, out on bail.

Her cell phone buzzed, bringing her back from her thoughts. She giggled when she saw the picture of Runner in the dog park with two tennis balls in his mouth. She immediately began to look forward to her date that evening and nothing was going to take away the excitement of that; not even a nerve-racking warning about a potential dangerous ex-whatever loose on the streets of Boston. Olivia didn't know what scared her more; that she was excited about seeing Alexander, or the warning Detective Wilder gave her about Simon. Both scared her to death.

~~~~~~~~~~

"Donovan, it's Cheryl."

"Cheryl, darling, please tell me you have some good news."

"Well, I do. Burnham is dating this Sarah Olivia Adler. Apparently, she goes by Olivia, though. I don't know how serious it is yet. They just met over the weekend, but you already knew that."

"Don't remind me."

"Martin dropped them off at the Sox game Sunday. Then took them to the North End for dinner. And later this evening, he will be taking him over to Miss Adler's house."

"Can you get her address for me?"

"I can do that no problem. Martin is very diligent about his travel logs."

"Wonderful."

"Is there anything else I can do for you, sir?"

Donovan thought for a moment and came up with a brilliant plan. "Yes. I'm going to try to spook Miss Adler. If what you're saying is true, if Burnham is interested in her, he will insist on her having a protection detail, not wanting to take any chances. And when that happens, I want you to try to get that assignment."

"Yes, sir."

Donovan hung up the phone before dialing again.

"Grant. It's Donovan here. I may have a job for you."

CHAPTER TEN

NEPENTHE

After returning home from the gym, Olivia looked at the time, wondering how it was suddenly only a few hours away from her date. She started to panic as she began to get ready, trying on practically every outfit in her closet. She was so nervous and really wanted to look good for Alexander, but nothing seemed to work.

She wanted him to like her. Hell, she wanted him to love her, and that was a strange feeling. She almost texted him to cancel no less than six times, her nerves getting the best of her. She even broke down and called Kiera to ask for advice.

"I'm going to cancel. I'm not going for oysters." Olivia plopped down on her bed covered in the vast majority of the contents of her closet.

"Bitch, I'm going to start charging you for all the shit you put me through."

"I know. But I have no one else to turn to." Olivia laughed anxiously.

"Okay, so why don't you want to go today? It's just oysters? Right?"

"Well, yeah. It's just oysters. But oysters lead to dinner. And dinner leads to kissing. And kissing leads to mind-blowing sex. And mind-blowing sex leads to marriage. And that will just end in disappointment for all involved." She started breathing heavy. Inhale. Exhale.

"Okay, crazy. You know I love you. You got over all your issues with me, so why can't you just let someone else in? Stop being a selfish bitch." Kiera laughed. "This is good for you.

And I swear to God, if I find out you cancel, I'm calling Dr. Greenstein!"

Kiera's threat to call her therapist was all Olivia needed. She really didn't want her doctor to think she was any more messed up than she already knew, considering she hadn't seen her in over five years. "Fine. I'll go. But I have nothing to wear."

"Bullshit. I'll be right over."

Kiera arrived within the half-hour and picked a gorgeous green Grecian-style dress that fell right above Olivia's knees. She paired it with gold sandals, gold bangle bracelets, and large gold hoop earrings. It was casual enough, but added a touch of dressy.

Alexander arrived promptly at seven that evening. When she opened the door, it felt as if all the oxygen was ripped from her body. The sight of him alone overwhelmed her very being as he smiled with a twinkle in his eyes, holding flowers for her. Olivia openly gawked at how good he looked in his dark jeans and light green shirt that made his eyes pop. *This is one attractive man*, she thought to herself.

Olivia was finally brought back to her senses after staring at Alexander for God knows how long. "Thank you for the flowers. Let me just put them in some water. Would you like to come in for a moment?" she asked, stepping into her foyer and allowing him to enter.

Nepenthe came up to greet Alexander, staring at him with a questioning look on his furry face. "Alexander, this is my cat, Nepenthe," Olivia explained before walking over to the kitchen island and grabbing a vase for the flowers.

Alexander looked down at the orange long-haired cat that was walking in and out of his legs. He bent down and scratched him near his tail. Nepenthe immediately started to purr. "Nepenthe. That's an interesting name," he commented.

"Yeah. Well, when I brought him home with me from the shelter, it was the first night I didn't have any nightmares for as long as I could remember. I wasn't even going to keep him. I just brought him to my place after volunteering one day because he wasn't feeling well and I wanted to keep an eye on him overnight. And, well, I had to keep him, especially if he kept the nightmares away." Olivia looked down at the wildflower bouquet she was arranging into a vase.

"How did you come up with the name Nepenthe?" he asked, staring at Olivia as she carefully placed the flowers in a vase, making sure it looked perfect.

"I lived out in Big Sur for a while after I graduated college and actually bartended at a great restaurant right on the coast with amazing views. It was called Nepenthe. In Greek mythology, nepenthe is a medicine or elixir for sorrow. I guess it was the first anti-depressant pill there was. So after not having nightmares that night when he was here, he became my own elixir for sorrow. My own personal Nepenthe." She smiled affectionately down at her cat.

Alexander just stood there, amazed by the woman in front of him. She had so many different layers. He desperately wanted to get to know each and every one of them. And to slowly become another one of her own personal nepenthes.

As Olivia sat in the car holding Alexander's hand a few minutes later, she was glad Kiera pushed her into actually going that evening. Her heart was beating so loud in her chest, she thought it was going to bust through and walk out of the car. Why did that man have such an effect on her?

She kept hearing Dr. Greenstein's voice in her head from all those years ago, pushing her to forge real relationships with people. She was engaged in a balancing act of self-preservation and selflessness. It was unclear which would win when it came to Alexander. Should she keep him at arm's length to avoid the emptiness she would feel when he left her, or should she just jump, feet first, into a new relationship because maybe it's something he needs or wants, and to hell with Olivia's selfish thoughts of being abandoned? She was starting to walk the tightrope and it was only a matter of time to see if she made it across or fell to the depths yet again.

"You look beautiful tonight, Olivia," Alexander said after they sat down at their table. When Olivia had opened the door earlier that evening, Alexander was stunned at the sight of her beauty. She looked like a Grecian goddess, her figure illuminated from behind by the setting sun streaking through her house.

"Thank you." She blushed as she opened the menu. Alexander chose to take her to Atlantic Fish, a restaurant that wasn't too far from Olivia's house. It was one of his favorite spots in the city to grab oysters and a great bottle of wine. As he ordered a bottle of Far Niente chardonnay and a dozen blue point oysters, Olivia glanced around the large restaurant at the mahogany walls adorned with various nautical themed prints.

"I hope I'm not being presumptuous ordering for you." Olivia snapped her head back to the table, her eyes meeting Alexander's. He was a man who liked control, she could tell.

"I don't mind. White wine and oysters go hand in hand, don't they?" She smiled before looking away.

Alexander recalled one evening from his childhood at the DeLuca's beach house with his father. They sat on their back deck, overlooking the Atlantic Ocean. He was eight years old and the DeLuca's daughter was six. They were all eating oysters, throwing their shells over the balcony onto the sand below. When the DeLuca's little daughter saw what they were doing, she snapped her crispy green bean snack in two, ate half, and threw the other half over the edge. Everyone roared with laughter and she continued to do that the rest of the evening. The memory caused Alexander to smile, wondering if the woman across the table from him would remember that. If it was even her.

The waiter returned with their wine, bringing Alexander back from his thoughts. It was a perfect choice, Olivia thought. Light and crisp but not too sweet. The perfect chardonnay.

"So I heard from Detective Wilder today," Olivia said, breaking a somewhat awkward silence.

"I thought you might. I spoke with her last evening. I want to make sure nothing bad happens to you…" he said, his voice trailing off, remembering his sister's warning and the promise he had made to a little girl all those years ago.

"Are you okay?" Olivia glanced at Alexander who had a look on his face as though he was searching the back of his brain for something.

"Yeah. Sorry. I'm just having a déjà vu moment, I guess."

Olivia smiled at his response. "I get those all the time. Mostly I just run into people I should remember that I knew years ago when I went to B.C., but I can't remember who they are for the life of me."

Alexander reached across the crisp white tablecloth and grabbed Olivia's delicate hand, caressing her knuckles. It was such a simple, chaste gesture, but it ignited sparks deep within both their bodies.

The oysters arrived, interrupting their moment. Olivia looked at Alexander, grinning, the corners of her mouth turned up in a mischievous smirk. "Umm, how are you with spicy cocktail sauce?"

"Ah, a woman after my own heart. Do it up, Love."

Olivia smiled to herself as her heart raced. *He called me Love!* She grabbed the cocktail sauce and added quite a bit of horseradish to it, as well as some hot sauce. She gingerly squeezed a lemon over the oysters. Once she was satisfied that the oysters were ready, she put a small amount of cocktail sauce on one of the large blue point oysters in front of her and, clinking shells with Alexander, slid one down her throat.

"Mmmm… I love oysters," Olivia said, relishing the salty taste in her mouth. "I remember watching my parents eat oysters all the time when I was younger. We would spend our summers at a beach house. Mom came from money. It was a family house." Olivia grabbed another oyster and Alexander stared as she prepared it and slid it down her throat again. The way she ate her oyster was strangely erotic, he thought to himself.

"I remember our beach house. It's one of the strongest memories I have of my life before the accident. And I remember them having friends over. I was so jealous of them because they would eat oysters on the deck. And it wasn't because they were eating oysters. It was because they would toss the shells over the side of the deck. And I wanted to do that. I couldn't wait until I got older and could toss my oyster shells over the deck, too."

Alexander couldn't believe his ears. Too many coincidences.

He kept telling himself that it was just a story. *I'm sure lots of people would throw their oyster shells over the side of the deck.*

They finished the rest of their meal engaging in relative small talk. After they left the restaurant, Olivia said she preferred to walk home. She didn't live far and the temperature had cooled down dramatically. Alexander grabbed her hand and they walked down Boylston Street in relative silence, a light breeze in the air.

"Sorry to bring this up again, but I want you to promise me something," Alexander said as they crossed over to Commonwealth Avenue and were about two blocks from Olivia's house.

"What is it?"

"I want you to always let me know that you're okay. I mean, with Simon out on bail, I just want to make sure he's not doing anything he's not supposed to." Alexander was worried. And he desperately needed to feel in control of her safety. He resented not feeling that control, but he didn't want to scare this girl off by setting up round-the-clock protection for her. Not just yet, anyway.

"I'll be fine." Olivia stopped walking and turned to face him, grabbing his other hand in hers. "And I'll let you know if I ever need anything. I promise." She smiled at him and a look of relief washed over his face. He pulled her close, embracing her. His warmth surrounded her. It felt so familiar to her, as if she had known that man her entire life. It felt like home.

"Okay. Can you do me one more favor?" He stroked her hair, not wanting to release her from his embrace.

Olivia caressed his back and felt the muscles rippling underneath his shirt. Her thoughts soon went to places that were unspeakable in public. "What's that?" She pulled out of his embrace to look into his eyes.

"Can I have a security system installed in your house? You live in Boston. You should have one anyway." At least if there was a security system installed in Olivia's house, she would be a little safer, Alexander thought.

"I have a security system and his name is Nepenthe." Olivia laughed. He simply smiled at her and remained silent, a stern look on his face as he waited for her to agree to his request.

"Okay," Olivia exhaled. "That's fine." How could she say no to those eyes?

"Great. Can I have my team come over Thursday? I have to head out of town later that evening and I'd feel better leaving you knowing that your house was secure."

"Thursday would be fine." She wondered why he had to leave town. *Probably some clandestine operation, Mr. Spy-Man,* she thought to herself.

They strolled the rest of the way to Olivia's house holding hands. Alexander walked Olivia up the steps to her front door and she turned to face him, dreading another awkward moment.

"Olivia," Alexander said breathlessly, pulling her body into his. He stroked her hair again. She could get used to the feeling of his body next to hers, warming her in the cool Boston night air. She leaned her head back to look up at him. *Would he freakin' kiss me already?* Olivia thought. She licked her lips as she stared into his eyes, hoping he would get the hint.

"Oh, Olivia." He pulled her face into his chest, resting his chin on her head as he gently caressed her back. "You have no idea how badly I want to put my lips on you." He exhaled loudly. "God. It's taking all of my resolve to not taste you right now."

"Then why don't you?" Olivia took a deep breath. He smelled so good.

"I don't think I'll be able to stop at just kissing you, and I couldn't live with myself. I mean, after what almost happened to you Friday," he floundered through his bullshit reason. He was more concerned with her being his long lost Olivia. How could he get close to her? Would she ever forgive him for letting her down all those years ago?

"But what if I want to kiss you?" Olivia looked up at Alexander again, a pout on her face.

"You will, I promise, Love."

She felt butterflies at his term of endearment. She wanted to hear that again.

"But when the time is right. And it will be amazing."

Alexander needed more answers.

"A little confident of your skills, aren't you?" Olivia laughed, pushing him away and taking a step back.

"Maybe. I mean…" He looked slightly exasperated as he ran his hand through his hair. It made his already disheveled hair look even sexier. Olivia started to feel a pulsating sensation between her legs as Alexander closed the gap between them once again. "Don't you feel this thing between us? The one thing I learned in my time overseas and after my father died was that life is precious." He stared down at the woman in front of him, his fierce green eyes intense. "I've never felt this way about someone after only knowing them for a few short days. I can't focus at work. I can't do anything without thinking about you. All these feelings are so foreign to me, Olivia. I don't know what to make of it. I normally couldn't give two shits about actually taking someone out, but with you, I don't know. I'm not only interested about getting you into my bed. I just want to see you smile. This is such a strange thing for me."

Olivia felt her heart drop into her stomach. She felt the same way. All thoughts were of Alexander. She had forgotten about Simon altogether until Detective Wilder brought him back to the foreground earlier that day.

"God, Olivia," he breathed, pulling her back into his arms, desperately needing to feel her small body against him again. "What are you doing to me? There's something about you that keeps me coming back to you. I can't explain it. And I'm not sure I want to." He took a step back, holding onto her forearms. "Let's just enjoy this thing, because I am."

"I am, too," she giggled, making Alexander's heart soar. He loved that sound.

"When can I see you again? I have to leave town Thursday, but maybe tomorrow?" He looked at her with a hopeful expression on his face. In the meantime, he was determined to get answers, even if that meant calling in some favors.

"Umm…" She hesitated, unsure of whether she should tell him about singing in a band.

Alexander's heart dropped, noticing her apprehension.

"What is it? Are you seeing someone? I mean, that's fine if you are," he rambled nervously.

"No. It's just, well… I kind of used to sing in a band when I was in college. And my friend Kiera tricked me into going to that bar last Friday and they were playing, and I sang a bunch of songs with them, and now I guess I'm part of the band again and we have a gig on Friday, but I have to go to rehearsal tomorrow." Olivia let out a huge breath, gauging his reaction.

His face turned pale and he had that look again. Like he was searching his brain for something.

"That's probably not your scene, huh?"

He snapped out of it. "No. No. Sorry, that's not it. Déjà vu moment again. Well, can I come and watch? I mean, one of these Friday nights? Do you mind?"

"No. Of course not. I'd love for you to come. You can meet Kiera. When do you get back into town? Will you be back Friday?"

"I don't think so. How about Sunday? Are you available? I'm hoping to get back into town late morning and I'd like to see you."

"I can do Sunday." Olivia smiled, happy that she had another plan to see him. She gazed at him, seeing the heat that was building behind his emerald eyes, and started to breathe heavier.

"Oh, screw it," he said, pushing Olivia against the door to her house, tilting her chin up. Before she knew what was happening, she felt his soft, full lips on her mouth. She opened her lips in response, giving him permission to enter with his tongue, his movements gentle but, at the same time, forceful, as if staking his claim. Olivia felt his growing arousal against her abdomen. She deepened the kiss.

Alexander traced his fingers up and down the side of her stomach, making Olivia moan into his mouth. He pulled away and they both stood on her front stoop, panting.

"Holy crap," Olivia exhaled, trying to catch her breath. In all her twenty-seven years she couldn't remember ever feeling so lightheaded after a kiss.

"You've got that right." He laughed. "You should go inside

before I pin you against that door again." He stared down at her, his eyes full of desire.

"I don't mind," Olivia said, playfully batting her eyes.

"Get inside, please," Alexander said softly, bringing his lips back to hers and planting a soft kiss on her.

"Okay," she replied, his lips still not leaving her mouth. "I have to get my keys."

"You can't do that from this position?"

"It might be hard not being able to look down." Olivia smiled.

"I really like the taste of your lips."

Olivia moaned at his words and he pulled his mouth away. She frowned from the loss of contact as she fished her keys out of her purse and turned to unlock her front door. Alexander was behind her immediately, wrapping his arm around her and caressing her stomach. Olivia backed into him, arching her neck to the side, giving him access to it. He brushed her hair away and kissed her neck, inhaling her scent. She wiggled her butt against him, feeling his growing erection.

He quickly spun her around. "You need to play fair, Miss Adler," he whispered in her ear, making Olivia's body tighten. "Or you'll regret it." He gave her one more quick kiss on her neck before she turned back around to open the door, her heart racing again.

"Are you sure you don't want to come inside, Mr. Burnham?" Olivia turned back toward him, giving him her most innocent smile. She was brimming with sexual tension and badly needed some release.

"Oh, you have no idea how badly I want to come inside," he replied, smirking at the double entendre. "But not tonight. For once, I want to do this right and not rush into anything," he murmured in her ear, kissing her cheek. "By the time I'm through sweeping you off your feet, you will be bursting at the seams, begging me to fuck you, never wanting another man inside you again."

Olivia gasped. He pulled back and she looked at him with wide eyes. He smiled and placed another gentle, moist kiss on her lips. "I'll be thinking of you." He turned to walk down the front steps to the waiting SUV that had arrived unbeknownst to Olivia. She watched him get into the car as she closed and locked her front door. She leaned her back against the door and tried to regain what little composure she had left.

In the car, Alexander grabbed his cell phone and made a quick call.

"Simpson, it's Burnham here. I need everything you can find on one Sarah Olivia Adler. Not really interested in anything recent. I'm more interested in the first ten years of her life. Get it to my sister as soon as possible. This is a top priority."

He hung up and texted Carol, asking her to do an age enhancement on a photo of Olivia as a child, something he had avoided doing for the past twenty-one years. He sighed, hoping he was doing the right thing. He just had to know one way or the other.

CHAPTER ELEVEN

HIGH AND DRY

Olivia felt sluggish the following morning as she made her way to work in order to teach her six a.m. circuit training class. She was happy once her morning classes were finished so that she could relax in her office and deal with some much neglected paperwork. She grabbed her cell phone to see if she had any missed calls, which was doubtful at eight o'clock in the morning.

Her heart skipped a beat when she saw a text from Alexander.

Alexander: *Good morning, Love. I hope you slept well.*

She quickly typed a reply.

Olivia: *I slept well enough, although it was difficult to get to sleep at first.*

Almost instantly, she received a response.

Alexander: *And why is that?*

Olivia: *I had a throbbing sensation between my legs from being left high and dry last night. Well, maybe not too dry. :-)*

Several minutes went by and she hadn't heard back from him. Olivia figured he was in a meeting or on his way to work, so she returned to sorting through the various financial statements she needed to review from the current quarter.

Out of the corner of her eye, Olivia saw a tall figure appear in her doorway. She felt her heart drop to the pit of her stomach. Never in a million years did she expect Alexander would show up at her office.

"May I come in, Olivia?" he asked politely.

God, this man is gorgeous, Olivia thought as she took in his tan suit, white button down shirt, and green tie. Green really was his color.

She simply nodded, unable to find her voice yet again. He stepped into the room and closed the door behind him. Olivia's heart fluttered when she heard the door lock. Not saying a word, he walked over to the windows and drew the shades closed, shrouding the room in relative darkness. The only light came from the small lamp on her desk.

"Now, what were you saying, Olivia? I left you high and, what was it?" he asked with an amused look on his face.

"Dry," she croaked out as she sat at her desk, unable to move or take her eyes off the man in front of her.

He walked over to the love seat in the office. Sitting and crossing his legs, he said, "No. That wasn't it." He draped his arm across the back of the couch, his eyes remaining glued on Olivia. "It was something else entirely, Miss Adler."

His grin made Olivia's body ignite with a foreign feeling. Just thinking about him and his devilish smile made moisture pool between her legs. "Wet. High and wet, Mr. Burnham," Olivia replied softly, her heart racing.

Alexander couldn't take it anymore. Her voice was deep and full of desire for him. He desperately wanted to make her feel good. "Come here, Olivia," he said, uncrossing his legs.

She gazed at him as he held his hand out to her. She rose from her desk and walked over to him, reaching for his hand. Electricity coursed through her veins as he pulled her down, forcing her to straddle him. Her excitement grew when she felt his erection against her body.

"Olivia, do you feel the effect you have on me?"

She stared into his eyes, unable to find her voice, the sensation of feeling him between her legs overwhelming her.

All she could do was nod her head.

"I want to know what kind of effect I have on you. It's only fair." He looked at her, raising his eyebrows as if asking for permission.

She nodded. "Yes," Olivia breathed out, finally finding her voice. "It is only fair."

"It's only fair, what?" He raised his eyebrows again.

"Mr. Burnham. It's only fair, Mr. Burnham," Olivia said, her breathing becoming more and more erratic.

"Good girl," Alexander said as he slowly slid his hands up her thighs, finally slipping one hand underneath the little gym shorts she wore. "Mmmm... No panties." Closing his eyes, he let out a little moan as he teased her folds. "I could get used to that." He opened his eyes and they were full of lust.

He slid his fingers further into her shorts, finding her most sensitive spot. "Oh, Olivia." He closed his eyes again as he started to gently stroke her wet clit. Desire began to pool deep in her stomach. She couldn't remember ever wanting anyone as bad as she wanted Alexander Burnham.

Opening his eyes, he whispered in a husky voice, "I do affect you, don't I?"

Olivia simply nodded and closed her eyes, reveling in the pleasure of his fingers on her, thousands of different sensations overtaking her core.

"Open your eyes, Olivia," Alexander demanded forcefully. She obeyed him, glancing down at his stomach, avoiding his eyes as he slowly entered her with his fingers. She moaned and her breathing increased. "Look at me, Olivia. I want to see your eyes when I make you come."

She straightened her head, her eyes meeting Alexander's as he continued to push in and out of her with his finger. "You're so tight, Olivia," he whispered, licking his lips. "I'm going to have to stretch you out a little before I can fuck you," he explained, his voice husky and deep as he kept his hungry eyes glued on Olivia's. "But I will fuck you."

His words sent her over the edge, causing her to explode around his expert fingers as waves of pleasure flowed through her body. She growled and leaned in, biting his neck softly.

"Holy fuck," she breathed, her heart racing with the aftershocks as he removed his hand.

Alexander placed both hands on her hips and flipped her onto her back. He loomed over her, his eyes burning into hers, searching. Leaning on his forearms, he nuzzled her neck, saying, "I hope you enjoyed that as much as I did." He nibbled on her earlobe before raising himself off the couch. "I'll be in touch, Love," he said, opening the door to her office. As he walked down the hallway, he chuckled to himself. He figured she would be begging for more in no time.

Olivia slowly got off her couch, trying to regain her composure, her body still trembling. She couldn't remember anyone ever making her feel so amazing from a simple touch. She didn't know whether she should feel satisfied or scared.

She looked at the clock on the wall and saw that it was close to nine. *Shit!* She had a few more classes to teach. After quickly changing into another pair of gym shorts, she ran down the hall into the studio. As she got her things together for the pilates class she was leading that morning, Kiera sauntered into the room.

"Hey, Libs! So, how was the date?"

Olivia immediately started to blush, smiling not about the date, but about just having a mind-blowing orgasm.

Kiera noticed. "Oh my god, Libby! Tell me! Tell me! Tell me!" Her excitement was infectious.

"Kiera, I like him. I really, really like him." *And I really, really like what he can do with just a few fingers.* "I've had a perma-grin on my face since he left me last night." *And my body is still shaking from him making me come.* "I just don't know what to do!"

"What is there to even think about?" she exclaimed, grabbing her friend's hands, jumping up and down. "Don't think too much into it. Don't let your fears ruin this for you, Libs." She sat down on the teaching platform, pulling her friend down with her. She draped her arm around Olivia. "Don't let your fears ruin this for me!"

"I know. I've already scheduled an appointment with Dr. Greenstein." Olivia glanced at her friend. She knew what that meant. Olivia had been hesitant to restart therapy, but she didn't want to scare Alexander away with her emotional inability to form meaningful relationships with people. She finally realized that she needed to get past her fear of abandonment.

"Good. Maybe she'll finally talk some sense into you. When do you see her?"

"Tuesdays and Thursdays. I start back tomorrow. God, Kiera. I can't stop thinking about Alexander. I'm gushing! Me! Sarah Olivia Adler! Gushing! Over a freaking guy! This is not me. What is going on?"

"Olivia and Alex sitting in a tree!" Kiera sang.

"No! Stop it. Act your age!" Olivia shouted, pushing her friend.

Kiera just continued, "F-U-C-K-I-N-G!"

"Oh my god! Shut up." People had started to file into the studio. "Get away from me. I have to get ready for this class." Olivia stood up, walking over to the sound system to set up the music she needed for her class.

"Fine, but drinks tonight."

"I can't. I'm rehearsing with Mo's band at around six."

"Then after."

Olivia thought for a moment. Maybe going out with Kiera and gushing over the new man in her life would be more healthy and productive than staying home obsessing over what to do about Alexander. "Okay."

"Good. Meet me at 28 Degrees. Nine sharp." She winked and went to take her place among the class.

As Olivia instructed her class, she cleared her mind of everything for a moment. Well, almost everything. Everything except Alexander Burnham. She couldn't stop smiling as she thought about him and how, in just a short time, he had already helped her overcome some of her fears. Fears he didn't even know she had. Olivia had started to change and she could only think that it was for the better.

Just nine floors above, Alexander stood against his large floor-to-ceiling windows, admiring the city buzzing below and impatiently waiting on the report from Simpson, when his sister came barreling through his office door.

"Alex!" she exclaimed, waking him from his daydream about how good Olivia felt as she clenched around his fingers in absolute ecstasy.

"Carol," he turned around. "What is it?" There was a file in her hands and her face had a look that Alexander had never seen before.

She handed the folder to him. He saw that it contained the background check he had asked Simpson to do. On the top was a photo of Olivia when she was a young child. It was the age enhancement he had asked Carol to do. He looked up at his sister, desperately needing an explanation for the strong resemblance between the computer enhancement and the woman he was falling for.

"Alex... It's her." His heart fell as he dropped his coffee mug, the brown liquid splattering all over the hardwood floor.

CHAPTER TWELVE

28 MARTINIS

Olivia finished teaching her mid-morning classes and returned to her office, hoping to get a little more paperwork done than she had gotten through earlier, although she thoroughly enjoyed her morning interruption. She checked her cell, hopeful that she would have a text from Alexander. It had only been two hours since she had seen him last, but she still ached for him. She smiled when she saw that he had sent her a text not even five minutes after he had left her.

Alexander: *I can smell you on my fingers. You have no idea what a turn on that is.*

Fuck. That guy loved to talk dirty and it was doing things to her.

Olivia: *Just wait till you get a taste, darling. You'll be begging me.*

She smiled, thinking two could play his game.

Alexander: *Oh really, Miss Adler? Is that a threat?*

Ha!

Olivia: *No. Not a threat. My money's on you cracking before me.*

Alexander: *Only time will tell, Love.*

Olivia got butterflies in her stomach thinking about his voice caressing the word, Love. She could hear the words leaving his mouth in his husky voice. How could she possibly be expected to concentrate the rest of the day?

~~~~~~~~~~

"Livvy!" Mo shouted when she opened the door to his house in Arlington later that evening, letting herself in and walking into his large living room. She had never knocked at Mo's when she used to sing with the guys and it felt like no time had passed at all since she left the band.

"So, who's the guy you were with at the Sox game on Sunday?" he asked, raising an eyebrow as he made his way to greet Olivia.

"Oh my god! Did everyone see that?" She punched his arm playfully as she followed him through the living room and into the kitchen, grabbing a bottle of water from his refrigerator.

"Well, fuck, you were like three rows behind home plate," he said, sitting down at the breakfast bar. "So, spill it. Do I have to kick some guy's ass?"

"No. It's all good, Mo," she sighed. "He's a guy that works in my building. And I think he could probably kill you and leave no physical evidence. He's an ex-SEAL and now runs a private security firm." She left the kitchen and headed up the stairs into her friend's spacious music room to wait for the rest of the band members to arrive. Mo followed close on her heels.

"Shit! I knew he looked familiar!" he exclaimed. "That's Alexander Burnham, isn't it?" He stared at her, wide-mouthed.

"Yeah," she answered sheepishly as she checked the tuning on her guitar. It was a tradition for her and Mo to play around a little bit with new tunes before the rest of the band arrived. Nothing really ever came out of it, but they had a chemistry when performing together they both cherished.

"So, what's the deal with you guys?" He started to sound concerned.

"We've gone out a few times."

"Do you like him? I mean, you don't date people, Livvy.

Not trying to sound mean, but that's never been your thing."

Olivia had always felt comfortable telling Mo everything. Sometimes his perspective was exactly what she needed. He never had a problem telling Olivia what he thought about anything. That was the cause of a few fights, but they would eventually get over it.

"I know. I usually don't. But there's something about him, Mo. I can't put my finger on it. I even called my shrink to schedule an appointment to start therapy again. All over a guy!"

"Livvy, I'm happy for you." He pulled her in, wrapping his arms around her. "But, remember. If he hurts you, I've got some moves of my own." He winked after he released her.

"Yeah, yeah. Sure. What are you going to do? Sing him to death?" Olivia laughed and Mo joined in before sitting behind a set of congas and grooving along to the song Olivia had begun to sing.

~~~~~~~~~

Just before nine, Olivia pulled up in front of 28 Degrees, tossing the valet the keys to her Audi. She walked in to see Kiera already sitting at the bar sipping a martini. Olivia joined her, ordering a martini as well.

"To breaking down those fucking walls once and for all," Kiera said, raising her glass.

"I'm working on it," Olivia smiled at her friend as she took a sip of her drink.

She glanced around the dark bar and noticed a tall man with dark hair and evil eyes, dressed all in black, walk into the trendy nightspot. He found a few empty stools at the bar opposite where Kiera and Olivia were sitting, giggling about something.

"Donovan. Grant here. I followed the girl to a bar called 28 Degrees. I left the car and came in to keep a closer eye on her."

"Great. Good work. I'll be there in five minutes."

Grant hung up, keeping his eyes trained on his target and

trying to pick up on her conversation.

"Wait a minute! You think Mo is cute? What?" Olivia nearly shouted as she took a sip from her second martini. *These drinks are going down way too easy tonight*, she thought. "I thought you were just flirting with him for fun! I had no idea!"

"Shut up. I mean, we started to get close when you left. We were the Olivia Adler Survivor's Club." Kiera winked.

Olivia punched her in the arm. "Stop it. You know I feel bad about that."

"You should. Bitch."

Kiera took a sip of her drink, finishing it, and stopped to get the bartender's attention. Suddenly, Olivia felt chills. Turning around, she watched a tall, muscular man with a shaved head walk into the bar, smiling at her as he passed. He walked over to the other side of the bar and joined his friend with the mean eyes. *Why are they both wearing black? Did they coordinate their outfits?* Olivia laughed at the thought.

"What are you laughing at?" Kiera interrupted her thoughts.

Olivia took a sip from her martini. "The thought of you and Mo in the sack."

"Stop it, Libby. And I call him Jack, anyway."

"That's right. I forget that's his real name."

"Why do you call him Mo?"

"Well, the night I first met him at Scotch, that bar we used to work at, he introduced himself and I didn't hear the first part of his name. All I heard was the Mo, and I guess it just kind of stuck. And plus, my Dad's name was Giacomo and he was Jack. I just couldn't bring myself to call him Jack, too."

"Oh. I didn't know that." Kiera rubbed Olivia's back, willing her to not freak out. Surprisingly, she remained relatively calm even though she had just spoken about her father. "Wow, Libs. You willingly spoke about your dad and didn't go storming off. Whatever Alexander is doing, he better keep at it."

Olivia blushed, wanting Alexander to keep doing the things he did to her earlier that morning. She looked across the bar and noticed the two guys staring at her. They weren't even trying to hide it.

"That reminds me. Open Mic mañana, chica?" Kiera asked, bringing Olivia's attention back to her.

"Absolutely! I'm going to get you up on the stage one of these days, I know it!" Olivia laughed at the look of horror on her friend's face.

"Oh, absolutely not. You can have the spotlight. But when you get discovered, just remember the little people, okay? I'm talking backstage passes, and you better make sure I get interviewed when you're on *Behind the Music*. Got it?"

Olivia smiled at her friend as she finished another drink.

The girls spent the next few hours catching up. They hadn't spent much time together lately, Olivia preferring to stay in most nights to Kiera's disappointment.

"Those two guys have been staring at us all night," Kiera slurred into Olivia's ear several hours later, gesturing with her eyes to the opposite side of the bar where the two guys in black sat, drinking their beverages of choice.

"Care Bear, they're creepy looking, not to mention probably about twenty years older than you." Olivia was more than a little drunk, having consumed about five martinis. "Take those fucking beer goggles off already." Olivia laughed. "Plus, I thought you wanted to bang Mo."

"Number one, they're martini goggles. Number two, I do. And I'm still working on that. And you already have Mr. Hottie. I need one, too. I'm going over there." She got off her barstool, almost toppling over.

"You're drunk," Olivia said, poking her arm.

"So are you," she replied, poking her back and heading across the bar. Olivia kept her eyes on Kiera, making sure she didn't slip off into a dark corner with either one, or, God forbid, both.

Olivia decided to take that moment to check her cell phone, noticing a few missed text messages from Alexander. Instead of texting him back, she decided to call him, wanting so desperately to hear his voice.

"Olivia," he answered, his voice sending shivers throughout her body the way he caressed her name. "Are you okay?"

"Of course I'm okay. Why wouldn't I be?" she slurred into the phone, giggling.

"Well, it's past midnight," he responded. In all actuality, that had nothing to do with it. He had texted her several times that evening and never heard back from her. He became rather concerned for her safety. When his phone rang seconds beforehand and he saw Olivia's name pop up, he finally breathed a sigh of relief for the first time all evening.

"Fuck! Is it really? Whoops."

"Olivia, are you drunk?"

She giggled again. Then hiccupped.

"Well, I think I have my answer."

"Oh, you think you have all the answers, don't you Alexander. And why Alexander? Why not Alex?" The booze had made her rather bold.

"We'll save that for when you're screaming my name. I guarantee you won't be able to pronounce my entire name when I'm making you come, Olivia."

She was silent for a minute, having no idea how to respond to his words.

"Are you still there, Olivia?"

She found her voice and squeaked, "Yes. I'm here."

"Who are you out with? Do I have competition for my affections, Love?"

There it was again. That word. *Love.* So full of hope.

"No. I'm with my friend, Kiera. She's over talking to two creepy guys sitting at the other end of the bar."

"Oh really? What makes you think they're creepy?" She could hear the humor in his voice.

"Well, they're wearing all black, which I mean, who does that? Are they in some sort of goth phase? Please! That was so ten years ago! Plus, they got to the bar almost immediately after I did and sat across the way from us. They've been staring at me this whole time. Kiera's over there talking to them and they're still looking at me. So, yeah. Creepy."

Alexander's heart dropped. After his discussion with his sister earlier that morning, he knew there was something going on. He didn't have all the answers, but he did know that the

woman he was falling in love with was the girl he failed early
on in life. And that his father had lied to him about her death
for some reason. He just didn't know what that reason was yet.
Until he figured out what was going on, he wasn't going to take
any chances.

"Olivia, I need you to do something for me." She could hear
the panic in his voice. "I need you to collect your things and
very casually walk into the ladies room."

"Why?" Alexander was starting to scare her. She guessed
that he saw everyone as a potential bad guy after all his years
in the security business.

"Please, don't argue with me right now, Love."

Ah, that word again. All he needed to do was say that and
Olivia was putty in his hands. Or his mouth.

"Can you do that for me? I am five minutes away. I will call
you when I'm there." Alexander sounded serious. He was
worried. But what could he possibly be worried about?

She got off the phone with Alexander and stood up from her
barstool, casually walking to the ladies' room as if nothing was
wrong. She wondered how he even knew what bar she was at.
Of course. He could probably track her cell phone.

A few seconds later, Kiera came barreling through the
bathroom door.

"Libby! There you are!" She dragged one of the creepy guys
in with her. "This is Donovan. He really wanted to get to know
you." She winked at her friend.

Olivia looked at Donovan. It was the guy with the shaved
head. He appeared rather intimidating. He was tall and
muscular with a mean expression on his face. She glared at
Kiera with a shocked look on her face. "Kiera! This is the
ladies' room! Get him out of here!"

Kiera looked around, finally realizing that she dragged a
man into the ladies' room, and giggled, saying, "Whoops!
What was I thinking?" She turned to Donovan and, placing
both hands on his chest, started to push him out the door.
"Out you!"

And then he spoke, making Olivia's skin crawl. "Okay. But
we'll be waiting." He glared at Olivia and left. Her cell phone

began to ring and she quickly answered it, seeing that it was Alexander.

"Olivia, are you safe?" Her hands were shaking.

"Yes, I'm safe. I'm in the ladies' room like you asked." She looked at Kiera who mouthed "What is going on?" Olivia held up one finger, signaling that she would tell her in a minute.

"There are two men dressed in black standing in the corridor. I have taken care of your bar tab. I will be in the hallway in one minute. Count to sixty and come out. Do you follow?"

"Yes." She hung up before turning to Kiera and, whispering, told her that Alexander was there because he was worried for Olivia's safety.

Kiera squealed. "Oh! That's so sweet. You're like a damsel in distress!"

"No." Olivia smacked her friend. "I just think he sees trouble in everything. It's almost like he has this hero complex." Would he still want to be with Olivia if he no longer thought she needed to be saved? The thought consumed her.

When enough time had elapsed, she told Kiera they were leaving and Alexander would meet them in the hallway to help them make their escape.

"Should I start humming the James Bond theme? Because I totally will!" Kiera laughed.

"Shut up, Kiera," Olivia responded as she pushed open the door to the restroom.

Alexander rushed up to embrace his Olivia. She steadied herself in his arms, deeply inhaling his scent, her eyes heavy. "Smell something you like?" he asked with humor in his voice.

She looked at him. "Oh, yes."

He glanced over Olivia's shoulder to the two men hovering in the hallway and whispered quietly in her ear, "We need to get you out of here." He was able to discreetly take cell phone pictures of the two men when he paid the girls' bar tab. He planned to run the photos through facial recognition later.

Alexander grabbed Olivia's hand and she, in turn, grabbed Kiera's hand. Olivia looked at her dumbstruck friend as she mouthed, "Holy shit, he's gorgeous."

Didn't she know it?

~~~~~~~~~~~

Olivia gave the valet her ticket and he quickly retrieved her car. Alexander opened both passenger side doors when the car was brought around, allowing Kiera to collapse in the back seat before helping Olivia into the front. He ran around, tipping the valet, and got in the driver's seat before taking off down the quiet Boston streets. Kiera had walked there because she lived around the block by the community gardens, but she was in no state to be walking anywhere at that moment.

After dropping Kiera off at her house, Alexander picked up his phone. "Burnham here. I want an overnight protection detail for a Ms. Kiera," he looked at Olivia, wanting her last name.

"Murphy."

"Kiera Murphy." He listed off her address and Olivia gazed into the distance. Those two men at the bar really did concern Alexander. She wondered why.

After he hung up the phone, Olivia glared at him. "What the fuck is going on?" she blurted out.

He reached across the console of her car and placed his hand on her leg. He took a deep breath. He thought about telling her. But how would she react? She was clearly intoxicated. Could she be rational? Would the information set her back? Would she never speak to him again? He wasn't ready for that to happen just yet.

"I'm not sure, Olivia. But I have a feeling. And my gut is usually right," he responded, his voice soft and sensual, causing Olivia to soften her glare and practically forget about the two men at the bar.

"Well, what is it you're feeling?" she slurred, trying to sound sexy.

He laughed. "What am I feeling? Well, if you really want to know, I am feeling a whirlwind of emotions right now, Love. I'm feeling that you're not just some girl I want to fuck and never see again. I care about you. Deeply. Which is a strange emotion for me, to be honest. I feel the need to protect you. To keep you safe. To make you happy." He smiled at her. *And to tell you that I finally found you after all these years.*

"But, you can't always keep me safe. No one could shoulder that burden." She hiccuped and he laughed, breaking the tension that was building in the car. She didn't know that he had made a pledge to protect her all those years ago and now that he found her, he could fulfill that promise.

Alexander pulled up outside of Olivia's house and parked the car on the side of the road. He walked her to the front door just as two black SUVs pulled in front. She noticed Martin driving the first but didn't recognize who was driving the second.

"Martin is here to take me home. And Carter will be parked out front keeping an eye on your place. It didn't look like anyone followed us here, but I need to be sure."

Olivia looked up at him, not ready to say good-bye just yet. "Stay with me, please." She didn't know what had possessed her to say that. She had never wanted anyone to stay over. Ever. Why now all of a sudden? Why that man? She couldn't believe her own ears. But she really did want him to stay.

He exhaled and pulled her against him. "I want to, but…"

"But what? I just want to fall asleep in your arms," Olivia said sleepily. "If you really want to make me happy, you'll stay."

"Ouch, Miss Adler. Using my words against me," he said in mock shock.

"I know. How very unfair of me, isn't it? I should be punished." She laughed and looked into his eyes. They immediately became hooded as desire flooded through them, making her entire body tingle. Alexander could think of some ways to punish her and they would both enjoy every minute of it.

"Okay. I'll spend the night." His heart warmed when he saw Olivia smile at his words. "I'd do anything to keep that smile on your face."

She turned to unlock the door. "Just knowing you're in the world makes me smile."

He pulled her into an embrace and sang a line from Elton John's *Your Song* in her ear. Her eyes glossed over, his voice and those lyrics stirring a memory that lay deep within her subconscious. She turned to get away from Alexander so that she could clear her foggy head. She stumbled across the doorframe, tripping on her own feet and falling to the ground, most likely due to all the alcohol she had consumed throughout the evening.

"Are you okay, Olivia?" She turned to look at Alexander who stood in the doorframe, looking down on her as she sat on the hardwood floor.

She laughed. "I'm drunk." All thoughts of that memory were now gone.

"We need to get you in bed before you do any more damage to that beautiful body of yours." He closed the door and locked it. "Just to remind you, my company will be here tomorrow to install your security system."

"Oh, I love it when you talk dirty to me." She giggled again. She couldn't stop.

He bent down and picked her up in his arms. "Where is your bedroom?"

Olivia leaned into his chest, enjoying the closeness of him. "Up the stairs. First door on the left." She was suddenly getting sleepy. He carried her up the stairs into her bedroom and gently placed her on the bed. She was so tired that she didn't think she could even muster the strength to find something to sleep in.

"Where are your pajamas?"

"Top drawer," Olivia mumbled, raising her arm to point in the direction of the dresser.

He opened the top drawer. "Now, this is hot, but if you wear this, I don't know how much sleeping you'll do." He winked as he held up a little black sleep slip. Olivia smiled.

He continued rummaging through her pajama drawer and found a black tank top with pink boy shorts. He walked over to the bed and helped her change into her pajamas, steadying her as she stood and lifting her shirt over her head.

"Like what you see, Mr. Burnham?" Olivia asked, raising an

eyebrow as he gawked at the pink lace bra she had on underneath her shirt.

His eyes bore into her and his breathing became erratic when she slowly removed her bra, letting it drop to the ground.

"Fuck…" he exhaled, staring at her perfect breasts.

Olivia grabbed his hand, pulling him closer to her, and pressed it against her chest. He began to knead, tugging gently on her nipple. Olivia threw her head back, moaning, as Alexander leaned down, burying his head in her neck. He groaned loudly before reaching on the bed behind him and grabbing the tank top he had found for her to sleep in.

"Please, you need to put this on, Olivia," he pled softly, handing her the top. "I want you so fucking bad right now, but you're drunk and I don't want our first time to be like this." He leaned down and trailed feather kisses against her neck. "I want you to remember every single moment that I'm inside you, filling you," he whispered, his warm breath against her skin sending waves of desire throughout Olivia's body. "Okay?"

Olivia remained speechless, shocked at his words. She loved how sensual and sweet he could be. She simply nodded as Alexander lowered the tank top over her head, helping her balance as she finished getting ready for bed. After helping her out of her jeans, he laid her down in her bed before stepping back to take off his clothes.

Olivia eyed him as he slowly unbuttoned his blue button-down shirt, keeping his eyes connected with hers. She didn't want to look away from his eyes but couldn't help glancing down at his body when he slipped off his shirt. She had been wanting to see what he looked like with no shirt on since the night they met and she was not disappointed. His wide shoulders led down to a well-defined chest and perfect washboard abs. Olivia wondered how much he worked out to maintain that physique. Then she noticed a faint trail of dark hair leading from his belly button down into his pants. Alexander's hands followed Olivia's eyes as he unbuttoned his pants, removing them and his socks quickly. He stood in front of her, wearing only a pair of boxer briefs. Olivia couldn't believe how lucky she was to share a bed with a man as beautiful as Alexander. She desperately wanted to see where that trail of hair led to, but knew it would have to wait. She was exhausted.

Alexander crawled into bed next to her after shutting off the lights. He pulled her to him, her back to his front. She could feel how turned on he was. "Sleep well, beautiful. I'll see you in my dreams," he said, his closeness causing her hair follicles to stand on end. Olivia drifted off to sleep, content to have a man sleeping next to her for the first time in her life.

CHAPTER THIRTEEN

NOT YET

Olivia sat in the back of her parents' car. She clutched Mr. Bear in her little arms. She knew what was going to happen. She knew her dad would tell her he loved her and then a car would slam into them from behind, forcing their car through a guardrail and then into a tree.

The green-eyed boy came to save her, just like he had been doing all week in her dreams. He placed her in a different car, telling her nothing bad would happen to her again. Then she saw a man dressed all in black come up to the boy and smash his head with the handle of the gun he was holding in his hand. The green-eyed boy stared at her and then fell to the ground.

"NOOOOOOO!" Olivia woke up screaming, covered in sweat.

The lights snapped on immediately as Alexander came rushing back to the bed, cradling her in his arms. "Olivia, Love. What is it?"

Her body convulsed from the aftereffects of her dream. Why was that dream becoming more and more vivid every day? She didn't understand it.

"I'm sorry, Alexander. It was just a stupid dream," Olivia trembled as he held her close, comforting her.

"Would you like a water?" he asked quietly.

"Yes, please."

He planted a delicate kiss on her forehead before leaving the bedroom in search of water.

Olivia was so angry with herself for asking Alexander to stay over. She hated that he had seen her freak out after having a nightmare. That was not the way to win a guy's heart.

"Do you want to talk about it?" Alexander asked when he returned with a bottle of water, sitting next to Olivia on the bed and wrapping his arms around her.

"It's nothing." She brought the bottle to her mouth, which proved difficult due to her shaking hand.

"Olivia, it is clearly not nothing. You're shaking." He looked at her, concern covering his face.

"I know. It's just a dream I've been having ever since I can remember. It's about my parents' death. I still can't believe it will be twenty-one years this Friday…"

Alexander's face went pale. Olivia had been dreaming about the crash. If she was able to dream about the accident, maybe she was able to remember more than she had let on.

"What's wrong?" Olivia asked. "Are you okay?"

"Yes, sorry. I just, well… I'm sorry you lost your parents." He couldn't bring himself to tell her. Not yet. It was still too soon. He turned to look at Olivia. "What happens in the dream? If you don't mind telling me." He needed to know if she had dreamt about him.

"I was at our beach house and my mama was rushing me, wanting to leave quickly for some reason. I don't think my mama felt well because she was asleep in the car. We sped through town before getting on the interstate. Finally, my father calmed down when we were far away from the beach house. I was in the back seat of the car holding Mr. Bear." She smiled. "Mr. Bear was my favorite stuffed animal growing up. That much I can remember about my childhood."

Alexander knew that bear well. Very well.

"My father looked back at me and told me how much he loved me. How much they both did. Out of nowhere, another car crashed into us from behind, pushing our car through a guardrail and into a tree. Usually that was where my dream would end, but recently it's been different."

Alexander remembered pulling up behind the DeLuca's crashed car. He and his father had been following them when they saw a large black SUV pull out of a highway turnout and careen toward their car, pushing it over the side of the freeway.

When his father saw the car, he thought they were dead. No one could have survived that crash. But Alexander saw movement in the back seat. He remembered rushing toward the car, searching for his best friend.

"How so?" Alexander asked, returning to the present.

"Well, last week, a little boy was in the dream and he's been there every night since. And then I saw my uncle with a scared look on his face when he was trying to help my mama."

"What was your uncle's name?" Alexander asked quietly, almost as if he didn't want to know the answer.

"Charles. Charles Wright." She looked at Alexander.

Now he knew that his father had used one of his alternate identities in order to protect this girl. He had found the paperwork on that alias when he was going through some of his father's things after his death. His father's real name was Thomas.

"What was the boy doing in the dream? Are you okay talking about it?" he asked, grasping her hand in his.

"Yes. I'm fine." She took a deep breath before continuing her story. "He pulled me out of the car. He ran me over to another car telling me that he would always protect me from then on. Suddenly, out of nowhere, a man dressed in black knocked him out with the butt of his gun. That's when I woke up."

Alexander started to rub the back of his head almost in the same place where the boy had been hit in the dream, recalling that moment like it was yesterday. He remembered the darkness, knowing that he could no longer protect his little Olivia.

Alexander got up and went to turn out the light. Climbing back into bed, he pulled Olivia close. "Go to sleep, angel, and forget about that dream. It was just a dream, like you said." He didn't sound too convinced. He knew it wasn't a dream. But he didn't want Olivia to know that. Not yet. Not until he had all the answers. Alexander had a feeling that he already had the answers in his possession, but he had just been too selfish to look.

The early morning sun awoke Olivia as it began to seep into her bedroom. She looked at the clock on her nightstand and saw that it was not yet six in the morning. It had only been a few hours since she woke up screaming, waking Alexander. She rolled over, hoping to snuggle with him, but he wasn't there. Olivia got out of bed and went downstairs, wondering if he was still in her house or if he left because he saw how clearly unstable she really was.

To her surprise, upon entering her living room, she saw Alexander sitting on the couch in his boxer briefs, a perplexed look on his face as he held an envelope in his hands.

"What's that?" Olivia asked. He looked up quickly, a hard look on his face that immediately softened when he took in Olivia's frame standing in the doorway.

"Hello, Love. I hope I didn't wake you." He smiled.

"No. You didn't," Olivia answered sleepily as she yawned. "The sun woke me up. I rolled over and you weren't there." Her face had a disappointed look on it. Alexander made a mental note of how beautiful she looked first thing in the morning, her hair slightly disheveled, rubbing her eyes.

Olivia walked over to the couch where Alexander sat with his elbows on his legs, holding the letter with both hands. Sitting down next to him, she noticed a brown leather messenger bag had somehow arrived during the night. He had files spread over the coffee table along with a nice journal with the year embossed on it in gold. *He keeps a journal*, she thought to herself. It warmed Olivia's heart that he felt comfortable enough with her to make himself at home in her house.

"Is that *the* letter?" Olivia recalled Alexander mentioning a letter his father wrote him before he died that he still hadn't opened.

"Yes, it is." He looked conflicted.

"What is it you're afraid of?" She was curious.

"I guess I'm afraid of what it says. I have a feeling I know what's in that letter. I don't know if I want my suspicions confirmed. That would mean that I had been letting my father

127

down since he died. I guess I'm hoping to remain blissfully ignorant." He laughed.

"Well, you need to do what you think is best. If you need more time, take it. If reading this letter will re-open old wounds, you're better off being prepared to deal with that." Olivia smiled.

He wanted to scream, *"It could mean that I've been letting you down! It could mean that I would have found you years ago! I could have saved you from your pain!!"* But he didn't. He just stared ahead, relishing in the closeness of Olivia.

"Come back to bed." She stood up and extended her hand to him. He placed the letter on the coffee table before taking her small hand in his.

They crawled back into the bed, a nice glow in the room from the sunlight creeping in. Alexander wrapped his arms around Olivia, enjoying the feel of her soft skin. She turned toward him, noticing he had a distant expression on his face. He was clearly still thinking about that letter. She made it her mission that morning to help him take his mind off it.

Smiling, Olivia pushed Alexander on his back, pinning him down with her legs on either side of him. His eyes flung wide open for a moment before becoming dark with desire. He placed his hands just below her hip bones, feeling her toned legs as she sat on top of him, unable to hide his erection. Leaning down, she brushed her lips softly along his jaw line. He moaned and a smile spread across Olivia's face, knowing that she made him do that.

She slowly started to move her hips in a circular motion, causing his erection to get even harder.

"Happy to see me this morning, Mr. Burnham?" Olivia smirked.

"Why Miss Adler, I'm always happy to see you. Haven't I made that quite clear?" He let out a small breath as she continued torturing him with her body. "God, Love. I can feel how wet you are through our clothes." Alexander found it hard to keep his head. He wanted to be intimate with her, but he wanted to be truthful with her first. He didn't know which one of his heads would win out. He had a feeling it would be the wrong one.

"Well, let's get rid of them, shall we?" She slowly trailed kisses down his chest and torso, taking her time to enjoy the taste of his skin. Olivia looked up and could see that he barely held it together, desperately looking for release.

She slid his boxer briefs down his muscular legs and he sprung free. Her eyes grew wide as she looked at him and gasped, surprised at his size. He smiled, stroking his erection.

Olivia pried his hand off, her hand taking its place. She slowly lowered her lips to him while staring into his green eyes, taking him in her mouth. He moaned with obvious pleasure as she continued moving her mouth over his length, slow and then fast, and then slow again.

"Fuck, Olivia," Alexander growled. He couldn't believe that his Olivia was there. And that she was doing *that* to him. It was so much more spectacular than anything he had ever felt before with any other woman.

Olivia started to pick up the pace. She felt him get harder, tasting the bit of pre-cum that escaped his tip. He wrapped her hair around his hand, helping to guide her as she continued torturing him.

Before long, he felt that familiar sensation, surprised at how quickly he reached that point. Something about Olivia's mouth and tongue on his most sensitive part made him feel things that he never thought possible. "I'm going to come," he breathed, warning her. She looked up at him, continuing her relentless motion. He gazed at her, wide-eyed, knowing what that meant. She gently bared her teeth, pushing him over the edge, and he released into her mouth as she continued to suck on him, the sensation overwhelming his entire body. He shuddered as he began coming down from his orgasm, trying to remember the last time anyone had made him feel that good. "Fuck," he exhaled, giving one last jerk.

Olivia slowly crawled back up to him when he grabbed her, throwing her onto her back and kissing her deeply, their tongues engaged in a passionate dance. Alexander was so incredibly turned on. He could taste him and Olivia. It was an intoxicating combination.

He released her and Olivia tried to catch her breath. Alexander collapsed next to her and they both lay on their backs, attempting to slow down their breathing after such an intense moment.

"Fuck," he breathed again.

"You've got that right, Mr. Burnham." She turned and smiled at him. She didn't know what had come over her. She would normally never do that for anyone, but there was something about Alexander that made her want to please him. She felt amazingly satisfied.

"Oh, Olivia. What am I going to do with you?" he asked, running his hand up and down her stomach.

"You keep saying that. What are you going to do with me?" She raised an eyebrow and leaned in, kissing him softly on his mouth. He pulled her in toward him, wrapping his arms around her small frame. She nuzzled against his chest and fell back asleep, listening to the rhythm of his breathing.

Several hours later, Alexander reluctantly got out of bed, needing to get into the office. Olivia walked him to the door to say good-bye. "I'll miss you this weekend." She embraced him, taking in his scent. She wasn't looking forward to her weekend without him.

He looked down at her and gave her a deep kiss. "I'll be thinking of you every day," he said sweetly. He pulled out of the embrace and looked out front where two black SUVs were parked, just like the night before. Olivia wondered if they were out all night. When his eyes returned to her, Alexander's expression was serious. "Carter is out front keeping an eye on things. I have two of my best men coming over this afternoon to install your security system. If you need to run any errands, Carter will escort you. Do you understand, Olivia? This is just for today."

"Yes. I understand. I just have an appointment at eleven, and then I was planning on going to the gym to work out."

"All that's fine. You can do whatever you need to do, just do not go anywhere without Carter. I cannot emphasize that enough."

God. Why is he treating me like a child? Olivia thought. "I got it, you overbearing ogre." She winked.

He glanced down at her, a menacing look on his face. "Oh, you have no idea how overbearing I can be, Love." He embraced her again and she was back in his arms. She never wanted to leave those arms. She could have died happy at that moment. He planted an affectionate kiss on her forehead before leaning down and quietly whispering, "I'm always going to protect you, Olivia." He turned to leave, closing the front door behind him.

Olivia's heart started racing, remembering her dream, that boy's voice, and those green eyes.

CHAPTER FOURTEEN

NUMBER ONE PRIORITY

"Miss Adler, ma'am. Where can I escort you to?" Carter asked as Olivia locked her front door later that morning before heading to her appointment with Dr. Greenstein. Carter was big, black, and very no-nonsense. Olivia wondered whether Alexander had anyone working for him that couldn't bench-press five hundred pounds.

"Um, hi. You can call me Olivia. Libby. Whatever." It wasn't the first time she had an escort. Her uncle had usually insisted on her having a chauffeur when she was growing up. Of course, that had become a point of contention between the two of them as she got older and wanted more independence to do whatever she wanted. Plus, she never really liked telling people what to do.

She immediately thought of all the romance novels she had read, having her very own escort ordered by her hot, rich, handsome whatever he was. She giggled before regaining her composure. *Carter must think I'm crazy*, she thought to herself.

"I have an appointment at the Prudential Center. I was just going to walk." She didn't live that far from the Prudential Center and she loved walking through the streets of Boston. Olivia thought there was no reason for Carter to drive.

"Ma'am, I have very strict orders from Mr. Burnham to drive you wherever you need to go. It's just a precaution." Olivia realized that she wasn't going to win that battle and she didn't want to disappoint Alexander so early on in their relationship, if it was a relationship.

"Okay," she said, walking down her front steps toward the

idling SUV. In a matter of minutes, they arrived at the Prudential Center. Carter proceeded to park in the underground garage.

He intercepted Olivia as she left the car to go into the center and up to her appointment. "Ma'am. I need to escort you into the building. Again, just a precaution. This should all be over by the end of today." She could tell that Carter knew she wasn't a fan of being subjected to constant security, but Olivia bit her tongue.

"Okay. But, just so you know, I have an appointment with my shrink. That's where I'm going." His face remained fixed with no reaction. He was probably trained to be rather discreet. "I guess that's better than having to accompany me to the gyno, huh?" She nudged him in the elbow as they walked into a waiting elevator, trying to get a laugh out of him.

He smiled at her. "Yes, ma'am. It definitely is better." He chuckled.

"This is her office," Olivia said as they stepped out of the elevator, nodding toward the office immediately in front of them.

"I'll wait out here," Carter said after assessing the arrangement. The doors to the doctor's office were all glass, so he would be able to keep her in his sights while she waited for her appointment to begin. And since she was seeing her therapist, he figured it would be good to give her some semblance of privacy.

When Olivia walked through the doors into the reception area, she received a warm greeting. "Olivia. It's wonderful to see you again." Dr. Greenstein had been waiting for her by the receptionist's desk. She was a middle-aged woman with short blonde hair and a tall frame. "Come on in." She followed the doctor into her office.

It didn't look like a typical shrink's office. It was large with floor-to-ceiling windows, black tile floor, and several comfortable white couches with green, orange, and yellow accent pillows. Dr. Greenstein had great decorating style.

She sat in an oversized white chair, motioning for Olivia to have a seat on the couch in front of her. "So, what brings you back to me, Olivia?"

"Well, I figured it was time." She laughed.

Dr. Greenstein picked up a notepad and a pen, looked at her patient, and said, "Do you think? What was the reason for you calling me? It's been quite a while."

"Yeah. Several years. I know."

"So, tell me. What's going on?"

"Well, I met this guy." Olivia smiled as she proceeded to give Dr. Greenstein a general overview of what had been going on in her life recently. About how she would refuse to get into a relationship with anyone but would hook up on occasion. She talked about Simon and how she met Alexander. She mentioned that she asked him to stay over the previous night.

"And how do you feel about that?"

She hated that question and her doctor knew it. "I don't know how I feel about it." Olivia glared.

"Okay, okay. Sorry. But we need to discuss your feelings, Olivia. What was going through your mind when you asked him to stay over? You've said that you never let guys stay over your place. If they were invited over, you would kick them out after sex. So, why Alexander?"

"Hold on. We haven't had sex."

"Okay. So you haven't been intimate yet."

"I didn't say that," she interrupted the doctor. "I mean, we've done some things, just haven't had sex yet."

"Hmmm… And do you think that's why you don't have a problem with him staying over?"

"No. I mean, I want to have sex with him. But, I don't know. We seem to be taking our time and I'm actually enjoying it. It's weird. Normally I just want to jump straight to sex so I can kick the guy out of my bed." Olivia looked down as she fidgeted with her skirt. She hated talking about her sexual habits with her doctor. Unfortunately, it was necessary for her to do so.

"Well, the act of sex is an intimate act, but you haven't made it so. When you jump right into things, you skip over the act of forming a bond with another individual. You use sex as a coping mechanism while, at the same time, keeping your subjects at arm's length so that you don't get attached. What is it about Alexander?"

Olivia looked up and met the doctor's eyes. "I don't know. Before me, he would kind of do the same thing I did, but I think his reasons are vastly different from mine. He doesn't have these attachment issues like I know I do. But now, I don't know. He said he wants more with me. He's sweet. He cares about me. He's always trying to protect me. He's incredibly sensual." Olivia's face flamed just thinking about some of the things he had said. "He's very gifted with words." That was the best way she could think to say he liked to talk dirty.

A smile crept across Dr. Greenstein's face. "So he's prolonging the seduction and you're enjoying it."

"Yes. Definitely." She was absolutely enjoying every fantastic minute.

"Olivia," the doctor said, removing her reading glasses from her face. "You, unfortunately, had your parents taken from you at such a young age. You never had the means to learn how to form a relationship with someone. You were so traumatized by that event that you pushed everyone away. When you were older and discovered sex, you wanted that without the emotional attachment. Now, you're experiencing a slow seduction for the first time. Most of us have experienced that early on in our development. Granted, early on, it's not necessarily about sex. But later in life, our bodies crave that release, so it becomes a slow seduction, which can sometimes last years before the actual act of intercourse.

"You need to embrace this. Enjoy it. Go for the ride and face your fears. Don't worry about whether Alexander will ever leave you or be taken from you. We can't control those things. But you can control your actions. If you want to have a meaningful relationship with this man, and it sounds like you do, don't push him away. Let him in. You're a beautiful, intelligent young woman. Let him fall in love with you. And keep yourself open to fall in love with him in return."

Olivia looked down. That woman was good. She was definitely worth every penny. Dr. Greenstein glanced at her watch. "Oh, I'm sorry, dear. We're out of time for today. We'll pick up again on Tuesday." She led Olivia toward her office door before giving her a gentle hug. "It's great to see you again, Olivia."

She turned to leave the office and really put some thought into what the doctor said. *I'll tell her about my dreams next time*, Olivia thought to herself.

~~~~~~~~~~

Shortly after she finished eating lunch that afternoon, Olivia heard a gentle knock on her door. Looking out the peephole, her heart fluttered when she saw Alexander standing there, a sexy smirk on his face.

She quickly opened the door and he swept her into his embrace. Olivia had missed that man and she had only been away from him for a few hours. "Miss me, Love?"

"You have no idea," she replied into his chest. He pulled back, giving her a chaste kiss on her mouth. "My security team is here to install your system."

"And I'm such a high profile client that the big boss man had to come supervise?" Olivia batted her eyelashes at Alexander.

He curved toward her, softly saying, "You are Burnham and Associates' number one priority, Miss Adler." He stepped aside to allow two gentlemen in the house to install the state-of-the-art security system Alexander had selected.

"Olivia, this is Arnold and Chase. They'll be rewiring your house for this system. It may take a few hours. Just let them know if you have any concerns. When they're done, they'll walk you through how to program and use it. They're also going to change your front door so that it's a punch-pad lock instead of a key. It's more secure." Mr. Businessman was back. The dichotomy of his sweet side and his business side intrigued Olivia.

The two men entered the house and started to do what they needed in order to secure her home. Alexander looked down on Olivia and grabbed her hand, placing a gentle kiss on her knuckles. "I have to return to the office. Carter is still out front should you need anything. What are you doing tonight? Any plans?"

"Actually, yes. And I'll take Carter with me, I promise. It's Thursday. Kiera usually drags me to Open Mic night at a bar in Davis Square called Johnny D's. It's a pretty good time."

"Ah, I've been there. Good bar. Great blues brunch on Sundays." His phone started buzzing. "One minute," he said to Olivia. He pushed the button on his phone, answering it. "Tyler. What's up?" He looked at Olivia and mouthed "brother" to her. She nodded and mouthed "okay" back to him.

"Yeah... After the meeting... I'm heading down afterwards... Okay... Hey listen, Ty, I have to go. I'm at my girlfriend's... Yes, you heard me... We'll talk about it later."

Holy crap! He called me his girlfriend! Olivia thought. Normally that would cause her to break out in hives, but the way the word rolled off his tongue did things to her. It made her burn for him.

Alexander hung up with his brother and dragged Olivia back into his arms, planting a kiss on her forehead. "I hope you don't mind that I called you my girlfriend."

She gazed up into his eyes. "No. Actually, it made me a little wet when you said that. I'm not going to lie."

He groaned and gave her a quick kiss. "On that note, sadly, I must leave you. I'll see you soon, angel." He walked out the front door, leaving Olivia feeling wonderful.

She collapsed on the couch, squealing. One of the installation men looked at her. Olivia thought it was Arnold. "I have a boyfriend!" she explained excitedly. He just looked at her and laughed.

"Oh my god! I need to call Kiera!" Olivia jumped off the couch and ran upstairs to her study.

"OHMIGOD! OHMIGOD! OHMIGOD!" Kiera shouted into the phone when Olivia told her the good news. For being in her thirties, Kiera sometimes failed to act a day over fifteen, especially when it came to the opposite sex.

"I know! And I let him stay over last night! I actually asked him to!"

"Holy crap. Where is my friend Olivia, and what have you done with her?"

"I know. I feel like I'm thirteen. Is this the honeymoon phase everyone always talks about?"

"Yes!" Kiera replied. "It is. And isn't it great?"

"Kiera, I feel like I'm on cloud nine. I'm happy. I'm smiling. He's all I can think about. For once, I'm not thinking about my past. All I'm thinking about is my future and how he could be a part of that."

"Aww, Libs! I'm so happy for you!"

"But what happens when the honeymoon is over? What happens when I don't feel like this anymore?" Olivia worried that she would become obsessed with that feeling and would be heartbroken if she didn't feel it anymore.

"Libby, when you're with the right person, the feeling will never go away. You will always have that person on your mind. You'll always miss them when they're not around. You'll always have this extraordinary excitement when you're together. That's how you know it's meant to be. And any relationship where you don't have that is not worth your time."

Olivia took Kiera's words to heart as she went through the rest of her day. The security system installation was finished by five that evening. Chase quickly walked her through everything, helping her set a code. They also set up the keyless entry. Olivia was thrilled to not have to lug her keys around anymore.

After getting back from the gym, she took a quick shower before Kiera was expected at her house to head to Open Mic.

"What the fuck is this?" Kiera asked when Olivia answered the door.

"Alexander put in a new system. He wanted me to feel safer. And Carter has to drive us to the bar tonight. Don't worry about the door and the alarm. I'll give you the code, but so help me God, if you set off the alarm and I have to deal with a panicky Alexander, I will murder you in your sleep. And I'll tell Mo that you have crabs." Olivia joked, grabbing her guitar case.

"You do that and I'll cut a bitch." The two girls laughed.

"Bye Nepenthe," Kiera said to the cat as he stalked the front door. "Your cat hates me," she remarked while Olivia armed the security system.

"Nepenthe doesn't hate anyone. He just has murder in his heart is all."

CHAPTER FIFTEEN

CONSTANT BUTTERFLIES

"I'll be here keeping an eye on things, ma'am," Carter said when he escorted Olivia and Kiera inside Johnny D's. He motioned to a table near the door where he would have a view of the entire club. To the right of the door was the bar area with a few high-top tables bordering the wall. To the left was a small dining area with a stage.

"Okay. Thanks Carter," Olivia said, walking toward the dining room area and up to the small front table. She added her name to the list. Open Mic night was getting started and there were already about ten people on the list. She figured it would be about an hour or so before she would go on.

"Hey, Livvy!" Mo said as he and Marcus made their way over to her and Kiera's table.

"Hey, Mo!" Olivia said, standing up and giving both guys a hug. "I didn't know you were coming tonight."

Mo met Kiera's eyes and they shared a look as if Mo finally realized Kiera was attractive.

"Oh, I get it," Olivia smirked, elbowing Mo.

The guys pulled up two chairs and joined Olivia's table.

"So, what are you going to do tonight?" Kiera asked as a server approached their table with their drink order.

"Well, actually, now that Mo's here, I think I may want to switch it up, if you're willing to back me up on percussion. Remember the song we were fooling around with last night?"

Mo nodded, his smile wide.

"That's the one, then," Olivia said.

"Sweet," Kiera said, taking a sip of her cocktail.

~~~~~~~~~~~

Across town, Alexander finally finished his meeting with his training strategist. Looking at his watch, he saw that it was half past eight. He rushed out the front door of his office building and climbed into the waiting SUV.

"Good evening, sir. Off to home then?"

"Actually, Martin. Let's make a quick detour. How fast can you get me to Johnny D's in Davis Square?"

"I can be there in fifteen minutes, tops."

"I'll give you five thousand if you can get there in ten."

Martin laughed. "Yes, sir." He peeled into traffic, heading toward Davis Square.

Less than ten minutes later, Martin pulled in front of Johnny D's and Alexander ran inside.

Carter saw him almost immediately and stood up from his chair. "Sir, is everything alright?"

"Carter, pretend I'm not even here please. Just go on with what you were doing and I'll be over at the bar. If either Miss Adler or Miss Murphy get up from their table, please intercept them and get their drinks."

"Yes, sir. Oh, and just so you know, she hasn't performed yet."

He smiled. "Thank you, Carter."

Alexander walked over to the bar and sat at a stool that hid him from most of the crowd sitting in the lower dining area that housed the stage. He still had a great view of the actual stage and that was all he cared about.

"Let's all give it up for the lovely Laura!" the M.C. shouted into the microphone. The crowd's response was mediocre at best, although Olivia cheered enthusiastically. She knew how difficult it was for anyone to get up on the stage and pour their hearts out to the audience. And anyone who had the courage to get on that stage deserved an enthusiastic response.

"Next up. Well, looky here. Miss Olivia Adler has graced us with her presence! Libby get your cute butt up here!"

Alexander shot daggers at the M.C., a decent looking guy in

141

his mid-thirties with a shaved head and a short beard. That cute butt belonged to Alexander. The thought of anyone else commenting on it made him wild with rage. He had never felt so possessive before and it was a strange feeling.

Olivia walked up to the stage, carrying her guitar and waving to the crowd as she made her way through the room. Alexander smiled as he took in her appearance. She kept her long dark hair straight and chose to wear a tight yellow halter tank with a pair of dark jeans and giraffe print heels. She looked hot. A guy followed her on stage and sat behind a set of congas. He was about the same height as Olivia and had very similar features. If Alexander didn't know better, he would have thought they were related.

She sat down at a chair positioned center stage and adjusted her microphone as she checked the tuning on her acoustic guitar.

"How's everyone doing?"

The crowd cheered.

"Awesome. Well, I've brought some backup with me today. My good friend Mo, oops, I mean Jack Distanzio, is going to help me out. Incidentally, his band, *Groove Delay*, is performing tomorrow night at MacFadden's in the Financial District, so come on by. And I'll be doing a few songs with them as well." The audience clapped. "This is *Sleeping to Dream* by Jason Mraz."

Alexander was transfixed on the woman holding the guitar and interacting with relative ease with the audience. It brought back so many memories of all those years ago.

And then she started playing, plucking at the guitar strings, a sweet melody amplified through the bar. As she sang, Alexander looked over the large audience sitting captivated by the woman on the stage. Her normally strong voice sounded sweet and light, matching the mood of the song.

Alexander listened to the lyrics of the song; a song he had heard many times before but had never paid much attention to. He absently wondered whether Olivia had realized that the boy she saw in her dreams was him. Whether she knew that he pulled her out of that car. Whether she knew that he swore he would always protect her. And whether she knew that he let her down.

Olivia and the guy playing the congas, Mo, as she introduced him on stage, were good together. It was clear they had been playing together for a while. When they reached the bridge, the back and forth between Olivia and Mo mesmerized Alexander. Olivia belted out the words leading to the final chorus, the audience cheering wildly as her strong voice hit a high note, the sound filling the bar and sending shivers through Alexander's body. She was good, he thought to himself. She looked so at ease in front of the large crowd.

He thought back to all those years ago, spending time with Olivia and her family and learning how to play piano and guitar from her mother, who would always sit in the great room at their beach house, playing for the kids. Olivia loved having the spotlight back then, singing and dancing to a pretend audience that consisted of mostly stuffed animals. And there she was, performing to a real audience. Alexander's heart swelled with pride.

The song ended and the crowd cheered. Alexander sat at the bar, clapping loudly for the girl on stage. The girl he knew all those years ago. The girl he loved all those years ago. The girl he never stopped loving. And the girl he was falling back in love with all over again.

"Thank you," Olivia said, walking off the stage and back to her table, the thunderous applause still going strong throughout the entire bar.

Alexander paid his tab, trying to get out before he was caught.

"Miss Olivia Adler everyone!" the M.C. shouted. The crowd went crazy. "Hey, Libs. How about one more? Have anything else ready?"

Olivia stared at the M.C., thinking about what she could possibly pull out of her hat. She conferred briefly with Mo before they both walked back to the stage. The crowd erupted in cheers again.

She sat down in the same chair, still holding her guitar. Pulling up a seat next to her, Mo took his guitar out of its case and checked the tuning. He nodded to her when he was all set.

"Okay. Here's one we'll be doing tomorrow night, so make sure you come and see it when it's the full band. It's a new one," she said into the microphone, smiling. "There's this guy that's kind of captured my heart these past few days and this song says it for me right now. This is *Brighter than the Sun* by Colbie Calait." Olivia glanced at Mo and he counted them off. Alexander stood motionless, not wanting to miss a minute of her performance. She was singing that song for him, although she didn't know he was even there. Maybe that was a good thing.

Olivia and Mo sat next to each other, strumming their guitars in near perfect unison. The crowd was getting into their performance, many people standing up from their tables and dancing along to the upbeat song. Olivia had heard it at the gym earlier in the week as she worked out. She immediately downloaded the song and listened to it repeatedly. She couldn't help but think of Alexander as she listened to the lyrics.

She had never expected to meet someone like Alexander. Olivia thought she would go through life having one short-term pseudo-relationship after another, never wanting to get close to anyone. But now, she wanted to have that. She remembered her mama telling her when she was a little girl that she would know when she was with the right person by the constant butterflies. Now, all these years later, Olivia wanted those butterflies. And she had them.

Alexander watched Olivia perform, thinking how perfect the song was. She was captivating, her enthusiasm contagious. *I've never felt this way before either, Olibia*, he thought to himself as she sang.

Olivia and Mo finished the song to roaring applause.

"Thanks everyone. See you all next week! And please come see us tomorrow night at MacFadden's!" Olivia jumped off the stage to her friend who gave her a massive hug.

"Oh, Libs. You were fantastic! And you are soooo falling in love with Alexander, I can tell."

Olivia began to blush. She knew Kiera was right. She was

torn about her feelings for him. On one hand, she had only known him a few short days so how could she possibly be falling for him so soon? But on the other hand, there was something so familiar about him. As if she knew him in a past life.

Once Alexander saw that Olivia would not be performing again, he discretely left the bar and climbed into his waiting SUV.

"Thank you, Martin. Now to my place, please. Then you're free of me for the weekend. I'll take my own car to Mystic."

"Yes, sir." Martin pulled into the street, heading toward the Waterfront.

Back in the bar, Mo and Marcus said their good-byes to the girls.

"Do we want to sail again?" Kiera asked, gesturing to their empty drink glasses after the guys left.

Olivia looked at her watch. "Probably not. I really should get some sleep. Early day tomorrow."

"And a long one, huh? You're playing with the guys, aren't you?"

Olivia laughed. "Kiera. That sounds so dirty." She grabbed her purse and stood up from the table, heading in the direction of the door.

"Oh my god. Stop it!" Kiera laughed.

Carter saw the two girls and stood up from his table.

"Are we all set ladies?" he asked.

"Yes, we are. Thank you, Carter."

"You were quite good, Miss Adler," Carter said, causing Olivia to blush.

"Thank you." Olivia looked outside and saw a downpour cloaking the streets of Boston.

Carter did a quick sweep of the bar. "Why don't you ladies wait inside for a few minutes while I run to grab the car." He hadn't noticed any suspicious behavior at the bar, so he figured they would be fine for the few minutes it took him to get the car and bring it around front.

"Okay. Thank you, Carter." He left, running into the rain.

"Well, I'm going to go use the little girls' room. Will you be okay out here?" Kiera asked.

"Yes. Go ahead." Kiera turned in the direction of the restrooms.

Olivia stood in the bar area, keeping an eye out the door for Carter and the SUV. As she stared out into the rain, pondering what Alexander was doing at that very moment, she felt someone approach behind her, sending chills down her spine.

"Livvy. Were you singing those songs for me?"

Olivia turned around quickly, knowing that voice all too well.

"Simon." Olivia's heart started to race. "You can't be here. You know that. Walk away and I won't call the police." She took a step back, trying to keep her distance.

"Don't worry. I'm not going to do anything." Simon glanced to the bar. "I saw your new little boyfriend here earlier. Thankfully, he was too self-absorbed to even notice that I was sitting just down the bar from him."

Olivia looked at Simon, confused. "What are you talking about, Simon?"

"You know. Your latest victim," he sneered. "Alexander Burnham. He came in right before you went on, sat at the bar, and left right after you finished."

Shit, Olivia thought to herself. *He saw me. And he heard those songs. Fuck! He heard me say that the last song was for him! Shit!*

"Well, I'll be off, Livvy. You enjoy your panic attack." He turned to walk out the door as Olivia began to breathe heavy, fighting for air. *How could I be so stupid?*

Kiera walked out at that moment and noticed that her friend had become very pale. "Olivia, are you okay? What's wrong?"

Olivia looked at her friend and responded, her voice almost a whisper. "He was here, Kiera. He saw me. He heard the songs I sang."

"Who was here?"

"Alexander."

"Wait. Shut the front door," Kiera interjected with a shocked look on her face. "How do you know that?"

"Ummm, well, Simon just came up to me and told me," she

replied nervously.

"Olivia!!!" Kiera screamed. "He cannot just come up and talk to you."

"I know that," Olivia admitted. "But he gets one. It happens again and I'll report him. But, Kiera. He saw. He heard those songs. How could I be so stupid?" She looked out at the rain pouring down, nervous about what Alexander would think.

"What are you so worried about? You sang a few songs. So what? If he has half a brain, he'll fall even more in love with you now that he knows you were singing to him. Relax. And stop worrying about it."

"What if he freaks out because of it? What if he leaves me?" Olivia couldn't believe her own words. She normally couldn't care less if a guy left her or not. But she had become attached to Alexander over the last few days, and him leaving scared her to death.

"Olivia, I saw the way he looked at you last night as he led us out of the bar. It was as if you're the most precious treasure on the face of the planet. As if he had been looking for you his entire life. He would never leave you, unless you do something incredibly stupid." Kiera winked as she spotted Carter standing in the bar doorway, holding an umbrella. "Okay, let's get out of here."

"Okay," Olivia exhaled, thankful to have someone like Kiera in her life to talk her down from the ledge.

Chapter Sixteen

Ice Cream Grins

"Mr. Burnham, it's wonderful to see you," a middle-aged woman said, greeting Alexander when he entered his family's house on the Mystic River.

"Good evening, Mrs. Carlson," he replied, walking in through the large living room decorated in a nautical theme.

"How was your ride down? I had expected you earlier."

"I'm sorry. I was detained in the city longer than I originally planned." He dropped his bags by the mahogany staircase before striding into the formal dining room. Alexander couldn't remember the last time that room had actually been used. The entire house seemed empty and cold.

"Can I get you anything to eat?" she asked, watching Alexander as he stopped in front of a large family portrait hanging on the expansive dining room wall. She always wondered who the little girl standing next to Alexander in the photo was.

"No. I'll raid the kitchen myself. You don't have to wait on me," he said dryly, his eyes remaining glued to the portrait.

"Well, then, I'll be right next door."

"Is my mother around?" he asked, snapping his attention back to Mrs. Carlson.

"No. She's still in Colorado. Let me know if I can do anything else for you."

"I will. Good night, Mrs. Carlson. I'll see you tomorrow."

"Good night." She turned and walked out the front door, heading to the guesthouse adjacent to the waterfront property. Finally alone, Alexander slowly walked through the house and took in his surroundings, thousands of memories of his younger days rushing back from being in his childhood home once again. He loved growing up in that house. Until his best friend was taken from him. Then the house stood as a painful reminder of all the happy memories he shared with his friend. Memories he would never be able to re-create anymore.

It always pained him to be in that house. He returned once a year. That year, however, he was hesitant about continuing his ritual knowing that Olivia was, in fact, alive. But he just couldn't break the tradition. Even though Olivia was alive, part of her did die that day, and he felt the need to continue to honor the memory of that little girl.

Alexander made his way into the large, airy kitchen to make a quick spring salad. It was a nice, breezy August evening, so he took his snack to the front porch of his family's house and sat down, looking at the darkness of the Mystic River.

He recalled spending hours on end swinging on the porch swing with his best friend at his house on the river. The estate was built in the early nineteenth century and used to be owned by an old ship captain. Olivia grew up right down the street from him and they had become almost inseparable since her birth. She spent practically every weekend at Alexander's house while her mother was in Newport, Rhode Island, where her family came from, attending one charity event or another. Her father, Jack, worked as a CIA analyst out of the Providence office and was never around that much, his work consuming most of his time. Alexander's father, Thomas, also worked for the CIA but had left before Jack worked for the agency in order to start his own private security company.

When Olivia's parents moved in down the street from Alexander's family, Jack and Thomas became fast friends, having both worked for the agency. Thomas was relentless in trying to recruit Jack to work for his company, but Jack refused, preferring the work at the agency. The two families shared everything, including celebrating holidays together, although Jack was never really around.

Alexander recalled walking down to Mystic River Park with Olivia and his dad on a warm weekend day, the downtown area teeming with tourists taking in the historic maritime town. They would always stop in one of the local shops for ice cream. As a young girl, Olivia loved ice cream. Alexander wondered to himself if she still did. She would always get a scoop of rocky road and a scoop of strawberry ice cream finished off with sliced pineapples. It was such a strange combination, but the look on her face when she ate that first bite was something he would never forget.

Alexander finished his salad and went upstairs to his childhood bedroom that his mother had redecorated years ago. Although that was his family home, no one really lived there, his mother choosing to spend her time between her Denver and South Beach properties instead. His father had hired Mrs. Carlson quite a few years ago to maintain and care for the house when he decided to relocate the main office of his security company from Providence to Boston. At that time, the house became somewhere they would go on the weekends. After his father died, Alexander thought his mother would live in the house again, but it was too painful for her to spend too much time there, the reminders of her husband and everything that family had lost throughout the years overwhelming.

He crawled into his antique four-poster bed and glanced at a photo on the nightstand of him and Olivia when they were children. They were at Mystic River Park and Olivia and Alexander were both covered in ice cream. They stood hand in hand with big ice cream grins on their faces. A smile spread across Alexander's face as he fell asleep.

~~~~~~~~~~

"Shit!" a young Alexander heard his father shout into a pay phone. Alexander stood inside a hospital room on his ninth birthday as everyone crowded the little baby boy that his mother just gave birth to the previous day. He was happy to have a baby brother but was upset that he was missing time at the beach with his friend, Olibia.

Alexander was surprised when his father walked briskly into the hospital room, meeting his wife's eyes. He bent down and whispered something in her ear. Her eyes went wide with concern. Whatever had upset his father worried her, too. He kissed her on the forehead before leaning down to do the same to the infant that lay in her arms.

"Alex, come with me," he said sternly as he left the hospital room. Alexander hoped he hadn't done anything wrong. He didn't think he did.

"What is it, Dad?" Alexander asked as he followed his father down the long corridor, nearly having to run to keep up.

"We need to get back to the Cape. I'll tell you on the way." They practically ran out to the car and within moments were on the freeway, heading away from New London, Connecticut toward Chatham, Massachusetts.

Alexander turned to his father, looking into the same green eyes that he had. "What's going on, Dad? You look worried."

Thomas took a deep breath. How could he relay that information to his now nine-year-old son? "It's Olivia and her parents. They're in trouble, son. Olivia's dad found out some things about some very, very bad people. They want to harm him and his family." Thomas looked down at the speedometer and pushed in the accelerator, urgently trying to cut down his time.

"Olivia's mother called earlier this morning and left a message on our machine at the house. I just checked it. She sounded scared." He didn't want to say anything else to his son. About how Marilyn said she didn't know who to trust. And that he was the only one she could trust. Marilyn wasn't one to overreact, so the fact that she was frightened worried Thomas. Taking a deep breath, he continued. "When I tried to call their house, no one answered. So we need to go check on them."

Alexander's heart began to race. What if something bad happens to his Olibia? She was his very, very best friend. He remained silent the duration of their excruciatingly long car ride to Cape Cod. Two hours later, they pulled up to the driveway at the DeLuca's beach house and frantically searched for their car.

"Do not get out of the car, Alex," Thomas growled as he leapt out of the car, running toward the garage and the house. Within a few brief moments, he ran back to the large SUV Alexander sat in.

"Did you find them Dad?" Alexander didn't know why he asked his father that. He could tell by his expression that he hadn't found them or their car.

"No. And it looks like they left in a hurry just a few minutes ago, so something obviously spooked them." Thomas put the car in reverse and

*accelerated toward the freeway, not wanting to tell his son about the blood
he saw in the kitchen. A wave of relief washed over him when he saw the
DeLuca's sedan further up on the freeway. He stepped on the gas, needing
to warn them before it was too late.*

*"Shit, no!" Thomas shouted when he saw a dark SUV pull out of a
turnabout, speeding toward the DeLuca's car, plowing into it and forcing it
through a guardrail and into a tree. The SUV continued on the freeway.
Slamming on the brakes, Thomas pulled off along the side of the road.*

*"Olibia! No!" Alexander swung the door open when the car came to a
stop.*

*"Alexander, get back here. It's too dangerous for you!" Thomas shouted,
trying to catch up with his son.*

*"I don't care about that, Dad. I need to help her." Alexander ran down
the short hill and stopped at the car. He looked in the back seat and his
heart sank. Olivia's eyes were closed and there was blood everywhere. Then
she stirred a little bit.*

*"Hey, Olibia. We need to get out of here, okay?" Alexander said,
unbuckling her seat belt, thinking that it most likely saved her life. He
smelled something and knew there was probably a gas leak. He rushed,
desperately needing to get her out of the car as his father attempted to help
her parents.*

"My mama and papa…"

"I know. But this is an emergency and you have to be brave."

*Alexander was able to get Olivia out of the car and quickly ran her to
the SUV. He gingerly placed her in the back seat. "I don't feel so well,"
Olivia said.*

*"I know. We're going to get you help. We're going to protect you
always, Olibia. Nothing bad will ever happen again. You can trust me."
Then Alexander felt someone approach behind him. He slipped into
unconsciousness.*

CHAPTER SEVENTEEN

HIDDEN

Alexander awoke with a start the following morning. He hated reliving that day in his dreams. He wondered if, had they been just a little quicker, maybe the accident never would have happened.

Getting out of bed, Olivia consumed his thoughts. *His Olivia.* He thought about the girl he knew all those years ago. And the girl he had met the previous week. It felt like two different Olivias. But they weren't. They were the same Olivia, separated by twenty-one years of secrecy.

August twenty-fourth. He hated that day more than anything. He thought it would feel different, knowing that Olivia was, in fact, alive and well. And in his life. But it didn't. It felt the same.

While he no longer mourned the loss of his best friend all those years ago, he still mourned not knowing Olivia during that time. He mourned not growing up with her. He mourned not being at her side.

He got ready for his day, not wanting to stray from tradition. He contemplated texting Olivia just to say hello, but decided not to. He needed to focus on his day. He made a cup of coffee and went out to the front porch to enjoy a calm minute before the day got away from him. Sitting at a small table on the porch, Alexander looked out over the same river that just the previous night was dark. With the rising of the sun, there was much more activity in the maritime community. He looked at the cemetery across the other side of the riverbank where, if he looked close enough, he could make out his best friend's grave.

"Alexander! Oh, it is you!" an elderly woman shouted as she walked her dog down the street. He wondered how Runner was getting along with the pet sitter.

"Mrs. Cunningham," Alexander shouted back, getting up to greet her on the sidewalk. "It's wonderful to see you."

"I had a feeling you'd be here this weekend." She gave Alexander a hug and kissed his cheek.

"Yeah. I'm a creature of habit, what can I say?" Alexander replied sheepishly, the normally confident man nowhere in sight.

"I think it's sweet you still come and pay your respects all these years later. I know it must be difficult for you. I mean, you and that little Olivia. God, the two of you were inseparable." She smiled at the memory. "I remember being over your mother's for tea years ago when she would look after little Olivia for her mama. She couldn't even walk yet and you would jump into her crib and just lie down next to her and watch her sleep, waiting for her to get up." A tear started to trickle down Mrs. Cunningham's cheek. "It was such a tragedy. I didn't know her parents well, but Olivia... She was too young." Mrs. Cunningham looked at Alexander, remorse etched across his face. "Well, dear me. I always bring her up. I'm sorry, dear. I'll be on my way. Stop by later for a cup of tea if you'd like."

She walked down the street and Alexander remained speechless. It was always so difficult to return to Mystic and see his old family friends who knew both him and Olivia. They would always talk about how lively and spirited of a girl she was and what a tragedy it was to lose her so young. He still had difficulty processing that she wasn't lost all those years ago. She was hidden.

An hour later, Alexander made his way to the cemetery. He grabbed his cell and noticed he had a missed text from Olivia. He ignored it, not wanting to deal with anything other than what he needed to that day. It was a nice day and he could use the time to think, so he walked the mile across the bridge and toward the old cemetery.

He stopped at a market and picked up two bouquets of roses

and one of sunflowers. He walked the rest of the way down Main Street and through the large iron gates of the cemetery before heading down the old dirt path to the DeLuca's graves set high up on a hill overlooking the river, the sun glimmering on the water creating a serene atmosphere. Placing a bouquet of roses on Olivia's parents' graves first, he made his way to Olivia's grave. He sat down and placed the sunflower bouquet at the gravestone, smiling at how his old friend loved sunflowers.

"Well, another year's gone by. And I just don't know what to do. I'm still talking to you like I do every year. But this year, well, I found you. Last week, actually. You're still alive, Olivia DeLuca. Except your name is now Sarah Olivia Adler. I don't know what the whole story is and why you were taken from me, but you were. And I'm scared to know the truth, Olibia.

"I love you, ya know. I mean, I love the girl I grew up with all those years ago. And you should see the woman you've become. You're a strong, beautiful, talented, exceptional woman. A woman I've always seen myself falling in love with, if you could believe that. Maybe the reason I never settled down before was because, deep down, I knew you were still out there somewhere and my heart was just waiting until I found you." A smile crept across his face, thinking about the previous morning with Olivia and the things she did to him.

"But, you're also scared," he said, returning from his thoughts. "Scared of losing people. You've lost so much in your life that now you just push everyone away, afraid that you'll lose them. And I don't want you to push me away. I want you to open up to me. I don't want you to be scared of losing me. I will never leave you. I've looked for you my entire life. And now that I know I was right, that you are alive, I will never lose you again."

Alexander looked down, unsure of what to say next, a gentle breeze rustling through the trees as the horn on the drawbridge sounded in the distance.

"I brought you sunflowers again. You always loved them when we were kids. You used to call them giant daffodils." He paused briefly, remembering arguing with Olivia when they were younger about the proper name for the flower that now lay in front of her gravestone. "You don't remember anything about your past," he said sadly. "You remember some things, but not much. It's as if you are this totally different person than the girl that I remember. And I know that's okay. I just wish you would remember, because it's breaking my heart to know that I'm going to be the one to tell you. To tell you that you were taken from the people that loved you. That you were taken from me. That your entire life has been a lie."

Alexander looked at the grave, his eyes brimming with tears. "And I don't know if I'm strong enough to do that." Taking a deep breath and trying to control his emotions, he stood up and placed his hand on the top of the gravestone. "I love you, Olivia DeLuca."

He turned to walk away and heard a slow clapping. He looked in the direction of the sound. He should have known.

"Adele. Why am I not surprised to see you here?" He walked toward a tall, thin blonde woman dressed in a short black dress, wearing an over the top black sunhat and dark shades.

"Alexander, darling. So happy to see you. I knew you'd be here." She walked toward Alexander and gave him a hug, which he returned weakly.

"Well, it's not that big of a surprise, now is it? I come here every year, don't I, Adele?" He glared at her.

"I know, darling. I know. Listen, Mummy and Daddy are having a thing today at the country club and I am in desperate need of a date, and I figure since you're in town and I'm in town, you'd be more than willing to accompany me."

"Adele, I don't think that's such a good idea. If I wanted to, I'd see you in Boston, but I don't. Plus, I'm seeing someone now. Someone that I actually care about more than just an occasional fuck. Don't get me wrong, it was fun while it lasted, but I'm not interested anymore." Alexander started to walk away.

"Come on, Alex. As friends," she said, running up to catch him, making him turn around. "I know you're still in love with Olivia even though she's been dead for like twenty years or something. Anyway, I'm not interested in dating someone who is in love with someone they can never have. No one can ever measure up to that pedestal you've placed Olivia on."

"You always have an ulterior motive, so what is it this time, Adele?" He crossed his arms over his chest and Adele visibly gawked at the rather impressive muscles bulging through his simple blue tee shirt.

"No motive, I promise." She held up her hands in defense. "I just miss my friend. We used to have fun together. Before things got complicated. Let's just hang out today. As friends, like we used to." Adele walked up to him and pushed a strand of hair out of his eyes. "I miss the old Alex," she crooned.

He was torn about what to do. All his thoughts lately had been of Olivia. The girl he once knew and the Olivia he now knew. Maybe some time away from it all was exactly what he needed to clear his head. "Okay," he exhaled. "I'll go."

"Great!" Adele exclaimed, clapping her hands. "There's a golf tournament that they're all at now, but want to call it noon? It's kind of an all day thing and I really didn't want to go alone. I hate all those pretentious high school bitches who are all married and all they talk about are their kids. If I have to look at one more baby photo and pretend the kid is actually cute, I may lose it, so thank you for doing this."

Alexander looked at his watch. It was only about ten in the morning. "Okay. I can do noon."

"Fantastic. Pick me up at my parents' place, okay?"

"Why don't you just walk over to my place? It's only three houses away."

"Alexander, darling. You can't honestly expect me to walk to you wearing heels, can you? You've been screwing trash for far too long, dear. You need to have higher expectations of the women you fuck."

"We're not fucking today, Adele." Alexander started to walk away. "I'll pick you up at noon." It was not worth the fight.

Alexander had known Adele and her family almost his entire life. She was the same age as Alexander and, even at a young age, was jealous of Alexander's relationship with Olivia. He remembered how inconsiderate she had been when she learned that Olivia died.

She wanted to become the new Olivia and had worked hard all during their school years to do so. Alexander and Adele had slept together on and off for the past decade or so. She was a distraction, but no emotional attachment ever came of the relationship. Adele had become a means to an end. She was more than willing to give up total control of her body to Alexander, which was what he needed and craved. But since he had met Olivia, he wanted more than just an occasional screw.

Adele's family came from old money, just like Olivia's mother. She was used to a certain way of living and refused to settle for anything less than marrying a man who had a heavily padded bank account, even though she also had one without working a day in her life. She was the polar opposite of Olivia, who, even with her wealth, still worked and volunteered her time to valuable causes. Adele preferred spending her time around Boston at night clubs with her friends from Wellesley College. She groaned every time her father insisted she attend one of the many charity events she was expected to be at, but attaching herself to Alexander's arm for the evening made it more bearable.

Adele quickly followed behind Alexander and jumped in her sporty white convertible, pulling up alongside Alexander. "See you at noon, Alex." She smirked. "Oh, and Happy Birthday, darling." She tore down the small dirt path in the cemetery and turned onto the street.

"Stupid bitch," Alexander murmured.

~~~~~~~~~~~

"Mr. Burnham, welcome back," Mrs. Carlson said when Alexander walked into his house. "Your sister is here, along with your brother. They're in the study."

"Thank you, Mrs. Carlson. I'll be going out in a bit and won't be around for lunch or dinner, so you'll only have to worry about Carol or Tyler, if they'll be around."

"Yes, sir."

Alexander made his way into the study.

"Happy Birthday, bro," Tyler said, walking over to Alexander as he entered the room, giving him a hug.

"Thanks, Ty," Alexander replied, staring at a younger version of himself. "What are you doing here? I thought you'd be hung-over from the big twenty-one celebration last night."

Tyler shrugged. "It's your birthday today. I needed to be here for you. I know how hard this day is for you." He leaned over and whispered in his ear. "Plus, that fake ID you got for me when I started college has been great. I feel like I've been twenty-one for years now."

Alexander smiled.

"Hey! I heard that!" Carol interjected.

Alexander looked fondly at his sister. "Hey Carol. How's it going?"

"Good. Good." She looked hesitant.

"What's going on? Why are you both here?" While it wasn't out of the ordinary for Tyler to show up in Mystic that weekend for Alexander's birthday, Carol normally stayed in Boston in case she was needed for work. Her being in town struck Alexander as odd.

"Umm, well, we need to talk, Alex," Carol said, looking nervously at Tyler. "I've been thinking that with all the new information that has come to light, it might be time to open that letter."

Alexander stared at his siblings with a wide-eyed look on his face.

"Alex, what are you so worried about? I know Dad sent the letter to you and it's your decision about whether to open it or not, but come on already!"

"You know what, sis?" he said, raising his voice, his face becoming flushed. "I love you. But I don't want to sit here and listen to this anymore." He turned to leave.

"Come on, Alex," Tyler interrupted, causing Alexander to spin back around to face his brother. "You've been sitting on that letter for over five years. Now you know that Dad covered up Olivia's death. He had her name changed. I guarantee that's what he was doing all those years when he was gone. He was with her. Protecting her. Don't you want to know why?"

Alexander looked at his sister, ready to kill her for telling Tyler about everything. "Of course I do!" he shouted, slamming his fist down on a nearby table. "But how the fuck do I tell her? I love her!" He couldn't believe the words that came out of his mouth. "Oh my God. I love that woman, guys," he said quietly, his lower lip trembling.

"I know you do," Carol said, laying her hand on his shoulder. "You loved her all those years ago when you were just kids. And you never stopped looking for her."

"It's like my heart knew she was still out there," he said quietly. "I just had to find her. Even though you all told me time and time again that she was dead. I have her fucking death certificate for crying out loud. How do I tell her that everything she has been told her entire life was a bunch of lies? How will she react? I just don't know if she needs to go through any more pain."

"I know, Alex. And when I read through the report you had Simpson prepare, I hoped that I could prove that it wasn't her. But too many pieces fell into place. The hospital records from the accident. The birth certificate that was dated the same date of Olivia's supposed death. School records. Signatures that were strikingly close to dad's signature. It was all too much. And then the photo enhancement of what she would look like now. We all still have questions. Questions that could probably be answered if you open that letter."

"I know guys. And thanks for coming to see me and all, but I need more time to think about all of this." The practical side of him was screaming at him to open the letter. But that side was at odds with the stubborn side that saw his refusal to open the letter as his one final act of defiance to his father. Sighing, Alexander looked at his watch. "I have to get ready. I promised Adele I'd take her to her parents' thing at the club."

"Oh, you're still talking to that bitch?" Tyler asked, surprised.

"She's not that bad."

Carol laughed and Tyler joined in.

"Okay, okay. Maybe she's a little cold."

"And calculated. She wants your money, Alex," Carol retorted.

"She's got money of her own. So she's not after mine."

"You haven't heard?" Tyler asked, raising his eyebrows.

"Heard what?"

"Well, word is, her family took a bit of a hit a few years back with the downturn of the housing market. They're still trying to keep up appearances that they have money as a way of attracting money to them, but, let's just say, they're practically broke."

"Gold digging whore," Carol muttered under her breath.

"Come on. I grew up with her. You guys didn't know her that well. And she liked me when they still had money. I'm not saying I ever saw myself with her long term, but she was always good for a distraction, and maybe that's what I need today. A distraction. So if you don't mind, I need to get ready to pick her up."

"Okay," Tyler said. "But you better hope she didn't pull some move like she did last time and call the photographers just to get her name and photo in the paper for a quick buck and a few minutes of celebrity."

"That was New York. We're in Mystic, for crying out loud. Not a hot bed of celebrity sightings, so I think we'll be fine. But thanks for your concern." Alexander turned to leave, pausing briefly. "Wait, I'm sorry guys," he said, spinning around, hating to leave his siblings on a sour note. "I'm just on edge lately. Stay the weekend. We'll go out for some drinks later. I haven't spent time with you all in a while with work being busy and all that. It'll be good for us."

"Yeah okay, bro," Tyler replied, giving Alexander a brief hug. "I know things have been rough lately."

"I can make that work. I'm off until Monday," Carol replied, giving Alexander a quick peck on the cheek before turning to her youngest brother. "Come on, Ty. Let's go get some oysters. My treat."

Alexander looked at his siblings, a hint of jealousy on his face.

"You can blow off Miss Fake Boobs and join us for oysters,

161

too." Carol winked.

He hesitated before answering. "I can't. I'll meet you all later and we'll have some drinks. Promise."

"Okay. But leave Adele out of it," Carol said.

"Got it. See you both later." Alexander walked out of the study, thankful that he hadn't left his siblings on a bad note. He was actually looking forward to spending some time with them during the weekend. He normally didn't get to hang out with them, although they all lived in the greater Boston area.

His younger brother went to Boston University and was in his last year there. His older sister, Carol, had joined the Boston Police Department nearly twenty years earlier. She had gone to college in Boston as well and never left the area.

Growing up, Alexander wasn't close to either one of his siblings, there being such a big age difference between both. Carol was in high school when Alexander was born. Tyler was born the day before Alexander turned nine. And for the longest time, he blamed Tyler for Olivia's death. If he and his dad weren't at the hospital visiting a newborn Tyler, maybe they could have gotten to the DeLucas in time to prevent their deaths.

CHAPTER EIGHTEEN

NO GOOD DEED

"Mr. and Mrs. Peters," Alexander said, standing from his seat at the bar. "Wonderful to see you." He shook Mr. Peters hand and gave his wife a quick kiss on the cheek.

"Oh, Alex, darling. It is wonderful to see you again," Mrs. Peters said with a fake smile on her face. Her bleached blonde hair was pinned back. She had the appearance of a woman who fought the aging process, with disastrous results. "We're so happy you and Adele have gotten back together. You really do need to date someone within your social status, you know. Your mother, God rest her soul, should have taught you that at an early age, but I don't mean to speak ill of the dead."

Alexander turned to the woman in front of him who had clearly received far too many Botox injections and lip implants. "First off, my mother is alive and well. Second, I am not dating your daughter. She begged me to accompany her today and I am here as an old friend. Last, I don't give a damn about dating someone in my social status, and you shouldn't comment on that either, given your family's precarious financial position of late."

Alexander threw back his drink and excused himself from the bar. He remembered why he avoided functions like that. It was good to go for business reasons, but, unfortunately, there were so many trust-funders who continued to jockey for position in New England Society just by associating themselves with Alexander, whose successful company had secured him a place as one of the most sought after bachelors in the country.

Alexander walked out the front entrance of the country club, hoping to get some fresh air, when a photographer snapped his photo.

"Hey. I thought I told you to leave, jackass." He walked briskly toward the photographer. He recalled just a few hours earlier, seeing the same photographer snapping photos of him and Adele as they entered the country club. He had an inkling that she or her mother had set it up in order to plaster Adele's photo all over the internet again, but he wanted to avoid arguing with her that day, if it all possible.

"I know you did, but I'm getting paid for the day. So make it financially beneficial for me to leave and I will. But just so you know, I've already sold some of the photos of you and blondie over there."

"What!?" Alexander exclaimed.

"Yeah. You're hot news. Who would think I'd get a good dish on you here in Connecticut?" The photographer lit a cigarette.

"You know what? I don't care. Sit out here as long as you want." Alexander turned to head back to the bar. *How low would Adele stoop?* he thought to himself.

Alexander re-entered the lounge area, happy to see that Adele and her parents had gone to the deck patio to have a seat. He needed a minute. Grabbing his cell phone out of his pocket, he saw one more missed text from Olivia. He thought again about responding, but with it being the supposed anniversary of her death, he simply couldn't do it. He didn't know why. He just needed that day.

After ordering another scotch from the bartender, he reluctantly returned to Adele and her parents. He thought her mother was a catty bitch, but actually got along quite well with her father. He was thankful to see Mr. Peters sitting alone at the table as he made his way across the deck patio overlooking the perfectly manicured greens of the golf course.

"Alex. You've returned. Don't worry. They've gone to find someone else to sink their claws into," Mr. Peters laughed, motioning toward a chair for Alexander to sit in.

"My apologies, Mr. Peters. I had no intention of being rude," he explained, sitting next to the gray-haired older gentleman. "But there are some things I cannot hold my tongue over. And I apologize for taking a dig at any financial difficulties you and your family may be going through."

"Oh, Alex. Don't you worry about that. I'm perfectly set for the remainder of my life." He smiled and Alexander could see the kindness in his eyes. He wondered how he could stand being married to such a fake woman. "My dearest Adele, however, having only viewed college as a way to find a wealthy husband, is going to have a difficult time once I pass. And I'm sure her mother will face the same problems."

"I'm sorry. I wish I could help, but I prefer to devote my time and efforts to real charity cases…"

"Oh, my dear boy. Of course, of course," Mr. Peters replied, placing his hand on Alexander's arm. "I would never ask you for anything like that. But that's me. My wife and daughter are a totally different story, I'm afraid." He paused briefly before continuing. "I've always been fond of you, Alex. I remember watching you grow up and play with that dear friend of yours, oh, what was her name?" Mr. Peters took a sip of his bourbon.

Alexander looked out over the golf course. "Olivia," he whispered.

"Oh, yes. Olivia. And if I remember correctly, you couldn't pronounce her name. You always called her Olibia, right?"

A lump formed in Alexander's throat. "Yes, Mr. Peters. That's correct. I guess it was a nickname that just kind of stuck."

"I'll never forget how jealous my Adele was of that girl. She wanted to be your best friend and just hated to share your affections with anyone." He sighed. "I love my daughter dearly, but that's not the woman for you. And I say that with all due respect to my Adele." Mr. Peters smiled fondly.

"Now what have you two been talking about? Hopefully not talking about me, Daddy!" Adele interrupted.

"Oh, you know I have nothing but wonderful things to say about the two most important women in my life," he said, standing up and kissing his daughter on the cheek.

"Alexander, darling. Let's dance," Adele said, turning to him and grabbing his hand. She dragged him inside the posh country club and toward a dance floor crowded with couples moving to a Dean Martin tune. He smiled as he weakly held her arm until they were away from her parents' eyes.

"I'm not going to dance with you, Adele," he growled, turning to face her. "I'm sure both you and your mother have those photographers selling their photos to the highest bidder to give you some internet juice. I won't have anything to do with that, so you can just cut the crap right now. I didn't want to say anything in front of your father because I genuinely like him, but I will not play your game." His voice grew louder. "So you can act as an old friend for the rest of the afternoon and we can enjoy each other's company, or you can continue to try to parade me around as your special friend and you will soon find yourself all alone." He looked around at the crowd that had gathered to eavesdrop on their conversation. "I'll be at the bar." He left Adele, her eyes wide.

"Dude, that was epic," Alexander heard as he took a seat at the bar. He turned to the source of the voice to see his brother sitting there, enjoying a beer.

"Hey, Ty. What are you doing here? You hate this scene." Alexander signaled the bartender to pour him and his brother another round.

"I know. But Ma is on my ass about getting out to more charity events, so here I am. Apparently we were all on the guest list. I figured I'd save you from yourself. Or at least from Adele." Tyler winked. "Carol had a work thing she needed to take care of. A conference call or something about a case, so I decided to drive out here and keep you company now that I can use my real ID to get a drink."

"I'm sorry I never officially wished you a happy birthday. I don't know where my head was before." He raised his drink to his brother and they clinked glasses.

"It's okay. I know how difficult this day is for you. I'm just here to try to make it enjoyable for once. And I promise not to mention the 'O' word at all."

"What 'O' word?" Adele interrupted, slinging her arm over Alexander's shoulder. He rolled his eyes, his annoyance with the fake blonde apparent. When neither Tyler nor Alexander responded, she raised her voice and laughed. "Oh, you must be referring to the multiple orgasms you gave me last night." She glanced over to a few photographers, smiling her best fake smile. "Alexander Burnham is an animal in the sack," she shouted, as if hoping the photographers would be quoting her.

"Adele," Alexander interrupted, pushing her arm away from him. "What did we just discuss? Do you really have no concept of class and dignity? You were a nice distraction all those years ago and it was great to blow off some steam with you when I was on leave from the Navy, but I could never date someone as superficial as you." Alexander stood up and slammed back his drink, clearly getting ready to leave.

"You know what, Alex?" Adele yelled as he walked away from the bar. "You need to get over your little obsession with Olivia DeLuca. She's fucking dead," she hissed. "And you still mourn her every fucking day. It's sad, really. You'd think that after twenty-something years you'd be over her. She's fucking dead! Move on!"

Alexander turned around, his eyes aflame with fury. "The difference between you and me is that I care more about people than whether they have a ten figure bank account. Olivia was an important part of my life when I was growing up. And, yes, I still mourn her death. She was a part of me that died. But you're too self-absorbed to understand. Good-bye, Adele." Alexander walked out of the clubhouse and handed his ticket to the valet who brought his car around rather quickly.

"Alex!" Tyler shouted as Alexander was getting into his Maserati convertible. "Wait a minute!"

"What's up?"

"Hey. Want to go to a real bar?" Tyler asked, his eyebrows raised.

"Yes. I need a drink after this," Alexander replied.

"Great. Meet me at The Tavern. I'll text Carol and tell her to meet us there."

Alexander got into his car and left the parking lot, making his way back to Mystic and The Tavern. It was a bar that he had frequented quite a bit when he was in town. The location right down the street from their favorite oyster place and near

Mystic River Park made it the perfect place to unwind.

Twenty minutes later, he pulled up in front of the historic brick building and walked inside the small dimly lit bar to see the place already buzzing at four o'clock on a Friday afternoon. He guessed everyone was getting an early start on the weekend.

"Alex!" Carol shouted as she downed a shot of some amber liquid.

"Hey, sis! How many of those have you had?" Alexander returned Carol's hug.

"Not nearly enough. Now let's get wasted. We can always walk back to the house later." They made their way from the bar to an open high-top table. A matter of minutes later, Tyler arrived and Alexander bought a round of beers and shots for his siblings. He was already feeling slightly buzzed from all the scotch he had drunk earlier at the country club.

"Come on, Carol. You need to play catch up!" Tyler shouted as he handed her another shot.

The three siblings drank and caught up, sharing with each other what was going on in their personal lives. Tyler was looking forward to his final year at Boston University, where he studied finance. He planned to go on to graduate school the following year as well. Carol told the guys about a few different cases she was working on at the moment. They all did their best to steer the conversation away from Olivia and their father.

Several hours later, they had consumed quite a bit of liquor. "She sings, ya know," Alexander said out of nowhere, slurring his speech, his eyes drooping low.

"What are you talking about?" Tyler asked, laughing.

"Olibia. She sings. I followed her to Open Mic at Johnny D's last night before I drove here. And she sings. It brought back a lot of memories."

"Alex, we don't have to talk about it tonight. I mean if you want to, we can, but you don't have to." Carol placed her hand on top of his.

"I know, Carol. But it helps sometimes. I know it's her, but it still doesn't feel real, ya know. And I mean, this is a girl who is so scared to get close to anyone. I'm just worried that finding out the truth will ruin her."

"But Alex, I don't know if that's your decision to make," Carol replied. "Imagine how she would feel if you keep that information from her. What's worse? Her learning about her past and needing some time to process the information, or her learning that you withheld vital information from her? I know you want to protect her, but I think you need to tell her and let her deal with the information as she chooses."

"Yeah. What Carol said," Tyler slurred.

"She's singing in a band tonight. I should have stayed in Boston to see her, but I just had to come here. It was weird this morning. I was talking to Olivia's gravestone as if she was still dead. And I was telling the young Olivia about the woman she's become. It's almost as if they're two different people. But they're not. They're the same person. And I know they are. But to me, they're two separate people. One girl died when she was six. And this new Olivia is who the other Olivia grew up to be, but I wasn't around to watch her grow up. And I think what's so heartbreaking for me is that I missed her all those years when she was so close to me." He looked at his brother and sister and felt the world starting to close in on him. "I need to go guys. I'll see you back at the house."

Alexander got up from the table and threw down several large bills to cover the tab and more drinks. He knew what he needed to do. He walked the quarter mile back to his house and headed straight to his bedroom. Sitting down at his desk, he pulled out his journal and wrote his daily letter to Olivia.

CHAPTER NINETEEN

GAMBLING THERAPY

"So, have you heard from him yet?" Kiera asked Olivia as she lounged on the couch in Olivia's living room on Saturday morning. Olivia had performed with Mo's band the previous night and had been in a rather snarky mood since then, having not heard from Alexander.

"No. I haven't. And it's killing me. It's so weird. He secretly watched me Thursday night at Open Mic. He said he had to go out of town this weekend for something. I texted him a few times, but I don't want to be that clingy girl, ya know?" Olivia took a sip from her coffee mug and glanced over at her friend.

"Fuck him. What kind of arrogant bastard is too wrapped up in himself that he can't at least send a quick text just to say hi? Men and their fucking mind games. And they say women are bad." Kiera flipped the cover on her iPad and started browsing the latest gossip websites.

"I think I'm just worried that he freaked when he heard the songs I sang. But he called me his girlfriend. And now he's just not talking to me. It's just... well, weird. I don't play games. This is why I don't do relationships."

"Holy shit!" Kiera shouted. "That fucking douche!"

"What? What is it?" Olivia asked, getting up from the table and running over to the couch to see what Kiera was looking at on her iPad.

"I'm not sure you want to see this, Libs," she said sullenly.

"Oh, come on. It can't be that bad." She pulled the iPad out of her friend's hand and turned to look at the screen in front of her. Her jaw dropped and she sank onto the couch. She felt her heart shatter into thousands of tiny pieces.

There was a photo of Alexander entering what appeared to be a country club, accompanied by a strikingly beautiful, tall blonde woman wearing a tight white sundress that accented her huge chest and tiny waist. Olivia continued to read the caption underneath the photograph. *"Alexander Burnham spotted entering New London Country Club with Miss Adele Peters. Burnham and Peters have been involved in a tumultuous on and off relationship for the past decade."*

"So this is why he couldn't be bothered to text me and why he was so secretive about where he was going this weekend," Olivia said quietly. She sat there for several long moments, Kiera knowing her friend well enough to not say anything. Sometimes saying nothing said everything.

How could I be so stupid? Olivia thought to herself. She finally let herself fall for a guy only to find out he was already dating someone else.

"See. This is exactly why I don't put myself out there, Kiera. Because this fucking hurts." Olivia stood up, tossing the iPad back to Kiera, and walked back to the kitchen table.

"Wait, Libs. I mean, you can't believe everything you read on the internet. Maybe there's a perfectly simple explanation for the photo." Kiera grabbed her iPad and looked at the photo headlining her favorite gossip website. She looked at Alexander and the woman beside him. They were smiling at each other and Kiera could almost see the affection between them. She did a quick image search and was bombarded with photos of the couple. "If it makes you feel any better, Libs, it looks like they've known each other since like forever," Kiera said.

"What are you doing?" Olivia asked.

"Just Googling your boytoy. Oh, that sounds so dirty." Kiera laughed, trying to lighten the mood.

"Kiera, I love you, but I am so not in the mood," Olivia said dryly.

"Libs. Stop it. Stop shutting down. You can't get like this. It's one photo on the internet. It doesn't mean anything."

Olivia stood up, walking over to the couch, and grabbed

171

Kiera's iPad from her.

"One photo on the internet?" Olivia shouted, looking at the screen with all the photos of Adele and Alexander in recent history. "There's hundreds of them together. Hundreds! And I am so not the jealous type, but I do not stand for being left in the dark. Even in my fucked up version of relationships pre-Alexander, the one thing I made damn sure of was that it was exclusive. I will not be strung along." She collapsed onto the couch.

Kiera hated to see her friend so upset. She knew how fragile Olivia could be at times and the last thing she needed was for her to retreat back into her shell. The shell that she struggled to get her out of for years.

"Relax, sweetie," Kiera said, rubbing her friend's back. "Even if he has no explanation, don't give him the satisfaction of knowing it upset you. You're bigger than this and much stronger than this. And you'll move on from this. There's someone else out there for you who will worship the ground you walk on."

"But I really liked him, Kiera." She buried her head in her hands, trying to subdue the lump that had started to form in her throat.

"I know, Libs." She continued comforting her friend. "Okay. Idea," Kiera said excitedly. "Let's get out of here for the weekend. Do something crazy."

Olivia thought about it for a minute. If she refused, she would just stay in her house, faced with constant reminders of Alexander. The more she thought about it, the more appealing getting out of town sounded. "Okay. Deal. What did you have in mind?"

"One word. Gambling therapy." Kiera grabbed Olivia's hand and before she knew it, they were on the road, heading for Connecticut and one of the Indian casinos.

~~~~~~~~~~

"Alex! Wake up!" Tyler shouted as he pounded on the door to his bedroom. Alexander rolled over, his head throbbing from

172

all the liquor he consumed the night before. He looked at the clock. He was going to kill Tyler.

"What the fuck, dude?" he shouted as Tyler barged into Alexander's old bedroom. "It's not even ten in the morning, asshole."

"No. That clock isn't right. It's after two in the afternoon. Get your ass up. We're going to the casino today. Carol's idea. Dave is coming down to meet us there. Birthday bash for us."

David was Carol's husband. They met when she enrolled in the police academy over twenty years ago. They had originally been assigned to different precincts and had started dating. They married a few years later. Now, they were both detectives, David working mostly homicides while Carol tended to work more domestic cases.

"Okay, okay. I'm up. Go find me some aspirin or a Bloody Mary." Alexander threw off the covers and shuffled into the shower. He couldn't remember the last time he drank as much. He normally would only have a few drinks when he went out. The previous day was an exception. Based on how he felt that afternoon, he wouldn't be consuming that much alcohol again for a very long time.

Alexander got out of the shower and walked back into his bedroom to find a tray sitting on his desk with a glass of water, two aspirin, and a Bloody Mary. "Love ya, Ty," Alexander shouted down the stairs.

"I know you do. Now get your ass in gear. The party bus leaves in twenty."

~~~~~~~~~~~

Kiera and Olivia sat at a trendy club having a few drinks before going back to try some more of their luck at the tables. So far, it had been a rather prosperous evening for the girls. Kiera had been trying to help Olivia forget about Alexander all day. They arrived at the casino shortly after lunch, checked into the hotel, and spent the afternoon by the pool. They were now enjoying the evening out at the casino. Sitting at the dark bar, Olivia actually felt okay. Not good. Not fine. But okay.

The skimpy black designer dress Kiera shoved at her to wear that evening probably helped. It was nice to see guys staring at her body, especially the long legs that the dress barely covered up.

"Give it to me, Libs," Kiera said when she noticed her friend looking at her phone yet again. All day Olivia had been constantly checking for some sort of contact from Alexander.

"Okay. Sorry. I promise to stop checking it. Just let me check my e-mail and then I'll turn it off." Olivia hated lying to her friend, but she wanted to do one more photo search.

On the drive down to the casino, Olivia found a multitude of photos online of Alexander and Adele. They just looked like they belonged together. Two of the most beautiful people in the world. Olivia wondered what Alexander could have possibly seen in her when he could be with someone as beautiful and stunning as Adele.

She clicked on the search button and noticed another recent photo, presumably from the same function. She clicked on the image and was brought to another gossip website. In the photo, it looked like Alexander was speaking to Adele, leaning into her ear and whispering. Olivia looked at Adele's face and could tell just by the expression on it that he must have been telling her something rather sweet and endearing.

"Fuck him," Olivia said, turning off her phone. "I'm swearing off men. Kiera, want to be a lesbian with me?"

Kiera laughed, handing her friend another drink. "Thanks for the offer, but I'm hot on Mo."

"You should probably do something about that then, Care Bear. He's one of the good guys. Apparently there's not a lot of them left."

"Oh, Libs. Don't rush to judgment so quickly. At least promise me you'll give him a chance to explain," Kiera said as she took a drink from her martini. "And then you can stomp on his balls."

"I'm not making any promises. All I know is that I need a drink and a distraction. Let's go dancing." Olivia got up from her barstool after downing her martini and headed in the direction of the dance floor. Kiera followed.

The girls found their way to the center of the dance floor, club lights barely illuminating the dark floor. The club was rather busy and there wasn't much room to move, but that was okay. Olivia moved to the rhythm of the music, trying to block out everything that had happened that past week. The girls danced for several minutes before a tall blond man wearing a black button-down shirt and jeans moved toward Kiera and started dancing with her.

"Are you okay?" Olivia mouthed. Kiera gave her the thumbs up signal, to which Olivia signaled that she was going back to the bar.

"Where you off to, beautiful?" a short, built man with blond hair and far too orange skin said to Olivia, standing in her way.

"Um, just off to get a drink, so if you'll please excuse me..." she replied, trying to move around him.

"Okay, hot stuff. I'll see you back here."

Olivia rolled her eyes as she continued to walk past the man, on a mission to get drunk. Kiera had tried her best to help Olivia keep her mind off Alexander, but he was all she could think about.

She approached the long circular bar and placed her drink order. As she waited for her martini, she heard loud laughing on the opposite side of the bar. She turned her head and gasped when she saw Alexander there with several other people, one being Detective Wilder, his sister. She looked a little closer, squinting through her eyes foggy from the alcohol, and noticed that hanging onto his arm was the woman from the photos, Adele.

She grabbed her drink off the bar, fuming, and returned to the dance floor, hoping that Alexander had not seen her. She was fairly certain he was too absorbed in the people he was with to notice her. Why would he notice Olivia when someone as beautiful as Adele clung to his arm?

She made her way through the crowds of people, finally finding Kiera.

"He's here!" Olivia shouted as her friend danced with another random guy.

"Who is?" she shouted back over the loud club music.

"Alexander. And the bitch is clinging onto his fucking arm."

Kiera immediately pushed the guy away. "Sorry. Girl problems. Thanks for the dance." Kiera turned to face Olivia as she finished her drink in one gulp, needing it to dull the pain. "Are you mother fucking serious?"

"Yes. And I'm so glad to know you have a degree in English. It makes me hopeful for the future of our country."

"Shut it, Libby. Where is he?"

"At the bar."

"Okay. Here's the plan. Two can play his little game. And don't yell at me and call me immature," she said, grabbing Olivia's empty drink glass from her hand. "We find you a hottie to dance with and just pretend he doesn't exist." Kiera scanned the dance floor and found a tall man with dark, brooding eyes and a chiseled face. He was very handsome.

"Hey! You!" Kiera shouted to her target, getting his attention. He walked over to the girls. "This is my friend, Olivia. I saw you checking her out like all night, so maybe you should grow some balls and ask her to dance." Olivia loved how direct Kiera was. She wished she could be like that sometimes.

"Olivia. It's wonderful to meet you," he said in a slight Irish accent. "My name is Collin." He reached his hand out for Olivia's and she gingerly placed her hand in his.

"Nice to meet you, too, Collin."

"Dance with me?"

"Yes." Olivia allowed him to lead her a few feet from Kiera and she got lost in the music.

At the bar, Alexander desperately tried to shake Adele off his shoulder. He had no idea how she knew he would be at the casino that evening. His luck was horrible as of late. She brought one of her college friends with her, who was shamelessly hitting on Tyler, not seeming to care that he was easily several years younger than her.

Adele wrapped her arm through Alexander's yet again. He was getting ready to lose his mind when Carol shot him a questioning look.

"Adele, how many times must I tell you? Get your hands off

me." Alexander reached for Adele's arms that were clasped around his and rid himself of her touch.

He signaled the bartender for another drink and saw a familiar silhouette walking away from the bar. He was seeing Olivia everywhere lately. Everyone with dark hair seemed to be her. He felt bad for not contacting her since Thursday, but he just needed some time to figure out what to do about that letter.

"So Alex, how's everything at the company going?" David asked.

"Pretty good. We're getting into air escorts and drone technology now. Still being contracted to train civilian forces overseas. Private security business is booming," he winked. "And there's still the domestic protection details we do. I have a new batch of recruits that start their training on Monday, so I need to go down to base camp for their first day."

"Good. Glad to hear it's all going well."

"And anytime you want to retire from civil service, there's a job waiting for you, man."

"Thanks for the offer, Alex. But I'll stick to homicide, if you don't mind." The men laughed. David had worked extremely hard to become a homicide detective. He had dreamed of that job nearly his entire life.

"Come on, Alex. Let's go dance," Adele whined, grabbing Alexander around the waist.

"Adele, I didn't come here to dance with you. I came here to spend some time with my family, which you will never become part of. If you want to dance, there is absolutely nothing stopping you." He gestured to the dance floor, signaling that Adele should go, when he stopped dead in his tracks.

He couldn't believe his eyes. Olivia and Kiera were on the dance floor. He watched as Olivia danced with a tall muscular man, her back to his front, her hips moving to the driving beat of the music in such a way that he felt himself immediately harden.

Olivia was enjoying the dance with Collin. He had been respectful of her boundaries and didn't try to touch her too much. All of a sudden, Collin grabbed her hair and pulled her head to the side, exposing her neck. Olivia gasped in shock as his other hand roamed her body from her waist up to her chest.

"Collin," Olivia whimpered as he kissed her neck. She immediately turned around to face him. "Look, I'm sorry if I gave you the wrong idea. I'm just not interested in you that way. Maybe if it was a few weeks ago, I'd probably take you back to my hotel room right now and fuck you…"

Collin's eyes grew wide. He pushed Olivia against the wall, crushing his mouth on hers as she fought against him, unable to finish her sentence.

Alexander felt his face flush with anger and rage. He slammed his drink down on the bar and rushed across the dance floor to the far corner where some guy had Olivia pinned against the wall.

Olivia pushed repeatedly against Collin, thinking how shitty her luck had been lately. She pushed one last time and Collin went flying to the side. She couldn't believe her own strength for a minute until she saw that familiar silhouette standing over her.

"What the fuck, man?" Collin exclaimed angrily.

"Do not mess with me, *man*," Alexander retorted.

"Whatever," Collin said, walking away. "Bitch isn't worth it."

"What did you say?" Alexander roared, his voice easily heard over the loud music. Olivia stood motionless, having trouble comprehending what was happening.

The two men stood glaring at each other. Kiera slid up to Olivia's side to watch the spectacle. "This is a dick waving contest, isn't it?" she whispered into Olivia's ear. Olivia hushed her friend, not wanting to miss anything.

"I said, the bitch isn't worth it," Collin repeated.

"First off, she is not a bitch. She is one of the most precious people to me. And second, she is absolutely worth it. She is worth every ounce of every effort anyone could give to her." Alexander's eyes met Olivia's and he could tell she was confused.

178

"Then why was she here dancing with me? Obviously she's not satisfied with you."

Out of the corner of her eye, Olivia saw a tall, skinny blonde stroll up to Alexander. Kiera elbowed Olivia in her side and they shared a knowing look. *This is definitely getting interesting*, Olivia thought.

"Alex, darling. Please. No need to fight for my honor tonight. I know you love me. Let's just go back to our family and enjoy our evening together."

Alexander heard Adele's words and he looked over into Olivia's eyes. Adele's eyes followed where he was looking, stunned at what she saw. She remembered those eyes, but it wasn't her. Olivia DeLuca was killed years ago. It was just an uncanny resemblance.

Alexander noticed that Adele was staring at Olivia and he worried about what she would say. Instead of putting up a fight, he retreated back to the bar, following Adele. Olivia's heart sank as she watched him walk away with her, his hand on the small of her back.

Tears threatened to fall down Olivia's cheeks. Kiera looked at her friend and saw how upset she was. "Men. Such jerks."

"Yeah," she agreed, attempting to regain her composure.

A man who Olivia recognized as one of the guys Kiera had been dancing with that evening approached the two women.

"Hey, are you okay?" he asked Olivia.

"Yes, thank you. I'm fine."

"Libby, this is Matt," Kiera said, introducing the smiling blond man standing to her left.

"Nice to meet you, Matt," Olivia said, shaking his hand before turning back to Kiera. "Listen, I'm going to head back to the room. I've had enough excitement for one evening. But you stay here, okay?" She knew Kiera was having fun dancing with Matt and she didn't want to be the one to rip her away from her good time.

Kiera looked at Olivia. "Are you sure? I can come back with you. We can order room service and a ridiculously expensive bottle of champagne and bitch about how much of an ass Alexander Burnham is." Kiera laughed.

"No. You have fun. You deserve it. And don't worry about me. I just need to be alone for a little bit."

Olivia left before Kiera could respond, quickly retreating from the dance floor, past the bar, and out the front doors of the club into the busy casino.

She was nearly at the elevators leading to her room when she heard a voice shouting. "Olivia! Wait!" She stopped in her tracks, refusing to turn around. She didn't know if she could look into those eyes again. Those eyes that once held such promise for her own future. Those eyes that she had become so accustomed to in just a week. Those eyes that remained the same, even when they were lying to her.

"Please. Olivia, Love…"

"Do not call me that," Olivia hissed as she spun around. "You lost that right, Alexander. I only ask for one thing out of people. The truth. And, well, I know it never came up, but you could have told me you were already fucking someone else."

"Olivia, please. Adele doesn't mean anything to me. She never has. We've known each other nearly our entire lives and she was more of a distraction for me than anything serious." Alexander moved toward Olivia. She held up her hand and took a step back, wanting to keep her distance from him.

"So, is that what I was, Alexander?" she asked quietly, her voice full of pain. "A distraction? I thought I meant more to you than that. I actually believed…" Olivia looked into his eyes, her own eyes brimming with tears. "I actually thought I could get close to you, something I have trouble doing. And this is what happens. I get hurt. You ripped my fucking heart out and stomped on it. I saw those god damn pictures all over the internet of you and her. And I was actually worried something happened to you and that's why you weren't responding to any of my texts. Stupid me. You were off getting fucked by some blonde bimbo who probably has more plastic in her body than anything else."

"Olivia, please. It wasn't like that. She found me yesterday morning and invited me to a thing her parents were putting on at the country club and I agreed to go. And tonight was just supposed to be me and my brother and sister and her husband.

180

Adele found us and just attached herself to our small little party."

Olivia thought about his explanation. Some of the things she had read about Adele made Alexander's story plausible. She was noted for being a gold digger, looking for a rich husband to marry, her father having lost a big chunk of his fortune in the recent recession. But one thing just didn't make sense to Olivia.

"If that's true, why did you follow her back? Why didn't you tell her you didn't love her? Why did you just stare at me, afraid someone would find out that I was your dirty little secret?"

Alexander opened his mouth, wanting to calm her fears but was unsure of what to say. He closed his mouth, hoping to formulate his thoughts. A few brief moments passed and he offered no explanation.

"That's what I thought," Olivia said, spinning on her heels and walking away from him into a waiting elevator car.

Chapter Twenty

Helpless

"Libs, you'd probably feel better if you talked about last night," Kiera said, interrupting the dead silence in the car as they drove back to Boston the following morning.

"I'd rather not," Olivia replied dryly.

"So, what are you going to do?"

"I'm just going to get back to the city and try to forget that Alexander Burnham even exists. Now you know why I don't date. It's not worth the heartache. It's not worth this totally helpless feeling I have right now."

Kiera looked at her friend briefly before returning her eyes to the road. "You're only helpless when your nails are drying and even then I'm sure you could still pull the trigger if you had to."

Olivia couldn't help but laugh. "You spend far too much time on Pinterest looking at all those e-cards. You know that, right?" Kiera always knew how to lighten a tense situation.

A few moments passed before Kiera spoke again. "But seriously. What do you think you're going to do? Has he tried to call you or anything?"

"Yeah. He has. I have about ten missed calls from him, a few voicemails, and a shit ton of texts. I just can't bring myself to listen or read or anything."

"Well, maybe you should. I mean, maybe closure is something you need here."

"I got enough closure last night when he couldn't come up with one simple explanation of why he chose to follow Bombshell Barbie back to the bar instead of stay with me. It was like last week was one big act for him to try to get in my pants or something."

"Did you sleep with him? You didn't tell me that!" Kiera exclaimed.

"No!" Olivia shouted. "That's the thing. We didn't even sleep together. We fooled around a few times. Wednesday night when he took me home and I was all drunk, he barely even laid a hand on me. Hell, I grabbed his hand and made him feel me up, but he felt like he was taking advantage of me because I was pretty far gone. He helped me get into my PJs since I was too wasted to even attempt it, but he was so sweet about it. It's almost like there's two sides to him. He can be rather forceful when he wants to be, but also sweet and caring."

"How so?" Kiera asked. "I see the way he looks at you and I'd give anything to have a guy look at me that way. Even last night. The heat between you guys was palpable." She fanned herself, making Olivia smile before her serious expression returned.

"Well, I didn't want to tell you," Olivia said, glancing over at her friend. "But I've been having those nightmares again. They're more clear now than they've ever been. And I see the person who pulled me out of the car. It's a boy who probably wasn't that much older than I was at the time, and he has those same green eyes as Alexander."

"Have you spoken to Dr. Greenstein about these dreams?" Kiera asked.

"Not yet. I mean, it's on my list of things to bring up with her, but we're still kind of playing catch up." Olivia fidgeted in her seat, hating to talk about her ongoing need to see a therapist with anyone, including Kiera.

"Did you have that dream when Alexander stayed over?"

"I did. And that night it changed again. The boy with the green eyes pulled me from the car, just like he had been doing. And he placed me in another car and then I saw someone come up behind him and hit him on the back of his head with a gun, knocking him out. I woke up screaming. And Alexander was so sweet during the whole thing. He jumped out of bed

183

and turned on the lights and just held me."

"Aww. I mean, he wouldn't do that if he didn't care about you."

"I know. And that's the part I'm struggling with. It's like he was a totally different person this past week than the person I saw at the bar last night. It's almost as if he's hiding something from me. I don't for a second believe that he and Adele are in a relationship. I mean, there are photos online of the two of them, but the dates are so random. If they were dating, there would be a lot more photos, ya know?"

"Exactly. So why are you ignoring his calls?"

"I want him to be honest with me," Olivia exhaled. "I don't want him to keep things from me. There was some reason that he wanted to get as far away from me as possible last night at the bar. And I want to know what it is. And until he comes clean, he can fuck off for all I care." Olivia crossed her arms in front of her body and looked out the window to see the Boston skyline appear in the distance. She was happy to be getting closer to home.

"Are you sure you're not just using this as an excuse to push him away?" Kiera asked quietly.

Olivia opened her mouth, surprised at her friend. She closed it quickly, knowing Kiera was probably right. Olivia was looking for a reason to push Alexander away. She was scared at how close they had gotten over the past week. And pushing him away seemed like a good idea, if only to save her the heartache.

~~~~~~~~~~

Alexander hung up his cell phone, swearing. He had called her countless times, left dozens of voicemails and texts, and still had yet to hear from Olivia. He was getting worried. What if something had happened to her?

"Hey, bro," Tyler said as Alexander walked downstairs into the kitchen in the early afternoon on Sunday. "Heading out?"

"Yeah. I need to try to smooth things over with Olivia. She's not answering my calls. I may have fucked things up."

"What happened last night?" he asked, leaning against the breakfast bar and drinking a coffee.

"I don't know," Alexander replied, running his hands through his hair. "One minute I was at the bar and then the next minute, I looked across the dance floor. She was dancing in the corner and some asshole had his hands all over her so I fucking snapped." His face flamed just thinking about anyone else touching Olivia. "And then," he continued, "Adele had planted photographers at the function Friday so there were photos of the two of us all over those gossip websites, and Olivia saw them. I never called or texted her all weekend, so she just thought the reason was Adele and that we're in some sort of relationship. This is one big fuck-up and I have no idea what I'm going to do." He opened the refrigerator and grabbed a bottle of water for the drive back to Boston.

"Well, good luck with that. I've been dying to meet the girl who stole your heart all those years ago. Drinks this weekend?"

"Yeah, sure. I'll be in touch." He gave his brother a hug, walked out the door, and within minutes was on his way back to Boston. During the two-hour drive back into the city, he thought about what he could possibly say to Olivia. He was new to this whole relationship thing, but he knew he fucked up. He dug himself into such a hole.

The weekend had started out perfect. Visiting Olivia's gravestone at the cemetery. Telling her all about the woman she had become. And then Adele happened. And, as usual, she clung onto him, wanting the entire world to see her name next to his to up her social status. Alexander knew he should have ignored her from the start, but he had a tendency to want to make everyone happy.

But, at that moment, the only person he wanted to make happy was Olivia and he would do anything to get her back. He would grovel. He would beg. He would do everything, except the one thing she wanted. He just didn't think he could tell her the truth yet.

Alexander pulled off the Mass Pike and drove straight to his office, needing to review the report Simpson had prepared before deciding what to do about Olivia. Sitting behind his desk, the sun shining through the large glass windows, he opened the file.

According to her birth certificate, Sarah Olivia Adler was born almost twenty-eight years ago on October sixteenth. The same day as Olivia DeLuca. Her medical records were fairly normal until twenty-one years ago. That year, according to a hospital report, she received a head injury and suffered from several cracked ribs as well as internal bleeding.

He compared the information on the medical records in front of him to the records of his other Olivia. Her death certificate listed the cause of death as blunt force trauma to the head causing severe cerebral bleeding. Then something struck Alexander. He looked at the signature of the medical examiner on the death certificate. He held it up next to the other hospital records from the same year belonging to one Sarah Olivia Adler. They were identical.

He pulled the financials of the doctor that had signed Olivia's death certificate all those years ago. He dug and eventually found records from the year of the accident. In August of that year, he noticed a transfer of over one million dollars into the doctor's account from an off-shore bank.

Whoever wanted to help cover up Olivia's death, or lack thereof, had big pockets. He reviewed his family's financials at that time and it couldn't have been his father or mother. They didn't have that kind of money just yet. His father's success didn't come until a few years after that. The only person Alexander could think of who would have had access to that amount of money was Olivia's mother.

Alexander looked at a copy of the trust Olivia's mom had set up several years before her death. Just a few days before the accident, the trust was liquidated and all the money was placed into several bank accounts in the name of Charles Wright. A few days after the accident, a beneficiary was named to the account - Sarah Olivia Adler. Alexander wondered if there was more to the cover-up than just protecting Olivia.

Charles Wright had made periodic withdrawals from Olivia's substantial bank accounts to pay for her private school and other various living expenses. She attended Charleston

Preparatory School for Ladies throughout elementary and high school and was involved in a wide variety of extracurricular activities ranging from lacrosse and field hockey to orchestra and drama club.

Olivia moved to Boston ten years ago and started at Boston College that September. She graduated five years later with a degree in exercise physiology and a minor in finance. She was named to the dean's list every semester and was the recipient of a wide variety of awards. Even though on her eighteenth birthday, Charles' name was taken off the bank accounts and she had millions at her disposal, she still worked. Throughout her time in Boston, she was employed at a bar called Scotch. Alexander knew the exact bar and had probably seen her there on a few occasions. That thought consumed him.

She graduated five years ago, the month Alexander's own father died. The man Olivia knew as her uncle. After that, Olivia seemed to have gone off the grid. She quit her job and never renewed the lease on her apartment in Boston. Bank records indicated that she bounced around from city to city all over the country. One month she was in Atlanta and the next in New Orleans. She even spent some time in Alaska. Olivia was clearly running from her past.

A year ago, there was a record of a sale of property to Olivia – the house on Commonwealth Avenue. A few months later, there was a transfer of money to a startup she was financing, which turned out to be the wellness center where she currently worked.

Simpson had done a rather thorough job of outlining Olivia's life from the beginning to that week. It was the early lack of medical records that caught his eye. And lack of any records, really. Something suspicious happened and Alexander wanted to know what kind of agreement his father had made. But digging any more may uncover information that could put Olivia in danger. He just didn't know if he was willing to do that. She had been safe those past twenty-one years and he wanted to keep it that way.

Closing the file, he knew he needed to speak with Olivia. He didn't know whether he would tell her everything or just some half-truth. Regardless, he knew he needed her back in his life and would stop at nothing to win her back, even if it meant telling her who she was. He knew he would only get one chance to persuade her to forgive him. He wanted to make sure he did it right.

Chapter Twenty-One

Self-Preservation

"He can spend as much fucking money as he wants to, but it means nothing without a mother fucking I'm sorry!" Olivia shouted at Kiera Friday evening when she picked Olivia up to head to MacFadden's.

"Oh, come on, Libs. Look at these earrings!" she said, holding up a pair of beautiful pink pearl tear-drop earrings. "They're gorgeous. If this doesn't say I'm sorry, I don't know what does!"

"Kiera, he has more money than he knows what to do with. All these gifts barely put a dent in his bank account. I want an explanation and an apology, and then, and only maybe, will I reconsider my position on Alexander."

Kiera giggled. "Ooh, Libby. Kinky."

Olivia couldn't help but laugh. "He is a little. Kind of dominating, but in a good way."

"What do you mean?" she asked, her eyebrows raised.

"Well, he has this way of just telling you what to do, and you can't help but obey. It's weird. And I kind of like it." Olivia blushed.

"Okay," Kiera said. "You need to get laid and Alexander needs to be the one doing it."

"Don't worry about me, Kiera. You need some ass just as much as I do."

The two girls laughed as they left Olivia's house and hopped in Kiera's car.

It was a busy night at MacFadden's. Word had apparently gotten out that Olivia was a regular with Mo's band. She was slated to do a few numbers with the guys in the second set that evening. The band had just started their first set as Olivia, Kiera, Melanie and Bridget sat by the bar on the second floor, ordering some drinks.

"So, whatcha got planned for tonight?" Melanie asked, excited to hear what her co-worker would be performing that evening.

"A few new ones and a few old ones," Olivia replied dryly.

"Hey, what's wrong with you?" Bridget asked. "You haven't been yourself this week. And then you blew off work today. Linda had to fill in and teach your classes. Don't tell her I said anything, but I think our clients prefer you leading the classes."

"Thanks, Bridget. I know. I've just been dealing with some personal shit, that's all. And I don't really want to talk about it right now." Olivia took a long drink of her beer. She secretly wanted to get her set over so she could continue to numb the pain the only way she knew how. With alcohol.

"It's boy problems," Kiera interrupted.

Olivia shot daggers in her direction.

"What kind of boy problems?" Melanie asked, her interest piqued. "With that hottie from the penthouse that came to visit you last week? Because OH. MY. GOD. I think I came just looking at him."

Olivia slapped Melanie playfully, not wanting to talk about her personal life with people she worked with. But she was barely ever at the office. Maybe their perspective would be helpful. So Olivia told them the whole story. How Alexander had been incredibly sweet the entire week before. How on the weekend things changed and he was seen with another woman. And how he shrugged off Olivia at the bar Saturday night.

"Maybe you're just overreacting, Libby," Melanie said as she took a sip of her drink.

"I don't think I am. He ignored me all weekend. I texted him a few times and didn't hear back and then I see photos of him on the internet with Bimbo Barbie at all those events. Then Kiera drags me to the casino Saturday night for some fun and, just my luck, he's there as well. With *her*. He didn't even acknowledge that I was alive until he got caught. When he tried to explain it, he couldn't."

"But tell them what he's been doing all this week," Kiera interjected.

"Oh, yes. What's going on?" Bridget asked excitedly.

"Nothing. Let's just say my apartment has enough flowers to last a lifetime."

"And don't forget about all the little blue boxes."

"Yeah. And he's sent me jewelry. But I don't need to be showered with gifts. I just want an explanation."

"I think she's trying to find a reason to not get close to him," Kiera said.

"You guys have no idea what it's like to lose someone so close to you. When that happens, it stays with you always, forever reminding you what it feels like to get hurt and be let down. So maybe pushing Alexander away is exactly what I need to do as my own act of self-preservation." Olivia turned to walk toward the bathroom, leaving her friends speechless.

Mo's band soon finished up their first set and took a thirty-minute break before having to start their second set. At that point, the second floor of MacFadden's was overcrowded with people.

The girl's conversation had gone cold after Olivia stormed off. She returned soon thereafter but was no longer in a mood to talk about anything.

"Hey, Livvy. You ready?" Mo asked, grabbing a beer from the bartender and checking his watch.

"Yeah. Let's do this." Olivia surveyed the audience hoping that, just maybe, Alexander would be there. Then she wondered why she even cared at all.

~~~~~~~~~~

"Tyler, hey," Alexander said as he walked up to the bar on the first floor of MacFadden's. The name of the bar sounded so familiar for some reason when Tyler had asked him earlier in the day to meet him there that evening. He shrugged it off, realizing that, after a while, the names of most bars in Boston seemed to run together.

191

"Hey, man. How's it going?" Tyler asked, giving his brother a hug and grabbing his beer off the bar. The downstairs area had cleared out once the band had started to perform.

"Okay, I guess," he replied.

"Listen, the band they have is wicked good, so let's head upstairs and check them out. I've seen them a bunch over the summer."

"Good. Anything to get my mind off Olivia," Alexander said.

The brothers made their way upstairs after grabbing another round. When he got to the second floor, Alexander couldn't believe his eyes or ears. He remembered why the name of the bar sounded so familiar. Olivia had mentioned it the previous week at Open Mic.

"Did you know about this?" Alexander shouted at his brother.

"What are you talking about?" Tyler shouted back, hoping his brother could hear him over the cheering and loud music.

"You really don't know?"

"No! What is it?"

"That is Olivia," Alexander said, gesturing toward the stage where a tall, dark haired girl belted out a Queen song.

"Are you shitting me?" Tyler exclaimed just as the audience erupted in cheers.

Alexander began to move through the crowd, wanting to get close to the stage. And to Olivia. "I knew she sang in a band, but I had no idea she would be here tonight," Alexander explained to his brother before returning his attention to the beautiful woman on stage that had been occupying his thoughts all week.

"Thanks everyone," Olivia said into the microphone, her voice sad. "I'm going to do one last song and it's a new one. My therapist always says that music helps me express myself, so I kind of feel like I need to do this one tonight. Even though I know the person it's aimed at isn't here, I need to sing this, if just for myself. So thank you." Cheers and whistles sounded through the large room.

Tyler looked at his brother. "Do you think she's talking

about you, jackass?"

"Shut it, Tyler." Alexander looked back to the stage and at Olivia.

"This is a Pink song. It's called *Misery*."

She stepped back and the band kicked in a slow, soulful melody. After the brief instrumental introduction, Olivia sauntered back to the microphone, closing her eyes and beginning the sad song. It was heartbreaking for Alexander to watch her, knowing that he was the reason she felt the need to sing that song. He could see the pain in her face as she sang about being all alone and missing something she almost had.

Her voice was strong and impassioned as she belted out the chorus with Mo singing backup. She thought about Alexander, as she usually did those days, and how she felt like a complete fool. The one time she actually let her heart get close to someone and she was met with excruciating pain.

Alexander watched Olivia interact with the guy he saw her sing with just the week before at Open Mic. They were good together. The crowd seemed to love them, too. Everyone swayed to the slow beat, cheering as Olivia belted out the melody. The hurt he caused her was clear and evident, not just with the song choice, but the expression on her face. He needed to explain himself. He wanted to give her space, but it had been almost a week. It was time to talk to her.

The crowd cheered and whistled as the band dropped out and Olivia sang the last line practically unaccompanied. Her voice rang through the bar before the entire place erupted in deafening applause. *God, she's good*, Alexander thought to himself as she bowed and left the stage to allow the band to continue their set. He watched Olivia practically run through the crowd.

Alexander tried to follow her through the mass of people but couldn't catch up. He saw her dash down the stairs, Kiera not far behind. It was more than obvious that she was upset and crying. And it was all his fault. He turned to face his brother, his mouth open, unsure of what to say.

Tyler saw the look on his brother's face and knew he needed to go smooth things over. "It's okay, man. Do what you have to do. I'll call you this weekend."

"Okay, Ty. Thanks." Alexander hurried after his Olivia.

~~~~~~~~~~~

Olivia and Kiera made a beeline toward the downstairs restroom. Once safely behind the locked door of the one-person bathroom, Kiera faced Olivia, wrapping her arms around her, knowing she needed to have a bit of a crying session.

As Olivia's tears fell, Kiera soothing her cries, there was a loud knock on the bathroom door.

"Fucker," Kiera said, her voice low. "We just got in here for crying out loud."

"Go away!" Olivia shouted.

"Olivia!" Alexander shouted through the door.

"Fuck," she said to Kiera.

"Who is it?" Kiera asked, taking a sip of her drink.

"It's Alexander," Olivia whispered, motioning for her friend to come closer to the door. "What do I do?"

"Do you want to see him?"

"Hell no!" Olivia shouted before realizing how loud her voice was. She instantly covered her mouth, hoping Alexander hadn't heard.

"Olivia! Open up! I know you're in there. I just want to talk to you. To explain things. I'm not leaving until you give me a chance to explain."

"Alexander," Olivia said through the door, a quiver in her voice. "You gave me all the answers I needed last weekend. It was clear from your inability to answer one simple question who you chose. And you chose wrong, so you have nothing to explain." Olivia sank to the ground, sitting on the cold tile of the bathroom floor.

"Olivia, please. Just come out and talk to me."

"No. Anything you need to say to me, you can say through this door. If I see you, I know I'll cave."

Kiera sat on the ground across from her friend as they continued to drink.

Olivia heard a chuckle on the other side of the door. "Then please, open the door. I want you to cave. But not for the wrong reasons. For all the right reasons. Because you know we're meant to be together, Olivia. You know it deep down in your heart. Last week was the best week of my life because of you." Alexander sat down in the hallway as Olivia continued to berate him.

"If it was the best week of your life, why did you go running to Plastic Surgery Barbie?"

Alexander laughed again and Olivia could just see the smile in his eyes. "That's a good one. I'll have to remember that."

"That's not an answer, Alexander." Olivia took a long slug of her drink, wanting to numb the growing ache in her heart.

"I told you last weekend. Adele is an old family friend. I am not interested in being with someone as self-absorbed as she is. I'm interested in being with a kind, loving, caring individual. Someone who doesn't care how large my bank account is. Someone who devotes her time to improving the lives of others around her, human and otherwise. Someone who makes my heart swell whenever I think about her. Who puts a smile on my face just knowing that she's out in the world. Who drives me all sorts of crazy when she looks at me with her beautiful brown eyes. I've been waiting my entire life to find you, Olivia. Please. Don't shut me out."

Olivia blushed and remained silent, unsure of how to respond. Kiera raised her eyebrows.

"What do I say to that?" Olivia whispered.

"Say what you think you should," Kiera whispered back.

"Is Kiera in there with you?" Alexander asked through the door.

The two girls giggled. "Yeah. She's here. Making sure I don't do something incredibly stupid like forgive you."

Kiera slapped Olivia.

"Hi, Kiera," Alexander said.

"Hi, Alexander. And don't worry. I'm actually hoping you can convince Olivia to forgive you so that I can go back to my own miserable existence and not have to be on Olivia-watch, fearful that she'll flee the city again."

Olivia slapped Kiera, nearly spilling her drink. "Shut up, bitch."

"What do you mean flee the city? Has she done that before?" Alexander asked even though he knew the answer.

"Yeah. Once before," Kiera explained. "But it's not my story to tell."

Olivia mouthed the words "thank you" to Kiera.

Alexander lowered his voice. "Olivia, Love. Please come out and talk to me."

She stared at Kiera, looking for advice on what to do. Kiera stood up, walked over to her friend, and grabbed her hands, pulling her up. "You need to at least start the conversation, Libs. You can't run all your life."

Olivia straightened herself up and handed Kiera her empty beer bottle before opening the door. Alexander scurried to his feet when he heard the door click open. He stared at Olivia. She looked beautiful as always, but there was a hint of sadness in her face. He would never forgive himself for causing that look.

Kiera walked out of the bathroom behind Olivia. "I'll leave you two to sort this out and, so help me God, you better buck the fuck up, Alex," she said before walking away.

Seeing Alexander up close made Olivia's heart ache all over again. Not wanting to listen to his empty lies, she stormed down the hall and out the front door of the bar. She continued walking down the sidewalk until Alexander caught up to her, the street bustling with people heading out to one of the many bars that dotted the area.

"Olivia, Love," he called out. Olivia turned around to face him, realizing Kiera was right. She couldn't run all her life.

Alexander moved toward her, the street lamp casting a glow on him, making his eyes shimmer.

"Please, stop. If you touch me, I don't think my heart could take it, so just say what you want to say," she pled with him, her eyes brimming with tears.

"I wanted to apologize for my behavior last weekend," he said softly. "I know it all looks so suspicious, but there really is an explanation for everything."

"Why did you go to Connecticut? What was there?" Olivia asked, crossing her arms over her chest.

"I grew up there, Olivia. My family's home is in Mystic and I go back once a year on the same day."

"What for?" Olivia was not going to back down. She wanted all the answers.

"It's hard to explain," Alexander answered.

"Well, try, Alex," she hissed. "Try real hard."

Alexander reeled. She had never called him Alex before, except when they were kids. But she wouldn't know that.

He took a deep breath. "When I was nine years old, my best friend growing up passed away. I went to visit her grave, as I do every year on August twenty-fourth."

"August twenty-fourth? That's the same day…"

"I know. That your parents died."

Olivia's heart sank. She immediately felt guilty for how she had treated him. But that still didn't clear up everything.

"Then why didn't you call me or anything?"

"I don't know, Olivia. I really don't. It was weird. I was at my friend's grave telling her all about my life and all I could talk about was you. And I know this may not make sense, but I just needed to focus on the weekend. On my friend. And I felt guilty, I guess, if I didn't devote the weekend to her memory."

Olivia took a step forward, placing her hand on his shoulder briefly, a look of compassion on her face. "I truly am sorry, Alexander. I know how difficult it is to lose someone you're close to. And it's wonderful that you still return home to honor her memory. It takes a strong person to do that. I know. I've never been able to pull myself together enough to visit my parents' graves. I don't even know where they're buried, to be honest. My uncle did, but he passed away." Olivia gazed off into the distance, a pensive look on her face.

"Hey," Alexander said, interrupting Olivia's thoughts. Her face snapped back to meet his eyes. "It's okay. We all mourn in our own ways. And this is my way. The Adele thing just kind of came out of nowhere. I thought maybe going to the event at the country club would help me take my mind off things, seeing old friends and what not. Then my brother and sister showed up, knowing I would be home that weekend. We ended up going to the casino Saturday night. And then when I saw you and I saw that guy with his hands all over you..." he trailed off, his face becoming red with anger, recalling how he felt when he saw another man with his hands on her body. "I lost it. I absolutely lost it, Olivia. The thought of anyone else touching you drove me crazy." Alexander lifted his hand and cupped Olivia's cheek, thankful when she didn't brush him away.

"Then why did you just let Adele drag you away? Didn't you see how hurt I was?" she asked quietly.

"I did. I'm so sorry. And if I could get a do-over I would take it in a heartbeat to spare you of that pain. The last thing I ever want to do is to hurt you, Olivia." He ran his thumb across the old scar on her forehead.

"Well, you did hurt me, Alexander," she said with a lump in her throat, her chin quivering. "More than I thought you could." A tear fell down her cheek.

Alexander exhaled loudly, dropping his hand. "I know, and I'm so sorry."

"You seem to be saying that a lot tonight."

"Well, I guess I have a lot to be sorry for. But I mean it. And I should have told you sooner, but..." Alexander hesitated. Should he tell her the truth or just some version of it?

"What is it, Alexander? I can handle it, whatever it is."

"Well, I don't know how to say this, and I don't want you to run or anything..." He paused, unsure of what to say.

Olivia looked at him, anxiously waiting for what words were about to come out of his mouth.

"You see," he exhaled. "My best friend when I was little, her name was Olivia, too." He decided against telling her the truth, at least for the time being. "And I didn't want Adele to know that you had the same name as her. I didn't want you to think the only reason I'm dating you is because of your name. And Adele knew my other Olivia and hated her. She was so jealous of her because I would always spend time with her instead of Adele." Alexander looked at Olivia, trying to gauge her reaction.

"Alexander, you could have told me. It's not that uncommon of a name. Hell, my first name is Sarah anyway. Not Olivia."

"I know. But the way Adele was looking at you, I was just worried she would do something spiteful. And I wanted to protect you from that. I will always protect you, angel." Alexander tilted Olivia's chin up, staring into her deep, dark eyes.

"Alexander, you can't always protect me. But you can just be honest with me. That's all I care about."

"And I will. I promise. From now on. I will be honest with you." Alexander regretted those words the minute he uttered them, knowing that keeping the truth from her was just as bad as lying. But he was doing it to protect her. "So, do you forgive me?"

She thought about it as she studied his vibrant green eyes. She exhaled. "Yes."

Alexander grabbed Olivia around her waist, pulling her body flush with his, crushing his mouth to hers. It was a fevered, passionate kiss, tongues dancing, communicating how much they had missed each other during their one week separation. Olivia's body was on fire from the closeness of Alexander to her once again, his mouth pressed against hers. She grabbed his head, running her fingers through his hair, not caring that people roaming the streets were whistling at them.

Alexander pulled away, grinning. "God, I missed your lips, Love," he whispered against her neck as he gently grabbed onto her hips, lifting her up and playfully spinning her around before planting her feet back on the ground.

"I missed you too, Alexander," she said, completely breathless from that kiss.

"Want to come back to my place? You can see Runner."

"Well, as long as I can see Runner. If not, you'd have to provide some other sort of incentive for me."

"Oh, Miss Adler," he said, leaning toward her ear, his husky voice sending shivers throughout Olivia's body. "I can definitely provide some sort of incentive." He pressed up against her and she gasped at his erection. He nibbled on her ear lobe and neck, making Olivia almost lose her balance.

Alexander held onto her hips, helping to steady her. "Is that a yes, Love?"

"Yes," she breathed out, her mind reeling from the overwhelming feelings coursing through her body from Alexander's touch. "Always. Yes."

CHAPTER TWENTY-TWO

LET LOVE IN

Alexander slammed Olivia against the back wall of the elevator when they got to his building after leaving MacFadden's. He had been thinking about those lips ever since he got a sweet taste earlier that evening. He devoured her mouth, his tongue tangling with hers. The kiss wasn't gentle. It was greedy.

Alexander lifted Olivia, his hands on her ass, and she wrapped her long legs around his mid-section, feeling his erection. "God, angel. I want you so bad right now." He dove in for another impassioned kiss, groaning. The elevator dinged, announcing its arrival on the twenty-fifth floor of Alexander's building.

Olivia followed Alexander out of the elevator into the foyer. He punched a five-digit code into the keypad and the solid black door buzzed, sliding open and allowing them access to his home.

"Additional security is never a bad thing, Miss Adler," he said, smiling down at her. "Come, let me show you around." He grabbed her hand, pulling her into the living room.

Olivia looked around, astounded. The penthouse was gorgeous. There were floor-to-ceiling windows throughout the open floor plan. The formal dining room was to the left, leading to a gourmet kitchen with all state-of-the-art stainless steel appliances. To the right was a long corridor leading to his home office and den. Immediately in front of Olivia was a palatial living room. It boasted a large black couch, matching love seat, and a pair of bright red wing-backed chairs next to a gas fireplace. The view from behind the couch was amazing, the lights of boats twinkling on the water twenty-five stories below.

"Runner!" Olivia exclaimed when he came pummeling down the hallway. The dog nearly knocked her over, showering her with his affection.

"Can I interest you in a glass of wine, Miss Adler?" Alexander asked, his tone sensual. The timbre of his voice made Olivia gulp. She released Runner and shook her head, staring into his deep green eyes.

"Good, because I have other plans for you."

"What did you have in mind, Mr. Burnham?" she asked innocently.

He laughed. "You'll see." He grabbed her hand and led her up the stairs to the master bedroom suite, leaving Runner behind. There was a short hallway before opening into a large room. An oversized four-poster mahogany bed sat in the center of the room with a writing and sitting area by the windows. The fireplace was directly across from the bed.

"Olivia, Love, are you on contraception?" he asked, pulling her toward the bed.

Olivia blinked, unsure she heard him correctly. That was not what she expected to hear come out of his mouth.

"Answer me," he demanded, staring down at her.

"Yes. I'm on the pill."

"And you're good at taking it."

Olivia became irritated. "Yes. Of course I am. I'm not a child."

A smile crept across Alexander's face. "Good. Men need to know these things, Love. Because I fucking hate condoms. I'm clean, don't worry. I can show you a copy of my last test results if you want."

Olivia looked at him, butterflies dancing in her stomach, excited about what they were about to do. "No. I believe you. I've only ever had sex using condoms before, but my last results were clear, too," she replied.

"Good," he said before changing his expression, the atmosphere in the room becoming heated. "I want to see you naked, Olivia," he said in a deep voice.

"Y-yes," she croaked out. He made her hair follicles stand on end whenever he was nearby.

"Sit down," he growled.

Olivia hesitated.

"I said, sit down." His green eyes were all aflame with desire and tenderness. It was an intoxicating combination. Olivia immediately sat down on his soft bed. He winked, picking up her left foot. He removed her heel and kissed the instep of her foot, slowly dragging his tongue across her arch, sending shivers throughout her body. He did the same to her right foot.

"Stand back up."

She obeyed, their bodies practically touching. She could feel his erection growing. Electricity coursed through her veins and she felt her body temperature rise from his stare. His eyes stayed locked on hers. She couldn't look away even if she tried.

"Lift your arms, Olivia."

She did as he commanded, remaining completely speechless in his presence, and he lifted her tank top over her head. He trailed kisses from one side of her neck to the other, tasting her silky skin as his mouth made its way down to her black lace bra.

"I like this bra," he murmured against her skin. "I'd like to see you in this more often." His fingers dipped into the bra and, finding her nipple, Olivia let out a low moan. He instantly fell to his knees and planted kisses down her stomach, dragging his tongue across her skin, holding onto her hips. "Do you have any idea what you do to me, Olivia?" he asked, his eyes still never leaving hers.

Sensation overwhelmed Olivia's entire body from the simple act of his lips on her stomach. She could barely form a coherent thought as her breathing increased.

"Answer me, Olivia," he said sternly.

"Yes," she exhaled. "I do." She was about to come unhinged as he continued tracing circles around her belly button with his tongue. She wanted that tongue on other parts of her body.

"And why is that, Olivia? Do I have the same effect on you still?" he asked with a hint of amusement in his eyes. He removed his hands from her hips and slowly unbuttoned her jeans. He raised his eyebrows as if asking for her permission.

She nodded quickly, biting on her lower lip. Olivia's heart raced with anticipation, her breathing heavy.

"Well, do I?"

Olivia nodded. She didn't know how much more she could take. "Yes. Yes, Alexander." She looked down and watched him slowly lower her skinny jeans down her legs, helping her step out of them.

Alexander raised himself up and stepped back to admire her bra with matching black lace panties. "God, Olivia. Do you have any idea how amazing you are?" He ran his hand through his hair, unable to control his desire for the woman standing in front of him. He couldn't remember ever being as aroused as he was at that moment.

She lowered her head, blushing, before returning her eyes to his. He rushed to her and claimed her mouth, wrapping his arms around her body. His kiss was needy. It was hungry. It was passionate. It was hot, Olivia thought. He deftly unhooked her bra and it fell to the ground. One of his hands went to her head, fisting her hair and pulling her head back, while the other tightly held onto the small of her back, pressing her to him. Their tongues did a delicate dance, communicating to each other exactly how desperately they wanted and needed each other.

He removed his hand from her back, sliding it down her side, and gently felt in between her legs. She moaned, letting him know it was okay to go further.

"Olivia, you're so wet." He stroked her through her panties.

"I know," she said breathlessly.

"What do you want me to do, Olivia?" He looked at her, his eyebrows raised.

"I want you…" Her thoughts were a complete haze. They were all over the place. She would do anything to just keep that man touching her. She needed his touch. She craved his touch. She would die without it.

"You want me to what, Olivia?"

She looked into his eyes and grabbed his hand, shoving it in her panties, hoping he would get the hint about what she wanted.

"I want you to say it," he whispered in her ear as he started to tease her clit. "Say it, Olivia."

Her breathing grew heavier as he continued to torture her. She felt as if she was about to explode.

"Come on, Love," he said, planting gentle kisses across her collarbone, his lips on her skin igniting the flames coursing through her body. "Say it," he pled. He needed to hear it. He needed her to beg him. It was what he craved. It was how he could remain in control.

He slowly removed his hand from her panties and Olivia was left panting, ready to burst without his touch. "FINE!" she screamed, her breathing heavy. "I WANT YOU TO FUCK ME!!!" She couldn't take it anymore. "God damn it! Don't make me beg!" He was so exasperating.

"I like it when you beg," he said, crushing his mouth to hers as his hand quickly pushed her panties down. Before she knew what was happening, Alexander pushed two fingers inside her. "Fuck!" Olivia moaned. He continued to rub her clit while he slowly teased her inside as well. She felt like she was going to explode.

Alexander needed to be inside of Olivia. He removed his fingers, leaving her wanting, and rid himself of his clothes. He wrapped his arms around Olivia's naked body, pressing his lips against hers again. He didn't think he would ever tire of kissing her. She gasped when she felt his arousal rubbing against her clit. He led her to the bed, his lips not moving from hers.

Pulling back the duvet, he lowered her down and stared at her, overwhelmed with a feeling he was scared to label. "Olivia, darling. You are one beautiful woman," he said, licking his lips. "I'm going to show you how much of a treasure you truly are, Love."

"Stop staring. You're making me self-conscious," she said, covering her naked body with the duvet.

"Oh, don't you dare," Alexander replied, crawling on top of her. She tilted her head toward him, their mouths meeting. Alexander pushed his knee between Olivia's legs, opening them. She wrapped her legs around his waist, feeling his erection against her cleft. She was eager to feel him inside her.

Alexander growled, pulling back as he hovered over her, admiring the beautiful woman lying sprawled out in front of him. He leaned down on his elbows and entered her slowly.

"Oh, God," Olivia moaned as he filled her, stretching her to match his size. It was such an amazing feeling. He hadn't even moved yet, but the simple act of him being inside her made her want to explode.

He slowly withdrew. "NO!" Olivia cried out, on the brink of becoming unhinged.

"I want this to last, Love. I felt that, you know," he smirked. "You're ready to come already, aren't you?"

She threw her arm across her eyes, wanting to hide from him. She was embarrassed that he could make her fall apart so quickly. She felt him lean down. Circling her nipple with his tongue, he slowly entered her again, causing Olivia to convulse around him, screaming out his name, her orgasm catching her by surprise.

"Fuck!" he exhaled, smiling, his mouth covering hers as he continued thrusting into her. "Don't worry. I'll make sure you come again," he said breathlessly. Alexander couldn't believe how good she felt. He had never felt so much pleasure with any of the other women he had slept with over the years.

Olivia wrapped her legs around his waist again, not wanting any distance between them. Legs and arms were entwined, hands caressing, nipping, pinching.

"You feel so good, Olivia," Alexander said as he moved inside her, filling her to the brim. "Do I make you feel good?" he asked.

"Yes, Alexander… Yes."

Her soft voice sent shivers through his body as her hands clutched onto his back, nails digging in. He pressed his lips back against hers, forcing them open with his tongue. There was something about kissing Olivia as he moved inside her that overwhelmed his entire being, igniting feelings he had repressed his entire life. He picked up speed, a tingling sensation coursing through his body and he knew he was close.

Burying his head against her neck, he gently nibbled, loving the taste of Olivia's sweaty skin.

Her breathing became more erratic and Alexander felt Olivia's body begin to tighten around him. "Again?" he asked, pulling back, his eyes searing down into hers.

She simply nodded, her voice nowhere to be found. Alexander pulled out.

"NO! Not again!" Olivia screamed, panting.

"I need to hear you say it, Love. Tell me you're going to come again," he said, ready to explode at any moment, his breathing labored. "Say I drive you wild when I'm inside you. Tell me I'm the only one who's ever made you feel this good."

Olivia tried to catch her breath. She had never come like that before and she was about to come again. She didn't know what to make of it.

"Damn it, Olivia. Just say it." He needed to hear it. He needed to know that he alone could make her feel that good.

"Yes. You're the only one, Alexander," she replied, her heart racing. "I've never had an orgasm like that in my life. Now, please. I want another one."

He leaned down and feathered kisses across her neck. "Ask me."

Olivia flashed back to the night they met. She knew exactly what he wanted. Smiling, she ran her fingers up and down his back. She felt him harden against her. "Please, Mr. Burnham. Let me come again."

"Fuck!" Alexander said, slamming into her, her sweet voice uttering those words sending him over the edge in just a few thrusts. Olivia felt him release inside her and came undone around him, her orgasm never seeming to end while the aftereffects ravaged her body for several long minutes.

"Holy shit," she said, finally able to find her voice as she listened to Alexander's heavy breathing.

"You are fucking incredible, Olivia," he said, nuzzling her neck. Of all the women he had ever slept with, he never felt as full and complete as he did in that moment. And he hoped Olivia felt the same way. He rolled over onto his side and wrapped his arms around her, pulling her against his body.

They lay there, their bodies covered with sweat, not wanting to put any distance between each other.

~~~~~~~~~~

Olivia had a dreamless sleep for once. She woke up in the middle of the night when she felt something poking her. Or someone. She turned her body to face the man lying next to her.

"Sorry, Love. Sometimes that thing has a mind of its own."

Olivia giggled.

Alexander pulled her mouth to his, kissing her deeply. "I love that sound."

She kissed him deeper and felt his erection harden.

"Olivia, get on top of me," Alexander ordered.

She obeyed, coaxing him onto his back and straddling his midsection. She leaned into his neck, her hips circling his arousal, whispering in his ear, "What should we do about that, Mr. Burnham?" She pulled back, looking deep into his eyes as she continued her relentless teasing.

He grabbed the back of her neck, pulling her lips back down to his mouth. Kissing Olivia was unlike anything he had ever experienced in his thirty years.

After an impassioned kiss, Olivia leaned back, raising herself over Alexander, and slowly took him inside her. The feeling was even more intense than it was before as he filled her to the brim. She wasn't going to last long, already starting to feel that tingling sensation all the way down to her feet.

He began to guide her up and down, over and over. Olivia stared deep into his eyes, knowing that he had total control of her body. And for the first time she could remember, she was okay with that.

Alexander gazed at the woman on top of him, her ample chest moving with the motion of her body. He was so deep in her. When he felt her body clench around him, he couldn't hold back any longer. He pumped harder, growling her name as he came undone inside of her. Olivia's body shuddered around him. Leaning down, she bit his neck to muffle her screams of pleasure.

As their breathing slowed, Olivia looked deep into his eyes. "I had no idea sex could be like that."

He brought his arms around her, pulling her off him and onto her side, her arm draped across his torso, and planted several kisses on her forehead gleaming with perspiration.

He thought to himself, *"That's because it's love."*

~~~~~~~~~~

Olivia awoke the following morning, shielding her eyes from the brightness of the sun. She looked at the man lying next to her, amazed that he could sleep so well with all the sunlight in the room. She quietly got out of the bed and went into Alexander's closet in search of a tee shirt and shorts to put on. She opened the door, walking into a closet any woman would be jealous of. Alexander had a thing for clothes, apparently. She found a chest of drawers against one wall and grabbed a pair of Navy shorts and a Harvard tee shirt that were both enormous on her, but she didn't care.

When she was dressed, Olivia made her way to the bathroom. After cleaning up a bit, she quietly left the master bedroom and walked down the stairs to the main floor. Runner attacked her, wanting to play and probably go outside. She put on his collar and found a pair of oversized flip-flops that would have to do for the moment. Grabbing his leash, she left the penthouse to take Runner for a walk.

She got down to the street below and walked around the block toward the water, allowing Runner to sniff and mark his territory as they went. After Runner had done his business, Olivia decided to head back to Alexander's place before he realized she was gone.

Back in the penthouse, Alexander woke up, feeling the bed next to him and reaching for Olivia, only to find her side empty. He quickly threw on a pair of shorts and went looking for her. After a search of his place turned up empty-handed, he started to panic. What if she decided to run?

He grabbed his cell phone and frantically dialed her

number. He heard her phone ringing. She had left her purse on the kitchen island. *Damn it! How could she be so careless?* He ran out of his apartment, fervently pressing the elevator call button, phoning Martin to help him find her. What if something had happened to her?

The elevator finally arrived after what had seemed like an eternity. After a painfully slow ride, he arrived on the bottom floor and ran out onto the sidewalk. Glancing up and down the street, he searched for his Olivia, his heart racing.

At that moment, Olivia rounded the corner, making her way back to Alexander's building with Runner. Alexander's heart dropped when he finally saw her. He rushed to her, his eyes wide with worry, and pulled her into a desperate kiss.

"Oh, Olivia. Thank God," he breathed a sigh of relief as he held her tightly.

"Hey, hey. What's wrong? Are you okay?" Olivia pulled out of his embrace and looked into his eyes before he wrapped his arms around her again, stroking her hair.

"I'm sorry. I woke up and you weren't there and then I couldn't find you. I was so worried something had happened. I thought you were taken from me again."

Olivia tilted her head back and looked at him, confused, her forehead wrinkled.

"Again? What do you mean by that?"

Alexander's heart started to beat rapidly. He thought his chest was going to explode. "Well, I mean with last week," he floundered nervously. "I just felt that you were taken from me then."

Olivia looked at him and, after a few intense moments, said, "Okay. I'm sorry I left. I saw Runner and figured he'd want to go out. I didn't mean to worry you." She looked down at her feet.

"Hey, look at me." Alexander grabbed her chin, gently leaning it back so he could see into her eyes. "I'm the one who's sorry. I didn't mean to overreact."

The elevator door opened and Martin ran out, slowing down when he eyed his boss. "Everything okay then, sir?" he asked Alexander.

"Yes. Sorry, Martin."

"Not at all." He turned and went back into the elevator.

"Does he live here or something?" Olivia asked.

Alexander ran his hand through his disheveled hair. "Yeah. He has a condo in the building just a few floors below me. I need to make sure he's close by, just in case. That's why I pay him very good money. Why don't we go back upstairs and have some breakfast?"

"Sounds good to me," Olivia replied, grasping his hand in hers.

Back in the penthouse, Alexander prepared Runner's breakfast before turning to Olivia. "Hungry?"

She wrapped her arms around his waist. "For you," she whispered in his ear.

Alexander leaned down, kissing her neck as he slipped his hand under the bottom of the shirt she was wearing, placing it on the small of her back. The gesture sent tremors through her body. She yearned for his touch.

"You look good in my clothes," Alexander said. "But you could make a paper sack look good, Love."

Olivia brought her mouth to his and kissed him, grasping his hair.

"Fuck it. Breakfast can wait." Alexander swooped Olivia in his arms and carried her to the enormous sofa in the living room. He stepped out of his shorts as Olivia swiftly removed her tee shirt and shorts. Alexander sat on the couch, his feet on the ground, pulling Olivia on top of him.

Alexander slowly lowered her down onto him, moaning with pleasure. He placed his hands around Olivia's waist, helping to guide the motion. When they met a steady rhythm, he removed one hand, bringing it to stroke Olivia's clit.

As if she wasn't overwhelmed with sensation as it was, when Alexander started to rub her, she couldn't take it anymore. It was all too much. She exploded around him.

"FUCK!" She exhaled breathlessly as he picked up a torturous rhythm, guiding Olivia up and down in swift movements. In a matter of moments, he screamed her name and emptied inside her.

In the aftermath of their lovemaking, Alexander gently stroked Olivia's back as she rested her head on his shoulder. "Stay the weekend," he whispered softly into her ear. He eagerly wanted her to agree.

"I don't know," she pulled out of his embrace and searched for her discarded clothes. She noticed the dog sitting a few feet from the couch. "Runner, you shouldn't have seen that, boy."

Alexander stood, put his shorts on, and grabbed Olivia around the waist, pulling her to him once again. "Why don't you want to stay? What is it? Talk to me." He noticed the look of concern on her face.

"I don't know. I just..." She trailed off trying to gather her thoughts. She couldn't keep her head straight when she was around him. "It's just that I think we're moving too fast. I mean, I enjoyed last night. And the middle of the night. And this morning. And I think I'm becoming too attached to you, and it scares me to death." Her lower lip trembled.

Alexander reached his hand out to her cheek. She leaned in, basking in the feel of his hand on her skin.

"Stop thinking too much into it, Olivia. I want to spend time with you. I want to get to know you. I want to share things with you. This is all new to me, too. Just don't shut me out. I beg you, Love."

Olivia looked into his deep emerald eyes, searching for the answer she so desperately needed.

She exhaled. "Okay. But I need to go back to my place to get some clothes and feed Nepenthe."

He embraced her, laughing. "That can be arranged."

212

CHAPTER TWENTY-THREE

SOMETHING YOU FEEL

"Come. I want to show you something," Alexander said to Olivia after they finished eating their dinner of salmon, roasted red potatoes, and asparagus. They had spent all day together after Alexander took Olivia back to her house to gather some things she would need for the weekend.

They had gone to Olivia's gym later in the morning after eating a breakfast of egg white omelettes with broccoli, spinach, mushrooms and feta cheese that Olivia had made. Alexander thought that she was a fantastic cook. The dinner reaffirmed that thought.

Olivia had spent most of the day snuggled up on Alexander's couch reading a book on her e-reader and scratching Runner's belly as he cuddled next to her. Alexander sat on the other end of the couch going over case reports. He disappeared into his study every so often, closing the door to make a phone call. Olivia didn't mind. She figured there were some things he was working on that were classified.

"Where are we going?" she asked when Alexander grabbed her hand, pulling her along with him down the stairs.

"You'll see," he winked. Olivia smiled at the twinkle in his eyes. He was so excited to show her wherever it was they were going.

He led her down a hallway past two spacious guest bedrooms before stopping outside a door. Beaming from ear to ear, he opened it, allowing Olivia to enter before him. She couldn't believe her surroundings. In the middle of the enormous room stood a beautiful Steinway baby grand piano.

213

Dozens of guitars hung on the walls. There were also amps, a drum kit, and various other instruments scattered throughout the room. It was a musician's dream come true.

"Why do you have all this?" she asked. "Do you play?"

"Yeah. You could say that," he replied, running his hands through his hair. "I started fiddling with the piano and guitar when I was a little boy. A family friend taught me." Alexander remembered Mrs. DeLuca teaching him how to hold a guitar. He remembered her showing him how to curve his hands around the keys of the piano. And most of all, he remembered hearing her daughter sing those beautiful melodies. "You can feel free to come down here anytime you'd like."

Olivia walked over to the piano, running her fingers over the keys, the cool ivory always a comfort to her. She saw a Martin guitar set on a stand next to the piano. She picked it up and checked its tuning, noting it was perfectly in tune. It must have been played recently. She wasn't expecting Alexander to have such a beautiful music room.

"And the walls are totally sound proof so you don't have to worry about disturbing me or anything." Alexander sat down on a love seat against the wall, watching as Olivia fiddled with the guitar. "Play something for me, Love."

Olivia smiled as she sat down in a chair in the middle of the room, bringing the Martin guitar with her. She remembered a song that she and Mo used to play quite a bit during her college years. When she was at B.C., she would often invite Mo and the guys over for beers to hang out with Kiera and some of their friends. Usually late at night, after lots of drinks had been consumed, Mo and Olivia would break out a few of her guitars and entertain their late night guests. This song was one of their favorites.

Olivia took a deep breath and closed her eyes as she began playing a beautiful melody. Alexander had heard the song before when he accompanied his brother to a Zac Brown Band concert. Her voice filled the room, the acoustics perfect, mesmerizing Alexander as she played the guitar, focusing solely on the music as if nothing else mattered. She sang an ode to the guitar she held against her body. As he listened to the lyrics, Alexander thought how appropriate the song was. Almost as if she could be talking about herself or the guitar she so lovingly played. Almost as if telling him how much she needed music in her life.

Halfway through the song, Alexander stood up and grabbed one of his other guitars. He watched Olivia's hands, getting the chords he needed to join her. Sitting in the chair next to her, he played with her, singing along to the chorus as she continued belting out the lyrics. Olivia opened her eyes, smiling at the sound of his soft, sultry voice next to her.

She finished the song and Alexander leaned over, placing a gentle kiss on her lips. "That was fantastic, Olivia. Did you study music in college?" He knew the answer, but she didn't know that.

"No, actually."

He looked at her, feigning surprise.

"I know. Everyone thought I would. I mean, I was constantly involved in music groups all through middle school and high school. Everyone thought it was what I would study. But I actually have a degree in exercise physiology."

"Ah," Alexander said. "Hence the health club."

She smiled. "Yeah. I don't know why I chose that. I mean, I was worried if I studied music, I'd start to hate it. And I didn't want to hate music. Anyway, music isn't something you study. It's something you feel."

Alexander flashed back. He remembered Olivia's mother saying those exact words to him as he learned to play guitar and piano all those years ago. And those words had stayed with him ever since.

~~~~~~~~~~~

That night, Alexander had trouble sleeping, thinking of the beautiful woman next to him and the letter from his dad. He knew the longer he waited, the worse it would be when he told her the truth.

He quietly got out of bed and walked downstairs to his office. He punched the code into the door, unlocking it, before he turned to close it, making sure it was secure. He hated keeping secrets from Olivia, but it was necessary at the moment.

He sat at his desk and looked down at one of the photos in front of him. It was of him and a beautiful six-year old Olivia. His parents stood behind them next to Olivia's mom and dad. *God, she looks just like her mother.* He sighed, still torn about what to do.

He recalled that he had a message from his sister to phone her immediately. Even though it was after three in the morning, he picked up the phone and dialed her cell.

"Alex," Carol answered, sounding wide awake.

"God, sis. Do you ever sleep?"

"Yeah. Sorry. I'm working the night shift tonight."

"They work you too hard. You know you'd make more money if you came to work for me full-time."

"Alex, I already make money off the company. And I just don't feel like taking orders from my baby brother round-the-clock." She laughed. "Plus, if I didn't work here, I'd never see David."

"So, what's up?"

"Well, I've been running the photos you took last week of the guys at the bar who you think were following Olivia."

"Oh yeah? Get any hits?"

"Well, at first I just thought you were being paranoid. But I got a hit. The taller one matched with a Mark Kiddish. And here's the weird thing. I've been looking into Simon a bit. Apparently, there was a wire transfer our guys had missed of $100,000 into Simon's bank account about two months ago from an off-shore untraceable account. According to Olivia's timeline, it was right around the same time Simon showed up to work the construction job on her gym.

"Now, this Mark Kiddish is the son of Jacob Kiddish." She paused for a minute. Alexander knew that name. Jacob Kiddish was a professional "fixer" or "cleaner" working mostly for politicians and other government officials. He had been suspected of a variety of crimes over the years, but he was so good at what he did that nothing ever led back to him or the people that hired him.

Alexander remained speechless as his heart raced, wishing his sister had said any name other than Mark or Jacob Kiddish.

"Apparently, Mark had taken over the family business after his dad disappeared all those years ago," Carol explained. "Just like his dad, they've never been able to link him to any crimes. Well, I cross-referenced who posted Simon's bail and the photo on the ID used matched Kiddish. But now he's going by a Donovan O'Laughlin."

"Sis, that's what Kiera said his name was."

"Well, we still can't connect him with any crime. But the money transfer worries me. Look, I don't want to go on about this, but you may want to think about reading that letter finally. Obviously, Dad was protecting Olivia and her identity. Maybe this has something to do with that. Maybe someone has realized it's her. If you were able to figure it out, I'm sure other people have, too."

Alexander sighed heavily. He knew his sister was right. "I know, sis. I'll tell her soon. I promise."

"Okay. Love you baby brother."

"I'm not the baby anymore."

"You'll always be the baby to me."

~~~~~~~~~~

It was the same dream again. The car crash. Her parents dying. The boy saving her. This time, when the boy was hit with the gun handle, Olivia saw him stare back at her and he morphed into Alexander.

"AAAAAGGGGHHHHHH!!!!"

Alexander sat in his office, contemplating the letter, when he heard a scream. *Shit.* "Olivia!" He ran out of his study. After the conversation he just had with his sister, he was on edge. He leapt up the stairs, taking them two at a time, before sprinting down the hallway and crashing through the bedroom door. Turning on the lights, he saw a shaking Olivia, sitting up and clutching a pillow to her chest as if her life depended on it. Tears streamed down her face.

He ran to her, wrapping his arms around her and pulling her close. "Olivia. What's wrong? Was it the dream again?" He caressed her back, trying to soothe the sobs that rolled through her body.

Olivia looked up at him. At those green eyes she had just seen in her dream.

"Do you want to talk about it?" he asked softly.

"I don't think I can."

"Come on, Love. It'll make you feel better." He placed a gentle kiss on her head, savoring the vanilla scent of her hair.

Olivia took a deep breath, finally getting her crying under control. Something about being in Alexander's arms had an amazing effect on her. It made everything seem okay. "Well, the dream was like normal. But when the guy smashed the boy's head with the gun and he stared back at me in the car, the boy turned into you." She looked at Alexander and saw the look of horror on his face. "What is it, Alexander?"

He quickly snapped out of it and pulled her body down so that she lay next to him, her head leaning on his shoulder. "It's nothing, Love. It's just a dream."

Olivia relaxed into him but couldn't help thinking that he was keeping something from her.

Something important.

Chapter Twenty-Four

Total Control

"Cheryl, what the fuck is going on?" Donovan shouted into the phone. "I thought for sure we'd have her spooked by now. It's October for crying out loud. We need to do something so that Burnham puts you on her protection detail. I need to get someone close to her to get more information."

"I know, sir. But he's been with her almost round-the-clock. I've had to keep my distance so that he doesn't catch on. I'm just as frustrated as you are."

"Well, get it done. I don't care what it takes. Follow her. Stalk her. Maim her. I don't care. Just get it done." Donovan slammed down his office phone just as a knock sounded on his door.

"What?" he shouted, his anger apparent.

"Sir," a petite blonde woman said, cracking the door open a bit. "I'm sorry to interrupt, but Paul Flinnigan is here to see you."

"Okay. Thank you, Susan. Send him in."

Paul Flinnigan strode into Donovan's office and placed his briefcase on the desk. "Let's get down to business," he said once the door was closed.

"Nice to see you, too, Paul."

"This isn't a social call, Mark," he said, sitting down. "I've got a deal worked out with the D.A. in Simon MacKenzie's case. He will agree to plea out to a lower assault charge. It's a felony, so it will stay with him for a while. In exchange for not mentioning your name or anything else, he requests a few things. First, he wants a sum of five million dollars, to be transferred into an off-shore account before he takes the plea."

"That's ridiculous. He may just be jerking my chain."

"I agree, so I got him to agree to a one million transfer as a sign of good faith, with the remainder due upon his release from prison. That brings up the next point. The only way I was able to persuade the D.A. to plea this down was to guarantee some jail time. It will be about a year, but considering he has no priors, he will probably be released early. Now, if the remainder of the money isn't transferred upon his release, he will go back to the D.A. and tell them about your involvement, so I suggest paying up."

"Yeah. No problem. That's doable." Donovan made a quick note to get in touch with his client who would be paying that money.

"One last thing. And I'll let you deal with this as you see fit," Paul said, standing up and closing his briefcase.

"What's that?" Donovan asked, his eyebrows raised.

"He wants to pull the trigger. I mean, when the time comes, and he's sure it will, he wants to be the one to, and I quote, 'Kill the bitch.'"

Donovan sat and thought about that for a minute. Could he trust Simon to do the job correctly this time? Then he realized that could actually work. Olivia knew Simon. She may be scared of him at first, but his previous incompetence could turn into an advantage.

After a few long moments of contemplation, Donovan finally spoke. "Okay. Agreed."

~~~~~~~~~~

Olivia woke up on a Tuesday morning in mid-October snuggled next to Alexander in his bed. Over the past several weeks, they had gotten to know each other fairly well. They spent nearly every free moment together, and Olivia was actually enjoying being in a real relationship for once. They had even planned to get away that coming weekend. Olivia had a marathon in Newport, Rhode Island and Alexander said he wanted to go with her to cheer her on as she attempted to qualify for the Boston Marathon. His reasons for doing so were two-fold. One, he really did want to support her. Two, he was still nervous about the connection between Mark Kiddish and Simon. He didn't want to let her go out of town unprotected, but he knew she would refuse to take any sort of protection detail with her.

"Good morning, gorgeous," Alexander said as he looked into her big, beautiful brown eyes. "Have I told you today how much I love waking up next to you?"

"No, you haven't," Olivia said sleepily.

"Well, I love waking up next to you," Alexander replied, flipping Olivia onto her back and hovering over her with a look of eagerness in his eyes. He leaned down and feathered a gentle kiss on her forehead as he placed his knee between her legs, pushing them open. "See, Love. Sleeping naked definitely does have its advantages."

Olivia reached up, grabbing the back of his neck, and pulled him down to her lips, kissing him deeply and communicating her need for him with her mouth. He moaned as she ran her fingers up and down his back, wrapping her legs around his waist, grinding against his erection.

"Oh, Miss Adler. You do not play fair," Alexander smirked.

"Yes. I know," Olivia replied, smiling.

"What am I going to do with you?" Alexander asked, kissing Olivia's collarbone.

"I have a few ideas," she said, throwing her head back, giving Alexander access to her neck.

He planted soft kisses on her skin and Olivia relaxed her legs around his waist. With his body freed, he slowly moved down Olivia's body, worshipping her with his mouth.

Lowering himself to her breasts, he took one nipple in his mouth, tugging gently as Olivia arched her back, squirming under his expert tongue. She reached down and ran her hands through Alexander's messy hair.

He looked up and his eyes met hers. "Mmmm... Your skin tastes divine, Love."

Olivia moaned with pleasure at his words.

"I have an idea," Alexander said, getting up from the bed.

Olivia pouted from the loss of contact. "What is it?" she asked.

"Close your eyes," he responded. Olivia looked at him, waiting for an explanation. "I said, Close. Your. Eyes." Alexander's voice changed from sweet to stern. Olivia obeyed. "That's better."

She heard some rustling from the closet and wondered what Alexander was doing. A few brief moments later, she felt him sit back down on the bed and instinctively opened her eyes.

"What did I just say?" Alexander asked forcefully.

"Oops. Sorry." Olivia closed her eyes again.

"Sorry, what?" he growled.

"Mr. Burnham. Sorry, Mr. Burnham." Olivia smirked, loving the little game they were playing.

"Are you laughing at me, Olivia?" Alexander asked, leaning down, his breath hot on her neck, making her body tremble in anticipation.

"No. I would never laugh at you, Mr. Burnham," she replied, the smirk gone from her face.

"Raise your arms over your head," he demanded.

Olivia complied with his command and felt a soft fabric being wrapped around her wrists before he fastened whatever he was using to restrain her to the headboard of the bed.

Alexander checked her restraints and was pleased with their security. He then grabbed a blindfold and placed it over her eyes. "You can open your eyes now," he said.

Olivia obeyed. "But I can't see anything," she protested.

"That's the point." She could hear the humor in his voice.

Olivia felt Alexander's breath lower from her neck down her body as his mouth hovered over one of her breasts. She moaned out in anticipation and tried to move her arms to touch Alexander.

"Fuck," she said. "This isn't fair."

"I know. I can be such a tease, can't I?" he asked, inches from her chest. He gently blew on her nipple, causing it to become erect.

Olivia wiggled beneath him, the darkness heightening the rest of her senses. "Hold still, Olivia," he said fervently. She immediately obeyed.

Alexander returned his attention to Olivia's breast, pulling her nipple into his mouth and sucking ever so gently. Olivia whimpered and raised her hips, desperately wanting him inside of her.

"What did I just say, Olivia?" Alexander demanded.

"Sorry," she replied meekly, lowering her hips back to the bed.

"Sorry, what?"

"Sorry, Mr. Burnham," Olivia choked out.

"One more move and I won't let you come. Do you understand, Olivia?"

"Yes. I understand," she said quietly. She loved when he was in total control of her body. It was as if he knew what she needed more than she did.

Alexander continued to kiss Olivia's body, trailing kisses down her stomach, gently circling her belly button with his tongue. He placed his hand between her legs and pushed them wide apart as he lowered his mouth to her sex.

"Mmmm… You smell amazing, Olivia." She could feel his breath on her clit. It drove her crazy. "I can see how wet you are for me." Olivia moaned out at the first stroke of Alexander's tongue, the surprise of his touch causing her to buck her hips.

"What did I say? Didn't I warn you about what would happen if you didn't lie still?" Alexander scolded, his breath still hot on her.

"Yes. You did."

He drove his fingers deep inside of her as he continued to tease her with his tongue.

"Fuck," Olivia screamed out, the sensation of Alexander's touch overwhelming her. She didn't know how long she would last.

"And what did I say your punishment would be, Olivia?"

She licked her lips. "That I couldn't come," she whimpered.

"Yes, Olivia," Alexander said, his fingers still teasing her insides. "This must be torture, then."

Olivia nodded her head fervently. Alexander removed his

fingers and she scowled, wanting him inside of her.

She felt Alexander lean down over her. "This is for me, not for you," he whispered into her ear. He immediately pushed into her. Olivia let out a loud gasp, surprised at the sudden invasion. He thrust mercilessly into her again and again, pulling out when he felt her tighten around him.

"What did I say, Olivia? No coming for you," he panted, looking down at her, her desire apparent from her heavy breathing.

He thrust into her again and she moaned loudly, setting Alexander off. He came inside her after only a few more thrusts. "Holy shit," he exclaimed, collapsing on top of her. He quickly unfastened Olivia's restraints and took off her eye mask.

"I like you all tied up," Alexander joked, kissing Olivia fully on the mouth. "And don't worry, Love. I plan on giving you more orgasms later on than your little body can handle."

Alexander got out of bed and went into the bathroom to take a shower. Olivia rolled over, feeling remarkably satisfied for some reason. She drifted off, warm and comfortable in Alexander's bed.

"Olivia, Love," Alexander said a short while later, waking Olivia up after his shower.

She opened her eyes and saw him standing over her dressed in his suit, apparently ready for the office. She wondered how long she had fallen back asleep for. "Hey," she said sleepily.

"Hey," Alexander said, sitting down on the bed next to her and brushing her hair away with his hand. "I need to get to the office. Stay as long as you need to. Runner has already been out this morning." He leaned down and planted a kiss on Olivia's mouth. " I'll miss you, Love."

"Come to my place tonight? Stay over?" Olivia lifted her eyebrows, giving him a sweet smile.

"I have a meeting, and then I promised my brother I'd go for a drink."

"After that?"

Alexander looked down at Olivia. "Okay. I can't say no to you." He kissed her one more time before he turned to leave the bedroom. When he reached the doorway, he turned back around. "Oh, and Olivia?"

She glanced up to see a devilish grin on his face.

"Don't you dare touch yourself today. I want your orgasm and I plan on getting it later." He spun around, leaving her completely speechless.

CHAPTER TWENTY-FIVE

PARANOIA

Olivia returned to her house after her morning appointment with Dr. Greenstein and sat to eat a light lunch before heading to the gym for her work out. She made a salad and sat in the little reading nook by her big bay windows as she ate. Her eyes focused on a black sedan parked across the street a block away from her house, the occupant clearly watching her. She thought it was strange but shrugged it off, not wanting her paranoia to get the best of her.

She quickly finished her lunch, grabbed her gym bag, and headed out the door. It was a sunny autumn day in Boston so she decided to walk and enjoy the brisk fall weather, the smell of burning leaves permeating the air. On her way to the gym, she just couldn't shake the feeling that someone was following her. But every time she turned around, all she saw were hoards of locals and tourists, shopping and going about their errands on the streets of Boston.

Within twenty minutes, she arrived at her building, thankful to get off the street. She wondered why, all of a sudden, she felt like she was being followed. After she swiped her key card and walked through the turnstiles, she turned around and looked through the floor-to-ceiling windows out onto State Street. She noticed a short man stop on the street and peer inside, searching for something until his expression settled on Olivia. His eyes locked on her, a snide smile creeping across his face. She was unable to break her own gaze from his even though her brain told her to turn and run.

"Libby? Dear? Are you okay?" Olivia heard a voice say. She

spun around and saw Jerry sitting at the security desk, a look of concern on his face.

"Oh, yeah. Sorry," she replied quietly. "I just spaced out for a second." She started to walk toward the bank of elevators, turning her head every few seconds to see if the man was still there.

The elevator car dinged, announcing its arrival. "Saved by the bell," Olivia muttered under her breath. She entered and pressed the button for her floor with shaky hands, ascending the twenty stories to the wellness center.

Jerry turned around as soon as the doors to the elevator closed and picked up the phone.

"Mr. Burnham, it's Jerry at the front desk. I'm sorry to bother you, but you should probably know... It's about Olivia... Yes, sir... She just went to her floor... There was a strange man outside on the street just staring at her... I'll have the video sent to you, sir... Yes, sir... You're welcome, sir..." Jerry hung up the phone, hating that he didn't wait for Olivia to mention anything to Mr. Burnham, but he'd rather be safe than sorry. He had been instructed over a month ago to report any suspicious activities surrounding her and he was pretty sure that had qualified as suspicious.

Up in the penthouse suite, Alexander's heart started racing. "Martin, I need you," he barked into his office intercom. Within a few seconds, Martin appeared in his office.

"What is it, sir?"

"Jerry from the security desk is sending up a video file. Get it to my sister and have her run facial recognition on it." Alexander stood up to leave.

"Yes, sir. Anything we should be worried about?"

"I'm not sure yet, but we may need to add some security for Miss Adler's safety. I have a bad feeling, especially after talking to my sister earlier today." Alexander dismissed Martin and strode out of his office, making a beeline for the elevators.

He had made Olivia promise that she would let him know immediately if she noticed any suspicious activity. She failed to do so. He was fuming. An elevator car arrived and he punched the button for the twentieth floor repeatedly, willing the doors to close quickly.

"Mr. Burnham," Melanie said, jumping up from the reception desk of the wellness center as Alexander walked through the front doors. "Libby is here. She just arrived a few minutes ago. I think she's still in her office."

"Thank you, Melanie." He continued to walk down the hallway he had grown so accustomed to in the last few months. He usually only visited her on the days she worked, stopping by to surprise her with lunch or just to see her smiling face. But that day, he was on another mission altogether.

Olivia sat at her desk, checking her messages from Melanie, when she saw an intimidating figure appear in her doorway.

"Olivia," Alexander said firmly.

"Alexander," Olivia responded, smirking at him.

"What did I tell you weeks ago?" He took a few steps into her office and closed the door.

"I have no idea what you're talking about, Alexander," Olivia replied, returning her eyes to her missed messages, not really reading anything as she was too nervous with Alexander towering over her.

She knew exactly what he was so upset over. Weeks ago, Alexander had made a point of telling Olivia, rather firmly, that if anything out of the ordinary had occurred, she was to contact him immediately. He didn't care what time of day. He ran a security company and the least he could do was make sure some of his assets were at her disposal so she was safe, particularly after Simon's attack and other information that had come to light Alexander was aware of.

He had been on high alert all day after receiving a phone call from his sister about Simon taking a plea deal. He didn't know if Olivia was aware of it yet, but he was certain the D.A. had been trying to reach her to let her know the details.

"Oh, Miss Adler, I think you do." He moved toward Olivia's desk and stood next to her, her eyes still avoiding his. He grabbed her chair and spun it around, forcing her to face him. His eyes bore down into her, wide with fury. She looked up and shot daggers at Alexander, willing him to back down.

I'm going to kill Jerry, Olivia thought. "So what?" she finally spat out, standing up and pushing Alexander out of the way before walking over to the windows. He quickly followed, grabbing her and making her face him again. "Some guy stared at me when I entered the building earlier. No big deal." She paused for a moment as those green eyes stared down at her. "He was probably just checking out my ass or something," Olivia joked, hoping to lighten the mood.

"I don't think you're telling me the whole story, Love."

After a brief moment, Olivia spoke again. "There's not much to tell, and don't go all Navy SEAL on me, *Alex*," she said with a hint of sarcasm.

His gaze softened. "Darling, I just want to make sure you're safe. And if I'm slightly overprotective, I'm sorry. But I can't even fathom losing you." He pulled her in close, needing to feel her body against his. He placed a gentle, affectionate kiss on Olivia's forehead. "Now, tell me what really happened."

"You're damn good at what you do, you know that?" Olivia whimpered into Alexander's chest, his warmth surrounding her and making her feel safe.

"I know."

She pulled away and walked over to her love seat, Alexander close on her heels. She told him about her morning as he sat next to her, his hand on her leg. She relished the flesh to flesh contact.

"Well, all day I felt as if someone was following me. I just thought your paranoia was contagious or something."

Alexander raised his eyebrows at Olivia. "You think I'm paranoid?"

"Yes. No. I don't know," Olivia said, irritated. "Maybe a little."

"Well, Love, it's my job to be paranoid where your safety is concerned. Now, tell me what else happened."

Taking a deep breath, she continued. "So I felt like someone was following me all morning. After I got back to my house from my appointment, I made some lunch and sat at my reading nook by the bay window in the living room as I ate it. I noticed a black sedan on the other side of the street a block or so down and thought that was odd. The driver's window was open and the guy was just staring at my house. A few minutes later, I got my stuff together and headed over here, and since it's such a beautiful day, I decided it would be nice to walk."

Alexander stood up quickly. "You WHAT?" he shouted. "You walked here? Are you out of your fucking mind? Do you have any idea what could have happened to you?" He strode over to the windows and peered down at the street, trying to control his temper and taking several deep breaths as he ran his hands through his hair.

"What's the big deal, Alex?" she shouted, walking over to the windows and glaring at him. "So what? I walked! It's not like it's the first time I've done that."

He realized how irrational he sounded. "I know, Love. I know." He smiled and grabbed her hands in his. "I'm being absurd. I'm sorry. Please, go on."

She eyed him suspiciously before she continued her story, wondering why he was overreacting. "Well, on the walk over here, I felt that feeling again. Like someone was following me. So I got here and went through the security gate and decided to turn around to see if I was just being paranoid. Outside on the street, there was a short man standing next to the building, scanning the lobby. His eyes met mine and he smiled. It was this creepy kind of smile and he just kept staring at me. I didn't know what to do. It was like he was looking for me. But why would he be looking for me? It didn't make any sense."

Alexander looked down, caressing her small hand in his. "I know. It doesn't. Have you heard from the D.A. about Simon's case?"

"I have a message from her. She wanted to talk to me about a plea bargain I guess Simon struck." Olivia looked up at Alexander. "Why? What do you know?"

"Just what my sister told me. That he pled down to a lesser assault charge and would be released in a year, maybe sooner. He did get some jail time, so that's good. I guess he got such a good deal because he had absolutely no criminal record."

"Yeah. The D.A. warned me that would probably happen," Olivia said. Alexander looked like he was deep in thought. "What? What is it? Do you know something?"

"What? Oh, no. It's nothing. Don't worry, Love. But humor me. Let me assign a protection detail. Please."

Olivia sighed. "I don't know, Alex. I think that's a bit of an overkill, don't you?"

"There's no such thing when it comes to you. At least have someone with you when I'm not around. That's all. Maybe this will be motivation for you to spend some more time with me."

"Can I think about it at least?" She looked at him, pleading with her eyes.

"Well, it's better than you flat out refusing," Alexander sighed.

"Okay. Good. I'll think about it."

"Fine. But under no circumstances are you to walk home. Come up to my office when you are done working out and I'll have Carter escort you home. Do you understand?"

Olivia glared at him for several long seconds before softening her gaze. It wasn't worth fighting over. "Yes. I understand."

"Good." Alexander embraced Olivia and looked down into her deep brown eyes. He pressed his mouth to hers. "I'll see you soon, Love." He walked out of her office, feeling better.

~~~~~~~~~~

Olivia went through her regular workout, taking it somewhat easy. She had a race that weekend and hoped to qualify for the Boston Marathon. As she was on the stationary bike, she decided Alexander was overreacting. She had called the D.A. immediately after he left and was told the same thing Alexander told her. So Simon was now in prison. There was no danger to her. She hated the idea that Alexander thought she needed him to protect her. She could protect herself.

Olivia finished her workout after an hour and a half and took a quick shower before grabbing her bag to head up to the twenty-ninth floor of the building, swiping her key card for access.

"Miss Adler," the cheery red-headed receptionist said when Olivia stepped out of the elevator. "Mr. Burnham is expecting you. Please go on in." She punched a security code into the door leading down to Alexander's office.

She walked down the long hallway, pausing when she heard a voice from within his office that didn't belong to Alexander. A female voice. The door was opened just a crack and Olivia could make out the conversation.

"Oh Alex, dear. I know you have no interest in going to Newport this weekend with that girl. Mummy and Daddy are throwing a charity auction. I know you'd much rather spend time with me than Olivia. You know she's not *your* Olivia, so stop wasting your time. I'll make it worth your while."

Olivia held her breath, desperate to hear Alexander's response.

"Adele. I have plans. So no. I can't go with you this weekend. Maybe some other time."

Olivia's heart dropped. Why didn't he just tell her off? Why was he being so nice to her?

She pushed open the door, anxious for Alexander to see that she had overheard. Tears formed in Olivia's eyes when she saw Adele in Alexander's embrace, planting a kiss on his neck.

Alexander pushed Adele away. His eyes grew wide in terror when he noticed Olivia standing in the doorway, his heart breaking from the look on her face. *Fuck. Not again*, he thought to himself.

Adele turned toward Olivia. "Hello, dear. You must be Alexander's friend, Olivia. Just so you know, I'm perfectly okay with him slumming it around with you for the time being. I don't mind sharing my man with anyone. I know eventually he'll get it all out of his system and then come crawling back to me." Adele pushed by Olivia and walked out of Alexander's office.

Alexander rushed to Olivia. "Darling, please. Don't listen to a word she says. She's crazy. I don't know what to do about her." Olivia put her hand up, willing Alexander to stop speaking. She knew what her eyes saw. The image of his arms around another woman were burned there.

"I'm going to leave now, Alex. And I don't want you to follow me." She turned and made her way down the hallway.

"Good-bye, Miss Adler," the receptionist called out as Olivia ran through the security door into a waiting elevator car.

She exhaled loudly when the doors closed just as Alexander appeared in the reception area.

"I guess he's upset about something," Olivia heard, realizing she wasn't alone in the elevator. She turned to face Adele.

"What do you want, Adele? You seem to be hell bent on breaking us up. Well, congratulations. You did it again." A lump formed in Olivia's throat as she struggled not to cry in front of her. She refused to let Adele see any weakness.

The elevator descended to the lobby in relative silence. When the doors opened onto the first floor, Olivia scrambled out, desperately wanting to get away from Adele.

"Well, just so you know. I'm not really sleeping with him or anything," Adele shouted, causing Olivia to turn back to the bank of elevators. "I just want you to think I am."

"Why the fuck would you want that?" Olivia spat out, glaring at the fake blonde.

"Well, if you think I'm fucking him, then you'll leave him. I mean, he is a good fuck, so I could understand why you'd stay just for that, but I have more long term plans with him."

"What are your plans? Take over his bank account?"

"I'm sure that's yours, dear. It's like the pot calling the kettle black."

"I'm not discussing this with you, Adele. But, just so you know, I'm not interested in Alexander's money. I'm interested in him as a person. A loving, caring person who worships the ground I walk on." Olivia took a step closer to Adele. "He's affectionate and kind, something you only wish you could be. And he deserves someone who treasures who he is. Not just the figures in his bank account."

"Oh, honey. He only worships the ground you walk on because your name is Olivia. He wishes you were his friend from all those years ago. That's all this is. It's just his childhood obsession with Olivia continuing into his adulthood. Soon, he'll realize that you're not his Olivia and leave you."

Olivia couldn't stand it anymore. Before she knew it, her clenched fist met with Adele's face. Adele fell to the ground, screaming, as Olivia stood over her, unable to control her laughter.

"Holy crap!" Alexander said, running out of the elevator car into the lobby. He rushed to Olivia and looked into her eyes. "Olivia, Love. Are you okay?"

"What about me?" Adele whined on the floor, clutching her cheek.

"Adele, I don't give a fuck about you. You should know that by now." Alexander turned to Jerry, sitting at the security desk, an amused look on his face. "Jerry, Adele Peters is no longer allowed anywhere in this building. Alert my security team that, should she try to make contact with Miss Adler in any way, she should be dealt with as they deem necessary."

"Yes, sir," Jerry smiled. "About time, sir, with all due respect."

Alexander nodded. "I agree." He looked down at Olivia who still looked rather shaken up. "That was incredible. I've been wanting someone to punch that little bitch for years now. I'm so glad it was you." Alexander laughed as he walked Olivia out of the building.

Once outside, he turned to face her, a worried look on his face. "Are we okay?"

Olivia sighed, running her fingers through his hair. "Of course we are."

A smile spread across his face. "Good."

A black SUV pulled up instantly with Carter at the wheel. Alexander opened the back passenger side door and helped Olivia into the car.

"I wish I could come with you, but I have some work to do. Carter will see you home safe. If you need anything, let me know."

"I will."

"I'll see you later, beautiful." Alexander kissed Olivia briefly before closing the door to the car. He watched Carter drive off before returning to his office, the image of Olivia standing over Adele with her fist clenched making his heart flutter.

CHAPTER TWENTY-SIX

OLIBIA

Olivia had a relatively uneventful remainder of her day. Carter dropped her off and did a quick sweep of the house to make sure it was safe. She made a delicious salmon dinner and settled onto her couch to snuggle with Nepenthe for a little bit. Her phone beeped at around eight. She looked at the text from Alexander letting her know that he probably wouldn't get to her until after midnight. She replied, giving him the code to the door as well as the alarm. She received a response immediately.

Alexander: *You really shouldn't be giving that to anyone. That defeats the purpose.*

Olivia: *You're not just anyone. You're my BOYFRIEND. :-)*

Alexander: *Say it again, Love.*

Olivia: *Later. XOXO*

Olivia fell asleep quickly that night. After midnight, she felt Alexander crawl in next to her. She could smell the alcohol on his breath.

"Livia, you smell great," he slurred. He was definitely drunk.

He snuggled into the girl sleeping next to him, his front to her back, wrapping his legs around hers. She felt his bare chest on her back, savoring the warmth of his body. His breathing became even, a perfect lullaby to fall back asleep to. When

Olivia was in that place between being asleep and being awake, she heard him whisper, "I'm going to protect you always, Olibia."

Her eyes flung open. She must have been dreaming about the crash again. The only person that had ever called her Olibia was the boy with the green eyes. The boy who haunted her dreams. She brushed it off and closed her eyes, dreaming of beautiful green eyes and the man sleeping next to her.

~~~~~~~~~~~

Olivia's alarm went off bright and early the following morning at five. She turned it off, hitting the snooze button. Alexander pulled her back to him. "Don't go, angel," he begged, his voice raspy from sleep.

"I don't want to, but I have to teach a six a.m. class today." Olivia nuzzled up to him, placing several kisses on his chest. He flipped her on her back and held her arms above her head with one hand, caressing the side of her body with his other.

"Well, I just need to give you something to think about the rest of the day then." He grinned, planting a deep kiss on her lips and lifting her tank top over her head.

"Olivia," he growled, gawking at her bare chest. It didn't matter how many times he had seen her with her shirt off. Each time still excited him as if it was the first. "It's almost like you were plucked from heaven just for me." He truly believed she was. He loved her since the day she was born. Even as a child, he loved making her happy. Because when she was happy, she would smile. And when she smiled, his heart would melt.

Alexander kissed her neck, savoring the taste of her soft skin as he moved his way down her chest. His breath was warm on her breast, making her nipple become alert. He teased it, tugging and licking. Olivia was about to become unhinged as his tongue circled her chest. She wanted that tongue on other parts of her body. She was on edge after not having an orgasm the day before and felt like she was ready to fall apart in a matter of seconds.

236

He slowly made his way down her stomach, lifting her butt so he could slip off her shorts. He lowered himself between her legs, Olivia's breathing heavy with anticipation. She moaned when he gave her clit a quick lick.

"You like that, Olivia?"

She nodded her head, not able to make a sound.

"I said, do you like that, Olivia?" he asked sternly.

"Yes," she replied, having trouble breathing through all the overwhelming sensations coursing through her body.

"Well, what should I do about that, Olivia? What do you want?"

"I want you. Now."

Alexander was being coy. He wanted to hear Olivia beg for him. He needed to hear it.

"I want your tongue on me. On my clit," she directed him.

He started gliding his tongue slowly over her swollen nub, sucking and licking gently.

"Is that all, Olivia?" His breath on her made her moan.

"I want your fingers inside me."

"Your wish is my command." He gently pressed a finger inside of her, making circular motions as he licked. Olivia's body was on fire from the electricity flowing through her core. "God, you taste sweet, Love," he said, taking a break before diving back in. "One of these days I'm going to make you fuck my face." His words were her undoing and she screamed out his name as waves of pleasure overtook her body.

He crawled back up to her and stared at the beautiful woman laying panting on her bed. Olivia was utterly spent. He propped himself on his elbow, kissing her. She deepened the kiss, invading his mouth with her tongue as she threw him on his back and straddled him, grinding against him, her breathing still uneven from her last mind-blowing orgasm.

"Say it, Olivia."

She knew what he wanted her to say. "No," she whispered into his ear. "You say it."

"So, it's a game then, is it?" She could feel his arousal getting harder. "Well, I must tell you, angel. I am very competitive. I'll do almost anything to win, including playing dirty."

She liked the sound of that. "Oh, really?" she asked with her eyebrow raised. "How dirty?"

"Oh, wouldn't you like to find out?" He flipped her onto her back and, stripping off his clothes, knelt between her legs, teasing her with his erection. "What do you want Olivia? I know what I want, but I just want to make sure we're on the same page."

"Oh, we're on the same page, Alexander," she smirked.

"Well, I wouldn't want to be presumptuous," Alexander replied, continuing to tease Olivia. She was still a bundle of sensation. Just the feeling of his arousal against her sex was turning her on.

"Fuck, Alexander," she exhaled, her breathing rapid as she stared at him, a devilish smile on his face. "OKAY!" Olivia screamed. "You win! I want you to fuck me!"

He slammed into her, groaning out. "I love when you say that, Olivia" he said, pumping into her, a fast rhythm.

Olivia wrapped her legs around his waist, deepening the sensation, and moved with the pace Alexander set.

"God, Olivia. There is nothing like being inside of you," he said, leaning down, softly licking and sucking on her neck.

She moaned out, the sensation of him being inside of her and licking her making her nerves stand on end. She still hadn't come down from her previous orgasm and felt like she was going to explode.

"Do you like me inside of you?" he asked, thrusting harder.

"Yes, Alexander. Yes," she breathed out, climbing higher and higher toward the peak she had just come down from.

"Say I'm the only one that's filled you like this," he commanded, his breathing becoming more and more erratic as he leaned back and stared deep into her eyes, his pace increasing.

Olivia could tell he was close. So she gave him what he wanted to hear. She wasn't lying. "You're the only one, Alex," she replied, moving with his rhythm, a familiar clenching sensation building through her core.

He felt it and nuzzled back into her neck, inhaling her

delicious scent. "Come with me, Olivia," Alexander grunted. He emptied inside of her, the warm feeling putting Olivia over the edge. She shuddered around him, screaming out his name in ecstasy.

His eyes met hers as they came down from their orgasms, their breathing slowly returning to normal. "I will never tire of being naked with you, Love," he said sweetly before feathering his lips against hers. She pulled his head toward hers, running her hands through his sexy morning hair, and deepened the kiss.

He slowly withdrew from her and picked her up, tossing her off the bed. "Shower, now," he growled, slapping her ass.

She jumped. "God. You can be so bossy."

"Oh, Miss Adler. You haven't seen bossy yet."

She laughed as she jumped in the shower, knowing she would probably be late for her first class that morning. When she came out, Alexander was sitting in her bed with his laptop, typing an e-mail and drinking coffee. He left a coffee for her on her nightstand. It all seemed so domesticated. And it didn't scare Olivia at all.

CHAPTER TWENTY-SEVEN

IN DEEP

"Libby!" Kiera shouted when Olivia walked into the empty pilates studio a few minutes before six that morning.

"Hey, Kiera. What's going on?"

"Not much. We need to catch up. I feel like I haven't seen you much lately, except for Friday nights. Do I have to start booking my time through Alexander? He's hogging you!"

"I know. I'm sorry. I'm free around nine if you want to grab coffee."

"I can do that," Kiera said.

"Great! It's a date." Olivia turned to boot up the audio system for the class.

The first three classes flew by and, before she knew it, Olivia was heading out to meet Kiera.

"Hey, Libby," Jerry said when he saw Olivia run from the elevator into the building's lobby. "Heading out?"

"Yeah. Meeting Kiera for coffee. I'll be back soon."

"Okay. Just tell Mr. Burnham, please. He'll have my ass on a platter if I don't tell him."

Olivia rolled her eyes as she continued past the security desk. "Okay, Jerry. I'll send him a text right now."

She grabbed her cell phone out of her purse and shot off a quick text to Alexander.

Olivia: *Heading out for coffee with Kiera. Back soon. XOXO.*

She felt her phone buzz as she turned the block, making her way through a crowd of people strolling the busy Boston streets on that sunny fall day. She read the text as she reached the neighborhood Starbucks.

Alexander: *Okay. Be safe. Carter will be on watch.*

Olivia groaned. He was so frustrating sometimes.

Olivia: *I haven't agreed to accept your bodyguard services yet, Mr. Burnham. ;-)*

Alexander: *Humor me, Love.*

There was that word again. Olivia didn't think she would ever tire of hearing that word fall out of his mouth. Even via text, she could just hear his lips caressing the word as he whispered in her ear. She began breathing heavy as she stood in line to order her coffee. She immediately snapped back to reality and returned Alexander's text when the barista asked for her order.

Olivia: *Fine. :-P*

Olivia dropped her phone in her purse and ordered two coffees while she waited for her friend. A few minutes later, Kiera walked into the shop, making her way toward Olivia's table.

"Hey, Libs," she said, sitting down as Olivia pushed the coffee cup toward her. "Thank God. I don't think there's enough caffeine in the world to get me through this day." She took a long drag of her drink.

"That bad, huh?"

"Yeah. Well, I had a late night last night, so I need it."

"Oh really? What were you doing?" Olivia raised her eyebrows.

"None of your business, slut. So what's going on with you and Alexander?"

"Not a whole lot, except he's still wonderful," Olivia blushed, looking at her friend.

"Okay, spill it."

Olivia hesitated and then told her all about her run-in with Adele the previous day. "God, it felt so good to just punch that bitch. I was proud of myself for not running. A year ago, if the same thing happened, I would have run as far as I could to avoid dealing with it. But yesterday, I just don't know what came over me. I knew she was talking shit and, well, she deserved it."

Kiera laughed. "That's fantastic. Maybe you've finally stopped trying to push Alexander away. He is definitely quite the catch." Kiera took another sip of her coffee. "So, he's going with you this weekend to Newport?"

"Yup."

"Nervous?"

"Yeah. A little. I mean, we're going away together for the weekend so there's nowhere for me to run to when things get bad."

"Oh, stop it. You're so negative. Things aren't going to get bad. He's going there to support you in your race. It's a big deal. Not everyone can run a marathon."

"I know," Olivia replied, nervously tapping her nails against the black bistro table. "But I've never gone away with a guy before. I am looking forward to spending some time with him away from the city. We've only done things around here, and most of the time lately we've just been going to his place. He feels better knowing that he's close to me. For some reason he's still all worried about Simon. Which reminds me…" Olivia said, sipping her coffee and lowering her voice.

"What is it?" Kiera asked, her interest piqued.

"I got a call from the D.A. yesterday. I guess Simon took a plea deal. He's pleading guilty to a lesser charge of assault and will serve about a year in jail. But with his lack of priors and over-crowding, they're saying he'll probably be out sooner."

"Hmmm…" Kiera said, looking at her friend. "How do you feel about that?"

Olivia glared at Kiera. She knew how much Olivia hated that question.

"Okay, okay. I'm sorry, Libs," she said, winking at a man

dressed in a business suit as he walked past their table to order his morning coffee. "I just want to make sure you're okay with it."

"I am okay with it," Olivia admitted. "What Simon did was wrong, but I just don't think I handled the break-up, if you can call it that, the right way and he snapped. I'm not making excuses for him, but he didn't seem like the violent type. So I'm sure this is the only time he'll ever be in prison, ya know? He made a mistake and he's paying for it. It's all good."

"Well, okay. As long as you're good with that."

"I am."

"So, getting back to Alexander all worried about Simon."

"Oh, yeah. He's still concerned about someone attacking me. It's sweet, but at the same time a little overbearing."

"I could see that." Kiera paused for a moment. "Have you ever thought that maybe he's hiding something from you? I mean, he runs a private security firm and has the ability to get any information he wanted. Maybe he found out something that has him on edge a bit."

"I don't know what he'd possibly find out. No one out there has any reason to want to come after me, so…"

"Yeah. I guess you're right." Kiera looked at her watch.

"Crap. I need to get to the office. I have a meeting with some new client about publishing their manuscript. I barely read the damn thing so this will be interesting." Kiera stood up and Olivia joined her, clutching her coffee.

"Well, you are the queen of bullshit. I'm sure you'll do just fine." Olivia laughed as she opened the door, leaving the coffee shop. She noticed Carter standing on the sidewalk and waved.

The two girls walked toward Olivia's office building, Kiera's being just a few blocks past that.

"So, what's with the bodyguard?" Kiera muttered under her breath.

"One word. Alexander," Olivia said. "He can be very domineering sometimes."

"Oh, I bet he can," Kiera laughed. "He looks like the type that would be into tying you up and having his way with you."

Olivia blushed. "KIERA!" she exclaimed, slapping her

friend.

Kiera looked at Olivia, her face bright red.

"Oh my God. I knew it! He's into that shit, isn't he?" The two girls stopped walking. "I mean, he's not fucked up and into beating you is he? Because that shit is so not cool. But hell, I'd go for being tied up and blindfolded."

"I am not having this conversation with you on the street." Olivia continued walking, a grin on her face, thinking about the previous morning.

"Dude. That is so fucking hot," Kiera laughed as she ran to catch up with her friend.

"Okay, you're right. It is so fucking hot." Olivia's face was flushed from the memories of Alexander restraining her.

"I bet it is."

"And he gets turned on when I call him Mr. Burnham," Olivia said, smiling.

"That's sexy. I'd call him Mr. Burnham. *Yes, Mr. Burnham. Whatever you want Mr. Burnham,*" Kiera said breathlessly, giggling. "I so need to find a man like that. I want to be dominated."

"It's not like that. It's almost as if he knows that I need that sometimes. And other times, he's so sweet and gentle."

"So sometimes you fuck and sometimes you make love."

Olivia froze in her place. "No, Kiera. We don't make love. That would entail…"

"What?" Kiera asked, interrupting Olivia. "That would mean you love him. And he loves you. And it's true. So the sooner you admit that to yourself, the sooner you can move past it. Stop freaking out. I see the way he is with you. Why do you think he feels the need to protect you? Because you're some girl he's banging? Hell no. Because he loves you."

"I don't think so."

"Fine, whatever. Keep denying it. You love him. Deep down. You may not realize it just yet, but you will. You're in deep already, girly, though I know you're scared to death to admit it. But you need to realize that your fear of getting close to people is not real. It's merely a product of choice, of thoughts that your mind has created. So get the fuck over yourself, Olivia, and let yourself be happy for once. Because no matter what happens, you are going to get hurt in life. But it's so much better to have jumped into the ocean and gotten stung by a jellyfish than to never have felt the salt water between your toes at all." Kiera turned and walked away, leaving her speechless.

Olivia walked through the front doors of her building and hurried to the elevator, wanting to get back to her office and some sense of normalcy, even though nothing had been normal about her life since she met Alexander Burnham. He entered her life in a whirlwind and had quickly implanted himself in nearly every facet of her existence. She thought about him every second of every day. And Olivia didn't know how she felt about that.

CHAPTER TWENTY-EIGHT

SOMETHING MORE

"Cheryl, I need some good news," Donovan said into his phone.

"I wish I had some, boss. We're getting there. He has Carter on an unofficial protection detail as of now. She noticed Matthew following her yesterday. It was good that he made it so obvious. That's got Burnham spooked."

"Yes, but I was hoping he'd assign you to the protection detail."

"I know. I'm working on that. But as of now, there's no official detail anyway. From what I've been able to find out, she seems hesitant to agree to it, thinking it's entirely unnecessary."

"Well, do something to make it necessary," Donovan growled into the phone.

"Yes, sir." Cheryl hung up and threw her burner phone into the nearest trash bin. She walked to a nearby drug store and bought a replacement.

~~~~~~~~~~~

"Hello, Mr. Burnham," Olivia crooned into her phone.

"Good afternoon, Miss Adler. Come to my place after practice at Mo's tonight?"

"Is that a question or an order?" she asked as she sat at the desk in her office, looking out the window at the bustling Boston streets below.

Alexander chuckled, listening to Olivia's voice, happy to

break the monotony of pouring over case files. "Maybe a little of both. We'll order sushi and watch a few movies. Take it easy. Keep you off your feet. You'll be pounding the pavement pretty hard this weekend."

"That's not the only thing I want to pound hard this weekend," Olivia said coyly.

Alexander inhaled quickly at her words, feeling a familiar twitching in his pants before regaining his composure. "Be there at seven, Love. And be ready to leave direct from my place tomorrow when we get up."

"So demanding."

"Don't you know it. Till then, Olivia..."

"Bye, Mr. Burnham."

"Good-bye, Miss Adler."

She hung up, collected her items, and headed out of her office. She sent Kiera a quick text reminding her to check on Nepenthe over the next few days.

"Bye, Libby! Have fun this weekend and good luck!" Melanie said as Olivia walked out the front doors of the wellness center.

"Thanks, Mel. See you next week."

When Olivia walked out of her building a few minutes later, a black SUV pulled up front.

"You've got to be kidding me," she mumbled under her breath.

"Miss Adler," Carter said, running around to open the rear passenger side door.

"Good afternoon, Carter," she said curtly as she stared into the passenger compartment of the SUV, hesitant about getting in. If she did, she was more or less agreeing to Alexander's ridiculous protection detail.

"Please, Miss Adler. It's just a ride home."

Olivia looked at her watch and noticed she was already running late. "Fine. But only because I'm short on time."

"Thank you, Miss Adler."

Olivia was home in record time and, after Carter did a quick sweep of her house, she began packing for her big weekend.

That evening, rehearsal with the band went by fairly

quickly. Before Olivia knew it, she was on her way over to Alexander's penthouse, courtesy of her chauffeur, Carter. She wasn't in the mood to start a fight with him, not when they were going away for the weekend. If he was providing her with her own personal driver for the evening, so be it.

"Olivia," Alexander said, rushing to her when he saw her walk through the foyer. She was dressed casually in a pair of jeans and a tee shirt, but she still made Alexander's heart skip a beat whenever she was near. He planted a long kiss on her lips. "Have I told you how much I missed you today?"

"Maybe once or twice, but you can tell me again." Olivia stared into his green eyes, reveling in the warmth coming off his body. He must have just gotten out of the shower. His hair was wet and he smelled of body wash and aftershave. He had changed out of his normal office attire and was wearing a white polo shirt and a pair of jeans.

"I missed you. I missed your eyes." His thumb ran over the corner of Olivia's eyes. "I missed your lips." He brought his mouth to hers, kissing her softly. "And I most certainly missed your tongue." He kissed her again, coaxing her mouth open as his tongue danced with hers before pulling back, leaving her completely breathless.

"Come, Love. Sushi has arrived." He led her down the hallway into the den. It was a spacious and homey room with a large pool table set in the far corner. Immediately in front of Olivia was a luxurious leather sofa and a giant flat screen TV. It was the one room of the penthouse that didn't appear to belong in a museum. Walking over to the couch, she noticed that Alexander had set up a small feast worth of sushi on the large coffee table. Runner sat next to the table, anxious for scraps. When he saw Olivia, he immediately ran up to her, his tail wagging.

"Hey, boy. Good to see you, too. Give mama kisses." She leaned down so Runner could give her a few kisses on her cheek.

They sat on the oversized couch and Alexander put on *Casablanca* as Runner sat back down, anxious for some food to be thrown his way. Alexander, being a total sucker for that dog, fed him the occasional piece of sushi when Olivia wasn't looking.

"I love this movie," Olivia said, her mouth full of yellowtail.

"I know."

"You do?" she asked, scrunching her eyebrows in confusion.

"Yeah. You mentioned it once and I just kind of remembered," Alexander replied nervously.

"I don't remember that. Oh well," she shrugged.

Olivia hadn't told him how much she loved the movie. Not since she was a kid. Alexander remembered sitting in the living room of his family's house with Olivia when they were younger and they would always watch *Casablanca*. Olivia couldn't understand what was happening in the movie, but she always loved the look on Ingrid Bergman's face when she looked at Humphrey Bogart. It was the look of true love.

She smiled at Alexander, leaned over, and gave him a quick kiss on his cheek.

He turned to look at her, his grin touching his eyes. "What was that for?"

"Nothing. I just love this movie." The look on Alexander's face at her words made her heart melt. She stared at him, their eyes not breaking from each other for several long moments. Runner walked over and started licking Olivia's hand, making her laugh. "Silly dog," she said, returning her attention to the sushi feast sitting in front of her.

They finished their dinner just as Ilsa asked Sam to play *As Time Goes By*. Alexander snuggled up next to Olivia, lying down next to her on the couch, his front to her back, and he sang along with Sam.

Olivia giggled as he kissed her neck. There was something so familiar about what they were doing, but she couldn't put her finger on it. It was as if she had been there before, had watched that movie with Alexander before, and he had sung those words to her before. But that couldn't have happened. She had only known Alexander for a few months. She shook off the feeling and settled in to watch the remainder of the movie.

Gently caressing her stomach underneath her tee shirt, Alexander shifted Olivia onto her back and hovered over her, gazing into her deep brown eyes, not saying a word.

"What?" Olivia asked, trying to break the tension.

"I just like looking at you. You're the most beautiful woman in the world."

Olivia blushed and turned her head to stare at the flat screen television, not really paying attention to the movie.

"Look at me, Olivia." She continued to stare at the television. "Come on, Love. Don't you realize how beautiful you are?"

She faced Alexander. "More beautiful than Plastic Surgery Barbie?"

He let out a laugh as he nuzzled against her, inhaling her scent. "Much more beautiful than her. Your beauty comes natural." He pulled back, gazing deep into her eyes. "She probably shelled out millions of dollars to look the way she does." He leaned down and kissed her lips softly. "Why do you get so shy when I give you compliments?"

"I don't know. I just don't take them so well, I guess. I mean, I'm not the most hideous thing on the planet," she laughed. "But, look at you. You're fucking hot."

Alexander laughed. "You think so, do you?"

"Hell to the fucking yes. You could have your pick of any woman out there who I'm sure wouldn't put you through half the drama I put you through…"

"Yes. But I want to be with you, Olivia." He trailed soft kisses along her collarbone. "It's you, Olivia. It's only ever been you," he whispered quietly.

His words caused an overwhelming sensation to surge through her core. She wrapped her legs around Alexander's waist and pulled his head to hers, crushing his lips with her own.

He pulled back briefly. "What made you change your ways, sweetheart?"

Olivia looked up at him. "What do you mean?"

Alexander rolled onto his side and Olivia followed, facing him, as he continued to caress her body from her hips to her shoulder. She loved his touch. Even a simple innocent stroke sent heat throughout her body. "I mean, when we first met, you mentioned how you always did the no-strings-attached thing. So why me?"

Olivia raised her hands to her face and covered it, not wanting to talk about her feelings. Her feelings petrified her.

"Look at me, Olivia," he demanded, pulling her hands away from her face and clutching them in his own. "I'm just trying to figure out what makes you tick. That's all."

"I could ask you the same question, Alexander," she replied.

He smiled. "Well, that's easy. I was waiting to find you. And once I did, I knew you were someone I wanted to get to know more than just a quick fuck." His words were actually true. He had been waiting to find his Olivia. "Your turn, Miss Adler."

"I don't know, Alexander," Olivia exhaled loudly. "I don't know if it was any one thing. We kept running into each other randomly. It was almost like someone was sending me a sign. And there was this feeling I had. I was so comfortable with you after spending just a short time with you. That's why I told you all about my parents' deaths. It normally takes me forever to open up to anyone, but there was something about you. I felt as if I had known you my entire life."

Alexander growled as he flipped Olivia onto her back. "Oh, darling. I felt the same way."

Olivia looked into Alexander's eyes and did her best Ingrid Bergman impression. *"Kiss me. Kiss me as if it were the last time."* She reached up and grabbed his face, forcing his mouth to hers, their tongues doing a frenzied dance. Olivia's body was on fire, her passion for the man on top of her at a fevered pitch.

He worshipped her body, caressing and nipping from her neck down her sternum, lifting her shirt over the top of her head. He gazed into her eyes, the dominating man she was so accustomed to nowhere to be seen. Instead, there was a look of affection, or maybe, just maybe, something more.

Alexander pulled her nipple into his mouth, sucking tenderly. Olivia let out a quiet cry.

"Do you like that?" He looked up at Olivia briefly before he moved to the other nipple.

She moaned again, bucking her hips, her body alert with

sensation.

Alexander grinned. "I'll take that as a yes."

Olivia pulled greedily at his tee shirt.

"Always so needy, Miss Adler. Patience, my Love," he whispered as he lowered down her body, licking her stomach, kissing her waist. "Let me worship you."

Olivia moaned again, her senses on overload. She bucked her hips once more, telling him to take off her jeans. Alexander smiled and obeyed the command Olivia gave with her body, unbuttoning her jeans and slowly unzipping them.

"God, Alex, you're killing me," she breathed, throwing her arm over her head. Blood coursed through her veins, lighting her body on fire from his touch.

"I told you already. Patience, darling."

Olivia exhaled before pushing Alexander off her into a sitting position, straddling him. "I'm done being patient," she growled. She reached for his shirt and yanked it over his head. Her eyes took in the beautiful man. She could feel his erection through his jeans as she circled her hips around his waist and kissed his neck.

"Oh, no you don't," Alexander said, flipping Olivia onto her back. "I'm driving." He unbuttoned his jeans and carefully stepped out of them.

"You like the control, don't you?" Olivia asked when Alexander climbed on top of her.

"Yes. And you like it when I'm in control, don't you?"

Olivia stared at Alexander, deep in thought.

He grabbed both her arms and pinned them over her head with one of his hands. "I know you do, Miss Adler. You love it when I tell you what to do."

Olivia blushed and turned her head to see the Germans invading France in the movie.

"Now's not the time to turn shy on me, Olivia. Say it. You like it when I'm controlling you."

"Yes. I do," she replied quietly. "It turns me on like I've never been turned on before." Her heart raced with anticipation, his brilliant eyes boring holes through her soul.

"Good girl," he said. "Now, remember what I like."

"Yes, Mr. Burnham."

"Oh God, Olivia," Alexander exclaimed, pushing into her, making her moan. But unlike so many other times, he went slow, his motions deliberate, filling her to the brim with pleasure and then slowly withdrawing before continuing with the same movement.

He was in control, but that time felt so different. It was as if he was trying to tell Olivia something with the way he entered her, planting kisses all over her body. She ran her fingers through his unruly hair and pulled his lips to hers. She knew she was falling for that man, but refused to admit it to herself or anyone else.

Her heart swelled with a strange emotion. She felt so fulfilled, she thought she might cry. Alexander was pushing her closer and closer to the edge with each slow movement inside her and her body began to quiver beneath his.

She drew his tongue into her mouth, the sensation of his lips on her mouth and him inside her a sensory overload. He retreated, pulling her bottom lip between his teeth, softly nipping it, sending her over the edge. She came undone, the aftershocks of her orgasm trembling around him as he found his own release.

Alexander continued to push gently into her until the last of her tremors ceased. He looked into Olivia's dark eyes, his breathing irregular.

"That was amazing," Olivia said. And it had been. She had never felt so fulfilled in her entire life. It was so much more than just sex. It was so much more than anything Olivia had ever experienced in her entire life. She thought that she may have found someone she could possibly spend the rest of her life with. And the thought scared her. She immediately wanted to run as far away as she could, but Kiera's words sounded in her head, telling her to just dive in.

She pulled Alexander's mouth back to her own, kissing him deeply and passionately.

"It was pretty fucking great," Alexander responded, his breathing still rapid. He slid off Olivia and positioned her on her side, facing the television again, his front to her back. He grabbed a blanket off the back of the couch and threw it over their naked bodies.

"Watch the rest of the movie, Love," Alexander whispered as he held Olivia in his arms. Within moments, she drifted off, feeling too exhausted to run.

~~~~~~~~~~~

Same dream again. The crash. The green-eyed boy. The boy getting knocked out. But instead of seeing black as Olivia normally did, she remained conscious. She saw the green-eyed boy fall to the ground and then stared into the eyes of a man. His eyes were blue and cold and he sneered as he moved toward Olivia in the SUV. Then a loud bang. The blue-eyed man fell to the ground, blood streaming from his head. Olivia screamed.

She heard footsteps running toward the car and she inched away from the open rear driver's side car door.

"Thomas! Help me with the body! We've got to get him back in his car!" Olivia knew that voice. It was her father's voice. She tried to call out to him, but couldn't.

"Jack! Let me take care of it. You're hurt. You need to get in the car! Now!" It was Olivia's Uncle Charles' voice.

"I can do it. Just help me."

"Get in the car and check on your Olivia. Get my son in the car, too. You're losing a lot of blood and you won't do much good to me if you pass out now. So move!"

Olivia opened her eyes when the green-eyed boy was placed in the car next to her.

"Olivia, are you okay?" her father asked.

She simply nodded, tears streaming down her face.

"Don't worry, Livvy. Stop crying," he said. "Everything will be okay." Her father closed the rear driver's side door and climbed in the front. He reclined the seat as far as he could and closed his eyes. "Everything will be okay. Your uncle is going to fix everything, I promise." It sounded like he was saying that more for himself than anything else.

There was a loud explosion and her parents' crashed car blew to pieces. Jack's eyes flung open as Thomas came running toward the SUV. The driver's side door opened.

"Where's Mary?" Jack asked, frantically looking at the car engulfed in

254

flames.

Thomas hesitated.

"Where's Mary, Thomas?" Jack asked firmly.

Thomas lowered his head, shaking it.

Jack cried out. "NO! No, Thomas. We need to go back for her!"

"No, Jack. It's useless. She's gone."

Jack covered his face with his hands and his body shook. Thomas turned around and met Olivia's eyes. But it was her Uncle Charles. Why was her father calling him Thomas?

"I'll take care of you, Olivia. I promise you that," Thomas said.

Olivia heard her father moan, apparently from pain.

"Shit!" Thomas said as Jack passed out. "We better get out of here." Thomas turned the ignition on the car and sped down the road.

Olivia cried until she slipped into unconsciousness.

~~~~~~~~~~~

"Olivia. Wake up. You're crying," Alexander said, shaking Olivia awake. She woke up suddenly, tears streaming down her face as she tried to catch her breath.

"Darling, are you okay? You were dreaming and muttering something about your father, I think. And then you started to cry."

Olivia sat up and took in the room around her. She was in the den at Alexander's place. They were watching *Casablanca* and then had amazing, mind-blowing sex. And then she fell asleep. It was after the accident. She was in the car. Someone shot the man that knocked out the green-eyed boy. Her Uncle Charles was there, but was going by the name of Thomas. And her father was alive. He made it out of the car wreck. And then he passed out.

"Please, Olivia. Talk to me. Was it the same dream again?"

Olivia stood up and walked over to her tee shirt and jeans. She pulled them back on, not wanting to feel so exposed anymore.

"Yeah," she said, wiping the tears from her face. "That's all it was. Just the same old stupid dream again. Every night of my fucking existence, reliving that crash over and over."

Alexander sat up and stared at Olivia, the room eerily silent.

"Bullshit," he said, breaking the silence.

"What did you say?" she asked, glaring at him.

"You heard me. I'm calling bullshit, Olivia."

She stared at him wide-eyed, her mouth agape.

"If you think I'm believing that lie, you obviously think very poorly of my abilities."

Olivia started to walk out of the den, not wanting to have that conversation. Alexander jumped off the couch and blocked her exit, distracting her with his very naked, very aroused body.

"You're using your body as a weapon, Alex," Olivia whimpered.

"I don't mean to, Love. And if you don't want to talk about it now, that's fine. I understand. But you need to trust me. Trust that I'm not going anywhere and no matter what you say to me, I'm staying put. Next to your side." He pulled her close. "It's where I'm meant to be."

She relaxed into his embrace, cherishing the closeness of his arms.

"Bed?" he asked after several moments passed.

Olivia looked up at Alexander and nodded. He bent down, swept her into his arms, and carried her out of the den.

"Alexander Burnham! You're naked!" Olivia screeched.

"I know. That's why I love living alone," he said, kissing her on the mouth.

Olivia giggled as he carried her up the stairs and into his bedroom, the dream now a distant memory.

CHAPTER TWENTY-NINE

THE OLIVIA

"Wake up, Olivia. Time to get moving," Alexander said, nudging Olivia awake the following morning.

She rolled over onto her stomach, trying to block out the sunlight, and groaned. "I don't want to. I want to stay in this nice soft bed and never get out of it."

Alexander smiled. "Well, that's a nice thought." He leaned down and nuzzled her neck. "I could think of a few things we could do. Maybe I'll just tie you to the bed and never let you out."

"That would be great," she retorted sleepily, still not wanting to open her eyes.

"I agree, but you've got a marathon to run on Sunday. Get your ass up so we can have breakfast before we hit the road."

"Make me," she said, a hint of snarkiness in her voice.

Alexander looked down at Olivia sprawled out on his bed, her naked body covered only by a thin sheet. He pulled the sheet back, exposing her soft flesh. She turned her head to look at him as he stood over her wearing a pair of boxer briefs. "You're going to have to do a lot better than that to get me out of this bed, Mr. Burnham." She closed her eyes, returning her head to the pillow.

"Oh really? Is that a challenge, Miss Adler?"

Olivia giggled. "You bet it is. Give me your best shot."

Alexander crawled on the bed and hovered over her, shivers running through her body at the closeness of his body to hers. She turned to look at him once more, wondering what he was doing.

"Face forward, Olivia." His voice was stern and demanding. It turned her on.

"Yes, sir," she mocked, a hint of sarcasm in her voice.

"I love how snarky you are in the morning."

He stared at Olivia's ass and slapped it hard. She jumped and yelped out. It hurt a little, but it caused her heart to race even faster.

Alexander plunged a finger inside her. "God, you're so wet, Love. Does spanking turn you on?"

Olivia turned her head again to look back at Alexander.

"What did I tell you, Olivia?"

"Sorry," she gulped, turning her head back.

"Sorry, what?"

"Sorry, Mr. Burnham."

"Good girl," he said, sliding another finger inside of her. "Now, tell me, do you like getting spanked?"

"Yes," Olivia replied breathlessly. Alexander slapped her ass again even harder.

"Yes, what?" he growled.

"Yes, Mr. Burnham," she said, raising her ass off the bed, squirming with pleasure.

"Do you have any idea how beautiful you look from this view? God, Love. Your ass was made for me," he exhaled, caressing her bottom. He removed his fingers from inside her before she felt Alexander get off the bed.

He walked over to the writing desk in the far corner of the bedroom. "Olivia, come here," he commanded sternly.

She turned her head and slowly got out of the bed, making her way over to where Alexander stood.

"I want you to lean over the desk here and hold on to the sides. Do you understand?"

"Yes," Olivia replied, bending her body over so her stomach was lying on the desk.

Alexander slapped Olivia's ass again. "Yes, what?" he barked.

"Yes, Mr. Burnham," Olivia whimpered, looking back at Alexander, relishing the severe look on his face.

Alexander slapped her ass again. "What did I tell you? Keep

your eyes forward."

Olivia snapped her head forward before she felt Alexander lower his shorts. He plunged into her from behind, a sudden invasion.

"Fuck," Olivia screamed out as he thrust into her, setting a punishing rhythm.

"I'm not going to last long this morning, Olivia," Alexander said, reaching around to touch her clit.

"If you keep doing that, either will I," she breathed out.

"Good, Love. Good." Alexander's breathing became heavy and labored. Olivia was happy that the sweet, caring side of Alexander was nowhere to be found that morning. She needed him like this, not affectionate. The affectionate side scared her. She needed the dominant side of Alexander. The one that told her what to do. The one that stayed in control. Because she felt as though she was losing control of the very thing she said she would guard with her life. Her heart.

"Come with me, Olivia," Alexander said when he felt her begin to tense around him. She closed her eyes and immediately spiraled down, her orgasm coursing through her entire being. He thrust a few more times and then emptied into her.

He stood, holding Olivia's hips as their breathing regulated. Once they both caught their breath, Alexander withdrew from her, leaving her exposed on the writing desk.

"Told you I could get you out of that bed, Love." Alexander winked.

"You jerk," Olivia joked, running to attack Alexander. They playfully fought until Alexander caught Olivia around the waist and drew her to him.

"I love waking up next to you," he said, kissing her full on the mouth.

Her heart raced at his words. "You're not so bad yourself," she replied.

"Okay. Shower now." Alexander slapped Olivia's ass one last time, making her jump.

After they showered, Olivia quickly got ready and headed downstairs where Alexander sat at the kitchen island, reading the newspaper. Runner sat by his side, anxiously waiting for table scraps even though there was no food being eaten.

"Runner, nobody likes a beggar. Just because we're sitting at the breakfast bar doesn't mean that we're eating." The dog twisted his head at Alexander.

"Oh, come here, boy," Olivia said, walking over to the kitchen counter. She opened a cookie jar and took out a treat. "Here you go." Runner sat, wagging his tail, waiting for Olivia to hand him the treat. He gently took it in his mouth and ran off to enjoy his doggie biscuit.

"What would you like for breakfast?" Olivia asked as she made herself a cup of coffee.

"Please, allow me," Alexander replied, standing up and ushering Olivia out of the kitchen. "You go relax and I'll take care of breakfast." He placed a kiss on her cheek and walked her into the living room. "Stay off those feet. You've got quite a few miles to run this weekend." He winked before turning and heading back to the kitchen.

Olivia gazed at Alexander as he made his way through the kitchen, pulling a few pans out. Over the past few months, Alexander had become accustomed to Olivia's tastes in food. She ate relatively healthy, liking to splurge on something decadent once in a while. It was a big weekend for her, so he made her one of her favorite breakfasts: egg white omelette with tofu, broccoli, mushrooms, spinach, and feta cheese.

"This is fantastic," she complimented a few minutes later as she sat at the breakfast bar next to Alexander, savoring the taste of her meal.

"I'm glad you like it," Alexander replied. "Are you looking forward to getting out of town for the weekend?"

Olivia took another bite of her omelette. "Actually, I am. I've never been to Newport before."

He stared at her, wide-eyed. She really had no idea about her past. "Oh really?" he asked after a long pause, trying to gather his thoughts.

"Yeah. Weird, I know. I've lived in Boston off and on for almost the last decade and I've never been to Newport. So it will be nice to have the extra time there to walk around a bit.

You've been before, I'm assuming?"

"Um, yeah, I have." Alexander remembered when Olivia mentioned she would be going to Newport that coming weekend. He didn't know what to think about that. Olivia still had some family in Newport, mainly on her mother's side. What if someone recognized her? He knew it was nearly impossible that someone would recognize this beautiful twenty-seven-year-old woman as that same six-year-old little girl who died in a car crash, but that still didn't settle his nerves.

Regardless, Alexander was worried being back in Newport could trigger some more memories and he wanted to be there to do damage control if it did. He felt guilty for keeping the truth from her, but maybe that was what had been keeping her alive.

~~~~~~~~~~

"Holy crap. This is a great car," Olivia exclaimed, getting into the passenger side of Alexander's Maserati Gran Tourismo convertible after packing their things and making their way to the basement garage of his building.

"Well, it's supposed to be a great weekend, so I figure we might as well take the convertible."

"I think the valet guys are going to cream themselves when you pull up with this bad boy," Olivia joked.

"I love how you sometimes speak like a trucker. Glad all that private school education and those etiquette classes paid off," Alexander laughed.

"Yeah, sure. I hated all that shit in high school. It was ridiculous. Imagine if my head mistress could see me now. Slumming it on Comm. Ave. in Boston. Oh, the horror," Olivia joked, knowing she lived in one of the most upscale areas of Boston.

Alexander pulled onto I-93 heading south and they rode most of the way to Newport in relative silence, the wind making it difficult to hold a conversation without shouting. He drove through the harbor town and gradually made his way down America's Cup Boulevard before pulling into a marina.

"Where are we?" Olivia asked.

"We're at the marina," Alexander replied, smirking.

"Well, I figured that much, smartass. But what are we doing here?"

"You'll see." Alexander had a huge grin on his face as he pulled up to an awning attached to a building that read "Newport Yacht Club." He threw the keys to the valet and instructed him to hold the car there for someone to come for the bags.

"What are you up to, Alex?" Olivia asked.

Alexander grabbed her hand and pulled her into his body. "Patience, Love," he whispered.

He led her down a dock as she gazed over the beautiful crystal water and all the boats. Stunning yachts lined the docks, the size of each one mesmerizing Olivia. She couldn't even fathom how much one of them would cost to buy and then maintain. That was some serious money.

Alexander stopped at the very end of the dock next to a yacht and turned to Olivia, beaming.

"What is this?" she asked skeptically.

"I don't want you to freak out, so just let me explain. This is my boat." He glanced to the enormous vessel behind him.

Olivia raised her eyebrows. "I don't know if you could call that thing a boat. It's more like a floating kingdom. That thing's got to be over a hundred feet," she marveled.

"Yeah. It is," he answered excitedly. "And I named her after my childhood best friend, who you recall shared your name. I didn't want you to freak out, but I really wanted to share this with you."

Olivia's heart raced as she looked into Alexander's brilliant eyes. There was an excitement in them she had never seen before. She returned his smile and planted a soft kiss on his lips. "Thank you for sharing this with me, Alex," she whispered.

He grinned as he clutched Olivia's hand in his, leading her toward the gangway. Martin appeared on the main deck and Alexander dragged Olivia up the ramp to where Martin stood. Olivia was surprised to see him there. She made a mental note to ask Alexander what his job description was.

"How was your drive, sir?"

"Great, thanks. Please go get our things out of the car. The valet is holding it for now."

"Yes, sir." Martin walked briskly off the yacht and onto the dock.

"After you, darling." Alexander led Olivia into the main cabin, his hand on the small of her back. He gave her a brief tour of his yacht. To the left sat the living room, which Alexander referred to as the salon. It was rather large with gorgeous wood flooring throughout. Just past that was an exquisite dining room complete with a state-of-the-art kitchen. To the right led to a small hallway with a rather large master bedroom. There was another small bedroom across the hall, as well as a study.

Downstairs, there were three guest rooms and the crew quarters. The upper deck housed another lounge area in addition to an outdoor dining area. The entire yacht was rather spacious and Olivia was floored at the largess of it all. She immediately felt overwhelmed by Alexander's wealth.

As they stood admiring the view off the main deck, she turned to him. "So, um, business must be good."

Alexander laughed. "Yes. You could say that. Lots of people needing my trained mercenaries," he winked. "But don't call them mercenaries. The U.N. doesn't really like that word."

She clung onto his arm as he led her toward the master bedroom suite. "Don't worry, *Love*. Your secret's safe with me," she said, mocking Alexander's term of endearment.

"Are you mocking me, darling?"

"I would never," she replied in faux shock.

"You better run, Olivia. I have plans for you."

She squealed and ran down the hallway into the owner's suite, tripping over Martin as he was dropping off their bags.

"Oh, Miss Adler. I apologize."

"Don't worry about it. Blame your boss." She laughed.

"I'd rather keep my job," he winked.

Alexander appeared in the doorway. "Thank you, Martin. Please co-ordinate with Carter. I have additional security arriving later in the day."

"Yes, sir." Martin turned to Olivia. "Enjoy your day, Miss Adler." He walked out of the master suite and down the hall into the study.

Olivia looked at Alexander when she was sure they were alone. "Additional security, Alex?" She raised an eyebrow at him.

"Yes. Sometimes it's an occupational hazard." He shrugged.

"Why? What's going on?"

"I can't really talk about it, Olivia." He turned to his suitcase and began unpacking his things. "It's nothing important and you shouldn't worry about it at all. It's more of a precaution than anything."

Alexander hated misleading Olivia. The additional security had nothing to do with him and everything to do with her. He always made it seem as though someone could come after him for a job-related issue, but the chances of that were slim to none. However, Carter had seen a black sedan tailing Olivia several times now. He wanted additional security in Newport, just to be on the safe side.

"Come on, Love. Get that worried look off your face," Alexander said, coming up behind Olivia as she put some of her toiletries in the bathroom. She looked up, gazing into his eyes through the mirror. He could see that her eyes were red and puffy. "Have you been crying?" He spun her around, making her face him.

"No. Don't be stupid," she stated, wiping her eyes. "Just let me finish unpacking." She tried to push Alexander out of the way. He stood in place, not letting Olivia pass, staring down at her for an explanation.

"What if something happens to you, Alex?" she asked, her chin quivering. "That scares me to death. I've lost too many people I was close to. I finally let myself get close to someone again and now I'm frightened I'll lose you, too." She started sobbing again as Alexander pulled her into his chest. She struggled to suppress the urge to grab her bags and run as far away as possible. A voice in her head was telling her to push Alexander away. And she started to think that she needed to listen.

"Hey. Hey. It's okay. You have nothing to worry about with me. I'm not going anywhere. Someone will have to drive a stake through my heart to ever take me away from you. I mean that. I promise that I will always be here to look out for you." He continued soothing her tears.

Olivia took a few deep breaths and pulled away from Alexander's chest, looking into his eyes. "I'm sorry. I don't know why that set me off. I'm just overly emotional for some reason. I think nerves about this weekend are getting to me a little," she lied, not wanting to admit to Alexander that she felt everything had started to spin out of control. She hated the feeling and could only think of one way to regain control. The only thing that had worked in the past. She wanted to run. But she kept hearing Kiera's words in her head telling her to take a risk for once. She wanted to, but at what cost?

"That's understandable, sweetheart." He grabbed a tissue and wiped Olivia's eyes. "Come. Let's go to lunch and then do something fun. Are you ready?"

"Yes."

Alexander took her hand in his and pulled her out of the master suite and off his yacht.

~~~~~~~~~~

"I have to say, Miss Adler. I'm looking forward to christening my yacht with you this weekend," Alexander said after the waiter dropped off a dozen oysters as they sat at an outdoor cafe right on the water.

"You've never had sex on it?" Olivia glanced at him, wide-eyed.

"No. I haven't," Alexander replied very matter-of-factly.

"Hmm."

"What is it?"

Olivia grabbed an oyster and slid it down her throat. "I don't know. I just figured you would have taken some girl on it at some time and, well, rock the boat."

Alexander laughed. "Cute." He exhaled loudly. "No, Olivia.

Sadly, she is still a virgin ship."

"Well, let's see what we can do about that." She winked.

Alexander felt his phone buzz again. He reached into his pocket and took it out. It was Martin. It was his fifth call within the hour. "I'm sorry, Love. I should take this."

"That's okay. I understand."

"Thank you." He pressed the answer button on his cell phone. "Yes, Martin. What is it?... What?!... When did this happen?... Okay... Yes... Handle it for the time being and we'll discuss how to proceed..." Alexander hung up, fuming.

"I won't ask if everything is okay, because it does not appear that it is," Olivia remarked, taking a drink from her wine glass.

"Well, something has happened," he replied, eyeing Olivia and taking a deep breath. "I don't mean to frighten you, but the alarm on your system went off about an hour ago."

Olivia looked down at her watch. "It wouldn't have been Kiera. She's at work. She's not supposed to feed... Oh my God! Is Nepenthe all right?" Olivia looked terrified.

"Yes. He's fine. A window triggered the alarm. Martin had another agent go over and check the house. They took Nepenthe to my place for the time being until we can sort everything out. I'll let my pet sitter know to keep an eye on him, too." He grabbed another oyster and tipped it back into his mouth.

Olivia stared off into the distance, breathing deep, trying to resist the urge to leave the table and run. With every passing moment, things were spiraling downward.

"Olivia, darling. Are you okay? Talk to me."

"What is going on?" she hissed. "I mean, really going on? I just feel like you're keeping information from me. And I would really appreciate it if you were straightforward and honest with me. If you don't think I've noticed your little protection details lately, you must think very little of my intelligence. I know you've been having one of your guys watching me whenever we're not together. So why? What is it?"

Alexander stared at her, contemplating what to tell her. "I'm just trying to keep you safe."

She glared at him. "If you really wanted to keep me safe,

266

you would tell me what the fuck is going on."

Alexander exhaled loudly, throwing his napkin onto the table in front of him. "I know. I should have told you this earlier. And I wish I had, but I was hoping it was nothing."

Olivia's heart began to race.

"Remember that guy from the bar all those weeks ago?"

She nodded.

"Well, he's the same person that bailed Simon out of jail and probably paid for his attorney as well. He's using a fake name, but his real name is Mark Kiddish and he is a very bad, very powerful man. He is a professional "cleaner." Do you know what that is?"

Olivia shook her head as she took in everything Alexander told her.

"A professional cleaner is someone who ties up loose ends, mainly for politicians and other high-ranking government officials. Why he's interested in you, I am not sure of, but he is not a good guy. So, yes. I am absolutely guilty of having some of my protection teams watching you. But I need to know you are safe, okay? This guy is a very real danger. I know no one has tried anything yet, but I don't want to take any chances with you." Alexander felt guilty for not telling her everything, but he just couldn't. Not yet anyway.

Olivia processed his words, trying to make sense of everything. Why would anyone want to harm her? She had money, yes, but that's no reason for a professional "cleaner" to target her. "I appreciate that, Alex. I really do. But you should have told me. You can't keep trying to protect me by withholding information from me. If you don't tell me these things, how can I trust you? I need to be able to trust you. You've never given me a reason not to, but you can't just make decisions based on what you think is best for me without asking." She still couldn't shake the feeling that he wasn't telling her the whole story.

"So you approve of the additional security?" Alexander looked at her, hopeful.

She thought about that for a minute before sighing loudly. "If it makes you happy, yes. Fine."

Alexander swooped her hand from the table and held it to his lips. "That would make me extremely happy." He placed a kiss on her hand as he stared at her. Olivia needed to do something to silence the voice in her head that was growing louder with each passing moment. She knew her time was running out.

~~~~~~~~~~

"Donovan. It's Cheryl. It worked. She is out of town this weekend with Burnham, but upon her return, I have been assigned to her security team."

"That's wonderful news. But we need to continue to give Burnham a reason to think she needs that security, so don't back off."

"I won't."

"Now that we can get you close to her, I need you to start getting information from her. The old man hid her identity and faked her death. I need to tie up these loose ends. That box containing all those documents is still out there somewhere. We need to get our hands on it. You'll need to help her try to remember where it is."

"And you're certain she'll know?"

"I'd bet my life on it."

CHAPTER THIRTY

MEMORIES

The sun filtered through the master suite, waking Olivia on Saturday morning. She rolled over and looked at Alexander as he slept, a peaceful look across his face. He didn't wake up in the middle of the night screaming or crying like Olivia did. She wondered how much longer he would want to be woken up every night with her cries. The little voice in her head was back, telling her to run before she fell too far. She needed to quiet that voice. So she did the only thing she knew would dull the pain of her constant nightmares and silence the voice. She swung a leg over Alexander, sitting on top of him, thinking she may already be in too deep.

His eyes flung open. A look of surprise crept across his face, turning into a mischievous smile. "Mmmmm... This is a nice way to wake up," he said sleepily.

Olivia could feel his erection grow. She leaned down and planted kisses down his jaw as she ground against his hips.

"Don't start anything you have no intention of finishing, dear," he groaned.

She looked at Alexander, his eyes hooded as he moved his hips beneath her, the voice in her head finally silent. "Oh, Mr. Burnham," she batted her eyes. "I have every intention of finishing." She lowered herself and pulled on his earlobe. "Again. And again. And again."

Alexander growled and flipped Olivia onto her back. She looked at him, a smile on her face. "I've been quite enjoying myself as we've christened your boat this weekend, Mr. Burnham."

"As have I, Miss Adler," he replied, positioning himself between her legs. He leaned down, kissing her neck. "As have I," he whispered as he slid into her. She gasped in surprise. "I'm glad to know I can still surprise you after all these weeks," he grunted, filling her to the brim.

Fire coursed through her body as he moved gently inside of her. His movements were slow and deliberate as he took his time, savoring every moment. Olivia didn't want him gentle. She wanted him to be rough with her. The voice was back and became louder with each soft thrust.

He gently nipped at her neck, tracing a line down her jaw and tugging at her earlobe. "You are one incredible woman," Alexander said. "God, I love being inside of you, Olivia." She ran her fingers up and down his back, her touch sending shivers through his body. "Just one touch and I'm ready to lose my mind."

"Faster, Alex. Please," she begged as she wrapped her legs around his waist, desperately bucking him with her hips.

"No, Love. I want you to feel me. Do you feel this?" he asked as he continued his slow movements, the closeness almost unbearable.

"Yes, Alexander. I feel it." And she knew he wasn't just talking about his erection inside her. He was talking about something else entirely.

The voice grew louder.

Alexander's breathing grew heavier as he picked up his pace, maintaining a quick but gentle rhythm. He leaned down and softly pulled on Olivia's nipple with his mouth, sending her over the edge, her orgasm taking her by surprise. She moaned out Alexander's name as she trembled around him. The feeling of Olivia pulsating around him in absolute ecstasy caught him off-guard and he soon found himself spiraling down from his own orgasm, collapsing on top of her. She held his head to her chest, stroking his hair and forehead beaded with sweat.

"That was a fantastic way to wake up," Alexander stated once his breathing slowed down.

"I'm glad I could be of assistance," Olivia smirked.

"Come on, beautiful. Up and at 'em," Alexander said, pulling Olivia up with him and leading her into the shower. "Big day today. Let's go get all your race stuff." He turned on the water, testing the temperature.

Olivia groaned, leaning against the bathroom wall. "Can't I just spend one day in bed with you all day?" *It's the only way I can try to dull this voice telling me to run*, she wanted to say to him.

"That sounds like heaven, but it will have to wait. At least until next week sometime," he replied, winking. He held out his hand and helped her step into the shower, the entire time, Olivia thinking she may not make it to next week.

~~~~~~~~~~

"Nervous, Love?" Alexander asked as they left the race expo, Olivia clutching her race packet.

"A little bit, I guess."

"Let's take a drive. It's a beautiful day, and you still haven't really done much exploring around this town." He opened the door to his car for Olivia, helping her in.

"Well, that's because someone's kidnapped me and used me as his sex-slave the past few days," she giggled. "Kinky bastard."

Alexander laughed, turning the ignition on his convertible.

"That I am."

A few moments passed as Alexander drove through the streets of Newport heading to the other side of the town. "I like it when you take control in bed," Olivia said out of nowhere, hoping he would take the hint and stop with the slow, emotional sex. She needed it rough. It was the only way.

Alexander looked at her, wondering what had brought that up.

"I used to never let anyone be like that toward me," she continued. "I always needed to maintain total control in bed. That way it was easier to kick out whoever it was. I guess I always wanted to remain a cold-hearted, detached bitch. It's less painful."

Alexander was floored by Olivia's admission. He knew she

had attachment issues, for obvious reasons. She had her family ripped from her when she was so young and had very few memories to fall back on.

"That's what I go to therapy for. You've been so good about not asking questions and I am thankful for that. I've been trying to get over my issues and my dreadfully overpriced therapist has been helping me get close to people again."

"I'm going to have to thank him or her, then," Alexander replied, grabbing Olivia's hand and kissing it. Several minutes passed as they drove around Newport in silence.

"You're my first boyfriend, you know. I would never date people before you." She stared out the window as the landscape changed from small houses to larger estates, wishing that talking about things would silence the increasingly loud voice in her head.

"Well, I'm glad you changed your outlook on the whole boyfriend thing," Alexander remarked. "I'm glad you gave me the opportunity to get to know you." He pulled the car into a parking lot. "We're here."

"Where are we?"

"Are you up for a little walk?" he asked, opening the door for her.

"Of course. It'll be a nice little warm-up for tomorrow."

Alexander led her out of the parking lot and down a few blocks onto a rocky path. "This is the cliff walk. It follows the beach and all the old mansions are on it."

Olivia had never seen anything like it before. As they walked, the ocean rolled in far below them. High on the cliffs they were walking on, gorgeous, sprawling mansions sat overlooking the coast. Olivia relaxed as she basked in the warm sunshine and ocean breeze, inhaling the salty sea air.

They walked for a while, Alexander pointing out the various estates. "This is the Breakers," he said after a while. "Probably one of the most famous of the Newport Mansions."

Olivia looked at the enormous estate. "It looks so familiar."

Alexander's heart stopped. He didn't want her to remember. Why did he bring her there? Her mother was part of wealthy Newport society. "Well, probably because of how famous it is,"

Alexander replied nervously.

"Yeah, you're probably right," she responded, deep in thought. Everything seemed so familiar to her. As if she had been there before. It wasn't just that mansion. It was all of it. The roads. The trees. The houses. The ocean. The cliffs. Everything. As they made their way down the walk, Olivia's mind raced with various scenarios of how she could know that area of Newport so well when she never recalled ever visiting there. The voice was back and Olivia had a strange feeling that her entire world was about to come crumbling down on top of her.

~~~~~~~~~~~

"Hey, do me a favor. Take a right up here. Onto Webster," Olivia ordered as Alexander drove on Bellevue, heading back to the marina half an hour later.

Alexander looked at her with a questioning look, his heart beginning to race. "Just humor me, please."

He hesitated before sighing loudly. "Your wish is my command, princess."

Olivia smiled weakly as Alexander put on his blinker and turned his car onto Webster.

"Here. Slow down a little, please," Olivia said, gazing out the car at the large estates on her right. "Okay, stop. Pull over," she ordered.

He obeyed, albeit reluctantly, and pulled the car to the side of the road before putting it in park. Olivia got out of the car and started walking up the street. "Where are you going, Olivia?" Alexander asked as he jumped out of the car, following her on foot. He cringed when he realized where they were.

"Alex. I know this house," she replied quietly, looking at a large home behind a wrought iron fence. "Why do I know this house?"

Alexander stopped and stared at the large estate. The massive brick pillars held a nameplate. "Harrison House." He knew the house well. Olivia had spent a great deal of time

273

there the first few years of her life. Her grandparents' home.

"I don't know, Love," he lied. "Please, get back in the car before someone hits you."

She continued to stare, pressing her hand against the brick of the pillars holding the entry gate and running her fingers against the nameplate bearing the name "Harrison House." She stood there for several long minutes, trying to remember why she knew that house. Finally, she shook her head and turned to get back in the car.

The voice grew louder.

The car was eerily quiet on the way back to the marina, neither person wanting to initiate conversation. Alexander knew his time was running out. Olivia had started to remember certain things. It would probably only be a matter of time until she put two and two together and realized who he was. She had already had a dream where the younger Alexander morphed into the older one. He needed to read that letter, if he could only build up enough nerve to do so.

The remainder of the afternoon passed with a relative unease between the two, neither one really wanting to address the elephant in the room; Olivia not wanting to talk about why she knew that house, fearful it would bring up shadows of the past, and Alexander worried that Olivia was starting to remember.

Olivia decided to lie down and take a nap before dinner. Alexander said he had some work to do, so he left her to sleep while he attended to some business.

Olivia curled up in the comfortable king-sized bed and pulled the covers tight around her. She dozed off within minutes, her brain exhausted from the afternoon.

~~~~~~~~~~

"Olivia, darling. Come get ready. Our guests will be here shortly," her mother yelled across a massive lawn to a young Olivia.

Olivia looked to her right where the green-eyed boy stood, covered in dirt. "I'll race you," she giggled. *"Loser has to worship the ground the winner walks on for all eternity!"*

"*That's not fair!*"

"*Ready! Set!*" Olivia ran through the large front yard of her family's enormous estate as she shouted, "*Go!*"

"*Olibia's a cheater,*" the little boy shouted, chasing the little girl.

Olivia reached the front steps first, jumping up and down, cheering for herself as she turned to watch her friend take the last few steps toward her.

"*She cheated, Aunt Marilyn,*" the boy complained.

"*Olivia, darling, you need to play fair.*"

"*I'm sorry, Mama.*"

"*You know better than that. That's no way to play with your best friend, now is it?*"

"*He cheats sometimes, too,*" Olivia said, winking at her friend.

"*It still doesn't make it right. Now upstairs with you. You're both filthy. Everyone will be here soon.*"

"*Where's Daddy?*" Olivia asked.

"*Oh, sweetheart. You know how it is. Your daddy has a very important job and he can't just leave it to be with us whenever we want him to.*"

"*Okay. But when can we go to the beach, Mama?*"

"*We're going to the beach house next week for the entire summer, Love. Now I mean it. Go clean up. Your grandparents are expecting you both to look like civilized human beings for once.*" She winked.

The two children stumbled up the stairs into the large playroom. Her mother entered the room a few minutes later to help them clean up and change. Soon, the two kids were dressed in their spring-time best. Olivia's mother grabbed the two kids by the hand and walked them down the hall to the music room.

"*One song before our guests arrive?*"

"*Yes! Mama! Play us a song,*" Olivia squealed with delight.

Instead of sitting down at the grand piano, she picked up an acoustic guitar and checked its tuning.

"*This one is for you, my two favorite babies…*" She looked toward where the green-eyed boy and Olivia sat, both kids excited about her performance, as she began playing the opening measures of the Beatle's 'I Will.'

"*Dance with me Olibia?*" the green-eyed boy asked, holding his hand out to her.

"*Okay,*" Olivia replied, grabbing his hand.

They danced awkwardly across the room as the green-eyed boy sang

275

along with Olivia's mother, never taking his eyes off Olivia. When the song ended, the green-eyed boy got down on one knee, morphing into an older Alexander. He opened a small ring box.

CHAPTER THIRTY-ONE

READY TO RUN

Olivia woke up, gasping for breath through the tears that flowed uncontrollably. She ran to the shower, needing to cover up her tears in case Alexander had heard her. She turned on the water and stripped out of her clothes before stepping into the shower, letting the water flow over her body. Tremors coursed through her as cries consumed her entire being.

It was that house. She remembered that house. It was in her dream. Was it there because she saw it earlier that day or did she really spend time there when she was younger? She didn't know.

Then she remembered how happy she was when she danced with the green-eyed boy. Who was the green-eyed boy? What happened to him? Why did everyone she was close to disappear from her life? Why was she so incredibly alone? What did it all mean?

Her heart beat rapidly as she tried to figure it all out. Alexander was there. The green-eyed boy morphed into him. And he got down on one knee. And there was a ring. She could see it in his eyes, not only in her dreams, but when Alexander looked at her on a daily basis. Kiera was right. The love Alexander had for Olivia was apparent. And that was the one thing that scared Olivia most. Love. It chilled her to her core. Because once you loved, then you could lose, and she didn't know if she could deal with that pain.

Her sobs overtook her again as she cried even louder. The voice was back and it was screaming at her to run. Something about that place and everything going on with Alexander made her realize she had lost all control. And she needed it back.

~~~~~~~~~~

Alexander hung up the phone in the study after getting a status update from Marshall, one of his top security agents. He thought about everything that had happened that weekend, wondering if Olivia was starting to regain her memory. He knew that some places could be triggers, but he hoped she wasn't remembering things. Her lack of memory could be the only thing that had protected her all those years.

As he was deep in thought, he heard a loud cry come from down the hallway.

"Shit. Olivia!" he yelled out, running toward the master bedroom. He looked at the bed and saw it was empty. He scanned the room when he heard more cries and the shower running. He walked quietly toward the bathroom, drawing his side-arm and taking off the safety. He kicked the door open slowly and saw that Olivia was alone in the shower, sobbing uncontrollably.

"Oh my god, Olivia!" Alexander cried out, putting the safety back on the gun before placing it on the counter. He jumped into the shower fully clothed. "Olivia, please. Talk to me." He pulled her into his chest, trying to soothe the tears that had overtaken her entire body. She cried into his chest, not caring how unattractive she looked at the moment.

After a few long moments passed, Olivia got her breathing under control, her crying mostly done. "Your clothes are all wet," she said quietly.

"Oh, Love, that's the least of my concerns right now. I'm worried about you. What happened?"

"It was just that stupid dream again," Olivia replied, her eyes shifting to stare at the soap dish.

Alexander knew she was lying. It wasn't the same dream. The dream was changing. He knew it. But he didn't know if he should bring it up with her at that moment. She seemed like she was ready to break at any second.

"I know how hard it must be for you to relive that day every night. Sometimes you just have to let yourself have a big cry to release all the pain you're holding inside. You always try to stay strong, ignoring the past, but you can't keep it all inside, Love. It will destroy you." He tilted her chin up so he could stare into her eyes, the water still cascading over her naked body. "It will destroy me, too."

Alexander's words chilled Olivia to the core. What was she doing to him? She didn't want to hurt him, but at the same time she couldn't cope with all the pain she had been dealt in the past. And at some point, Alexander wouldn't want to deal with all the drama anymore. No one would. And he would leave her. Just like everyone else in her life.

It was at that instant that everything became incredibly clear. She knew what she had to do. She needed to listen to the voice.

Olivia resolved to do the one thing that she could in order to maintain control over the situation. She needed to distance herself from Alexander. She had gotten too close to him, too fast, and the only one who would end up hurt would be her. She couldn't let that happen again. She would get through the weekend. Then she would push him away. It wasn't what her heart wanted, but she needed to do this for her own survival.

"I'm sorry I'm such a mess," she said, a blank expression on her face, devoid of any emotion.

"Don't apologize, Olivia," he said, brushing her hair out of her face. "You're a beautiful mess." He winked.

"I feel better now after that," Olivia said dryly.

Alexander saw her face and realized the panic had passed. "Good," he said, kissing her deeply, which she only half-heartedly returned. He looked at her, pulling away. "Are you sure everything is okay?"

"Yes. I'm sure. I'm just cold and pruning. I need to get out of this shower."

He turned off the water and stepped out of the tub before grabbing a towel and wrapping Olivia in it. He rubbed her arms, warming her up. "Feel better?"

She gazed into his eyes. She was going to miss those brilliant green eyes. A tear escaped at the thought of not seeing those eyes first thing when she woke up in the morning. Alexander reached out, catching the tear.

"Sorry. Just a straggler," Olivia explained, leaving the bathroom. She turned to look as Alexander stripped out of his wet clothes. She stared for a moment, wanting to savor everything about the man in front of her. She knew her time with him was limited.

"See something you like?" Alexander asked, placing his hands on his hips and showing off his manliness. Olivia couldn't help but laugh. "There. I knew I could put a smile on your face," he joked as he grabbed a towel to dry off, unable to shake the feeling that Olivia was slipping from his grasp.

~~~~~~~~~~~

That evening, Alexander took Olivia to a quaint restaurant right on the marina where they had a pleasant dinner, albeit relatively quiet. Thankfully Olivia was able to brush off her silence and blame it on nerves about the following day. That eased Alexander's fears somewhat. It made sense.

After their main course and before dessert arrived, Olivia excused herself to use the ladies' room. She walked through the crowded restaurant, finding the hallway where the restroom was located. As she pushed open the door, she nearly ran into an older woman who was trying to exit.

"Oh, I'm so sorry," Olivia exclaimed, staring at the woman in front of her.

"Oh, it's…" The woman stopped when she saw Olivia. She stood still for several long, uncomfortable moments.

"Are you okay?" Olivia asked. The woman was probably in her seventies. Her graying hair was pinned back, keeping her gentle facial features clear. She was just a few inches shorter than Olivia. Her eyes seemed so familiar, but Olivia couldn't place where she could have possibly seen the woman before. But nothing that day seemed to be making any sense. Everything had spiraled out of control almost overnight.

The woman snapped out of her thoughts. "Yes, I'm sorry.

You just remind me of someone." A smile spread across her face, touching her eyes as if thinking of a fond memory. "Do you live around here?"

"No. I'm in town for the marathon. I live in Boston."

"I see. I have some family members running tomorrow as well. Gosh, you just look so familiar. Are you sure you're not from around here?"

Olivia thought the elderly woman looked familiar, too. "No. I grew up in Charleston. This is actually my first time in town here."

"Well, welcome to Newport. My name is Rose. Rose Harrison."

"Olivia Adler," Olivia replied, extending her hand.

Rose looked at Olivia, a look of surprise on her face. "I'm sorry. What did you say your name was, dear?"

"Olivia."

The older woman's face went pale.

"Are you okay? You don't look too well. Do you need to sit down?" Olivia held her arm, walking her to a chair in the vanity area of the restroom.

"Thank you, dear." She sat down, her hands shaking.

Olivia sat next to her. "Are you sure you're okay? Do you want me to help you back to your table?"

"I'm fine, dear. I was just reminded of someone I knew long ago. My little granddaughter was named Olivia."

"Was?"

"Yes. She passed away. And you look just like her mother."

"Oh. I'm sorry about your loss, Ms. Harrison."

"Please, child. Call me Rose."

"Okay, Rose. Can I help you back to your table?"

"Would you?"

Olivia reached out, helping Rose stand up, and walked her back to her table where her husband sat. After making a little small talk with both of them, Olivia excused herself to return to her own table.

"Well, that was interesting," she said dryly, taking her seat.

"What was, Love?"

"I nearly toppled some poor woman over in the restroom

281

and then when she heard my name, she looked as if she had seen a ghost." Olivia looked out at the harbor, the lights of the yachts twinkling on the dark ocean.

"Oh, really? Why's that?" he asked, taking a drink from his wine glass.

"She had a granddaughter named Olivia who I guess passed away, and apparently I look like the girl's mother."

"What was her name?" Alexander asked. Olivia looked at him with a questioning look. "Reason I ask is I spend some time here and I'm just wondering if it's someone I know."

"Her name was Rose Harrison." Olivia returned her gaze to the marina, wanting to shake the feeling that she was supposed to know that woman for some reason.

Alexander remained quiet, his face showing no emotion at the fact that Olivia had just met her grandmother.

CHAPTER THIRTY-TWO

THE VOICE

Olivia woke up at five the following morning so she could have enough time to get ready and walk the mile to the start line. Alexander continued to sleep while she got ready. As she went about her routine, she kept glancing at him sleeping so calmly and peacefully. She wondered if she should really push him away. But she had to. Ever since she made her decision, the voice had gone away. It was the only way. She had to regain control of the situation and the only way to do that would be to leave him. And eventually he would move on and be happy. Happiness wasn't in the cards for Olivia, but that didn't mean Alexander couldn't be happy. So she needed to leave him. And she knew the only way to do that would be to leave Boston as well.

Looking at her watch, she saw it was time to head to the start line. She grabbed her race stuff and walked over to the large bed. Alexander stirred, opening his eyes and looking at Olivia.

"Getting ready to leave?" he asked, rubbing his eyes.

"Yes. I should get a move on," she replied.

He threw off the covers and stood up. Olivia gaped at his naked body. *God, I'm going to miss looking at that,* she thought to herself. He found a pair of shorts and slid them on before walking over to Olivia.

"Good luck, darling," he said as he pulled her into his arms. "You'll do great." He gave her a quick kiss on the lips. Olivia returned the kiss, deepening it and kissing him as if it would be the last time she ever kissed him. Because she knew his kisses were numbered and she wanted to remember every single one.

She pulled away and walked out of the master bedroom, leaving Alexander behind. She would have to get used to walking out on him, thankful that she had already worked out an escape route that the additional security she had agreed to would not be aware of.

The weather was a bit chilly on her walk to the start line, but the crowds of people congregating on Newport made her excited. There was something about the buzz of adrenaline at the start line of a marathon that Olivia had become addicted to over the years. She loved the feeling in the crowd of runners right before the starting gun went off. There were people who were running their first marathon and there were runners who were running their hundredth. Everyone had their own story about why they ran. And she loved it.

She got to the starting line area and encountered thousands of runners already milling about in the darkness of the early morning. She found a spot to sit down and ate her bagel as she waited for the race to start. She relaxed and mentally prepared herself for what she was about to do. Before long, they were calling the runners to line up in the starting corrals. It was a sea of people and Olivia loved it.

"This is it," she said just before the starting gun went off. Once it sounded, she made her way to the starting line and began running at a conservative pace, not wanting to go out too quickly and burn out halfway through.

She had a lot to think about on her run. Many times, she tried to talk herself out of leaving Alexander. But every scenario she came up with only ended with him leaving her in the end. She just had too many issues and it would be inconsiderate for her to make anyone sit around and wait for her as she dealt with them. The voice grew louder every time she began to reconsider fleeing. She knew she had to leave. She had gotten too close to Alexander. And her feelings petrified her. She needed to leave before she could no longer silence the voice.

The miles zoomed by as she thought about leaving Boston. It would probably be for the best. She would leave Monday and drive until she was tired. A beach in Florida would be good that time of year.

She hit mile twenty-five and looked at her GPS watch. She was right on pace for a sub three-thirty finish. She still had some juice left in her legs, so she went for the final push, picking up her speed.

She neared the finish line and saw Alexander in the crowd cheering her on. It warmed her heart to see him there supporting her. But she knew it was only fleeting. She pushed harder and crossed the finish line with a final time of three hours and twenty-eight minutes. She qualified for the Boston Marathon. She knew she should be happy, but she wasn't. She didn't feel anything. She felt empty. And she knew it was because, after tomorrow, she would no longer see Alexander. And it made her heart ache. But there was no other way. She would only destroy him, too.

As she made her way through the finish line chute, she grabbed her finisher's medal and found Alexander just outside of the runners area. He ran over to her, picked her up, and swung her around. "You did it!!!" he exclaimed. "I'm so proud of you, Olivia." He put her down and kissed her full on the mouth.

Olivia pushed him away. "Gross. I'm all sweaty and salty."

"I like you salty," Alexander said, grabbing her hand and leading her out of the crowd. His enthusiasm was infectious and she couldn't help but smile weakly. Olivia cherished that moment. She knew it would be one of her last moments of joy.

Back on the yacht, Olivia emerged from the shower and saw Alexander sitting on the bed. "Feel better now, Love?" he asked, taking in her beautiful silhouette as she walked through the master bedroom in only a towel, her long hair dripping with water.

"Yes. Thank you," she responded dryly.

There was something off about Olivia. Alexander had noticed it the day before. She seemed like an empty shell. No emotion. There was nothing there anymore and he didn't know what to make of it. The previous day, Olivia had said it was nerves about her upcoming marathon. But now, that was over. She had qualified for Boston. He thought she would return to her normal self, but even at the finish line, when he thought she would be thrilled for achieving her goal, she was distant. Aloof. She was empty. He could see it in her eyes. The spark was gone. He needed that back.

Olivia sat at a small reading table in the master bedroom. She could feel Alexander's eyes glued to her. She turned her head to look out the expansive windows, not wanting to look into his vibrant green eyes. The eyes that she knew she would be leaving the following day.

Everything still seemed so familiar as she watched sailboats float by. In the distance, she could faintly make out a military fort. She knew she had been there before. It was Fort Adams. She knew that. But why did she know that?

A lump formed in her throat as she thought about what it could all mean. The house yesterday. The dream. The green-eyed boy. She was losing her grasp on things. Her life was fine before Alexander walked into it on that night back in August. Since then, she slowly began to lose control of her own feelings. She had started to let him in. And she regretted that. Life was better before when she kept everyone away. And that's what she needed to do again. Keep everyone away. And get her heart back from Alexander.

After Olivia had finished brushing her hair, Alexander watched her walk back into the bathroom, throwing her long locks into a ponytail before slipping into a pair of yoga pants and tank top. He looked into her eyes through the mirror, although she was unaware of it. The emptiness was there. He hadn't seen that look since the night he first met her. At that instant, he knew she was slipping from him. There was only one way for him to regain that control he so desperately needed.

"Olivia," he said sternly, waking Olivia from her thoughts as she finished getting ready in the bathroom. "Get out here."

Alexander's voice was powerful. She couldn't help but obey. The past few days something had changed in Alexander and it scared Olivia. Whenever they had sex, he was gentle and sweet. The normally dominant lover was nowhere to be found.

But at that moment, she needed that. She wanted to turn it all off. So that's what she did. With a blank expression on her face, she walked out of the bathroom, staring into Alexander's brilliant eyes, hooded with an emotion Olivia had never seen before. She could almost see the struggle within through those eyes.

"Come here, Olivia," he said forcefully. She obeyed, walking over to the edge of the bed where he sat waiting for her.

The emptiness was still there in her eyes. He couldn't bear to look into the cold eyes that were void of any emotion. Getting up from the bed, he strode over to the chest of drawers.

Olivia turned around to see what he was doing.

"Face forward, Olivia," he barked.

She obeyed again, thousands of different sensations running through her core. She liked it when he told her what to do. *That* she could deal with. She could turn everything off and just submit to Alexander. What she couldn't deal with was the slow, emotional sex that seemed to occur more and more lately.

As Alexander strode back behind her, she felt his body heat, the proximity overwhelming her senses. She could do this. She would do whatever he said. And then she would leave him. She knew he saw it in her eyes. The emptiness. He always was observant, knowing how she felt before she even did. At that moment, Olivia realized that Alexander thought he was losing control. And he was. This was his way of regaining that. Olivia would play the part he needed her to play. It was the least she could do. She would make him think that he had control of the situation and that she wasn't going to leave. But no matter what, she had to leave him. She would only destroy him, too. He had said that himself.

Alexander placed a blindfold over Olivia's eyes. The room was silent except for their breathing.

"Lift your arms, Olivia," Alexander said. Olivia obeyed and Alexander quickly lifted her tank top over her head.

"Place them at your side," he commanded.

She obeyed again, her heart racing and her breathing becoming heavy.

287

Alexander grabbed one hand and brought it behind her back, joining the other hand and wrapping a silk tie around her wrists, binding them together.

"Good. I like you tied up," he whispered against her neck, causing her hair follicles to stand on end. Her body tingled in anticipation. She heard the rustling of clothes around her and could only assume that Alexander had stripped out of his tee shirt and jeans. Seconds later, she felt two strong hands on her waist. Instantly, a tongue was on her stomach, circling, sending tremors through her core.

Alexander swiftly lowered her yoga pants, helping Olivia step out of them, holding her steady at her hips. He pressed against her and she could feel his erection.

"Kneel, Olivia," he ordered.

Olivia lowered herself onto the ground, Alexander helping her maintain her balance. She knelt on the hardwood floor.

"Don't sit back on your heels," Alexander commanded. "That won't work for what I need from you right now."

Her heart raced madly in her chest. She raised herself tall on her knees.

"Open your mouth," Alexander said quietly. Olivia could feel him right in front of her. She immediately obeyed. Alexander slowly slipped his arousal into her wet mouth, pushing in and out in a slow rhythm, the sensation of Olivia's tongue on his most sensitive part overwhelming his entire being.

Alexander pressed his hand against the back of Olivia's neck, holding her head in place, thrusting into her mouth. Olivia met his motion, licking and dragging her tongue across his length, moaning every so often because she knew that he liked that. And this was all about convincing Alexander that she wasn't going to leave. So she gave him exactly what he wanted. She felt him harden and knew it was only a matter of time before he lost it. She gently bared her teeth.

"Fuck, Olivia," Alexander exhaled, pumping into her mouth even harder before pulling out. She frowned from the loss of contact. She was actually enjoying being able to please him like that.

"Ask me, Olivia," he demanded.

The room remained silent as Olivia tried to gather her thoughts. Alexander reached down and grabbed her ponytail, tilting her head back roughly.

"I said, ask me, Olivia," he growled. "Beg me. Olivia. Beg me to come in your throat."

Fuck, Olivia thought to herself. She loved it when he told her what to do. How could she possibly even think of leaving him when he was like this? His words set her entire body on fire.

"Please, Mr. Burnham," she said sweetly. "Please come in my mouth."

Alexander moaned at her soft voice begging him. It's what he needed at that moment. It's what he always needed. That way he felt in control of a situation that he knew he was losing all control over.

He rubbed his erection against Olivia's lips, commanding her to open her mouth wider. She did so and he pumped mercilessly, finding his release in seconds and exploding into her throat. There was nothing like coming inside Olivia, but coming in her mouth was a close second.

When the last of the aftershocks ceased, he withdrew from her mouth and helped Olivia to her feet, crushing his lips against hers, his tongue exploring the place his arousal had just been, tasting himself in her mouth. It made him harden again. He led Olivia, blindfolded and bound, over to the bed. He swiftly readjusted her restraints over her head and helped her lie down.

Alexander looked down at Olivia, her breathing becoming erratic. Her body was on fire with excitement. She could feel Alexander's eyes searing down into her body. She felt like she was going to come from the anticipation alone.

Her mind raced, desperately needing some sort of release. She felt Alexander hover over her body. He planted rough kisses against her neck, his tongue trailing down her chest. He bit down on her nipple, causing her to scream out from a combination of pleasure and pain.

"You like that, Olivia?" he asked with a hint of amusement in his voice.

She simply nodded, unable to form a sentence from the unique sensations running through her core.

"Tell me you like it, Olivia. Say the words. Tell me I'm the only one who can set your body on fire like this." He continued torturing her with his tongue, tracing circles around her nipple, sucking and biting gently. Her body shook from the amazing feeling of absolute ecstasy. His words rang through her brain. And she knew this was his way of reminding her how much she needed him. She knew he was the only one who could make her feel like that. But it didn't change anything. Still, she said the words he so desperately needed to hear. It was the only way.

"Yes, Mr. Burnham. It's you. You're the only one who makes me feel this way," she exhaled.

He could tell Olivia was on edge and about to go over. It was working. He was regaining his control. He could feel it. He pressed his lips against Olivia's, softly at first before deepening the kiss into an impassioned exchange.

She moaned, Alexander's tongue invading her mouth and sending sparks throughout her entire being. She needed some sort of release. Wrapping her legs around his waist, she began thrusting her hips against him, hoping he would get the hint.

"Oh, no, Olivia. I don't think so. I'll fuck you when I'm good and ready and not a moment sooner." He looked down at the girl laying on his bed, ready to fall apart at any minute. And he knew he had her right where he wanted her. Where he needed her. He lowered his mouth to her neck, nipping gently as he made his way down the rest of her body, sucking and biting as he went.

Alexander positioned his mouth between her legs and Olivia could feel his hot breath on her. "Mmmmm... You're so wet for me," he said.

"Fuck..." Olivia exhaled. She didn't know how much more she could take. She was ready to agree to anything if he would just make her come.

"Ask me, Olivia," he said.

She knew what he wanted and she was happy she could give it to him. For a moment, all thoughts of running quickly disappeared. She was living in the moment of complete and utter ecstasy. Nothing mattered at that point. Not her past. Not her dreams. Not the memories threatening to come forward at any minute. No. The only thing that mattered was Alexander and making him happy.

"Please, Mr. Burnham. Lick me…"

Her breathing became heavy, her flesh on fire from the proximity of Alexander's mouth to the most sensitive part of her body.

"Lick you where, Olivia?" he asked. "I need you to tell me where."

"You know where," Olivia responded, a grin on her face.

Alexander's heart warmed. For the first time since the previous day, she looked like her old self. There was a smile on her face. He wanted that smile to stay. He slowly lowered his mouth back between Olivia's legs and softly licked her clit.

"Fuck!" Olivia breathed out, the simple act of his tongue on her sex about to make her unhinged. Her nerves stood on end and she knew she was on the brink of falling over the edge with Alexander. And the thought didn't scare her at that moment. Because she knew he was the type of person to catch her, no matter what.

"Come on, Olivia. Don't fight this," he breathed between licks. "You know you need this. Now give me your pleasure." He returned his tongue to her clit and slid two fingers inside her.

She shuddered around him, her orgasm consuming her entire core as the aftershocks coursed through her body. At that moment, she knew no one else could ever make her feel as full and complete as Alexander.

He raised himself up to her mouth and crushed his lips to hers, forcing his tongue in her mouth. Taking the blindfold off, he gazed into her eyes. He smiled at the beautiful woman laying beneath him. It worked. The spark was back.

But so was that voice.

CHAPTER THIRTY-THREE

TIME TO GO

The following morning, Olivia woke up early, thinking about what the day would bring. The voice returned the day before and she knew she couldn't stay. It became louder and louder. The only way to silence it was to go far away.

Throughout the previous day, she went through the motions, giving Alexander what he needed so that he didn't become suspicious. She smiled during the extravagant celebration dinner he had arranged on the veranda of the yacht. She giggled at his affectionate words as they shared a bottle of champagne. She was playful during the multiple times they had sex throughout the course of the evening. She played the part she had to play so that she could run. Her survival depended on it.

During the night while Alexander was fast asleep, she wrote him a letter explaining everything. She planned to slip it into his suitcase after they were done packing. She didn't want to leave him with no explanation. She just couldn't do it face-to-face. She knew it was cowardly, but she didn't care.

She looked over at Alexander and ran her fingers up and down his chest, playing with the little tufts of hair. It was the last morning she would be waking up next to him and the thought broke her heart.

"Mmmmm…" Alexander groaned sleepily.

"Ssshhhhh…" Olivia whispered, placing her finger over his mouth. "Don't talk." She climbed on top of him. "I'm in control this time."

She wanted one last time with Alexander, but she needed to

be in control. It was the only way she could distance herself from her feelings. She knew she cared deeply for him and that made leaving him even more difficult. But she had to. There was no choice. He said it himself. She would only destroy him, too, and she could not have that on her conscience.

Her hips circled Alexander's waist and she felt his erection grow. She slowly eased herself onto Alexander, taking him inside of her, relishing the feeling of completeness. She began to move against him, trailing kisses down his chest and grabbing his hands in hers, holding on as she said good-bye to him the only way she knew how. She took her time with him, wanting to cherish every feeling.

Alexander looked at her and noticed there was something different about Olivia that morning. She was slow and deliberate in her motions. There was a closeness that had never been there before, but when he looked into her eyes, they seemed distant and empty again. He held on for as long as he could, but once he felt Olivia shatter around him, he joined her. There was no screaming or moaning of names as there usually was when they had sex. This time it was quiet, the only sound in the room their heavy breathing.

Olivia stared down into Alexander's eyes for several minutes, neither one of them speaking. Alexander knew there was something wrong, but he didn't want to bring it up. He wasn't ready for that conversation. He just wanted to get Olivia back to Boston.

~~~~~~~~~~

"Come back over later, Love?" Alexander asked, helping Olivia bring her luggage up to her house. "I've had Nepenthe brought over so he'd be here when you got back."

"Thanks. Maybe I'll just stay the night here if you don't mind. I'd like to spend some time with Kiera. I feel like I've been a bad friend lately."

Alexander pulled her into him, kissing her forehead. "Of course. I understand. Thompson is out front, keeping an eye on things. I'll miss you terribly, but you deserve some time to yourself."

"I'll miss you, too," Olivia whispered. Alexander had no idea how much she would miss him. This was the final good-bye and she couldn't really even say everything she wanted to. No. She put all that in the letter. If she didn't do it this way, he would convince her to stay, only to leave her broken-hearted later. This had to happen.

She punched her code into the keypad and opened her front door, quickly disarming the alarm system. "I'll see you in my dreams," Olivia said, turning to Alexander as he was getting into his car.

Alexander blew her a kiss before she closed her front door. She leaned against the door and all of her emotions over the past few months came flooding forward as tears began to flow.

She cried for all the missed kisses. All the nights she decided to stay at her house instead of going over Alexander's place. All the times she could have gone up to his office to see him but instead stayed in her own office. All those missed opportunities to be close to him. She cried for herself. But mostly, she cried for Alexander. Her beautiful Alexander.

She wasn't in love with him, but even if she was, she didn't know what love felt like. If it felt like the way she was feeling at that moment, she was okay with running from it. She had never been in so much pain in her life. But if she stayed and got even closer, that pain would be even worse. She needed to leave before the pain became so unbearable that she couldn't survive.

Nepenthe came up to Olivia, purring as he rubbed against her. "Ready for a new adventure?" she asked, drying her eyes with her sleeve. Nepenthe continued to rub against her, purring even louder. "I'll take that as a yes."

Olivia went up to her room and grabbed some clothes and her running sneakers. She packed up her acoustic guitar and left everything else as it was. She made a mental note to let her money manager know she would be out of town and to take care of her bills until further notice.

Looking out the front window, she saw a black SUV sitting watch. She didn't recognize the person behind the wheel.

Grabbing her bags, she walked down to her basement and out the back door to her Audi sitting in the back alley, loading the few items she chose to take into the car. She went back inside and put Nepenthe in his large cat carrier, packing his food and some toys. Placing her cell phone on the kitchen counter, she left behind the only life she knew.

She drove her car down the back alley, her heart beating wildly that her protection detail would notice her. When she finally merged onto the Mass Pike and determined that no one had followed her, she let out a breath she didn't realize she had been holding.

Looking at the city she had grown to love in the rear-view mirror, she knew that she had made such a mess of everything.

It was time to go.

Again.

CHAPTER THIRTY-FOUR

THE RIGHT THING

Alexander went to the office on his way home to brief the security team that would be assigned to Olivia. There were a total of six people assigned to her, with Carter taking the lead in delegating jobs and duties.

"Sir, if it's okay, I think it might be best if we have a female look after her at night. It just might make more sense, especially considering we would be staying in one of her guest rooms."

"Yes. That will only be necessary on the nights that she is not with me. But absolutely. And you're one of my best agents, so you'll be on this full time, if you're okay with that. I don't want anything to happen to her."

"Of course not, sir," Marshall replied, the other agents nodding their heads in agreement.

"Okay then. I think we're all set here. Carter, you'll take the first shift tomorrow. Thompson is over there now, but since she's comfortable with you, I'd like for you to arrange a time for her to meet the rest of the team."

"Yes, sir," Carter replied as Alexander walked out of the conference room. A few minutes later, he was on his way to his penthouse, looking forward to seeing Runner.

He was nearly knocked over when he opened the door to his home. "Hey, buddy. Happy to see me?" Runner kept jumping up, trying to lick Alexander's face, his tail wagging. "Easy buddy. Let me unpack and then we'll go for a walk, okay?"

Runner heard the word walk and started running around like crazy. "Silly dog," he said, bringing his suitcase upstairs into the master bedroom. He threw it on the bed and slowly started to unpack.

When he was almost done, an envelope caught his eye. It had his name written on it in Olivia's handwriting. He looked at it, confused. His heart sank as he read the letter contained in the envelope.

Alexander,

I hate that I'm writing this letter, but I now know that it needs to be written. First, let me say that the few months I've known you have been the best in my life. You have opened my eyes to new things and my heart to new feelings. And I treasure every moment that I was able to spend time with you. My only regret is not spending more time with you.

I realized something over the weekend. Something I wish I hadn't come to terms with. But, the truth is, I will never be able to make you happy. And I wish that wasn't true. I have so much baggage and I know in the end I will only hold you back. I want you to be happy, but you will never have that with me. I will always be pulling away from you, scared that you'll leave me. It's hard enough for me to write this letter knowing that my heart is aching. But this heartache is nothing compared to what it will be when you have to move past me.

When I look at you, I see this beautiful, normal human being. And then there's me with all my craziness. And I know at some point, you won't be able to handle all the crazy anymore. I'm just preventing you from wasting your time, waiting for me to sort out my issues. Because I don't think I'll ever be able to.

I just have one wish and that's for you to move on. Forget about me. I know it will be hard. It will be painful for me. I may not be able to forget about you. But one day, eventually, the sun will shine a little brighter and someone new will walk into your life that can make you happy. Who will fill that missing piece of your heart. But it isn't me.

This is more than just good-bye. I know I will never gaze into those eyes of yours again. Those beautiful green eyes that have haunted my dreams since we met. I need to let you go. Those eyes are no longer mine to gaze into, your lips not mine to kiss, your heart not mine to possess.

What we had was beautiful. But then I come and make a mess of everything with all my baggage. And that's what this all is. One big beautiful mess that I need to walk away from. Call it self-preservation.

297

I wasn't lying when I said I would see you in my dreams. It's where I can always hold you close and dear and never let go. And from now on, I will cherish those dreams.

Olivia

Alexander sank onto the bed. Why was she doing this? It wasn't her decision to make. How could she try to control his happiness? He was happy with her. And he didn't care how many times she closed up or tried to push him away, he would never leave her. Why couldn't she believe that?

He ran downstairs and grabbed his cell phone off the kitchen island. He pressed Olivia's contact, his heart beating rapidly as the phone rang. After several rings, the voicemail picked up. "Shit!" he yelled. He grabbed Runner's leash and called for the dog to follow him. After descending down to the garage, Alexander ran to his car, Runner close behind. He knew it was a desperate move, but maybe if Olivia saw Runner, she would reconsider.

Alexander sped through the rush hour downtown Boston traffic and slammed on the brakes outside of Olivia's house. He grabbed Runner.

Thompson ran out of the black SUV, catching up with his boss. "Everything okay, sir?" the ex-marine asked.

Alexander had a grim look on his face. "I'm not sure, but you're free to go. I'll take over for now." He took the steps up to the front door, banging on it.

"Olivia!" he yelled. "Open up! We need to talk!" He listened. Nothing. He knocked again. Still nothing.

He punched the numbers into the keypad on the door and then disarmed the security system.

"Olivia? Are you home?" He scanned the house, letting Runner loose. He ran up to the master bedroom. It looked as though someone left in a hurry, clothes scattered all over the place and hangers thrown on the ground. He ran back downstairs before throwing open the door to the basement. He had never been down there. Dashing down the stairs, he saw how she had gotten away unnoticed by the protection detail sitting out front. Opening the back door, he looked into a small back alley that ran behind the entire block.

"Fuck!" he screamed as he ran back upstairs and looked for Nepenthe. She wouldn't abandon an animal, no matter how desperately she wanted to disappear. His heart sank when he saw that his food and bowls were missing. He walked into the kitchen and let out a loud sob when he saw her cell phone sitting on the counter.

He fell to the floor, leaning against the kitchen cabinets. Runner came up, nuzzling into him. "She's gone, boy. The only woman I've ever loved and she's gone." He pulled the dog close to him and they sat there processing what had just happened for what could have been seconds or hours.

~~~~~~~~~~~

"Olivia? Are you in there?" a female voice sounded, bringing Alexander back to the present. "Libby?"

Alexander stood up and saw Kiera walking into the kitchen. "Oh, Alex. I'm sorry. Where's Libby?" Alexander just stared at her, his eyes swollen and sunken from crying. "What happened? Is something wrong?" Kiera asked.

"You could say that," Alexander replied, his voice an empty shell. "She left, Kiera. She ran. I don't know where she is." He sounded so lost. He stared out the windows, still processing everything that happened.

"What do you mean she left?" Kiera asked, the panic sounding in her voice. "When will she be back?"

"I don't think she will." He looked back at the clock in the kitchen and saw that it was past nine at night. He had been sitting there for nearly four hours. Four hours he could have been looking for her. He started to do the math in his head. She probably had about an eight-hour head start on him. That was such a long time. She could be anywhere.

"I need to go, Kiera," he said, snapping back to it. "I need to find her."

"Alex, wait. She's done this before. And, well, she just doesn't want to be found. Give her time. She will come back. I went through this with her right after she graduated from college. She will come back. I know it. But if you try to find her, you might just push her even further away."

"How do you know she'll come back?" he asked, his eyes filling with tears once more. "She told me to move on and I just don't think I can do that, Kiera."

"I know, Alex. I know. But she will come back. She always does. It may not be tomorrow or next week or next month or next year."

"Why? I don't understand," Alexander said, trying to subdue the knot in his throat.

"Running away is the only thing she knows how to do when she's scared. When she was growing up, everyone who said they would always be there for her left. So she pushes everyone away."

"But, I love her. I'll never leave her. I need to find her…"

~~~~~~~~~~

Around three in the afternoon the following day, Olivia pulled her Audi in front of a beach house. She found the rental when she stopped for gas the previous night and immediately agreed to pay for six months up front, sight unseen.

"It's perfect," Olivia said.

She grabbed Nepenthe out of the back seat, thankful that he didn't mind car rides all that much.

"You must be Miss Adler," an older gentleman said, walking down the front deck to meet Olivia.

"Yes. Mr. Robinson?"

"That's me."

Olivia grabbed the envelope with the cash for the beach rental and handed it over to Mr. Robinson. He gave her the keys and left Olivia to take in her surroundings.

Amelia Island, Florida. It was perfect. Small and quaint. Not overrun with tourist traps that plague most Florida beaches. And she found a great three-bedroom house on the north end of the island right on the water. It was exactly what she needed to help clear her mind and move on. A little sun and sand could do wonders for the soul.

Then why was the only thing on her mind Alexander? She wondered how he had reacted when he got her letter, if he even found it. She felt guilty for leaving town without telling Kiera and Mo, but it was necessary. It had to be done.

She unpacked the few things that she brought with her, setting up Nepenthe's food bowls and pouring him some fresh food and water. He ran over and began to eat, purring in appreciation. She collapsed on the couch in the large open living room, exhausted from her long drive. She hadn't eaten since breakfast the day before, but she had no appetite.

"If this is what a broken heart feels like, I did the right thing, didn't I, Nepenthe?"

The cat looked up from his bowl, a scowl across his face from his meal being interrupted. She grabbed a blanket off the back of the couch, thankful that she found a fully furnished rental, and pulled it over her. She fell asleep, listening to the crash of the waves from the Atlantic Ocean, thinking to herself how that was her worst birthday yet.

To Be Continued...

A BEAUTIFUL MESS PLAYLIST

Honky Tonk Woman - The Rolling Stones
Paradise By the Dashboard Light - Meatloaf
Something Like Olivia - John Mayer
Pride and Joy - Brandi Carlile
The Blower's Daughter - Damien Rice
Your Song - Elton John
Sleeping to Dream - Jason Mraz
Brighter than the Sun - Colbie Calait
MoneyGrabber - Fitz & The Tantrums
Misery - Pink, featuring Steven Tyler
Gorilla - Bruno Mars
Martin - Zac Brown Band
As Time Goes By - Dooley Wilson
Never Gonna Leave This Bed - Maroon 5
I Will - The Beatles
Beautiful Goodbye - Maroon 5
Go Your Own Way - Fleetwood Mac

A Tragic Wreck Excerpt

Anticipated Release date - February 4, 2014
(Unedited and Subject to Change)

As Sarah Olivia Adler sat on the front deck of the beach cottage she had been hiding in the past few weeks, the glow of the setting sun behind her casting beautiful shadows over the ocean, she thought about all the decisions she made that led her to that point in her life. *This would be a perfect oyster throwing deck*, she thought to herself, fighting back the tears that threatened to fall at the memory of eating oysters with Alexander. She sighed as she grabbed her wine glass and retreated back inside her beach house.

As far as rentals, she had found a pretty good place. The two-story ocean-front cottage on the north end of Amelia Island had an old-school beach house vibe to it that made her feel safe. She loved listening to the hardwood floors creak as she walked through her refuge on the coast. The salty air blew into her house through the large windows that adorned each wall. There was an open and airy quality to her new home that she relished. It was peaceful. No one there knew her name. And she liked it that way.

Olivia had been avoiding all sorts of technology since she arrived in Florida, not wanting to deal with the reality of what she had done. She got scared and she ran. Again. Her shrink was right. At some point, her friends would give up on her, sick of her always leaving and running. *They'd be better off without me in their lives*, she thought to herself.

October gave way to November and the weather began to

cool off a bit. Olivia spent her days reading on the beach, trying to avoid all romance novels. She kept to herself, content to be a recluse in her little beach house. She ran a lot. It helped to clear her head of everything to do with Alexander Burnham. Most nights she ate dinner on her deck, watching the waves roll in.

She dreaded nighttime. The nightmares always found her. Often, she woke up screaming, clutching her heart, and then began to cry when she realized that Alexander was no longer there to soothe her sobs. His arms were no longer there to calm her breathing. And every night she continued to see Alexander's face in her dreams, uttering those five little words that had changed everything. *It will destroy me, too*.

Olivia loved the mornings as the sun rose over the Atlantic Ocean, the sky a soft orange. If a storm was coming in, the street by her house would be lined with cars of surfers hoping to catch a few waves before the rain hit.

"Good morning," a voice called to her one day, catching her eye as she sat on her deck enjoying her morning coffee. He untied a surfboard from his Wrangler parked on the side street and made his way to the beach.

Olivia took in his surfer boy appearance, watching as his tall, lean body walked away from her. Her heart stopped a little when he turned around and smiled, his teeth bright against his tan skin and sandy hair. *No, Libby. Never again*, she reminded herself before getting up from the deck and retreating inside her house.

Her heart beat madly, all from a simple smile. Maybe a distraction was exactly what she needed to forget about Alexander. But the problem was, she just couldn't forget about him. He was permanently ingrained in her mind and her heart. She wasn't sure she would ever get over him. She wasn't sure she wanted to.

~~~~~~~~~~

"Come on, Alex, you need to get out of this funk," Tyler said to his brother as they sat at a dimly lit bar on Boylston Street in

Boston. "You need to get your mind off of…"

"STOP!" Alexander roared. "Do not say that name. I can't bear to even hear it." He slung back his shot glass and signaled the bartender for another one. His eyes were fuzzy and he wasn't sure another shot was such a smart idea. But he didn't care. He needed to numb the pain he felt. He lost her. How could he miss the signs? She had become so aloof that weekend in Newport. But he ignored it and she left. He had searched for any sign of where she might be but couldn't find her. Not yet anyway.

It was as if she simply vanished. He didn't know what happened that day back in October. He wasn't thinking. He was so torn about the fact that Olivia was gone that he failed to act. By the time he had finally come around and was able to function again, hours had passed. It was all his fault.

"Okay. Okay. I won't say the name. But you can't go on like this. You know that, right?" Tyler was worried about his brother. He had never seen him so upset before. Olivia had been gone for almost a month and he was still angry and hurt over everything that had happened.

"Whatever," Alexander replied, downing yet another shot as he attempted to stand up. "I gotta take a leak." He stumbled away from the bar and in the direction of the restrooms.

"If it isn't Alexander Burnham," a soft, sultry voice called out.

Alexander turned a little too fast and had trouble steadying himself. He squinted, trying to make out who had called his name, his vision blurry from the excessive liquor he had consumed that night. She took a step forward and Alexander took in her brilliant auburn hair, long legs, killer rack, and deep brown eyes. Eyes almost as deep and brown as…

"Chelsea Wellington," Alexander slurred, propping himself up against the wall. "It's been a while."

Chelsea smirked, throwing her wavy hair over her shoulder as she sauntered across the dark hallway to stand near Alexander. "It sure has. I've missed you, Alex," she exhaled. "I heard you were dating someone, though. I couldn't believe my ears at first…"

"Well, you heard wrong," he barked.

Chelsea grinned, crossing her arms over her too tight black dress. "I was hoping the gossip mills were wrong. I mean, Alexander Burnham and girlfriend in the same sentence? There's something wrong with that statement, if you ask me."

Alexander stared off into the distance. There was nothing wrong with him having a girlfriend. He missed his girlfriend more than life itself. But she left and the gap in his heart was threatening to kill him. He needed a distraction.

His eyes narrowed in on Chelsea's chest. "Wanna get out of here?" he asked, his eyebrows raised.

"I thought you'd never ask."

He led Chelsea through the bar and past Tyler who simply gaped, wide-mouthed, at his brother. He couldn't believe Alexander was actually resorting back to his old ways.

Martin pulled up outside of the bar and ran around to open the car door for Alexander. "Sir," he said in greeting, eyeing his boss suspiciously.

"Take us back to my place," Alexander demanded.

Martin exhaled loudly as he closed the door to the SUV and ran around to get in behind the wheel. Out of all the women he used to bring home, Martin couldn't believe Alexander chose to get back together with Chelsea Wellington. At least it wasn't Adele, he thought to himself as he maneuvered the Escalade through the busy Boston streets.

When Martin pulled up in front of Alexander's building, Chelsea waited for Alexander to run around and open the car door for her. *Olivia would have just opened it herself*, he thought. He took a deep breath, half-heartedly regretting his decision to invite Chelsea over, but, at the same time, feeling that he needed to move past Olivia. And this was the only way he knew how. She wanted him to move on. That's what he was doing.

"I just love the view from your place, Alex," Chelsea said as they entered his penthouse. She kicked off her heels and made her way toward the staircase, turning back to look at Alexander standing at the entrance, a dumbfounded look on his face. "Are you coming or not? I don't have all night."

Alexander contemplated what to do. Yes, he did invite Chelsea over for the sole purpose of fucking her until Olivia never again entered his mind. But now that she was there, could he really follow through? Just a few months ago, he wouldn't even be having second thoughts. He'd bring her upstairs and bury himself inside of her. Now, after Olivia, and after everything they had been through, it felt wrong.

Chelsea slinked toward the doorway where Alexander stood, deep in thought. "Stop thinking," she whispered, brushing her ruby red lips against his neck, gently nibbling on his earlobe. "This is just sex, Alex. Nothing more. Come on. I know what you need. You need to forget about her. I can help you." She pressed her body against his. Alexander wondered how she could tell he was thinking about a girl.

It all felt so different. There was no spark. Hell, he was even having a little trouble getting an erection. That never happened with Olivia. He was always ready to go when she was around. And even when she wasn't.

Chelsea grabbed Alexander's belt, pulling him toward her, quickly unbuckling it before unzipping his pants. Her small brown eyes met his as she reached into his boxers and helped spring him free.

"There's my boy," she smiled.

He exhaled loudly, desperate to feel something other than the excruciating loss that he had been feeling those past few weeks. "Just make me forget, Chelsea. Please," he pled with her.

"Okay, Alex." She pressed her lips to his.

Alexander grabbed her by the neck, deepening the kiss. Slamming her against the wall, he tore her panties from her body and got lost inside of her, the whole time thinking about his Olivia and what she was doing at that exact moment. Wondering whether he should have looked harder. Thinking about whether or not Kiera was right. Would she ever come back? Maybe Olivia needed to know that Alexander would fight for her, no matter what. But he didn't fight for her. He just let her walk away from him. Now it was November and the trail had gone cold. Olivia disappeared without a trace.

Even with all the resources he had at his disposal, there was nothing. Not one clue.

He thrust even harder into Chelsea, needing to find some sort of release. Release from the hold Olivia still had over him. Would he ever be rid of that? He didn't see how. Olivia always had a hold over him. Everything he had done throughout his life had been for her. Growing up, he just knew that she wasn't dead. She couldn't be. And his lack of serious relationships was due to that, always holding out hope of finding Olivia. And once he found her, he didn't want to let go. And she left him.

"That's it, Alex. Let go!" Chelsea screamed as Alexander bit into her neck, pulling out as he came in his hand. He just couldn't bring himself to come inside of Chelsea. The last person he came inside of was Olivia and he wanted to keep it that way.

He turned and walked briskly down the hallway to the bathroom to clean himself up, leaving Chelsea alone in the living room. Looking in the mirror, he saw a shell of his former self. Maybe it would have been better if he had never found Olivia. Maybe he should move on, like she asked. Maybe he should just forget all about her. He *needed* to forget her.

He splashed some water on his face, enjoying the coolness of the liquid, before walking back down the hallway into his living room.

"Feel better now, Mr. Burnham?" Chelsea asked coyly as she sat on his sofa.

"Yes, I do. Thank you." He strode over to the couch and took a seat next to Chelsea. The air was thick in the room, Alexander not really wanting to initiate conversation.

Chelsea sighed loudly. "So, want to talk about it?"

Alexander looked over at her. "No. Not really. I'd rather just forget about everything that went on these past few months and pretend none of it ever happened."

She grinned. "Would you like my help doing that?"

His eyes met her small brown eyes. How could he possibly forget about Olivia's big brown eyes? He would always see them in his dreams. He knew that. But maybe, with time, he could forget. "Yes, I would, Miss Wellington." His eyes became hooded as he pushed her down on the couch, grabbing both her arms and pinning them above her head.

"Oh, Mr. Burnham, I love it when you tie me up," Chelsea whispered.

"Stop talking. Don't say a word until I tell you to," he growled. He just couldn't listen to her voice. Every time she spoke, all he felt was betrayal. And he didn't want to feel that. He didn't want to feel anything.

Alexander ripped off his tie and wrapped it around Chelsea's hands, binding them together, before pulling out a condom and sinking back into her.

~~~~~~~~~~

Olivia didn't even know his name, but every morning she looked forward to seeing surfer boy park his Jeep in front of her house and untie his surfboard before hitting some waves with his friends. He would smile at her and she would feel heat coursing through her body. It wasn't the same as what she felt when Alexander smiled at her, but at least she felt *something*. And *something* was better than the nothingness and pain she had been feeling since she ran.

The mid-November sun shone through the thick clouds one morning as she sat on her beloved deck and drank her coffee like she did each morning. Olivia actually started to look forward to seeing surfer boy. She was surprised that he surfed every day, even when the waves were fairly non-existent. Regardless, like clockwork, his Jeep pulled up in front of her house early every morning just as the sun rose.

One of Olivia's favorite things about her new home was the location. It was so peaceful being able to wake up and watch the sun climb up the horizon over the crashing waves. There was something about the sunlight reflecting on the ocean that made everything seem okay. Not good. But okay. And Olivia was content with just okay. Nothing would ever be extraordinary. Only Alexander was extraordinary. So she settled for okay.

Just as the sun rose on that November morning, the Jeep

pulled up as usual. And, as usual, surfer boy untied his surfboard and smiled. Nothing ever changed. A smile. A drink of coffee. A sigh. That's what her mornings were composed of.

"My life is pathetic if my only excitement is some guy whose name I don't even know," she said to herself as she read a book on her e-reader, drinking her coffee.

"Cameron. My name's Cameron Bowen, but most people call me Cam."

Olivia jumped, looking for the source of the voice. Surfer boy stood to the right of Olivia's deck in his wetsuit, carrying a surfboard. She hadn't noticed him walk up to her deck, desperate to finally make an introduction.

Cam turned the corner and stood by the steps leading to Olivia's deck, watching as she quickly raised herself off her lounge chair, turning to her front door and frantically trying to open it, sticky with the beachy humidity. "You see, usually, when someone gives you their name, they may want you to return the favor. At least where I'm from they do."

Olivia listened to his accent, noticing a hint of a southern drawl. "And where is it you're from, Cam?" she inquired, turning around and crossing her arms.

"All over really. But truth be told, born and raised in South Carolina." His eyes sparkled and Olivia couldn't help but to respond to him.

"Me too. But I haven't lived there in well over a decade."

"It's a pity." He smiled a small but infectious smile that made Olivia want to melt. "I bet you used to sound too cute for words with a little southern drawl." He beamed, showing Olivia a perfect set of teeth.

God, he's really handsome. This was bad. This was very, very bad. She was trying to get over Alexander. It still pained her to think about what she had done, leaving him. She couldn't string someone else along, knowing full well she could never give that person her entire heart. She gave her heart to Alexander and he still held it, although he probably didn't realize that.

Cam took a few steps closer, still on the sandy road by her deck. He was rather attractive and had a good body underneath his wetsuit. Olivia had noticed how handsome he was several weeks ago, but up close, he was even more so. His silver eyes beamed as he smiled, staring up at her. The ocean breeze gusted, blowing his wild sandy hair in front of his eyes. But she was off men. And no matter what, she couldn't get Alexander out of her thoughts, as much as she tried.

"So, are you going to tell me your name, or do I have to try to guess it?" He cautiously stepped up the stairs of her deck, making sure he wasn't intruding.

She uncrossed her arms and took a few steps toward Cam, holding her hand out to him as he climbed the remainder of the stairs onto her deck. "My name's Olivia. People call me Libby, though."

Taking Olivia's hand in his own, Cam felt her soft skin. There was something so tragic about the woman standing in front of him. He couldn't put his finger on it, but she just seemed so alone. He had been watching her every day since mid-October when she appeared out of nowhere, renting old man Robinson's beach cottage. He figured she would only be there for a week, but every day, without fail, she sat outside, drinking her coffee and staring out at the ocean as if it held the answers to all her questions.

The first week, she barely smiled. As she drank her coffee, he noticed tears streaming down her face. Something made her sad. The waves were killer that week, a big storm brewing off the coast. The second week, the waves died down a bit and, after checking the surf report, he thought about blowing off surfing in the morning. But something about the sad girl who sat on her deck and drank coffee made him put on his wetsuit and go. And every day, even when the waves were more or less non-existent, he drove down to Ocean Avenue in the Fernandina Beach section of Amelia Island and smiled at the girl with the sad brown eyes.

"Libby. It's wonderful to finally put a name to the face."

Olivia took in the man she had grown accustomed to seeing every morning. His silver eyes had a depth to them. And a kindness that she had never seen before. She felt as if she could spill her entire life on him and he wouldn't judge her. His smile was infectious and before Olivia knew it, she smiled back. She couldn't remember the last time she smiled. It felt good.

"Do you surf?" Cam asked.

"I've tried it a few times. I lived in Hawaii for a bit and I didn't want to stick out as a haole, so I learned to surf." She looked over the horizon at the dozen or so bodies bobbing up and down, waiting to ride a wave into shore.

"What's a haole?" he asked.

"It's a Hawaiian term for mainlanders." She took a long sip of her coffee, wondering whether she should offer him a mug.

"Aah, I see." He smiled a genuine smile at the quiet woman. "So want to catch a few waves?" he asked, gesturing toward the water.

"I don't have a board. Or a wetsuit."

"Just grab a bathing suit. The waves are pretty calm today so you'll be fine without one."

Olivia hesitated, thinking about it.

"Come on. I see you sitting here every morning, drinking your coffee, and you just look so sad. Please. Let me at least show you some fun."

She looked at him, shocked that in just those few seconds each morning, he noticed how empty she was. "Okay," she said after a few seconds of deep thought. "Give me ten minutes. I need to shower."

"Great. I'll go try to catch a wave or two. I'll see you out there." He ran toward the water, holding his board.

It was a relatively warm morning for mid-November, but Olivia knew the water would be freezing. She had been there several weeks and still hadn't put a foot in the water. Even if she didn't get on a surfboard, at least she would finally feel the salt water against her skin.

She took a quick shower, making sure to shave fairly well. Pulling her hair back, she threw on her two-piece swimsuit she used when training for triathlons. Before heading out her door, she grabbed a towel and walked between the sand dunes down to where the water met the shore.

Cam ran up to her when he saw her walking down the beach. "Hey. You made it."

"You look surprised," she mumbled dryly.

"Well, a little. I thought you would blow me off, maybe go for a run and then just sit in your house the rest of the day."

His statement caught Olivia off-guard. "How do you seem to know so much about me?"

"You caught my eye. I have a thing for beautiful women," he winked, grabbing her hand and pulling her toward the water's edge.

"Holy crap that's freezing!" Olivia squealed when her foot hit the cold ocean, stopping dead in her tracks as Cam pulled away.

"Come on. Stop being a baby," he shouted back. He was already up to his knees in the water.

Olivia took a deep breath before running into the ocean, knowing that once she was fully submerged, she would feel better.

"Here. Grab onto the other end of the board," Cam said when Olivia finally caught up to him.

"Thanks." They swam out to just beyond where the waves crested.

"Hey! Cam-Bam!" a guy on a surfboard yelled.

"Come here. I want you to meet the guys," Cam said to Olivia. They swam over to a group of three guys.

"Hey! Who's this?" one of them asked.

"Everyone, this is Olivia. Olivia, this is Chris, Benny, and Jason."

Olivia waved with little enthusiasm. "Hi."

"Are you going to try surfing today?" Chris asked, trying to spark up a conversation with the girl who seemed so distant.

"Yeah. Might as well," she shrugged. "I've surfed before, so I'm not totally useless."

"Why don't you catch the first one? I'll hang back here on one of the guys' boards," Cam said as he swam over to Benny's board and hung on to it. He grinned while he watched Olivia swim away with the board.

"She's hot, man," Jason said, nudging toward Cam in the water. "Is she the one you've been talking about?"

"Yeah. That's her. I'm glad I worked up the nerve to finally

313

talk to her."

"You're such a pussy," Benny laughed. "For a guy pushing thirty-five, you have no balls when it comes to talking to women."

"Suck it, man!" Cam joked back. "Whatever. There's just something kind of sad about her. I couldn't help it." He returned his eyes to Olivia as she climbed on the board, throwing her legs on either side, getting ready to catch a wave.

After a few minutes, she saw a wave coming in that was ideal for her to ride. She positioned her hands and quickly hoisted her legs onto the board, balancing it perfectly as she rode into the shore.

Along the coast, a few people were milling about, collecting shells. As the sandy beach got closer, she started to space out and thought she saw Alexander. She saw him everywhere lately. Her heart began to race and she panicked, losing her balance. The board slipped out from underneath her and she toppled off, hitting her head as she sank below the water.

"Shit!" Cam exclaimed when he saw Olivia sink beneath the surface. He swam quickly toward where she went under, desperately searching for her, worried that in the few minutes it took him to get to her, she hadn't resurfaced. He dove into the water, his eyes stinging from the salt. A few feet away, he saw her, her eyes closed, bubbles coming out of her mouth.

He reached her and grabbed her around the waist, kicking toward the surface. "Come on, Libby. Stay with me, here." He pulled her toward the shore and laid her on her back. The rest of the guys finally joined him.

"I think she hit her head pretty hard." Cam leaned his ear down over her nose and couldn't hear any breathing, but she still had a pulse. He started rescue breathing, frantic for her to cough up the water that appeared to be stuck in her lungs. After a few long breaths, Olivia gasped, coughing. Cam helped roll her onto her side, getting the water out of her mouth.

"You scared me there, sweetheart," he said softly, gazing down at the woman lying on the sand.

Olivia looked around, trying to get her bearings. She went surfing. She tried to make a new friend and now she looked like an idiot. She tried to stand up, but her legs were weak, causing her to lose her balance. Cam caught her. "Hey. Take it easy," he said softly. "You bumped your head pretty good. Let's get you back inside your house. You should probably go lie down."

Cam led Olivia up the beach to her house, helping her to the couch. Once she was settled, he walked through her living room and into the kitchen, searching the freezer for some ice. He assembled a make shift icepack and brought it to Olivia.

"Here," he said, leaning down and placing the icepack on her forehead. "You should probably keep this on your head. There's a little bit of swelling." He brushed a piece of hair out of Olivia's eyes.

"Thanks."

"Anytime." He looked around the house, noticing how minimalist everything looked. As if she had just rolled into town with a suitcase. There was nothing personal aside from a guitar case leaning up against a wicker chair. He walked over and sat in the chair. "Do you play?" he asked, gesturing to the case.

Olivia took the ice off her forehead and sat up, facing Cam. "Yeah. A little, I guess. In a former life. I really haven't played lately, though. Since I got here. The guitar's just been sitting there, collecting dust."

Cam looked into her eyes. She seemed so empty.

Out of the corner of his eye, a large orange long-haired cat walked down the stairs into the living room. The cat stalked, determined, toward Olivia, jumped up on her lap, and curled up in a ball. "This is Nepenthe," Olivia said.

"Ahh," Cam breathed. "The ancient elixir of depression."

Olivia turned her head. "How did you know that? Not a lot of people know what nepenthe is."

"I have a brain full of useless information." Cam laughed. There was a long awkward silence. He was attracted to the woman sitting across from him, snuggling up with her cat. But she seemed so distant and uninterested in anything. He didn't know much about her, but he wanted to learn more. "Can I take you to dinner tonight? There's this great place on the

315

other side of the island right on the water."

Olivia looked around. "I don't know. I don't think that's such a good idea."

"Come on. It'll be fun. I promise. Just as friends. No pressure. I just want to get to know you. Be your friend."

Olivia had been avoiding all social situations for the past several weeks. Certain things set her off, triggering a panic attack. Looking out her large front windows into the ocean, she hoped for some guidance about what to do. She was getting to like her new home. And if she got involved with Cam, she would just leave him, too. That's what she did. She ran. Always. That was all she knew.

"Hey, Libby. The answer isn't there in the ocean."

Olivia looked back at Cam, a smile still on his face, but also something else. She couldn't quite put her finger on it, but it was almost like a look of compassion.

"I just want to get to know you. That's all. I want to spend some time with you."

"But, why?" Olivia asked, her brows furrowed.

"What? Why wouldn't I?"

"I could give you a thousand reasons," she mumbled under her breath.

"As friends. That's all, Libby. Come to dinner with me. Let me be your friend."

Olivia sighed, petting Nepenthe in her lap. "I don't need any friends. I'm perfectly happy in my little oasis here on the beach."

"Oh, come on. Don't make me beg."

Olivia's heart stopped. Alexander's husky voice flashed through her memory. "*I like it when you beg.*"

Her lip started to tremble and she quickly jumped off the couch, walking toward the stairs and away from Cam, desperately trying not to fall apart in front of him. She had finally gotten through an entire week without breaking down and crying when she thought about Alexander. But that memory was too much. She couldn't take it. Her heart was in pieces and she knew it was all her fault. But it still didn't make it hurt any less.

Cam caught up to her and grabbed her arm, noticing he had upset her somehow. He didn't want to leave it on such a sour note. "Libby, please. Whatever I said, I'm sorry."

She turned to face him, tears running down her face.

"I just want to make you smile, please. Just come to dinner with me. I promise I'll help you forget about whatever it is that has you so upset."

She looked up at Cam, surprised at his height. He was even taller than Alexander, a feat at six-foot-five. Maybe he was right. Maybe what Olivia needed was someone to help her forget. She couldn't possibly go on living her life as she had been. Every day was a struggle to get through. And she felt *something* when she looked at him. It wasn't sparks and shivers and tremors as it was when she looked at Alexander. But at least *something* was far better than *nothing*.

Cam pleaded with her with his eyes, desperate to find out more about this mysterious woman who had come to the island and captured his attention so quickly.

"Okay. I'll go out with you."

A smile spread across Cam's face and Olivia couldn't help but giggle a little at the look of excitement.

"Great!" he exclaimed. "I'll pick you up at seven." He left before Olivia could protest.

She fell back onto the couch. For the first time in weeks, she actually had something to look forward to that evening. She was unsure how to feel about that. Would she just find herself in the same situation as she did with Alexander? No. Impossible. She refused to let it get that far. She couldn't. It nearly tore her apart when she had to leave Alexander. And she vowed to never have to do that again. Even if it meant spending the rest of her life alone.

"Damn it, Nepenthe. What have I gotten myself into?" Her cat stood up and stretched before settling back down on Olivia's stomach.

ACKNOWLEDGEMENTS

Writing these books has been a labor of love. This all started out back in January, 2013 when I got the crazy idea to just start writing. I've always loved to read, something I think is becoming lost on the younger generation these days who prefer to sit in front of a game console. Where's the adventure in that?

Growing up, I remember my father taking me and my two sisters to the library every week, and we were so excited to be able to pick out new books to read. So I guess the first people I need to thank are my parents, Don and Linda Martin, for instilling a love of reading at such an early age. I recall being able to read when I was barely out of pre-school, and I don't think I ever stopped. I've always preferred it to watching movies, which is ironic considering I work as a producer, but there's something magical about reading. It's like being able to direct your very own movie in your mind.

And I can't leave out my support system since I was in diapers. My two sisters, Melissa Morgera and Amy Perras, who, when I told them I had written not one but three novels, didn't look at me like it was the craziest thing in the world. They were so excited that they both wanted to read it immediately. A lot of our antics growing up made its way into the book, as did the basis for a few of the characters. I couldn't imagine life without my two sisters.

Another huge thank you is to one of my oldest and dearest friends, Kerri Deschaine. Without Kerri in my life, there would have been no Kiera in these books. Kerri was my inspiration for the character. She is a fierce friend who would bend over backwards for you, and support you no matter what. And I'm forever grateful that we met in a dingy fraternity basement at UMASS Lowell.

And of course, I need to give a huge huge thank you to my betas who enthusiastically agreed to help, not really knowing what they were getting themselves into. Your words of encouragement stayed with me during this whole process, even when the little doubt fairy paid a visit saying I'd never sell a copy, except to maybe my mother.

Lynne Ayling, Karen Emery, Natalie Naranjo, Stacy Stoops, thank you all for your thoughts on what worked and what didn't. I have to admit, I was so nervous sending my manuscript out to you all. My hand was literally shaking as I hit send on each of those e-mails. I was so worried that I just wasted the last six months of my life on something that totally sucked. So thank you girls for telling me that it doesn't suck and for your enthusiasm about the project!

Last, but certainly not least, I need to thank the love of my life. My husband has been nothing but supportive through all of this. When I finally told him that I had written three novels, he stayed up almost round-the-clock reading all the books. Then he began reaching out to all his friends and acquaintances and convinced them to check out my Facebook page. Instead of doing any of his work, he became my very own publicist. When I was going through my manuscript, editing it like a madwoman so I could get it published ahead of schedule, he made breakfast and lunch for me on a daily basis, bringing it up to me on a tray, while I toiled away over my manuscript. I'm so happy that he believes in these books as much as I do. His support has been overwhelming. Stan is my Alexander.

Can't wait to do it all over again with *A Tragic Wreck*.

About the Author

T.K. Leigh, otherwise known as Tracy Leigh Kellam, is a producer / attorney by trade. Originally from New England, she now resides in sunny Southern California with her husband, dog and three cats, all of which she has rescued (including the husband). She always had a knack for writing, but mostly in the legal field. It wasn't until recently that she decided to try her hand at creative writing and is now addicted to creating different characters and new and unique story lines in the Contemporary Romantic Suspense genre.

When she's not planted in front of her computer, writing away, she can be found running and training for her next marathon (of which she has run over fifteen fulls and far too many halfs to recall). Unlike Olivia, the main character in her *Beautiful Mess* series, she has yet to qualify for the Boston Marathon.

Follow her online at:
www.facebook.com/tkleighauthor
www.tkleighauthor.com

CPSIA information can be obtained at www.ICGtesting.com
Printed in the USA
LVOW13s0120210214

374547LV00009B/930/P